JANE FEATHER

AN UNSUITABLE BRIDE

POCKET BOOKS

New York   London   Toronto   Sydney   New Delhi

Pocket Books
A Division of Simon & Schuster, Inc.
1230 Avenue of the Americas
New York, NY 10020

This book is a work of fiction. Names, characters, places, and incidents either are products of the author's imagination or are used fictitiously. Any resemblance to actual events or locales or persons, living or dead, is entirely coincidental.

Copyright © 2012 by Jane Feather

All rights reserved, including the right to reproduce this book or portions thereof in any form whatsoever. For information, address Pocket Books Subsidiary Rights Department, 1230 Avenue of the Americas, New York, NY 10020.

First Pocket Books paperback edition August 2012

POCKET and colophon are registered trademarks of Simon & Schuster, Inc.

For information about special discounts for bulk purchases, please contact Simon & Schuster Special Sales at 1-866-506-1949 or business@simonandschuster.com.

The Simon & Schuster Speakers Bureau can bring authors to your live event. For more information or to book an event, contact the Simon & Schuster Speakers Bureau at 1-866-248-3049 or visit our website at www.simonspeakers.com.

Manufactured in the United States of America

10 9 8 7 6 5 4 3 2 1

ISBN 978-1-4391-4526-5
ISBN 978-1-4391-5551-6 (ebook)

A lady's secret . . .

"Do you have the first idea what you've done?" Alexandra demanded. With cold clarity, she thought, *It's over.* All the work, the misery of the charade, all for nothing. Blind rage filled her, and her palm cracked against his cheek.

Peregrine grabbed her wrist. "*No.* You won't do that again."

Under his steady blue gaze, Alex felt the rage die down. "You've ruined *everything*," she said in a low voice.

"How?" he demanded. "I don't intend to spoil your game. I'm only curious. Will you tell me your first name, at least?"

"Alexandra. Let go of me, *please.*"

"Do you promise not to run?"

She shook her head impatiently. "Where the hell would I run to?"

That made him smile, dissipating the tension. "Much better. Now I feel I'm in the company of the real Alexandra . . . whoever she may be." He released her. "How can I be of help?"

"You can pretend this never happened."

He shook his head. "Oh, no. I'm afraid I could certainly never pretend I didn't see you frolicking on the beach, with your hair flying in the breeze." He trailed his fingers through the cascade of chestnut hair, as the mystery of who Alexandra Hathaway was suddenly lost its importance.

He cupped her face, and his mouth hovered over hers, his breath brushing against her cheek.

*Turn the page for rave reviews of
Jane Feather's wonderful stories . . .*

A Wedding Wager

"This compelling read delivers an unforgettable cast of characters and places them in an irresistible story . . . that only an author with Feather's talents can pull off."
—*Romantic Times*

"Vivid protagonists, appealing secondary characters, and a passionate romance."
—*Publishers Weekly*

"A page turner. . . . A thoroughly enjoyable novel."
—*Romance Reviews*

Rushed to the Altar

"Gathers momentum much like a classical opus that ends in a resounding crescendo. . . . Ms. Feather certainly knows how to titillate the imagination with some sizzling scenes set in a tapestry of bygone days."
—*Winter Haven News Chief*

"Fun and intelligent. . . . I am completely captivated."
—*Fresh Fiction*

"An ingenious story line, witty prose, and charming characters . . . a well-written addition to the historical romance genre."
—*Romance Junkies*

A Husband's Wicked Ways

"A consummate storyteller, Feather rises to new heights in her latest Wicked novel of intrigue and desire. Her utterly engaging characters and suspenseful plot combine to hold you spellbound."
—*Romantic Times*

"Filled with recurring quirky characters, truly evil villains, and a fearless heroine who is definitely an equal to her hero." —*Booklist*

To Wed a Wicked Prince

"Enchanting and witty . . . sizzling." —*Publishers Weekly*

"A poignant love story . . . strong characters, political intrigue, secrets and passion . . . it will thrill readers and keep them turning the pages." —*Romantic Times*

A Wicked Gentleman

"Will enchant readers. . . . Filled with marvelous characters—and just enough suspense to keep the midnight oil burning." —*Romantic Times*

"Intriguing and satisfying. . . . The captivating romance is buttressed by rich characters and an intense kidnapping subplot, making this a fine beginning for Feather's new series." —*Publishers Weekly*

All the Queen's Players

"Beautifully moving . . . rich in period detail."
—*Booklist*

"A truly fantastic novel."
—*The Romance Readers Connection*

"Terrific." —*Genre Go Round Reviews*

Also by Jane Feather

An
Unsuitable
Bride

Prologue

JANUARY 1763

"But I don't understand." Alexandra Douglas stared at the two objects the lawyer had placed on his desk in front of her. "These are our inheritance?" She touched the heavy gold signet ring and the diamond fob before looking up at Lawyer Forsett, her clear gray eyes bemused. "Sylvia and I were to have ten thousand pounds each on Papa's death. He told me so himself."

The lawyer pulled at his chin and stared down fixedly at the blotter on his desk. He cleared his throat. "Mistress Douglas, yours and your sister's circumstances changed when Sir Arthur divorced your mother."

"I'm well aware of that, sir," Alexandra responded somewhat tartly. "When my mother ran off for the last time, I was sent to St. Catherine's Seminary and Sylvia to live with our old nurse. Quite different circumstances from our previous life at Combe Abbey. We were under no illusions, sir."

The man looked at his visitor with a hint of compassion. "There was another aspect to your changed circumstances, Mistress Douglas, that perhaps you did not fully understand." He cleared his throat again. "Your legal status changed as well."

A little needle of apprehension pierced Alexandra's customary composure. "Legal status?" she queried.

The lawyer sighed. It was a damnable business. He'd told his client, Sir Arthur Douglas, many times that he owed it to his daughters to explain what his divorce meant for them, but Sir Arthur had waved away any urgency. "All in good time, my good man." The lawyer could hear the brusquely dismissive tones as if the man were sitting right in front of him, instead of dead and buried in the family mausoleum. In essence, Sir Arthur had not had the courage to inform his daughters of the ghastly situation his own selfish actions had put them in. And now it was up to his lawyer to do his dirty work for him.

"Your father obtained a divorce from his wife, your mother, *a vinculo matrimonii*," he began.

"What does that mean?" his visitor interrupted before he could continue.

"It means, ma'am, that the marriage in question was null and void from its inception, either because of an improper blood relationship, insanity, or . . ." He paused, a slight flush on his cheek. "Or because of nonconsummation. On such grounds, the marriage is dissolved as if it had never been, and all children of the union in the first two causes are declared illegitimate. Your father had your mother declared insane in absentia."

Alexandra began to see where this was leading, and the needle of apprehension became a knife of fear. "So Sylvia and I are bastards, sir? That is what you're saying?"

His flush deepened, and he coughed into his hand. "In a word, ma'am, yes. And as such are not legally entitled to inherit anything from your father's estate, unless specific provision has been made."

The young woman was very pale now, but her voice was steady, her eyes focused. "And am I to assume that no such provision was made?"

"Your father intended to do so, but his death was rather sudden, before he had managed to settle anything on you or your sister. However . . ." Lawyer Forsett opened a strongbox which stood on a small pedestal table beside his chair. "Sir Stephen Douglas, your father's heir, has agreed to allow you and your sister fifty pounds apiece from the estate, just to tide you over until you find some means of employment." He pushed a bank draft across the table to Alexandra.

She looked at it in disgust. "Cousin Stephen? That's what he considers fair?"

The lawyer's distress increased visibly. "I did suggest to Sir Stephen that he honor your late father's intentions and make a one-time payment to each of you in the sum of ten thousand pounds. Unfortunately, Sir Stephen did not see the matter in the same way."

"No, of course he didn't," she returned with a bitter little smile. She had never met this distant cousin, but her father had never had a good word to say for his putative heir. The need to disinherit Sir Stephen by producing a male heir of his own was the main reason, she had always assumed, for her father's hurried second marriage.

She folded the bank draft and tucked it into the deep pocket of her muslin skirt. The signet ring and fob followed it as she rose to her feet. "I thank you for your time, Lawyer Forsett, but I won't take up any more of it."

He rose himself, saying awkwardly, "Have you considered your next step, ma'am? You must find gainful employment. Perhaps the seminary would employ you as a teacher, or maybe you could hire out as a governess in some respectable family. Your education will stand you in good stead."

"No doubt that was my father's intention when he sent me to the seminary in the first place," she stated, her eyes burning. "And I presume it will be up to me to earn sufficient for my sister's care in addition to my own?"

"I could approach Sir Stephen again, ma'am, appeal—"

"Indeed not, sir," she interrupted his awkward speech. "I would not ask my cousin for the parings of his nails. I bid you good day."

The door closed on her parting vulgarity, and the lawyer shook his head, mopped his brow with a large linen handkerchief, and sank back into his chair.

Alexandra went out onto the freezing wind of a London winter's day. Chancery Lane was busy with traffic, iron wheels splashing through puddles, sending up sprays of dirty water from the kennel. For a moment, she stood, heedless of her surroundings, numbed by the prospect of a future that was no future. She had been brought up to believe that her world would never significantly change, that she would tread the path well trodden before her by other young women of her position in Society. Not even her parents' divorce, an almost unheard-of circumstance among her peers, had caused undue alarm over the prospect of the next stage of her life. She had settled happily enough at St. Catherine's, close enough to her sister, who was being well cared for by their former nurse, and waited patiently for the doors to the life to come to swing wide.

Instead, they had been slammed shut.

Chapter One

The Honorable Peregrine Sullivan drew rein on the high Dorsetshire cliff top and looked out over the calm waters of Lulworth Cove. The sea surged through the horseshoe-shaped rock at the entrance to the cove in a flash of white water and then smoothed out as it rolled gently to the beach.

Perry was not familiar with this southern coastline, having spent his own growing in the rugged wilds of Northumberland, where rough mountains and hilly moors were the usual scenery, but he found it rather soothing, the expanse of water sparkling under the Indian summer sun, the rough grass of the cliff top, the air perfumed with the clumps of fragrant pinks crushed beneath his horse's hooves. It was altogether a softer part of the world, and none the worse for that, he reflected.

His weary horse raised his head and whinnied. Perry leaned over and stroked the animal's neck. "Almost there, Sam." He urged the horse forward with a nudge of his heels. It had been a long ride from London, three days in all. The Honorable Peregrine was not overly flush with funds and had decided a post chaise would be an unwarranted expense, and he didn't wish to change horses on the road, leaving Sam in an unknown stable, so they'd taken it slowly, at a pace that the gelding could comfortably manage, but now they were within two miles of Combe Abbey, their final destination.

The gray stone building stood on a slight hill, easily visible from the road that wound across the cliff above the Solent. It was an impressive turreted building, with arched mullioned windows glowing in the setting sun. Well-tended green lawns swept down to the cliff top, and a stand of tall pines served as a windbreak along the boundary of the grounds and the cliff.

Perry felt a little surge of anticipation. In that impressive building was a library, and in that library were treasures, some known, such as the *Decameron,* which set his literary juices running, and many, he was sure, unknown and equally priceless. His good friend Marcus Crofton had assured him that he could spend as long as he liked in the library. Its owner, Sir Stephen Douglas, had given him carte blanche to browse as much as he chose.

Peregrine turned his horse through the gates, which were opened at his appearance by a robust gatekeeper. "Dower House is just around the first bend in the drive, sir," he informed Peregrine in answer to the latter's question. "They's expectin' you. Master Crofton told me to look out for ye."

"Thank you." Perry nodded his thanks with a smile and rode on up the drive. He was looking forward to this visit with his old friend, and not just because of the opportunity to see the library. Since his twin brother, Sebastian, had taken his new wife, the Lady Serena, on an extended honeymoon to the Continent, Perry had to admit that the house they had shared on Stratton Street seemed far too big, and very lonely. It had surprised him how lonely he had been. He'd always considered himself perfectly self-sufficient, perfectly content with his own company and that of his books. But he'd been mistaken, it seemed.

Now he nudged Sam into a trot as the Dower House came into view. It was a pleasant thatched building in the Queen Anne style, nowhere near as impressive as the Abbey itself but rather inviting. Smoke curled from the kitchen chimney, and the windows on both levels were opened to catch the freshness of early evening. Perry dismounted at the front door and pulled the bell rope beside it. He heard the chime within the house, and the door was opened almost instantly by a white-haired steward, who bowed and murmured, "The Honorable Peregrine, I assume, sir?"

"You assume right," Perry agreed with an amiable smile, drawing off his gloves.

"Perry, is that you?" A cheerful voice hailed him from the cool depths of an oak-floored hall, and a young man of around Perry's age appeared behind the steward. "Welcome, m'dear fellow." He extended a hand in greeting.

Perry shook his hand warmly. He had known Marcus Crofton since their school days. But whereas Perry had had the protection of his oldest brother, Jasper, and the constant companionship of his twin, Sebastian, Marcus had been thrown into the brutal waters of Westminster alone and left to sink or swim. The Blackwater brothers had extended their protection and friendship, and Marcus and Peregrine had quickly become fast friends once they had discovered a shared passion for science. A passion that the less rigorously academically minded Sebastian had found hard to understand and after a few attempts had given up trying to share with his twin.

"I've been expecting you for the last two days. You rode?" Marcus peered over Perry's shoulder to where his horse stood patiently behind him.

"In slow stages," Perry returned. "Where should I stable Sam?"

"Oh, up at the Abbey," Marcus replied. "My mother didn't wish to go to the expense of opening the Dower House stables, and Sir Stephen offered to extend the hospitality of the Abbey's whenever we need it. For a not so small stipend, of course," he added with a cynical note that Peregrine didn't miss.

"Mother keeps her barouche up there," Marcus continued. "But, except when I'm down here for some hunting, we don't trespass further on his generosity." The cynical note was again difficult to miss. "Except for our visitors, who also use the stables. Roddy will take him up and see him settled. See to it, will you, Baker?"

"Of course, sir." The butler disappeared into the back regions of the house.

"Come into the parlor," Marcus urged. "You must be dying of thirst after all that riding." He led the way into a square parlor. It had an intimate, family feel to it, the air scented with great bowls of roses planted on every available surface. "You'll have to excuse my mother, Perry. The Dowager Lady Douglas suffers from ill health and spends much of the day on the chaise in her boudoir. She's resting now before dinner." He poured two glasses of ruby claret, passing one to his guest. "You'll meet her at dinner, of course."

Peregrine raised his glass in a toast of thanks before saying, "I hope the dowager doesn't consider my visit an imposition."

"Oh, good heavens, not a bit of it, dear boy. There's nothing my mother likes better than visitors. She just don't like to exert herself. But Baker and his wife, the inestimable Mistress Baker, run the house between 'em, and m'mother has to do little more than wave her sal volatile in their direction and miracles occur." Marcus chuckled, clearly not considering this less than respectful description of his parent to be in the least offensive.

Peregrine smiled knowingly. His own mother had been of the valetudinarian stamp, and he understood the situation well. "I'm most grateful to the dowager for her hospitality. I confess I can barely hold my patience until I can see the library. Your stepfather was known as the most skilled antiquarian book collector in the country. And his father before him," he added, his blue eyes sparking with enthusiasm. His fatigue seemed to have left him now that he was at journey's end and so close to the object of his passionate interest.

Marcus chuckled. He knew well the depths of his friend's literary enthusiasms, even though he could not himself summon up such intense interest for anything outside the realm of science. "I doubt the library will expand under Stephen's caretaking. Sir Stephen Douglas doesn't appear to share the literary interests of his two predecessors. But you should be able to see the collection soon. We shall dine quietly at home, and I should warn you we keep country hours, but afterwards we are bidden to the Abbey for an evening of cards. Every evening, Sir Stephen has card tables set up, either with his own houseguests or members of the local gentry." Marcus shook his head with a slightly rueful smile. "I give you fair warning, my friend. If 'tis not whist, then 'tis fierce gaming. Sir Stephen plays for high stakes."

Peregrine had neither the desire nor the funds to play for high stakes, but he would cross that bridge when he came to it. He shrugged the issue aside. "As long as there's an opportunity to look at the volume of the *Decameron,* I'll do the best I can."

"Oh, no one will trouble you on that score, although you'll have to beard the librarian."

"Librarian? There's a librarian?" Perry was surprised that a man with no interest in books should employ someone simply to take care of them.

"Yes, she's been there for a while. Stephen has little interest in the collection, except in terms of its monetary value, so he employed this Mistress Hathaway to catalogue it with the aim of selling it to the highest bidder. 'Tis a damn shame, and I'm sure my stepfather is turning in his grave." Marcus shook his head. "Such a waste of a lifetime's assiduous collecting, and, as you said, not just Sir Arthur but his father before him. Some of the works are priceless. Anyway, Mistress Hathaway is just a dab of a thing, although I think she knows what she's doing. She's so shy and retiring, she'll probably run a mile if you speak to her."

"It's hard to believe Sir Stephen doesn't appreciate such a treasury," Peregrine observed, sipping his claret.

"Truth to tell, m'boy, Sir Stephen Douglas has more than a little of the Philistine about him," Marcus declared. "Money is his major passion, as far as I can tell. And social climbing is that of his lady wife, the inestimable Lady Maude," he added with a sardonic grin. "Stephen does his best to further her aspirations, riding to hounds with the County set, offering generous hospitality to everyone who is anyone in Dorset, but the lady doesn't appear overly appreciative of his efforts." He drained his glass. "Let me show you to your chamber. You'll want to wash off the dirt of the road before dinner."

Marcus led the way upstairs to a commodious chamber at the back of the house. "John will valet you. I'll send him up straightway." He gestured to a pier table by the window. "Claret and Madeira should you feel the need. I'll see you in the drawing room in half an hour." The door closed behind him.

Peregrine surveyed his surroundings. His portmanteau had been unstrapped from his horse and unpacked, and his clothes were hanging in the armoire. A knock at the door brought a manservant with a jug of steaming water and an array of fresh towels over his arm. "Good evening, sir."

"Good evening, John . . . I believe it is." Perry stripped off his coat. "I'm covered in dust from the road, and I need a shave. Would you sharpen my blade?"

"Aye, sir." The valet set to work with blade and strop while Perry stripped to his undergarments.

Half an hour later, he presented himself in the drawing room, dressed appropriately in a suit of wine-colored velvet, plain white stockings, buckled shoes. His only jewelry was a turquoise stud in the froth of lace at his throat and a clasp of the same stone confining the fair queue at the nape of his neck.

"Ah, there you are, Perry. Everything to your satisfaction, I trust." Marcus poured claret and handed a glass to his guest.

"Perfectly, I thank you." Perry took the glass, raised it in a toast, and wandered to the bow window that looked across the sweep of lawn to the glittering blue sliver of sea glimpsed through the windbreak. "Exquisite setting, Marcus."

"Don't I know it," the other responded, coming to stand beside him. "My stepfather was a careful landowner. His death was very sudden, a fever out of nowhere, and he was dead within two days." He shook his head. "The physicians couldn't fathom it. He seemed as strong as a horse when he was struck down. They muttered about a weak heart after the fact, but 'tis still a puzzle. Anyway, he left the estate and the accounts in immaculate order.

"Unfortunately—" He stopped abruptly, cleared his throat, and changed the subject. "If you care for a day's fishing, Perry, the trout stream is well stocked."

"One of my favorite country pastimes," Perry said casily, even as he wondered what his friend had been about to say.

"Lady Douglas is descending, gentlemen." The steward spoke from the door behind them.

Marcus nodded. "Thank you, Baker." He went to the sideboard, where glasses and decanters stood, and poured a small measure of ratafia into a delicate crystal glass.

"Ah, dear boys, you're down before me." The light voice emanated from what to Perry's bemused gaze appeared to be a billowing ball of silks, chiffons, and paisley shawls. From within the depths of these fabrics, a pair of light brown eyes glimmered, and a small, very white, heavily beringed hand appeared. He bowed over it. "Lady Douglas, I am most grateful for your hospitality."

"Nonsense." She waved the hand airily. "My dear Marcus's friends are always most welcome." The ball of material flowed to a chaise longue and reposed itself in elegant folds, which, when they had finally settled, revealed the plump figure and doll-like countenance of a lady of early middle years. She smiled amiably at Peregrine and dabbed a lavender-soaked scrap of lace at her temples. "I am something of an invalid, unfortunately, so you must forgive me if I keep to my own chamber most of the time." She sighed. "'Tis such a trial, but we must be grateful for what we have, isn't that so, Marcus?"

"Indeed, ma'am," her son agreed gravely, handing her the glass of ratafia. "I trust this will give you a little more strength before we dine."

"Oh, yes, such a tonic I find it." She sipped with a complacent smile. "So, tell me, Mr. Sullivan, what is the gossip from London?" Another little sigh, before she said, "I do so miss the bustle of town, but I no longer have the strength for it."

Perry caught Marcus's smothered grin and concealed his own amusement while he racked his brains for a suitable tidbit. His sister-in-law, Lady Serena, was always a fount of useful *on dits,* and he remembered a particular one concerning the Duke and Duchess of Devonshire.

Lady Douglas listened with bright-eyed fascination. She was really a very pretty woman, Perry reflected, with her pink and white complexion and rounded chin. Certainly younger than her invalid manner would imply. She was well pleased with Peregrine's attempts to amuse her, and when dinner was announced, she rose with unexpected energy from the chaise, taking his arm for him to lead her into dinner.

Marcus followed, smiling to himself. He was very fond of his parent—only sixteen years separated them—but always delighted when the burden of her entertainment was assumed as competently as Perry was assuming it.

Mistress Hathaway paused at her dressing mirror to take stock of her appearance before descending to the salon of Combe Abbey to obey her employer's summons to make up a four at one of the whist tables. She had dined as usual with the family and their houseguests but, as usual, had escaped rapidly to her bedchamber the moment the ladies had left the table for the drawing room. The unwelcome summons had followed when the gentlemen had repaired to the drawing room, replete with port, for an evening at the whist tables.

She was called upon to make a four whenever there were uneven numbers among the guests, and Mistress Hathaway cursed her stupidity in revealing her skill at cards one afternoon, when her employer wished for a game of piquet. She had always been too competitive for her own good, she reflected irritably. If she had let Sir Stephen win, she wouldn't be in the abominable position of having to obey every summons to the table that her employer issued.

She glanced sideways at her reflection, at the small but unsightly hump at the base of her neck. The candlelight caught the faint brown birthmark below her right cheekbone and the scattering of gray hairs above her temples. Mistress Alexandra Hathaway sighed, even as she nodded her satisfaction. Everything was in order. She picked up her pince-nez and her fan from the dresser, drew on her black silk mittens, and went downstairs.

She was crossing the hall to the drawing room as the butler opened the door to two young men. She recognized Marcus Crofton, but his companion was unknown to her.

"Good evening, Mistress Hathaway." Mr. Crofton greeted her in his customary genial fashion. She dropped a curtsy, lowering her eyes, murmuring a greeting in a barely audible voice.

"Allow me to introduce my guest, ma'am. The

Honorable Peregrine Sullivan." Marcus gestured to his companion, who was handing the butler his hat and cane. "Mistress Hathaway is the genius in residence, you should understand, Perry. As I explained earlier, she is cataloguing Sir Stephen's magnificent library."

Peregrine was eager to meet the guardian of the library and bowed with a warm smile. "Mistress Hathaway, an honor."

"Sir." She bobbed another curtsy, not meeting his gaze.

Peregrine frowned a little. What a strange little dab of a creature she was. Not at all what he'd expected of someone capable of appreciating and cataloguing such an intellectual treasure house as Sir Arthur Douglas's library. However, looks could be deceiving, he told himself.

"I am most eager to view the volume of the *Decameron,* ma'am. I understand it is part of Sir Stephen's collection." Mistress Hathaway seemed to wince a little as he said this, but perhaps her misshapen back was paining her, he thought with a flash of sympathy.

"Indeed, sir," she responded after a barely perceptible pause. She raised her eyes for the first time. Large and gray under surprisingly luxuriant dark lashes. "I would be delighted to show it to you at some point. But at present, my employer is expecting me at the whist tables." She moved away to the double doors to the salon.

There was something puzzling about the lady, Peregrine reflected. Something slightly off kilter, but it was none of his business. He followed Marcus into the salon.

"Lady Douglas, may I present my houseguest, the Honorable Peregrine Sullivan?" Marcus bowed over the hand of an angular woman in a saque gown of magenta silk that hung from her thin frame as if from a coat hanger. Her décolletage revealed an expanse of sallow freckled skin, and her pale red hair was dressed in an elaborate coiffure of frizzed curls on her brow and tight ringlets curling to her sharp bare shoulders.

She greeted Peregrine's bow with a nodded curtsy, subjecting him to a scrutiny that seemed to find him wanting. "Mr. Sullivan. You are welcome, I'm sure," she murmured with a distant twitch of her lips that Peregrine thought could have been a smile with sufficient imagination.

"An honor, Lady Douglas," he responded with impeccable courtesy.

Sir Stephen Douglas was a tall, well-built man of florid complexion. His belly pushed against the silver buttons of his striped waistcoat, and the seams of his green damask breeches strained against the fullness of his thighs.

A sportsman who was also a little too fond of the pleasures of the table and the decanter, Perry guessed, bowing as he greeted his host. In his late middle years, he would run to seed. It was an uncharitable reflection, but something about the man put his back up, even though he couldn't pinpoint the cause.

"The Honorable Peregrine Sullivan, eh? One of the Blackwaters, I believe." Sir Stephen took snuff as he responded to Peregrine's bow. "I am slightly acquainted with your brother, the earl. We belong to the same London club. I don't, however, believe I have met *you* there."

"I'm sure I would have remembered had we met there, sir," Peregrine responded with a smooth smile. "But I am not overly fond of cards. Blackwater, on the other hand, is quite taken with 'em."

"Not overly fond of cards . . . Gad, sir. What *gentleman* is not fond of cards?" Stephen exclaimed, sneezing snuff into his handkerchief in vigorous punctuation.

"We are a rare species, Sir Stephen, but you find us in all the best circles," Peregrine responded with an amiable smile that did nothing to conceal an edge of disdain to his voice. He became aware of a strange sound over his shoulder. A slight choking noise. He turned his head sharply, but only the librarian was close by, and she was plying her fan, gazing into the middle distance.

"Oh, good . . . good." Belatedly, it seemed to occur to Stephen that he might have implied that his guest, a scion of the august Blackwater family, somehow lacked gentlemanly attributes. Disconcerted, he blinked and stuffed his handkerchief into the deep pocket of his coat. "Well, we have three whist tables set up. Mistress Hathaway has agreed to make a fourth at the third table. I trust you have no objections, Mr. Sullivan."

"How could I?" Peregrine asked blandly. "If the lady has no objection to playing with a self-confessed amateur." He glanced at the librarian with an inquiringly raised eyebrow.

"Maybe I will not draw you as partner, sir," the lady murmured from behind her fan. "In which case, I can only be delighted to find myself playing against an amateur." She moved away to one of the card tables set up on the far side of the salon.

Peregrine swallowed his surprise at this riposte. His host clearly hadn't heard the sotto voce response and was busily allocating players to tables. The party divided, and Perry took his place at the third table with a keen-eyed gentleman in a suit of a vivid shade of turquoise and a lady of an uncertain age, dressed in a fashion too youthful for her slightly raddled countenance, the décolletage of her crimson gown revealing too much wrinkled flesh, none of it improved with copious applications of paint and powder. Mistress Hathaway took her place rather diffidently, keeping her eyes down as they cut for partners.

Peregrine was more than happy to draw the librarian as his partner. Not only would her skills offset his own inadequacies, but she had piqued his curiosity with that sotto voce riposte. Had he really heard her correctly?

"I fear you have drawn the short straw after all,

ma'am," he murmured as he moved into the chair opposite her. "I shall do my best not to let you down." He hid a smile as he waited to see if she would rise to the bait.

Mistress Hathaway glanced across at him. "If you play as well as you are able, sir, I must be satisfied," she responded, her voice as soft as ever, her expression as demure as before. "But I do beg you to remember in your bidding that a librarian's purse is not particularly plump."

There was an unmistakable glimmer of amusement, of challenge even, in the gray eyes. Perry's lips twitched. She had not disappointed him. But he was still deeply surprised by such a sharp undertone that seemed completely out of keeping on the lips of this dowdy, downtrodden woman. And there was something about those eyes that did not match the face. They were young, bright, and very sharp. He leaned closer, his own gaze sharpened, but she instantly dropped her eyes to the cards she was sorting in her hand, and he sat back, for the moment prepared to bide his time.

Why on earth had she allowed herself to respond like that? Alexandra cursed herself roundly for such a foolish impulse, but there was something about the Honorable Peregrine that piqued her, that drew from her an urge to engage with him in some way. Maybe it had something to do with his knowledge of the

Decameron—she longed to discuss the library with someone who might share her delight in its treasures—and maybe it had something to do with his sharp put-down of Sir Stephen's pretensions. Whatever it was, it was as ridiculous as it was dangerous. She bit the inside of her cheek hard until the pain distracted her.

Perry realized quickly that his partner was indeed an expert. It was true that he'd never seen the appeal in cards—there always seemed more interesting ways to pass an evening—but he had a mathematical mind, and after a few hands, he found an unexpected pleasure in the intellectual exercise of memory and calculation at which Mistress Hathaway appeared to excel. There was something supremely satisfying in finding that they were completely in accord, each knowing how the other would follow a lead.

Once or twice, his partner would glance at him when they took a game, and he would see a light in her gray eyes that seemed at odds with the slack, faintly dark-shadowed skin beneath them. But she never spoke except to call her bid. She laid down her cards with the same brisk purpose with which she added up the scores and the wins and losses at the end of each rubber.

A formidable lady, whose outward appearance completely belied the efficiency of her play. Peregrine wondered if anyone else noticed the paradox as the evening finally broke up and he rose from the table with a respectable sum in his pocket. He shook hands with his opponents and then turned to where Mistress Hathaway had been standing, a smile on his lips, his hand outstretched, only to discover an empty space behind him. The librarian was nowhere to be seen, and Marcus appeared at his elbow, yawning.

"Stephen's gathering a fishing expedition tomorrow at sunrise," Marcus said. "D'you fancy joining it?"

"Certainly," Perry responded with enthusiasm. "I've more stomach for fishing than for whist."

Marcus chuckled. "You had a profitable evening, though, I gather."

"Yes," Perry agreed thoughtfully. "Not in some small measure thanks to Mistress Hathaway."

"Yes, she's an unusual woman. Don't find too many of the dear souls with wits to match hers," Marcus agreed, yawning again. "Still, with such an unfortunate appearance, 'tis good she has the wit at least to compensate."

"Yes, I suppose so," Perry agreed as they went out into the starless night to walk down the drive to the Dower House.

Chapter Two

Alexandra Douglas reached the haven of her own bedchamber, closing the door behind her with a sigh of relief. She leaned against it, listening to the sounds from the hall below as the party broke up. She had made her escape so abruptly as to be considered discourteous, but she doubted anyone would have noticed. Except perhaps for her fair-headed whist partner, the Honorable Peregrine Sullivan. Those deep blue eyes had a disconcertingly penetrating quality that made her very uneasy. But what could he have seen?

Of course, she hadn't helped matters with her impulsive responses. For some reason, the man had brought out the carefree Alexandra Douglas she used to be. She'd always enjoyed verbal challenges and lively sparring with anyone willing to engage with her. But she'd learned to quell the urge, or, at least, she thought she had. It was so difficult sometimes to hide her self in this dim carapace. Beneath the dull gray surface of her outward guise, the flame that was Alexandra Douglas burned just as brightly as ever, and not a day passed without her longing at least once to be free of the whole wretched business.

She straightened from the door, checking that it was securely locked, and then went to examine her reflection in the long pier glass. Her appearance was still in order. There was nothing untoward. Surely the Honorable Peregrine couldn't have detected anything out of the ordinary. Her reflection showed a hunched, middle-aged dormouse in a dowdy bombazine dress of nondescript color, an unsightly birthmark disfiguring her cheek.

And once again, that wave of resentful depression washed over her. She didn't want to look like this. What would the Honorable Peregrine have thought if he could see her as she really was? She had a sudden unreasoning longing to show him that this incarnation was merely a charade, and with a muttered imprecation, she reached up to take the pins out of her hair, shaking it free of the tightly braided plaits knotted at her nape, running her fingers through it to ease the tangles.

And then she wondered why on earth it should matter to her that a perfect stranger should see only an ugly old woman in a shabby gown. It was exactly what she wanted him to see. Even when she was resenting it, she triumphed in the success of her disguise, feeling a welcome sense of superiority to all those she was deceiving. So what was different about the Honorable Peregrine? Not that it mattered in the least, she told herself fiercely. Only the plan mattered. She must never lose sight of that.

Leaning closer to the mirror, she peered closely at the strands of gray artfully woven into the dark chestnut mass. They would need retouching in a day or two. She unbuttoned her gown, letting it fall to her ankles, and untied the tapes of the small pad that sat between her shoulder blades, before sitting in her shift at the dresser and cleansing her face with a soft cloth dipped in water from the ewer. The dark smudges under the eyes came away with one sweep of the cloth, the birthmark took a little longer to remove, but eventually, Alexandra Douglas looked upon her own face and not that of Mistress Alexandra Hathaway.

It was a relief to have herself back, even if only for the night. She would begin the whole laborious process again soon after dawn, but for now, she could feel the tension of deception slide from her as the disguise was removed.

She rose from the dresser and slipped a woolen night robe over her shoulders, wrapped it tightly before pouring herself a small glass of Madeira from a bottle she kept hidden in the bottom of the armoire. It wouldn't do for the servants to discover that Sir Stephen's secretary and librarian was a secret tippler. Not that she ever allowed herself more than this one solitary nightcap a day. It relaxed her after the day's stresses and loosened the tight controls that she had to live with every minute away from the safety of this corner bedchamber.

Alex sat on the deep windowsill, looking out over the lawn to the silver glimmer of the moonlit sea. It was a beautiful night, but soon the leaves would turn and fall, and the winds of winter would blow strong from the sea. She had always loved the winters at Combe Abbey, the crisp frosty fields, the bare trees bending beneath the gusting wind, the smell of burning logs in the great fireplaces. Her own bedchamber, once she and her sister had left the nursery floor, had been at the front of the house, Sylvia's adjoining it. Lady Maude, Stephen's wife, kept them both as guest chambers these days. But Alex was happy enough in her small corner chamber. It was secluded from the rest of the house, more easily reached by the backstairs than from the grand staircase leading up from the front hall.

Only a few short months before, she had been contentedly moving from day to day in a world where everything followed an accustomed pattern, until that early December afternoon . . . could it possibly have been only eight months ago?

Resting her chin in her elbow-propped hand, she let her mind drift back to that chilly afternoon . . .

◁∽▷

"Mistress Alexandra? Oh, there you are. I've been looking all over for you." The young maidservant adjusted her cap as she ducked beneath the bare branch of an apple tree. She was somewhat breathless, pink-cheeked from the brisk winter wind.

"Well, now that you've found me, Dorcas, what can I do for you?" Alexandra closed her book over her gloved finger and smiled up at the girl from the bench beneath the apple tree in the relatively sheltered orchard.

" 'Tis Mistress Simmons, miss. She wants you."

Alexandra uncoiled her lithe frame from the bench and drew her cloak more tightly around her. "Then she must have me. Where is she?"

"In her parlor, miss."

Alexandra nodded. "Thank you, Dorcas." She walked quickly away down the avenue of apple trees, her stride like that of a restless young colt eager for the pasture. She broke through the neat rows of pollarded fruit trees at the foot of a sweep of green lawn leading up to a pleasant gray-stone house, the pale sun deepening the hue of the red-tiled roof. She paused for a moment, enjoying the vista. The house had been her home for the last five years, and while she still had moments of longing for her childhood home, Combe Abbey, standing high on its Dorset cliff top overlooking Lulworth Cove, St. Catherine's Seminary for Young Ladies had given her much to be thankful for.

She strode off towards the house, heading for a side door. The narrow corridor was filled with familiar scents of beeswax and lavender, and she could hear the girlish chatter of young voices coming from one of the schoolrooms as she passed a closed door. She smiled faintly—not so long ago, her voice would have joined those. She crossed a square, sunlit hall and tapped on a door.

"Enter."

Alexandra entered the room, smiling a greeting. "Dorcas said you wished to see me, Helene."

"Yes, my dear." The middle-aged woman behind the desk took off her pince-nez and rubbed her eyes wearily. "Sit down."

Alexandra obeyed. She had spent many hours in the last five years in this room, part parlor, part office, part schoolroom, avidly inhaling every scrap of knowledge Helene could impart. Now, however, she felt a tremor of alarm. Her friend and mentor for once seemed to be at a loss for words . . .

Helene Simmons regarded the young woman in compassionate silence for a moment. She had owned St. Catherine's Seminary for Young Ladies for more than ten years and was accustomed to trying, and failing for the most part, to educate young and frivolous female minds to respond to the stimulation of the intellect. The young girls who came under her tutelage were generally the daughters of the landed gentry, for whom lay ahead only good marriages, the amusements of the Season, the long heartbreaking years of childbearing. They had little interest in the finer pursuits of the mind, although they were eager enough for dance classes, music lessons, and instruction in deportment. Alexandra Douglas was very different.

From the first moment the fifteen-year-old girl had arrived at St. Catherine's, Helene had known she had a potential protégée at last. Alexandra's curiosity knew no bounds, and everything fascinated her, whether it was a mathematical equation, some finer point of agriculture, the intricacies of beekeeping, or the poems of Catullus. Helene, with sheer joy, had honed the girl's undisciplined mind and seen her grow into the highly accomplished young woman sitting across the desk from her on this chilly December afternoon.

And now she had to give Alexandra news that would have who knew what consequences for her future.

Alex became increasingly uneasy as the silence stretched, until Helene said simply, "I have some bad news, my dear." She took a sheet of parchment from her desk. "This is from your father's lawyer in Chancery Lane. I'm very sorry to have to tell you, Alexandra, but your father has died very suddenly."

Alex blinked and swallowed the lump that had grown in her throat. "Papa is dead?"

Helene nodded, pushing the letter across the desk to her. "Read for yourself, my dear."

Alexandra stared down at the black, lawyerly script, the seal of an inn of Chancery at the bottom. It was a simple statement of the death of Sir Arthur Douglas on the fifteenth day of November, in the year of our Lord 1762. The following paragraph merely said that there were estate matters to discuss with Sir Arthur's daughters, and Lawyer Forsett would be happy to make the journey into Hampshire to impart these matters to Mistress Alexandra and Mistress Sylvia Douglas, unless they would care to wait upon him in his chambers in Chancery Lane.

"I am so sorry, my dear," Helene repeated, seeing the girl's pallor, the sheen of tears in her eyes.

Alexandra shook her head as if to blink the tears away. She hadn't seen her father for five years. Every Christmas, there had been a token of some kind but never a letter or anything really personal. She had wondered at first what she and Sylvia had done to cause their father's hostility, but as time went on, she had learned to shrug it off. Their mother's final romantic escapade had probably been sufficient for their father to cut himself off from their shared offspring, and when news of the divorce and his remarriage had reached them in a terse note from this same lawyer, his daughters had accepted the situation. Alexandra's upkeep and tuition at St. Catherine's was paid for regularly, and Sylvia's financial needs and her care under their former nurse continued uninterrupted. Alexandra had vaguely assumed that their father had made some provision for their future and ceased to question his silence.

Until that freezing January afternoon in Lawyer Forsett's chambers.

Alexandra brought herself back to the reality of the present, the moonlit evening, the quiet chamber at her back, the oh so familiar surroundings of her familial home. So familiar and yet so unfamiliar now. She felt the old, cold anger begin to spiral within. She had learned painfully over the years the need to control her mercurial temper. She was a natural hothead, and it had taken many unpleasant lessons to teach her both the need and the tools to keep it on a tight rein.

Injustice had always been the first trigger, and the injustice that presently tyrannized herself and her sister constantly threatened to overwhelm those hard-won controls.

She fought her silent battle for a moment, until she felt the anger subside under the equally cold but twice as useful determination. Her loathsome cousin Stephen was, all unwittingly, paying for his avarice, and he would continue paying until she had safe the ten thousand pounds apiece that her father had intended to leave his bastard daughters.

Not that the money would confer legitimacy on either herself or Sylvia, she reflected with a renewed burst of fury, this time directed at her father. *How could he have done that to his daughters?* Alex remembered him as an affectionate parent, somewhat distracted at times, and she remembered the many hours he and she had spent in the library . . . the library downstairs at Combe Abbey where she now spent the better part of her day.

Her father had introduced her to all of his literary treasures, those acquired by his father and by himself. As much a bibliophile as his own parent, Sir Arthur had recognized the same passion in his daughter, and from the moment she had learned to read, he had encouraged her to have free rein among his books. She couldn't remember his ever raising an eyebrow at the volumes she roamed through during long winter afternoons curled up in a corner of the sofa. And he'd always answered her questions about the content of the books, even when, as she now understood, neither the content nor the questions had been appropriate for a young girl's mind.

That knowledge stood her in good stead now, she reflected grimly. Who else was better suited than she to catalogue the volumes in the library for their new owner? Stephen's interest was only in their value, but Alexandra had every intention of turning that to her own and Sylvia's advantage.

She yawned suddenly and stood up with a sigh, slipping the robe off her shoulders before climbing into the high bed. She leaned sideways to snuff out the candle and then lay back, watching the play of moonlight on the wall opposite the window, listening to the faint sound of waves breaking on the shore of the cove. A sound that had lulled her to sleep throughout her childhood.

But tonight sleep proved elusive. She wondered whether Sylvia was asleep in the modest cottage in Barton, in the neighboring county of Hampshire. The sisters had never been this far apart. When Alexandra had been sent to St. Catherine's just outside Barton, Sylvia had remained with their former nurse, who had continued to care for the invalid girl long after Sylvia no longer inhabited the nursery at Combe Abbey. Someone—their father, they had always assumed—had provided a small cottage in Barton, only a quarter-mile from the seminary, for his second daughter and her nurse, and from then on, Sylvia, like Alexandra, had had no contact with her parent.

Matty was devoted to Sylvia, who had been in fragile health since birth, and the stipend she received from Sir Arthur Douglas to continue caring for the girl was a welcome addition to her miserly income. Without that stipend, she would not be able to keep Sylvia or afford the medicines and tonics she needed.

Alexandra tossed onto her other side. She was always worried about Sylvia now. She knew that Matty would not abandon her, and the fifty pounds Stephen had been willing to part with would keep her for almost a year, but after that, if Alexandra was unable to put things right, to restore justice to this muddle of their lives, Sylvia's future didn't bear thinking of.

Alexandra had given some thought to the lawyer's suggestion that she take up employment as a governess or teacher. Helene had accompanied her to London but had remained at the hotel during Alexandra's meeting with Lawyer Forsett. When she'd heard the full story on Alex's return, she had instantly offered her protégée a position at St. Catherine's. She'd stressed how it was an ideal solution. Alex would be able to stay in the home she'd grown accustomed to, in the company of her best friend, and within a mile of her sister.

But resignation did not come easily to Alexandra Douglas, and she had considered the possibility and dismissed it in the next breath. It was not right, it was not just. She and Sylvia had been deprived of their due through a trick of the law, and she would get it back for them. Stephen could well afford to honor Sir Arthur's intentions, and sheer avarice kept him from doing so. Well, his avarice would turn the tables on him, and he'd never know.

She smiled a little and felt sleep creep over her at the familiar resolution.

❧

Peregrine slept the deep, untroubled sleep of a man who has spent the last few days on horseback. He was woken at dawn by John, bringing hot shaving water and coffee.

"Master Crofton will meet you in the breakfast parlor in half an hour, sir," the valet informed him, setting down his burdens and drawing back the curtains.

Perry struggled up against his pillows, blinking in the gray dawn. "At this god-awful hour? The sun's not even up," he muttered. "Oh . . . fishing, I remember now." Reluctantly, he swung his legs from the bed and stood up, stretching, glancing longingly at the warm sheets behind him. "Riding breeches, then, John, and the green worsted coat." He soaked a cloth in hot water and held it to his face, feeling the blood begin to flow again.

He dressed swiftly, pulling on leather boots sturdy enough to withstand the damp and mud of a riverbank, and went downstairs. Marcus was already attacking a plate of sirloin in the breakfast parlor. He greeted Perry with a wave, his mouth full, and gestured to the sideboard, where covered dishes steamed gently.

Perry helped himself to kidneys and bacon, poured himself a tankard of ale, and sat down. "I hope you have a rod for me, Marcus. I didn't come supplied."

His host swallowed his mouthful. "Oh, no difficulties, dear boy. I have rods aplenty. The trout should be biting this morning."

"Where do we meet Sir Stephen?" Perry buttered a thick slice of wheaten bred.

"Up at the Abbey. There'll be quite a party of us. Very fond of country pursuits is Sir Stephen. Anyone would think he'd been a country man all his life."

"He hasn't?" Perry was curious.

Marcus shook his head. "Not a bit of it, and believe me, it shows where it matters."

"Oh?" Perry raised an inquiring eyebrow.

Marcus took a swallow of ale. "Shouldn't really talk out of turn, but the man hasn't the first idea about estate management and husbandry. Sir Arthur knew every blade of grass on this estate, decided which crops to plant where and when, took care of his tenants and laborers . . . even down to whose roof needed repairing. He always said to me, if a man doesn't look after his own people, he'll come to ruin."

"And Stephen doesn't believe that?"

Marcus shrugged. "I don't think he gives it a moment's thought. Believes that basically the estate runs itself, and all he has to do is take what he wants from it. If it weren't for the agent, good man that he is, who knows how matters would stand."

"So where did Sir Stephen come from, then?" Peregrine speared a kidney.

"Bristol, I think. He's a townie, that's for sure. I think his branch of the family had something to do with shipping, but they were definitely the poor relations. Social pretensions aplenty, Lady Maude in particular, and they do enjoy lording it over the County gentry around here."

Marcus spoke with all the casual derision of one who had no need for pretension. Perry knew that his friend's late father, the Dowager Lady Douglas's husband before Sir Arthur, had been a baronet of considerable lineage and estate. Marcus, as the younger son, had inherited an enviable competence.

"There are children, presumably?"

"Oh, mewling brats . . . I don't know how many, but Lady Maude is always sending for the physician or demanding that Sir Stephen sack the nursemaid because she's neglecting one or other of them." Marcus chuckled. "Hate to say it, but I wouldn't be in Stephen's shoes for all the tea in China."

Peregrine absorbed this as he cut a rasher of bacon. "The librarian, Mistress Hathaway, how does she fit into the household?" He kept his tone casual, hoping to conceal the depths of his curiosity about the woman, whose rather lovely gray eyes held a deep spark of liveliness that belied her appearance.

"Not quite sure," Marcus confessed. "I think she's more than a librarian these days. I gather she handles Stephen's business affairs. He's a gambler through and through and loves to play on 'Change. Our librarian is apparently quite an expert at such matters, odd though it may seem."

"Mmm." Perry chewed reflectively. It did seem odd. "So where does she come from?"

"No idea." Marcus tossed aside his napkin. "If you're done here, Perry, we should head up to the Abbey. Stephen will be champing at the bit."

Perry finished his mouthful, wiped his mouth with his napkin, took a final draught of ale, and pushed back his chair. "At your service, sir."

They walked up the driveway to the Abbey. The morning air had a chill to it, and a sea fret blanketing the gray waters of the Solent rolled in over the cliff top. On the circular drive in front of the Abbey, a group of men waited, buttoned into their coats, servants behind them carrying rods, hooks, flies, and all of the usual fishing paraphernalia.

Sir Stephen greeted the new arrivals with a pointed look at his fob watch. "Good, you're here at last. If we don't hurry, we'll miss the first rise. They bite best before sunup."

"Forgive us, Sir Stephen," Perry said with a concilia-tory smile. "Your hospitality was too good last even. I found it hard to leave my bed this morning."

Stephen looked somewhat mollified. "Well, let's be

going." He waved an encompassing arm at the other men. "I daresay you'll make your own introductions, but Marcus knows most of the company." He strode towards the rear of the house, and the rest fell in behind them.

～∞～

Alexandra watched them pass the house from the corner window of her chamber. Her gaze went unerringly to the tall figure of the Honorable Peregrine. He walked with a long, loose stride, his fair head bare, the golden locks gleaming in the early-morning gloom. He carried his gloves in his hand and was in animated discussion with Marcus Crofton, walking beside him.

He wanted to see the volume of the *Decameron,* she remembered suddenly. Was he a collector? Certainly, such a desire indicated a literary turn of mind, a bibliophile, even. A little thrill of excitement ran through her as she moved to her dresser to begin the long process of assuming her disguise. Combe Abbey these days was a den of Philistines, in her admittedly jaundiced opinion. The conversation was exclusively limited to the affairs of local society, the complaints of Lady Maude, and, in the private conversations that Alexandra had with her employer, the handling of accounts, the value of books, and the acquisition and manipulation of stocks and bonds on the Exchange.

She so desperately missed talking to anyone who shared her own passions that she'd be happy to spend time in the library discussing its contents with any-one, even a snuff-covered ancient with rheumy eyes, a stained waistcoat, and a beard to his knees, but Mr. Sullivan came with his own undeniable attractions. Those wonderful blue eyes, the color of a summer sky, she thought fancifully. And that golden head of hair coming off a broad forehead with a deep widow's peak. Dear God, what was she thinking of? She sounded like some half-daft romantic without a sensible thought in her head.

Fixedly, she gazed at her reflection in the mirror, deftly shading the skin under her eyes with a stick of moistened charcoal, smudging it with her finger until it was barely there but there nevertheless. She was going to have to be very careful in the Honorable Peregrine's company.

She must keep her mind fixed upon the plan. A few hours wrestling with Sir Stephen's investments would chase all unwelcome distractions from her mind. It was an activity she loved; it stretched her mental abilities, satisfied her love of figures and calculations, and gave her the glorious satisfaction of funneling profits here and there into her own private fund. When she reached the exact sum their father had intended to leave them, Mistress Alexandra Hathaway would disappear from Combe Abbey, never to be seen again. Sir Stephen and Lady Maude would be none the wiser, and certainly not injured in any way. She now had a very firm grasp of her father's estate and the fortune he had left and knew to the last penny what every necessary expenditure cost the estate.

She leaned closer into the mirror. The birthmark was a little more difficult to achieve than the shadows beneath her eyes, but a thin paste of rouge applied with the tip of a quill pen created the desired effect. She was always careful to keep out of the direct light, and her downcast eyes and hunched posture helped to draw attention away from her face.

She and Sylvia had so enjoyed charades as children. They had developed the most elaborate scenarios. On one of her infrequent visits to Combe Abbey, their mother, in a moment of benign distraction, had been persuaded to donate to her daughters whatever items of her wardrobe no longer pleased her. Swathes of velvets, silk ball gowns, ostrich plumes, heeled kid slippers, even discarded powder and paint from her own paint box, had provided all the props they had needed. Alex had always been the instigator, the creator of the scenarios, and her main pleasure was seeing how her sister came out of herself and seemed to take on a flush of health in her enthusiasm for the play. Sylvia was always exhausted afterwards, but even Matty had refrained from more than minor grumbles at the toll such games took on the girl's strength.

So where is our mother now? Alexandra began to braid her hair into tight plaits. The Contessa Luisa della Minardi, once Lady Douglas, was presumably somewhere on the Continent with her second husband, unless she'd moved on to a third. Alex and Sylvia remembered vividly the times when Combe Abbey would fall ominously silent, and their father would never be in evidence, shut up in his business office or the library. Alex had known whenever their mother had made one of her not infrequent disappearances to keep away from the library unless she was certain her father wasn't there. She and her sister hadn't known what took their mother away, but servants' gossip was impossible to miss.

The first Lady Douglas had had a roving eye and was susceptible to beautiful young men. And, a beautiful woman herself, she had attracted the adoration of many an Adonis.

At first, Sylvia and Alex had thought their mother's escapades excitingly adventurous. But that delusion had not lasted long, their father had made sure of that. And Luisa's final flight, with the Conte della Minardi, had been the last straw for Sir Arthur.

Alexandra tied the tapes of the pad between her shoulder blades and stepped into a gown of faded gray muslin, almost colorless now. She took a last careful look in the pier glass, making sure everything was in place, and stepped out into the corridor. Once the door closed behind her, she became Mistress Hathaway, a person of no importance, no status in the household. Automatically, her head drooped a little, her eyes were downcast, her shoulders hunched up against the ugly humpback.

The most irksome duty of the day lay ahead, breakfast in the morning room. If she was lucky, Maude would be occupied with some minor disaster in the nursery, but if she was unlucky, then she would be ensconced at the table, with weak tea and toast, ready to launch into a catalogue of complaints that a patient-seeming Alexandra would have to comment on with appropriate understanding and sympathetic murmurs, always careful not to overstep the boundaries defining the relationship between an employer and her servant. Maude had a certain malicious cunning, and she was all too quick to sense a slight where there was none and all too willing to invent insolences and incompetence when it suited her.

If she suspected for a moment that there was more to the dowdy librarian than met the eye, she would nose it out, poking, probing, questioning, until she came up with something that suited her. Sir Stephen lived in trembling fear of his wife's ill temper, and if Maude came up with a reason to get rid of her husband's librarian, he would find it hard to resist her. And that would be the best-case scenario. Alex didn't want to consider the worst—an accusation of fraud, of fictitious references, anything that could put her on the wrong side of the law. Just a few questions could untangle the entire web of deception that maintained the charade. And the consequences for both herself and Sylvia were unthinkable.

Chapter Three

Peregrine watched the silver flash arc gracefully through the air as he reeled in his fourth catch of the morning. The trout were plentiful in this river-fed stream. All three Blackwater brothers were practiced fishermen and had spent many a silent but companionable dawn or dusk fly-fishing on the family estate in Northumberland. Perry was relieved to find that his present companions were not talkative, either, and in the gentle rhythm of casting and reeling, he slipped into a meditative trance.

His mind went, as it so often did these days, to his uncle, Viscount Bradley, and the vexed issue of his will, or, rather, of the one stipulation in the will that would make his three nephews equal heirs to his massive fortune. Peregrine felt the familiar surge of anger whenever he thought of the old man, who, while insisting that he was dying, still contrived to make the lives of everyone around him miserable with his malicious manipulations.

Three brothers, three wives. It sounded reasonable on the surface. One could believe that Viscount Bradley was looking out for the future of the Blackwater family, except, of course, that he was doing the opposite. Perry's line twitched, and he began to reel it in slowly. Bradley had decreed that the three wives had to be fallen women in some respect—An incautious movement made his rod jerk abruptly, and he cursed as he watched the fish on the end of his line wriggle, twist, and vanish back into the green-brown water below.

Damn Bradley. He pulled in his line and rebaited the hook. Just the thought of the viscount's twisted malice broke his concentration. Somehow, his brothers seemed to find it easier to accept than he did. Jasper was probably right that Bradley had his own good reasons for wanting to rub the noses of the Blackwater family prudes and sticklers for convention in the ordure of a city kennel. But it was still a pact with the devil. Maybe he did want revenge on the family, maybe he was even entitled to it, but Bradley didn't give a damn what his nephews thought about being compelled to marry women of less than stainless reputation, women they wouldn't ordinarily find themselves in the same room with, unless, of course, it was a brothel. And his nephews had never done him any harm.

Perry walked a little way along the riverbank and cast his line again, watching the hook sink below the surface, smooth as silk. Jasper, of course, had no reason to complain, he thought with a wry smile, trying not to indulge in the familiar little niggle of resentment at the ease with which the fifth Earl of Blackwater, Peregrine's eldest brother, had managed to beat the old gentleman at his own game. The wife he had chosen, Clarissa Astley, had been practicing her own deception in London when Jasper had met her. On the surface, she was a whore, a denizen of one of the most renowned Covent Garden nunneries, and thus perfectly suited to satisfy Viscount Bradley's condition. However, Clarissa was not at all what she seemed.

The titian-haired beauty had fooled Bradley, or at least forced him to accept her for what she appeared to be, and she was now ensconced as Countess Blackwater, and the love of her husband's life.

Which left Jasper's younger twin brothers to fulfill their own obligations if the heavily mortgaged family estates were to be towed out of the River Tick. And Jasper had made it very clear that he expected his brothers to do what was required, one way or another. Once in a while, Perry thought, with a flash of exasperation that made him jerk his rod again, his eldest brother could acknowledge the difficulties in the task. Just because it had been so easy for him . . .

But then Sebastian had managed it, too. Perry raised his rod and recast. His twin hadn't had to look very far, either, to find a woman whose peculiar circumstances made her fit the viscount's criteria of a fallen woman. Like Jasper's bride, she, too, was not all that she seemed, but the circumstances of her life made her a perfect bride for Sebastian to fulfill the conditions of the will. And since he'd been in love with Lady Serena Carmichael from the moment he'd first stepped into London Society as a callow youth, it was a perfect match in every respect.

Which left Peregrine.

He'd tried, God knows he'd tried. He'd experimented with an orange seller at Drury Lane and for a while had thought he might be able to make it work, at least for long enough to satisfy his uncle, but he'd been fooling himself. He'd explored the better class of brothel in the hopes that he might come across another Clarissa but to no avail. And every time his eldest brother asked him how his search was going, he'd prevaricated, implied that he might be making progress, anything to stave off Jasper's steely anger that Peregrine would put his own wishes above the honor of the Blackwater family, standing by while the family estates were sold off piecemeal.

It might be easier if he'd ever been in love, Peregrine thought gloomily. And then at least he'd know what he was looking for. He'd had his dalliances, certainly, but he knew in his soul that he needed a woman who could be his intellectual match. It might be arrogant of him, but it was the truth. He could not possibly contemplate sharing his life with a wife who could not give him intellectual companionship. He had little interest in the conventional pursuits of Society, found small talk a complete bore, unlike Sebastian, who could charm the birds out of the trees when he chose. His friends all shared one or more of his passions, be it science, literature, philosophy. And he knew that his distant manner put off the young debutantes who might otherwise have set their caps at him. And how in the world was he to find an intellectual match in the stews of London?

The pleasant morning was suddenly spoiled, and he yanked his rod roughly from the water, bringing it up in a shower of glittering drops, the empty hook swinging.

"That's not like you, Perry," Marcus observed cheerfully as he reeled in his own rod. "You're usually the soul of patience."

Perry shook his head with a rueful smile. "Something disturbed my concentration." He glanced around and saw that their companions were taking in their own rods, handing them over to the accompanying gamekeepers. The accumulated catch thrashed around in several large baskets.

"Breakfast, gentlemen," Stephen announced. "Fresh trout and good ale."

A chorus of agreement greeted this, and the men moved away towards the house, leaving the gamekeepers to bring up the rear with the morning's spoils. Perry strolled at the back of the group, his mood still somewhat clouded by his earlier reflections.

"You'll be able to take a look at the *Decameron* this morning," Marcus observed, falling in beside him. "Mistress Hathaway should be in the library by the time we get to the house."

"Ah." Perry's mood lightened instantly. "For a moment, I'd forgotten about that. I wonder if she'll have time to show me some of the other rarities."

"I'm sure she'll be happy to. She's a woman of little conversation in general, but I've seen her eyes light up when the topic turns to any of her treasures, and she does seem to consider them to be hers." Marcus chuckled. "Fortunately, Stephen's not particularly possessive about the contents of his library. His main focus is what he can get for 'em. So the lady can live her fantasy possession to her heart's content."

Perry nodded absently. Mistress Hathaway must have had a most unusual education in order to acquire such rarefied knowledge. What must it feel like to lavish love and care upon objects that you found precious knowing that their owner did not appreciate them? Frustrating, certainly, maybe even a little hurtful, he thought. And then he remembered that hastily suppressed gurgle of amusement the previous evening when he had snubbed Stephen, and he thought that perhaps Mistress Hathaway found her employer's Philistine indifference to the beauty of the library something to despise rather than personally painful.

The party tramped into the house through the gun room. A fire had been lit in the massive inglenook in the great hall, where a table groaned beneath sides of beef and ham, jugs of ale, and bread hot from the oven. The morning's catch disappeared to the kitchen to make an appearance on the table very soon.

Peregrine approached his host. "Would it be possible for me to see some of the rare volumes in your library, Sir Stephen? I own to a fascination with unusual acquisitions, and I'm told you have a magnificent collection."

"Oh, yes . . . yes, so I believe. Doesn't mean much to me, don't have time for much reading," Stephen responded, taking a tankard of ale from a passing footman. "But they're valuable, I'm told. I'm thinking of selling 'em. Not doing much good moldering away on those shelves." He drank deeply. "But by all means, dear fellow, take a look. Crofton told me of your interest, and Mistress Hathaway'll be glad to show you around. She knows what's there." He gestured with his free hand to the library towards the back of the house. "You'll find her in there, I'll be bound."

"Thank you." Perry smiled his appreciation and made his way to the rear of the house. He opened the door very quietly and stepped into a large, dimly lit room.

Floor-to-ceiling bookshelves lined the walls, and a small fire burned in the grate. The windows looked out onto the rear gardens, which were in shadow at this time of day. A single lamp burned on a massive oak desk, where a woman sat intent on the sheet of parchment in front of her. She was so absorbed in her work that she didn't at first notice her visitor, who stood by the door watching her. The light from the lamp caught shades of tawny gold and darker chestnut in the smoothly braided hair. As she worked, she moved an impatient hand up to brush aside a wisp of hair that was tickling her cheek.

Something about the gesture struck Peregrine as strangely out of place, oddly youthful somehow. She was frowning slightly as she bent to her task, and then a slow smile spread across her face, a smile of naked triumph and satisfaction. She gave a low chuckle, light and melodious, and wrote briskly for a few seconds. When she reached across the desk for another sheet of parchment, the lamp illuminated her face, and Peregrine stared, startled. Her expression seemed to change the contours of her face, softened it, rounded it out in some way. It was an almost imperceptible change, and yet it made the fine hairs on the back of his neck stand up and a little thrill of excitement course down his spine.

Abruptly, she looked up towards the door, only just aware of her audience. Her mouth formed a little *oh* of surprise, and uncertainty flashed across her face. Uncertainty and a degree of apprehension, Perry thought. *What is she afraid of?* But then it vanished, and he was bowing to the dowdy Mistress Hathaway, aware of a prickle of disappointment that the momentary appearance of someone else beneath the dowdy surface had merely been an illusion.

"I didn't mean to startle you, ma'am, but Sir Stephen said I might disturb you at your work if you could spare a little time to assist me. I'm most anxious to see the *Decameron* . . . and any other treasures you could show me."

"Indeed, sir," she responded rather distantly. How long had he been standing there watching her? It was so difficult to be on her guard when she was alone, and she could easily have betrayed herself with an unwary expression or a gesture not in keeping with the character of the downtrodden librarian. She overcame the flicker of fear with sheer effort of will and continued casually, "I am rather busy at the moment, but the shelves are at your disposal, of course. Please feel free to browse." She bent her head to her papers once again.

Peregrine frowned at this cool dismissal. It was not her place to refuse her assistance when her employer had promised it. "I don't wish to interrupt your work, Mistress Hathaway, but . . ."

She looked up at him again with a little sigh of exasperation that would not have been out of place on a vexed schoolmistress. For some perverse reason, it overcame his irritation. It just wasn't convincing. He gestured to the shelves with a comically perplexed air. "Where am I to start? You must admit 'tis a daunting exercise if one doesn't know how they are categorized. Are they alphabetical? If so, by title or author? Are they in order of rarity or shelved according to subject? I have even seen libraries where the books are arranged according to size."

"Surely not?" Mistress Hathaway exclaimed. "What barbarian would do something that idiotic?"

He laughed. There was nothing of the schoolmistress about her now or, indeed, of the diffident librarian.

Her indignation had brought a flush to her cheeks and a sparkle to the gray eyes, quite at odds with the subdued mien Mistress Hathaway generally presented to the world. Her shoulders had straightened imperceptibly, and her chin was lifted in that slightly challenging manner he remembered glimpsing the previous evening. "A barbarian rather like our friend Sir Stephen, I imagine," he observed lightly, giving no indication of his fascinated reflections. "I understand he's interested in selling the collection."

Her expression darkened, and the fleeting impression of youthfulness vanished. "That is so. Are you in the market, sir?"

He shook his head ruefully. "Alas, no. I have nothing like the necessary funds for such treasure. I may only gaze and admire at a distance."

She cast him a covert glance as if assessing the truth of what he said. "I am hoping to find a buyer who will appreciate what is here for itself rather than for its monetary value. Do you know of anyone, perhaps, whom I could approach privately before the collection goes to auction?"

"I know plenty of men who would kill for this library, but none I know has the necessary funds to acquire it intact. Are you prepared to break it up?"

Again, a look of distress crossed her face, and she turned aside for a moment before responding. "*I* would not wish it, but I doubt Sir Stephen minds how it's disposed of as long as it goes to the highest bidder."

Peregrine wandered across to the nearest row of shelves and glanced along them, fingering the leather spines. "I understand Sir Arthur Douglas and his father before him were responsible for the acquisitions. They must have been as shrewd as they were book lovers."

Something unreadable flashed again across her eyes, but her voice was flat, her face expressionless. "I wouldn't know, sir. I work for Sir Stephen. My job is to catalogue the library and do what I can to secure the best price for it. That is my sole interest."

Peregrine looked at her in disbelief. "Oh, come now, ma'am, you can't expect me to believe you get no personal pleasure out of being among these treasures."

"They don't belong to me," she said with an unmistakably bitter edge to her voice. "I cannot afford to have any personal feelings for the books."

Perry suddenly felt as if he was intruding on something very private. He didn't know why he felt that, but he decided it was time to leave well enough alone for the moment. He said cheerfully, "Could you at least point me towards the *Decameron,* ma'am? I don't wish to take up too much of your time."

Mistress Hathaway rose from her chair and came out from behind the desk. "'Tis over there, in the far corner." She moved a tall library ladder to the shelf in question and climbed up, reaching to the top shelf.

"May I help?" Perry asked, coming swiftly to her side. Ladies past their youth were usually not too agile when it came to ascending rickety ladders.

"No, I have it, thank you." She drew the volume from the shelf and jumped down from the top step of the ladder. "See how fine the binding is." She walked swiftly to the desk and put the volume under the light. "This copy is from 1492."

Peregrine followed. Maybe years of practice had given Mistress Hathaway the ability to climb up steps and jump off them without giving a thought to the maneuver.

And maybe it is snowing in Lucifer's inferno.

He stepped up beside her. Mistress Hathaway had drawn on a silk glove and was opening the volume with practiced skill, turning the pages with the utmost delicacy and a reverence that made nonsense of her earlier statement about taking no personal pleasure or interest in the books themselves. He became aware of her scent, a most delicate flowery fragrance that seemed to emanate from the back of her bent neck, where a heavy coil of gold-flecked hair lay against the very white column. He inhaled deeply, trying to identify the particular flower. A lemony scent, he thought. Very light and fresh, almost girlish.

As if aware of his concentration, she looked up at him, her expression both puzzled and wary. "Is something the matter, sir?"

"Not in the least." He bent over the volume.

Alexandra forgot her unease in the sheer joy of sharing this treasure with someone whose awe and reverence matched her own. Her delight bubbled in her voice as she showed him the illustrations. "Don't you think Bacchus is delightfully mischievous here? He's so often portrayed as rather malevolent, but this depiction shows a quite different interpretation. At least, I have always thought so."

"Yes, indeed." Peregrine took the magnifying glass from her and peered closely at the illustration. "He does have a wicked look about him, and you're right, 'tis not malevolent."

"You must see my fa—" Alex caught herself in time. She moved away from the desk. "Let me show you this edition of the *Canterbury Tales*. It was thought to be a first edition, but unfortunately, 'tis not. However, 'tis a very early one." She hopped up the ladder again and came down as swiftly as before, bringing the volume to the desk, opening it with the same reverence.

Perry examined the exquisitely illustrated volume with all the pleasure of a connoisseur, but he was aware that a significant part of his pleasure came from sharing it with his like-minded companion. There was something immensely appealing about the way her voice vibrated with enthusiasm when she talked about the finer points of the illustrations, the beautifully formed letters, and the ease with which she followed him when his thoughts were sidetracked to early printing methods and the different types of ink the monks would have used for different types of illustrations. It occurred to him with something of a shock that Mistress Hathaway knew at least as much as he did, if not more, about the intricacies of manuscript creation.

Neither of them was aware of time passing until a discreet cough and the steward's apologetic voice shocked them out of their absorption.

"Sir Stephen was wondering if you'd be joining them for breakfast, Mr. Sullivan. The trout is fresh from the kitchen."

"Oh, yes . . . yes, of course." Reluctantly, Perry raised his head from the book. "I hadn't realized the time." He stepped back and bowed to Mistress Hathaway. "Forgive me, ma'am, I have taken up too much of your time, but thank you for sharing these with me. May I visit you again? I'm sure there are treasures aplenty to view."

"Indeed there are, sir," she said with a formal curtsy. "Of course, you should feel free to use the library whenever you wish. You are Sir Stephen's guest."

Gone was the sparkle, gone the glow to her complexion. She was suddenly as plain, dull, and mousy as she had ever been. He nodded with a brief smile and left her to her papers and her volumes, returning to the lively gathering in the hall.

Alexandra sat for a long time behind the desk, staring into the middle distance. She was unnerved, unsettled, uneasy. Afraid she had let something slip in her pleasure in sharing her passion. And what a pleasure it had been. She could still feel the sense of his body as they had stood so close together turning the pages.

She could still smell the faint aroma of lavender from his shirt, the slight tang of fresh sweat on his skin, the morning's freshness on his cheek.

Sweet heaven, she hadn't thought it would be so difficult to maintain the charade. And indeed, it hadn't been until the Honorable Peregrine Sullivan had walked into the house.

She had anticipated many of the difficulties with this game she was playing and had thought she was ready to deal with anything that came up. But she hadn't anticipated the loneliness. She could never let down her guard long enough for any meaningful contacts with the people around her. Everything had to be superficial; she could permit herself only the most banal of conversational exchanges, revealing nothing at all about herself, not even her likes and dislikes, in case she slipped up. As a result, she felt as if she were living in solitary confinement, locked inside her own head.

She missed Sylvia dreadfully. She and her sister had been inseparable companions from earliest childhood. Only eleven months separated them, and in many ways, they were more like twins than regular siblings. Their mother paid little attention to them even when she was in residence, and soon after Sylvia's birth, she had started on her series of romantic escapades that had culminated in the elopement with the mysterious Italian count.

Alexandra still vividly remembered one fight she had overheard between her parents, soon after Sylvia's ninth birthday. Their mother had just reappeared after three months' absence, laden as always with gifts for her "precious girls," as she insisted upon calling them. And on this occasion, her husband had received her with open anger instead of his usual apparent indifference.

Alex had been curled in her habitual corner of the library sofa, struggling with a book of Latin verse. At first, she had felt a frisson of guilty excitement at eavesdropping on her parents, but as their voices had risen and the angry, hurtful words buzzed like wasps in the usually tranquil room, she had become alarmed and then terrified that they might discover her.

Their mother had made it clear that she couldn't stand the peace of the countryside, absolutely refused to become pregnant again—pregnancy and childbirth had nearly ruined her body. She needed the attention she could still command, and who would deny her the right to take what life offered her? She could still inflame a man, and no one could blame her for taking advantage of her gifts, since her husband had no interest in them. All he wanted was a brood mare and a housekeeper, and she had no intention of servicing him in either capacity.

At the time, Alex hadn't understood all of this, but she had understood that somehow she and Sylvia were responsible for their mother's frequent absences and their father's growing distance. From that moment, she and her sister had become all and everything to each other, sharing confidences, hopes, and fears, trusting only each other.

Alexandra sighed and reached for her quill again. She had heard that sometimes when a limb was lost, the person felt it aching like a phantom limb. Her sister's absence from her life was just like that. Sometimes she caught herself turning to say something, share some thought, only to realize that there was no one there. If she could just spend an hour with Sylvia now and again, she wouldn't mind the loneliness the rest of the time, but her sister was a day's journey away in the neighboring county, and there was no way Alex could engineer such an absence, let alone find a way to get there.

Letters were their only means of communication, and Sylvia was a faithful correspondent, but they had both agreed that it would be too dangerous for her to write about anything except the most innocuous subjects in any letter coming into Combe Abbey. Alex would have dearly loved her sister's advice, her sympathetic ear, her delicious sense of humor, which would make light of some of the trials and tribulations of this charade. But Sylvia allowed herself only the most oblique and seemingly anodyne comments. Alex took her own letters to the post herself, so she had greater freedom of expression. No one in the house knew to whom her letters were addressed. Letters coming into the house were left in plain sight on the table in the great hall to be picked up by the intended recipient, and while it was far-fetched to imagine anyone breaking the seal on something addressed to the librarian, the risk was not worth taking.

Restless, Alex got up from the desk. She couldn't concentrate on her work. A brisk stroll along the cliff path would refresh her mind, concentrate her thoughts properly. She went up to her chamber for her hooded cloak and gloves and took the backstairs to the kitchen. Preparations for dinner were in full swing, and no one acknowledged the almost insubstantial presence of the librarian. She was so self-effacing, so reluctant to draw attention to herself, that over the months, she had succeeded in moving around the house almost as if she was invisible. Now she let herself out the back door into the kitchen garden and took the path to the gate in the brick wall that led to the side path.

The wind was quite brisk, and she was glad of her cloak as she took a narrow alley between rows of fruit trees in the orchard and from there to the cliff top.

She walked for half an hour, enjoying the fresh air, the buffeting wind, the white-capped waves beyond the horseshoe entrance to the calmer waters of the cove. She had often swum in the cove in the summer. Even on the hottest days, the water had been chilly, and Sylvia had remained huddled in a blanket on the beach, enviously watching her sister. Sea bathing was forbidden the invalid, as was any exercise more strenuous than a sedate trot in the pony cart. Alex loved to gallop but had forced herself to keep her pony to a walk beside the cart when Sylvia took an outing. No one really knew what ailed Sylvia, but it was decided that she had a weak chest and a less than robust heart. It was true that she tired easily and often developed a persistent cough that could last most of the winter, but Alex often wondered if the strict precautions were really necessary. Sylvia certainly chafed against them.

After a while, she turned back towards the house, this time taking the main driveway up through the grounds. She was just passing the Dower House when her stepbrother and his guest rounded the corner of the drive in front of her on their way back to the Dower House.

"Good morning, Mistress Hathaway." Marcus swept off his hat with an elaborate flourish as he bowed. "Well met. Have you been taking the air?"

"Just a little stroll on the cliff top, sir," she responded, curtsying.

"Don't blame you. All those dusty books must give you a headache," he commented cheerfully.

"Oh, I doubt Mistress Hathaway finds the books in the least dusty, and I should be most surprised to find they gave her a headache," Peregrine declared with a conspiratorial smile at the lady, even as he doffed his own hat. "Mistress Hathaway and I find libraries most stimulating places to spend time. Is that not so, ma'am?"

Alex felt words of eager agreement rush to her tongue, as an answering smile set her eyes dancing and her lips moving. And then she bit back the words, swallowed the smile. "I'm sure your scholarship far exceeds mine, Mr. Sullivan. I merely do what I am employed to do."

Perry felt a wash of disappointment. He had sensed that she had been about to say something quite different. His pleasure in seeing her again so soon had surprised him, as had the ease with which he had slipped into the chatty, companionable ease they had adopted in the library. Mistress Hathaway, however, seemed to have forgotten that. She was avoiding his eye now and had taken a sideways step on the path as if to increase the distance between them.

"Will you come in for a moment, Mistress Hathaway? My mother was asking after you just the other day. She would enjoy a visit, if you could spare the time, ma'am." Marcus's smile was cajoling. He spent much of his time finding entertainment for his parent, and it was true that the Dowager Lady Douglas had expressed curiosity about the Abbey's librarian after meeting her at dinner a week or so earlier, when the dowager had been dutifully invited to the Abbey by the current Lady Douglas to join a select gathering of local society.

Alexandra hesitated. She was curious herself about her stepmother, whom she'd only met the one time, and she knew that Sylvia would be agog to hear her sister's opinions of the lady who had supplanted their own mother. But if she went in, she would find herself in the company of the Honorable Peregrine again. And her earlier unease had come back in full force the moment she'd seen him on the drive. It sounded far-fetched, and yet she couldn't deny the conviction that the gentleman's company was dangerous. Not only did he seem to see too much, but she found it very difficult to maintain her charade under the inviting gaze of those penetrating blue eyes. Perhaps she was imagining it . . . no, she wasn't.

"Do come in," Marcus urged, seeing her hesitation. "Just for a few moments. My mother is an invalid and sees so few people."

The hesitation had been her undoing. An instant refusal on the grounds of a pressing engagement with Sir Stephen would have been sufficient excuse, but now it would appear so churlish as to be discourteous and would certainly draw unwelcome attention to herself. She really had no choice but to satisfy Sylvia's curiosity.

"Of course, I should be delighted to call upon Lady Douglas, sir." She bobbed a curtsy.

Marcus beamed and offered her his arm up the path to the front door. Perry followed, reflecting that it would be interesting to see how the reclusive Mistress Hathaway conducted herself on a social visit. She had not shown herself to be much of a conversationalist at the whist table the previous evening. He knew she could more than hold her own in a private conversation, but he suspected that no one else at Combe Abbey had experienced that spirited tongue. *Why?* Why did she keep it on a leash?

Marcus ushered Alexandra into the hall. "Is Lady Douglas down, Baker?"

"She came down to the yellow drawing room an hour ago, sir. May I take your cloak, ma'am?"

"Thank you." Alex let the butler assist her with her cloak and then accompanied her stepbrother to a cheerful, firelit salon at the rear of the house.

"Mama, I have brought you a visitor." Marcus ushered Alexandra ahead of him into the salon. "Mistress Hathaway was passing the house, and I persuaded her to pay you a morning visit."

"Oh, how delightful." The light and rather youthful voice emanated from an astonishing assortment of scarves, silk draperies, and fringed shawls elegantly disposed upon a day bed before the fire. A white hand emerged from the drapery. "Mistress Hathaway, do take a seat, and we shall have a comfortable coze. Ratafia, Marcus. I'm sure Mistress Hathaway must be chilled to the bone out there in all that wind."

Alex took the proffered hand and curtsied. "Lady Douglas, I'm sorry to see you unwell."

"Oh, 'tis nothing, Mistress Hathaway. I am always in ill health. Such a nuisance, but one must play the cards one's been dealt," Lady Douglas said with a vague wave of the white hand. "I'm a martyr to rheumatism, and when the wind blows, 'tis like being tortured on the rack."

"You have my sympathies, ma'am." Alex took the slipper chair beside the day bed. "A member of my own family suffers from persistent ill health, and I know what a trial it is."

"Oh? And who is that?" Eliza Douglas's gaze sharpened with interest. "A close relative?" She took the glass of ratafia her son placed at her elbow.

"A cousin, ma'am." Alexandra took a sip from her own glass and then hastily put it back on the table. For a moment, she had forgotten that the cordial was revolting.

"How old is she, this cousin?" Eliza nibbled a sweet biscuit.

"She has twenty summers, ma'am. But her ill health has persisted since childhood."

"Oh, what a trial. Poor girl." Eliza sighed. "And where are you from, Mistress Hathaway? Not from these parts, I'm sure."

Alexandra became aware that Peregrine had removed her glass of ratafia and was replacing it with a glass of tawny liquid. "I feel sure you will prefer sherry, ma'am," he murmured, setting the glass down beside her.

"Thank you," she muttered, taken aback. Had her distaste been that obvious? She must remember to watch her facial expressions—as well as everything else—around this man. He was watching her too closely again.

"A little village just outside London, Lady Douglas," she said, averting her head slightly so that he could not read her expression. "My father was the vicar. A very scholarly man."

"I see." Eliza nodded sagely. "That would explain your own bookishness, then."

"My father taught me himself. His stipend was too small for a more formal education," Alex continued fluently. This narrative she could sustain for as long as necessary. She and Sylvia had rehearsed it for days before the game had started, and her unease receded a little.

"And what of your mother? Did she approve of such an extensive education? My own dear parents considered it quite unnecessary for their daughters to learn anything beyond drawing, the pianoforte, the harp perhaps, and, of course, dancing and deportment."

"Indeed, ma'am." Alex suppressed a slight shudder at the prospect of such a dull and mentally constrained existence. "For a lady destined for marriage, such skills are indeed necessary."

"Unlike the pursuits of the mind, Mistress Hathaway?" Perry inquired, leaning his shoulders against the mantel, a slightly derisive smile on his lips as he watched her. "Do you believe an educated wife is undesirable?"

"I have no opinion on such a subject, sir. How should I? 'Tis a question best asked of one of your own sex. What think you, Mr. Crofton? Would you look for education in a wife?" That smile annoyed her. The Honorable Peregrine was challenging her. Of course, he knew she couldn't have no opinion on the subject, not after their session in the library, but why couldn't he just leave her alone? His pointless little games were making the charade even more difficult to maintain, and one slip, and she would be lost. Everything would be lost.

But of course, he didn't know that.

Marcus seemed startled by her question. He shared many of Perry's intellectual interests, science first and foremost, but he would be the first to admit that they were not always paramount in his pursuit of enjoyment. Perry, he had always thought, had a mind of a higher class altogether. "I doubt I would enjoy a wife who had no interest in things of the mind. But I would not wish for a bluestocking, either."

"Indeed. Such ladies can be infuriatingly opinionated on occasion," Peregrine observed.

Alexandra shot him a look of scornful disbelief and then saw too late that he was grinning. She realized to her chagrin that he was teasing her, and she had fallen neatly into the trap. And then it came to her that he was teasing *her*. Not Mistress Hathaway, the librarian, but herself. She took an overhasty gulp of sherry and spluttered as it went down the wrong way.

Peregrine removed the glass before it spilled in her lap and solicitously proffered his handkerchief. She shook her head, waving it away as she fumbled for her own, her cheeks scarlet.

"Oh, poor Mistress Hathaway," exclaimed Lady

Douglas. "Fetch water, Marcus, at once, before she chokes."

"No . . . no, indeed, ma'am. It will pass." Alex gasped into her handkerchief. It was all too absurd. She felt foolish and childish, the shell of her carefully constructed character disintegrating into a million cracks.

Once the paroxysm had passed and she had herself in hand again, she rose to her feet. "I fear I must go back to the Abbey, ma'am. Sir Stephen will be looking for me. We have some business to deal with this afternoon, and I have been absent from my duties for too long already."

"Oh, I was hoping you would stay and have a light nuncheon with me," Eliza said with a moue of disappointment. "I am so starved of company, sometimes I think I will begin talking to myself. And that, you know, is a sign of madness. I'll probably end my days in Bedlam."

"Oh, ma'am, don't be absurd," Marcus declared, half laughing. "You know perfectly well I will not countenance such a thing. Besides, you have an engagement to play cards this evening with Lady Lucas, her sister, and her cousin. They'll talk the hind leg off a donkey, given half a chance."

"Oh, for shame, Marcus. Such vulgarity," his parent exclaimed.

"Thank you for your hospitality, Lady Douglas." Alexandra curtsied and made for the door.

"Allow me to accompany you to the house, Mistress

Hathaway." Peregrine, with alacrity, had reached the door ahead of her and was bowing her through.

"There is no need, sir. I know my way perfectly well," she said, ducking her head in the manner she had acquired as she resumed the part of the dowdy Mistress Hathaway. It had the advantage of concealing her eyes where she knew he would still read her anger at him for playing with her when he had no idea what was at stake.

"Oh, I wasn't presuming to guide you, ma'am," he said, taking her cloak from the hook by the door. "Allow me." He draped it around her shoulders, his fingers for an instant brushing against her neck, sending an electrifying tingle down her spine. "But I intend to protect you from bears and any other evil creatures lurking in the woods."

"There are no bears in Dorset," she retorted, feeling her character slip again. Firmly, she set her lips and determined to say not a word on the walk back to the house if he insisted on accompanying her.

Chapter Four

Peregrine made his way back to the Dower House after his silent walk with Mistress Hathaway. Infuriatingly, she had refused to answer any of his conversational sallies, however outrageous they had been. He had been trying to provoke the swift comeback she had given to his provocative comments in Lady Douglas's salon, but the sparkling challenge of one Mistress Hathaway had been replaced with the dull monotones of the other. Did no one else see this dichotomy? How could they miss it? But then, he reflected, perhaps she didn't show it to anyone else. Now, that was an intriguing thought. Could it be that in his company, the lady found it hard to resist revealing her other self? Just as he found it impossible to resist trying to ferret that other self out of the burrow in which she had so thoroughly buried it? The reflection put a spring in his step and a smile on his lips, although it did nothing to answer the question of why she needed to pretend to be someone she wasn't.

"Did you enjoy your stroll with Mistress Hathaway?" Marcus asked as Perry rejoined them in the yellow drawing room.

"Not much," Perry confessed, picking up his neglected sherry glass. "For some reason, the lady refused to open her mouth beyond the barest platitudes. Maybe she allows herself a certain quota of words a day, and she reached that already." He shook his head with a resigned shrug and sipped his sherry. Whatever his suspicions about Mistress Hathaway's true incarnation, he was prepared to keep them to himself. She must have her reasons, and until he knew for certain that they were not good and sufficient for this game she was playing, he would not risk exposing her.

"She's an odd creature, I grant you that." Marcus brought over the decanter to refill his glass. "Can't make her out at all."

"She seems very shy," the Dowager Lady Douglas put in, waving the vial of sal volatile beneath her nose. "But her background is rather obscure. She's clearly from a rather bourgeois family, but at least she doesn't give herself any airs. I might cultivate her, when I feel a little stronger." She wafted the vial languidly. "I can't imagine why a parent would ruin a girl's chances of marriage by educating her out of the market. But then, I doubt a respectable *parti* could have been found for her. Such an unfortunate appearance . . . that crookback and the birthmark." She shuddered. "Poor woman, to be cursed in such a way." She set aside the vial. "I shall be kind to her, offer her a little distraction. It will help to pass the time. Marcus, assist me into the morning room. I told Baker to lay out a light repast, and I'm feeling a little faint."

"Of course, Mama." Marcus helped his mother rise from the sofa in a soft billow of silks. "I doubt Perry and I could manage another mouthful. We had an enormous second breakfast up at the Abbey with the fruits of our morning on the river, but we'll be happy to keep you company."

"Indeed, ma'am," Perry said hastily. "More than happy."

He was amused to see how Lady Douglas interpreted a light repast. The dining table in the morning room groaned under an array of savory tarts, a glistening ham, a dish of scalloped oysters, and a marzipan confection with crystallized fruits. The dowager took her place, accepted a cup of watered wine, and began languidly to eat her way through the offerings. Perry gazed in growing astonishment at the food that disappeared into that dainty mouth. On her insistence, he toyed with a cheese tartlet and drank a glass of claret. Marcus followed suit, while Lady Douglas ate and engaged Perry in a detailed examination of his family history.

"Your brother, the earl, he's recently married, I understand." She nibbled a piece of marzipan.

"Yes, ma'am. And my twin brother also. I'm the only bachelor among us now." He tried for an easy smile to accompany the statement but found it difficult to produce. It brought to the forefront the one issue he was trying to forget, at least for this weekend.

"Oh, yes, you have a twin. The Honorable Sebastian, is it not?"

"Yes, ma'am." He sipped his wine and tried to change the subject. "How long has Mistress Hathaway been in residence at the Abbey?"

"Oh, a few months, I believe. But tell me, how do you find your brothers' wives, Peregrine . . . I may call you Peregrine, may I not?"

"Of course, ma'am . . . I wonder how Sir Stephen found such an accomplished librarian. Did he consult an employment agency, d'you think?"

"Oh, I wouldn't know about such things. I make it my business to leave all matters of hiring staff to Baker, and I really don't know how one goes about finding suitable people." Lady Douglas waved a hand in dismissal of such an irrelevancy. "But do tell me about your sisters-in-law."

She leaned forward slightly, her brown eyes shining with curiosity in her smooth, rather plump, but undeniably pretty face. "Lady Lucas was asking me just the other day, when we passed in our carriages in the village. She was agog to know that we were hosting the Honorable Peregrine Sullivan." She smiled and nodded encouragingly at Perry.

"I hardly think I'm worthy of such attention, ma'am," Perry demurred.

"You are a Blackwater, Peregrine," Eliza stated with a degree of satisfaction. "Of course you are."

"Indeed, Perry, you're an exotic in our little backwater," Marcus put in with a mischievous grin. "Satisfying local curiosity really is a case of noblesse oblige."

Peregrine shook his head, half amused, half annoyed. "My sisters-in-law, ma'am, are both beautiful, a credit in every way to themselves and to their husbands."

"Are their families well known? I'm always interested in how these matches are made." Eliza sipped her watered wine. "'Tis time Marcus looked for a bride. A little advice might not come amiss."

"Ma'am, I have no need of advice on such a matter," Marcus expostulated, taken aback by his parent's swift thrust.

"And indeed, Lady Douglas, I would be ill equipped to provide it," Perry said, his eyes dancing. "As would my brothers."

"Oh, and why would that be?" Eliza looked puzzled.

"My brothers both made love matches," Perry said simply. "As I understand it, such unions are made only with celestial intervention."

Marcus gave a shout of laughter. "Outplayed, Mama. You must admit it. If the heavens are good enough to drop the perfect love match in my lap, then I shall give up all hopes of a confirmed bachelorhood and welcome love and marriage with open arms."

"Oh, you are absurd, both of you," Eliza declared

crossly. "'Tis a serious matter. I don't know why you think 'tis so amusing."

"Forgive us, Mama." Marcus leaned over and kissed his mother's hand. "We are but callow youths. Will you take the air in the barouche this afternoon? I would be delighted to accompany you."

Peregrine admired his friend's masterly handling of his mother. Having barely known his own mother, he found the relationship a mystery. Marcus's patience was clearly underpinned by affection, and Perry was conscious of a prickle of envy. He and Sebastian had been inseparable growing up, and Jasper had been their mentor, their protector, their inspiration. Their father had died when the twins were barely out of petticoats, and their mother had taken to her own apartments, showing little or no interest in her offspring.

"Well, a little outing might do me some good," Eliza was saying, mollified. "Maybe I will take some preserves and some of Mistress Baker's calves-foot jelly to the vicar's wife. She's expecting another child, poor woman. She must have a dozen at least, by now."

"Not half as many, Mama," Marcus said, laughing. "But I will gladly accompany you. What of you, Perry? Will you accompany us, or do you have something else planned for this afternoon?"

"I have some correspondence to attend to," Perry said. "If you'll excuse me."

"Of course, dear boy." Marcus nodded his comprehension. There was no need for his guest to participate in Marcus's filial duty. "We are bidden to the Abbey for dinner this evening, if you've a mind for it."

Another evening in the company of the fascinating Mistress Hathaway? Most certainly, he had a mind for it. "I should be delighted." Perry rose from the table and bowed to his hostess. "Lady Douglas. I hope you have an enjoyable afternoon."

"I daresay it will be well enough," the lady responded. "But I had forgotten about my engagement with Lady Lucas this evening. Perhaps I should spend the afternoon on my bed, otherwise I may not have the strength for it. Roddy shall take the preserves and the calves-foot jelly to the vicarage. See to it, will you, Marcus?"

"Immediately, ma'am." Marcus helped his mother up and escorted her upstairs to her boudoir.

Peregrine chuckled. It would probably be infuriating to live with such a valetudinarian, but for a short visit, the lady's affectations were quite entertaining. He went up to his own chamber, looking forward to a quiet afternoon with his books and letters.

⚬⚬⚬

Alexandra passed a sheet of parchment across the desk to her employer, who was sitting and tapping his fingers. "You will see here, Sir Stephen, that these stocks"—she indicated with her quill—"have lost value in the last two months, but wool from Flanders has gained in value, and I believe that if you buy at this price, you will be able to sell in about six months at a considerable profit."

Stephen looked at the rows of figures, the columns of profits and losses. He couldn't fault his advisor. Mistress Hathaway had steered him well over the three months that she had been in his employ. "So you would advise selling the shares in the Burnley mine and buying shares in Scottish fleece."

"Yes, sir." Alexandra sat back, surreptitiously easing her shoulders. Maintaining the hunched shoulders to accommodate the pad grew tiring after a few hours. "But most important, I think you should expand your holdings in the new Bridgewater Canal. After its opening last year, traffic on the canal has increased tenfold. If you also buy into the new Turnpike Companies that maintain the roads into and out of both Liverpool and Leeds, you will have an interest in every aspect of transport between the two cities. The number and variety of goods being passed along the roads and the waterways can only increase. I don't see how this could be anything but a wise investment."

Stephen stroked his chin and considered. "How much profit d'you anticipate, Mistress Hathaway?"

Alex did a swift calculation. If she told Stephen six thousand guineas and the transaction finally netted eight, then she would have two thousand to invest for herself. The trust fund she was building for herself and Sylvia was also benefitting from her expertise. The profits she skimmed from Stephen she was reinvesting for herself. It seemed entirely reasonable that she should use her own expertise to benefit herself and her sister. Sometimes she had the urge to embezzle much more. Stephen was so greedy, he was only interested in profit, and he really didn't fully understand the markets in which she played. As long as she kept him satisfied, she could fiddle with the books to her heart's content. But greed led to mistakes, and she wasn't going to risk that. Sometimes she fantasized about ruining Stephen—she could do it easily enough, greed had made him so gullible. But that would ruin the estate. However angry she was at her father for forcing this impossible situation upon his daughters, she couldn't see Combe Abbey fall into rack and ruin.

She glanced at her cousin and saw his little eyes fill with predatory anticipation as he awaited her answer. He licked his lips, a snakelike dart of his tongue. Maybe she would dip a little deeper just this once, she thought.

"Four thousand within six months," she said, keeping her gaze lowered to the paper in front of her. *Four thousand to be invested for myself and Sylvia. In an industry that cannot help but succeed.* She bit the inside of her cheek again to keep from showing the slightest indication of triumph.

Stephen appeared satisfied. "Good . . . good." His eyes shone. "And then, if I reinvest the profit in the further development of the canals, there would be no end to the possible profits from the commodities that could be transported so cheaply."

"Coal, pottery, wheat . . ." Alex gave an expressive shrug. "The barges and canals are transforming the way goods are transported. A wise investor could make a killing."

She bit her cheek harder, hearing how decisive she sounded. Sometimes when she was talking to Stephen in this way, she forgot to maintain her diffident character in her voice. So far, Stephen, in his own acquisitive excitement, seemed not to notice or, if he did, to accept that his librarian had a different manner when she was talking about financial speculation. But she must be more careful.

"Excellent . . . excellent," he said. "Do exactly what we've discussed, Mistress Hathaway. You do very good work. I'm most pleased with you."

"Thank you, sir," she responded softly, once more self-effacing.

Stephen got up from his chair. "How soon will you have finished cataloguing the books?"

Alex had tried to draw out the process. Even though she intended to profit from the sale herself, her soul still revolted at the idea of selling the product of years of loving labor by her father and grandfather. Books she had grown up with, books that informed the person she was. But if she was to succeed in her plan, she could not prevaricate much longer. "Within two weeks, sir. Maybe less."

"Excellent," he repeated, rubbing his hands together.

"And with the money from this collection, Mistress Hathaway, I shall be able to invest in every up-and-coming stock. Get in on the ground floor, that's what they always say. Isn't that so?"

"So I believe," she responded without expression, reaching for her quill once again.

"Well, I leave you to your work. Very satisfactory, ma'am. I'm pleased." The door closed behind him, and Alexandra dropped her head into her hands. She was exhausted but also exhilarated. The mental gymnastics fascinated her, and the results as she saw her own funds expanding filled her with triumph. But the energy required to maintain the deception drained her.

Lady Maude crossed the hall with the firm step of one intent on a particular goal. She had seen her husband leave the library, which meant that Mistress Hathaway was now alone. There was something about the librarian that irritated Maude, but Stephen couldn't see it for some reason. There was something sly about her, and Maude sometimes felt as if the woman looked down on her. Which, of course, was ridiculous. She was merely a servant, an educated upper servant, certainly, in the same league as the governess, but despite her namby-pamby ways, the downcast eyes, and barely whispered responses, something didn't sit right in Maude's opinion. She was too clever. Of course, it was that cleverness that made Stephen so blind. He couldn't see anything wrong with the woman, couldn't catch that flash in her eye sometimes, the derisive twitch of her lips, or the strength in her voice when she laid down a winning card. As long as she continued to direct his investments into paths of greater riches, he would never see any of that or listen to his wife when she tried to point it out.

She opened the library door quietly. Mistress Hathaway was sitting at the desk, her head resting on her hands, which were otherwise idle. Maude smiled. "Ah, I'm glad to see you're unemployed, Mistress Hathaway. I had thought you must have some free time—you spend so many hours alone in here." She gestured slightly contemptuously to the bookshelves. "Anyway, I have some other employment for you, to fill your spare hours."

Alexandra raised her head abruptly, her heart beating fast, as if she really had been startled out of sleep. She regarded the lady of the house with mingled astonishment and trepidation. Maude remained an unknown, but Alex sensed her malevolence and hadn't yet discovered a way to neutralize it. She contented herself with a quiet "Indeed, ma'am?" and a raised eyebrow.

"Yes, I need you to tutor Master George," the lady declared. "He will be going to Eton next year, and he needs to brush up his arithmetic and Latin. I understand from my husband that you are proficient in both, so you'll be pleased to assist Master George with his preparations."

"I am not a governess, ma'am," Alex protested, keeping her tone soft but failing to quell the spark of outrage in her gray eyes. "Your husband employs me as his financial advisor and librarian. I have little time for anything else, I assure you."

"Nonsense," Lady Maude declared, waving her fan. "When I came in here, you were dozing at the table. If you have time to sleep in the afternoon, Mistress Hathaway, you have time to tutor my son."

Alex's jaw dropped at this outrageous statement. "Forgive me, ma'am, but I was *not* asleep. Sir Stephen has just left me after an intensive session with his financial affairs. I was merely preparing myself to return to the cataloguing of the books."

"Well, that's as may be. I still wish you to take on this additional task. You will find Master George an excellent and attentive pupil. He will await you in the schoolroom after breakfast tomorrow."

Alexandra stared at the woman, for the moment lost for words. Lady Maude's gown of pale yellow silk opened over an underskirt of tangerine damask and did little for her sallow complexion, despite the thickly caked powder that covered her freckles. The color of the underskirt clashed rather horribly with her hair, Alex thought with an almost vicious satisfaction. How anyone could have so little sense of what suited her, she couldn't imagine. Maude was a very plain woman, but her pinched lips and little green eyes also gave her an air of spite, the look of a deeply disappointed woman. Life had not given Maude what she considered her due, which at this point gave Alexandra a degree of pleasure.

"I would need to discuss this with Sir Stephen, ma'am. I believe he is my sole employer," she said.

Maude's nostrils flared at her tone, at the look of disdain in the clear gray gaze. She snapped, "There will be no need for you to do so. I will inform my husband of the new arrangement," and exited the library in a rustle of yellow and orange.

Alexandra wanted to leap to her feet and fly after Maude, hurling her indignant fury in her miserable face. But she couldn't do that, in fact had probably done more than enough damage already. That unpleasant exchange would have repercussions, she had no doubt. But she'd have to face them when they materialized. She looked at the papers in front of her with a twinge of distaste. They seemed to have lost their appeal for the moment.

She put them aside and drew a fresh sheet of vellum in front of her. Composing her weekly missive to Sylvia could never lose its appeal. It had been a more interesting week than usual, she reflected. It would amuse her sister to read side-by-side descriptions of their stepmother and the woman who had supplanted her at the Abbey. Two such very different women, one whom both Alex and her sister could like, the other whom Sylvia would detest as heartily as did Alex.

And then there was the arrival of Peregrine Sullivan. Would Sylvia be interested in that? No particular reason she should be, Alex thought. He was no different from any of the other visitors to Combe Abbey. Or at least, no different from any of the younger visitors from London. Of course, he was a friend of their step-brother, and Alex liked Marcus and knew that Sylvia would, too. That was good enough reason to include his arrival in the week's events at Combe Abbey.

Alex stroked the feather tip of her quill, staring down at the blank sheet. How to describe the Honorable Peregrine? Fair-haired, striking blue eyes, tall. Understated clothes, but he wore them well. Nothing flamboyant about him, just an air of natural, unobtrusive elegance, a sense that he was totally comfortable in his skin, never likely to second-guess himself. And most important, he had an educated mind. He enjoyed intellectual pursuits, which did set him apart from the usual run of visitors to Combe Abbey.

She dipped the quill into the inkwell, took it out, and shook surplus ink from the point. Should she tell Sylvia of the uncomfortable curiosity Peregrine seemed to have about herself? Should she mention the sharpness of those blue eyes, the ready glint of amusement, the strange and disturbing feeling she had sometimes that he was seeing more than he should? And the even stranger and more disturbing feeling that she, Alexandra Douglas, wanted to spend time in his company, meet him on equal terms, be her true self when she was with him?

But she couldn't tell Sylvia that. Not in a letter—it was far too complex to describe. She didn't understand it herself. Why did she have this urge to risk everything by engaging in some verbal sparring that was quite out of character for Alexandra Hathaway and quite *in* character for Alexandra Douglas? What was it about Peregrine Sullivan that brought out the devil in her, the spark of mischief that she had worked so hard to quell? And now, *here,* where it was so dangerous. If he asked questions, pushed for further information, he could ruin her . . . ruin Sylvia. She'd end up in prison, and Sylvia would starve.

It didn't bear thinking of. From now on, she must have no private conversations with the Honorable Peregrine. If he was in a room, she must leave it. She mustn't even look at him, since that seemed to start the damage, and once they began to talk, it just got worse, her resistance fading inexorably.

Alex drummed her fingers on the desk. She had always been truthful with Sylvia. Her sister found it difficult to be helpless, unable to be a concrete support while Alex took all the risks. If Alex so much as hinted at a difficulty, she would worry herself into a shadow. Somehow she must choose her words carefully, giving nothing away. Amusing descriptions of Maude and Eliza would be well and good, along with an account of her latest financial triumph and maybe a brief mention of Marcus and his friend. That would be sufficient. Nothing at all about how attractive she found the Honorable Peregrine Sullivan. *Nothing at all.*

It took her an hour before she was satisfied that she had struck the right note for her sister, sufficiently informative while revealing none of her own confusion. She sanded the sheets, folded and sealed them, and took them with her to her own chamber to dress for dinner.

On her way, she passed Lady Maude's boudoir. Raised voices came from behind the door, and she paused, unable to help herself. In another life, she would consider eavesdropping a dishonorable activity, she reflected with a sardonic smile, but in her present circumstances, it was an essential tool. And most particularly when, as on this occasion, she heard her own name.

"Georgie needs help, Sir Stephen. He struggles so with his lessons, and he will never manage at school without more preparation."

"The boy struggles because he won't concentrate," Sir Stephen stated, his tone dismissive. "He's lazy and distracted, and that tutor has no control over him at all. You coddle him, ma'am, always have done. The slightest sniffle, and you send for the damn leach. If he doesn't want to do his lessons, you find excuses for him. 'Tis no wonder he can barely read, let alone construe Latin or add up two and two to make four."

"You are too harsh, sir. The poor child has always suffered from ill health, and he needs a little more help. Mistress Hathaway has time on her hands. I found her sleeping in the library this afternoon instead of at her work. She's overpaid, and she can certainly devote some time to Georgie."

"Sleeping?" Sir Stephen exclaimed, his voice rising. "I'll have you know, ma'am, that Mistress Hathaway and I had a most fruitful session with my business affairs this afternoon, and if you think the lady is overpaid, you don't know what you're talking about. Her financial acumen is worth a lot more to me, indeed, to both of us, than any suitability she might have as a governess. I'll not hear another word. You leave well alone, Lady Douglas. Mistress Hathaway works for me."

Alexandra whisked herself away and around a corner of the corridor as Lady Maude's door opened, and Sir Stephen, rather red-faced, emerged from his wife's room. In the safety of her own chamber, Alex stood for a moment in frowning thought. Maude already resented Alexandra's presence in the household, and matters would not be improved if she fell out with her husband over the librarian. Maybe Maude resented the time Stephen spent with her, Alex thought, but she'd seen no indication that the lady pined for her husband's company in the usual course of the day. Was there something about herself that put Maude's back up?

Whatever it was, Stephen's castigation would only make it worse. If Maude was obliged to acknowledge defeat in matters concerning the librarian, her natural vindictiveness would be given free rein.

Still, she reflected, drawing an evening gown out of the armoire, at least she wouldn't have to deal with Master George. Alex liked children in general, but Stephen's son and heir was a whining brat, hopelessly spoiled and indulged by his mother. Any attempt to teach him would fall on stony ground, and the governess would get the blame. It would put her in a worse position vis-à-vis Maude than Stephen's intervention.

She held up the gown and wrinkled her nose. The

dove-gray taffeta was barely an improvement on the dull brown twill she was wearing at the moment. She had a fleeting memory of her mother, who always looked wonderful, richly dressed and ornamented, her coiffure always perfect. For a moment, she could almost catch the fragrance that seemed to envelop the first Lady Douglas. Gardenia, she remembered, seeing in her mind's eye the little vial on her mother's dresser. What would Luisa think of her elder daughter now?

And where was she, anyway? Presumably still in the land of the living, Alexandra thought, stepping into the dove-gray taffeta. Surely she and Sylvia would have heard of their mother's demise. There might even be an inheritance of sorts. But that brought a cynical smile to her lips. Luisa never had two pennies to rub together. Her extravagance had been another cause of the fierce quarrels between her and Sir Arthur. And as far as Alex and Sylvia had been able to gather, Luisa's romantic escapades had been just that, flights for romance and excitement rather than the wealth of a new suitor. Not that their mother had ever appeared short of a guinea, Alex reflected as she fastened her gown. Presumably, she and her lovers lived on credit.

Of course, it was possible that Luisa had occasionally sold herself for money to keep both herself and her current lover in funds. It should be a shocking idea, but Alex didn't find it so. She and Sylvia had long given up expecting anything as dull as conventional morality from their mother.

Dressed, she made her way downstairs. Another long evening to be endured in mousy silence before she could attain the peace of her bedchamber for the precious hours of solitude the night gave her.

As she reached the bend in the stairs, she heard a voice from the hall below that brought her up short. No one had told her that the Honorable Peregrine was to be a dinner guest tonight. But then, of course, why should they?

Could she escape, plead illness and retreat to her chamber? Despite her earlier resolution to avoid the man, she knew that such a move would merely postpone the inevitable. Peregrine and Marcus would be frequent guests at Combe Abbey while they were staying in the Dower House. If she didn't confront the situation tonight, she would have to another night. Somehow she must learn to maintain her customary diffident reticence despite his provocations; she must ignore the conspiratorial gleam in the blue eyes, the inviting twitch of his full lips. She must pretend that he wasn't telling her that he knew she was not what, or rather who, she seemed. And she must pretend that she didn't find that assumption of inside knowledge immensely appealing. With Peregrine Sullivan, she couldn't allow her guard to slip for an instant. But why did her own defenses against him seem so fragile?

She hesitated on the stair, waiting until the group gathered in the hall had entered the salon, so that she could slide into the room without drawing attention to herself.

Chapter Five

Peregrine was standing with a glass in his hand, trying to make conversation with Lady Maude, when he noticed Mistress Hathaway sitting on an armless chair pressed into a corner of the room. Her hands were folded in her lap, and she seemed to be concentrating on the pattern of the Turkey carpet at her feet.

He excused himself from his hostess with a word of apology as one of the other guests came up to make his bow. He took a glass of sherry from a passing footman and made his way to the corner. "Mistress Hathaway. I believe you take sherry." He bowed before her, holding out the glass.

"I do not care to drink overmuch, sir," the lady demurred, not taking the glass.

"I'm not suggesting you do, or should, ma'am," he returned, continuing to proffer the glass. "But I can't help thinking that a little stimulant in this company might not come amiss." He raised his eyebrows in a gesture of conspiratorial amusement and saw to his satisfaction an answering glimmer in those lovely gray eyes. Somewhere underneath that façade was a very beautiful woman, with a personality to match, unless he was much mistaken.

Alexandra took the glass with a murmur of thanks. "I trust the Dowager Lady Douglas was feeling well enough to attend her card party this evening."

"Indeed. She rested upon her bed the whole afternoon to gain the strength for it," Perry said solemnly, watching her over the lip of his glass. He was not mistaken, her eyes danced, although she dropped them immediately into renewed scrutiny of her gray taffeta lap.

"Country life can be quite fatiguing," Alex murmured, taking a sip of sherry, hoping she had managed to conceal her involuntary amusement. It was happening again, however hard she tried to fight it. The wretched man either deliberately or accidentally made her want to laugh aloud. She suspected it was the former and once again knew that prickle of danger. It would be so easy to become her real self in these exchanges. He was such an attractive man, and she wanted nothing more than to respond to him in kind, to allow those playful and penetrating blue eyes to draw her into the private conspiratorial world he was offering. But she daren't play games. She *had* to conceal the urge to respond to him, to meet and match him, however tempting it was . . . however unfair it seemed when, for the first time in her life, she could glimpse what it would be like to enjoy a man's company and instead had to run from it.

"Yes, indeed. Charitable visiting, card parties, and the like," Perry agreed. "Did you enjoy your walk this morning?"

"Very much, sir. I find when one spends as much time within doors as I do, 'tis necessary to take the air on a regular basis." Sweet heaven, how much longer could she keep this up with a straight face? It didn't seem to matter how sternly she took herself to task, the concealed Alexandra kept coming out of hiding. In desperation, she opened her fan and retreated behind it.

Peregrine took a sip from his own glass and regarded her in a thoughtful silence that she found even more unnerving than his conversation.

"I wonder if it will rain tomorrow," she said. "There's been no rain for over a week. I daresay the gardens are very dry."

Peregrine's expression became one of astonishment at this inane non sequitur. She glanced up at him over her fan with an air of mild inquiry and saw to her relief that she had rendered him momentarily speechless. She plied her fan, averting her eyes.

Perry struggled for a moment to find a suitable response but in the end accepted defeat. For a few moments, he had thought he was about to break through, but she had now retreated, and he could sense that any further pursuit would be pointless. He would return to fight another day. "I daresay, ma'am." He turned on his heel and walked over to join the group around Marcus, leaving Alex to resume her solitary silence.

When dinner was announced, Peregrine was directed to take Lady Maude into dinner, and Alexandra was left to bring up the rear with a callow youth suffering from a terminal case of shyness, which suited her very well.

She was perfectly willing to draw out the young man at the dinner table and put him at his ease. He was far too nervous himself to see in his table neighbor anything but a rather drab spinster with a kind disposition, who was willing to engage him in talk of his life at Oxford and allow him to tell tales of his escapades with his fellow students without making him feel either foolish or too young for adult company.

Henry Dearborn obviously thought of her as like a kindly old aunt, Alex thought rather ruefully. It was one thing to play the part so successfully but paradoxically quite another to see herself through the young man's eyes. This charade was definitely not good for her self-esteem.

"So, Mistress Hathaway, do you care to ride?"

The unexpected question startled her. The Honorable Peregrine was addressing her across the table, rather against established etiquette, but she supposed he could get away with it where others couldn't.

"We are discussing a riding expedition tomorrow, to Durdle Door," he continued with a bland smile. "I understand 'tis one of the most famous rock formations in the area. I was wondering if you cared to ride. You were saying earlier how taking the air and some exercise refreshed your mind." Part of him regretted indulging the impulse to force her into the limelight, but only part of him.

"Ride?" Alexandra was taken aback, and even more so when she became aware that she had drawn the attention of others around the table. *Damn Peregrine Sullivan.* Her eyes flashed fire at him across the table.

"Of course Mistress Hathaway don't care to ride," Lady Maude declared from the bottom of the table. "I'm sure she has never learned, and even if she has, I doubt she would find it easy to sit a horse. One needs a certain posture."

The mean-spirited reference to her humpback took Alex's breath away as she imagined what she would feel like if it really was a deformity and not a strategically placed pad between her shoulder blades. How could the woman be so insensitive, so blindingly malicious? Even if Maude was getting her own back for her earlier failure to compel Alexandra into the schoolroom, it was still a wretchedly unkind vengeance.

She was at a loss for words for a moment, and then Peregrine said, as if Maude had not spoken, "So, Mistress Hathaway, what d'you say?"

She was angry enough now to say, "Had I a mount, sir, I would be delighted. I have always enjoyed riding."

"Then I'm sure a suitable mount can be found for you," Peregrine declared. "Sir Stephen, surely you have something in your stables for Mistress Hathaway."

Stephen looked nonplussed, but as he hesitated,

Marcus, as indignant as Perry at Maude's appalling jibe, entered the lists. "Oh, come now, Stephen, you have a stable full of horses eating their heads off. Lady Maude doesn't ride much, and she has the prettiest dapple gray just aching to shake up her heels."

"No . . . no, please." Alex shook her head vigorously before Maude could vent her indignation. "I couldn't possibly impose. Indeed, I am perfectly happy to take a walk along the cliff top when I need fresh air."

"Yes, I'm sure that's so," Stephen said, visibly relieved, seeing his wife's color mount to an alarming shade of puce. "But should you ever wish to ride, Mistress Hathaway, there's an old mare in my stables who needs a little gentle exercise. Jackson, my head groom, told me so the other day. A perfect mount for you, nice broad back, gentle gait. You just take her out whenever you wish. I'll tell Jackson. He'll make sure you have an experienced groom to accompany you."

"You are too kind, Sir Stephen," Alex murmured, dropping her eyes to her plate.

But not before Peregrine saw the look of horror cross her face at Stephen's description of the mare and his solicitous offer of a guiding hand. He smiled to himself. Mistress Hathaway had no more interest in riding a sedate, broad-backed, elderly mare than he would have had. So where had she learned to ride? A bookish childhood spent in an impoverished country vicarage wouldn't usually provide much access to spirited horseflesh.

"Ladies." Maude rose abruptly from the table, her color still high. "Let us withdraw."

With relief, Alexandra followed Lady Douglas from the dining room. She glanced longingly at the stairs, wondering if she could make a discreet escape, but Maude instructed sharply, "You must play for us, Mistress Hathaway."

Playing in the drawing room after dinner and making a fourth at whist were two tasks that had somehow devolved upon her, and Alexandra could see no way of avoiding either without causing serious offense and making her position even more uncomfortable. She didn't need to antagonize Maude any more today.

"Of course, ma'am." She sketched a curtsy in subdued acknowledgment and followed the ladies into the drawing room, where she took her place at the pianoforte.

She didn't consider herself more than an adequate performer, but Maude and her company seemed to have no complaints. If, indeed, they listened, she thought with a dour smile. She selected a Bach prelude, which would provide a pleasant background to their chat, but after five minutes, Maude called, "We'd prefer something livelier, Mistress Hathaway. One of those French folk songs, perhaps, or a country dance. That music is so dreary."

Without expression, Alex put aside her music and flexed her fingers.

"Do you have music? May I turn the page for you?"

She looked up, startled once again by the almost silent appearance of Peregrine. A quick glance around the drawing room told her that he was the first of the gentlemen to leave the port decanter. "There's no need, sir. I know the music by heart." She began to play, acutely conscious of the man standing at her shoulder, a teacup in his hand. She could feel his eyes upon her, could sense the long, supple lines of his body as he leaned closer. Every inch of her was suddenly vibrantly aware of his physical presence, and she almost had to catch her breath.

Her fingers slipped on the keys, and she took her hands away, pressing her fingertips to her temples.

"Won't you go on?" he asked quietly.

She shook her head, staring down at the black and white keyboard. "There's no need. No one's listening."

"I was."

"You're too kind, sir." Her voice was distant as she rose from her stool. "But I'm sure you've heard many superior performances."

"Maybe so." He could see little point in denying it. She wouldn't believe him, anyway, and she clearly had no interest in flattery.

"So, who's for cards?" Stephen came in on a wave of port, his inebriated guests crowding behind him. "What shall it be, gentlemen? Bassett, piquet, backgammon?"

"Chess," Peregrine said suddenly. "Mistress Hathaway, I challenge you." He bowed.

Despite her earlier perturbation, Alexandra felt a

rush of excitement. Chess was her game. She played a good game of piquet, but she excelled at chess. And then reality reasserted itself. Was this another of Peregrine's traps? Every time she accidentally revealed her true self, he was there. And every time it happened, she lost a little of the desperate resolve that enabled her to maintain the charade. She could not afford to weaken herself any further.

"I find myself a little tired, sir. If you'd excuse me." She made to move past him, but he laid a hand lightly on her arm.

"Afraid, Mistress Hathaway?" The penetrating blue eyes were quizzical, but there was a hard determination behind them, and the accompanying smile only increased her dismay. "I may not be your match at whist, but I'll lay any odds you name that I can take your king."

Anger at his persistence swept through her. *To hell with it,* she thought abruptly. If he thought he could break her guard, he was in for a surprise. She dipped her head, blinking rapidly. "I do beg you to believe, sir, that I will give you but a sad game."

Will you, indeed? he thought with an appreciative smile. Unless he was much mistaken, Mistress Hathaway was incapable of playing a bad game of anything competitive. "Then, if necessary, ma'am, I will weep. But I insist upon a game."

On your own head be it. Alex inclined her head in demure acknowledgment. "Very well, sir. If you insist."

She moved aside to a small table in the window, where a chess board was set up. "Will you choose?" She took a white piece and a black piece and held them behind her back.

"Your right hand," he said.

Alexandra uncurled her right hand. "You have the first move, sir." She put the white pawn on the table and took her seat behind the black pieces.

Peregrine opened with the standard pawn to king four, and she responded with the customary counter-move. Perry brought out his queen's knight, and for a few moves, they played according to the book, but then Alexandra moved her bishop, exposing her king. Perry blinked. What trick did she have up her sleeve? He examined the board carefully but could see no possible move she could make to recover from the bishop move. He brought his queen into play, threatening her king. "Check."

Alexandra frowned and cast him a look of distress. "Oh, dear, I didn't see that. Now what should I do?" She gazed at the board, her hand hovering tentatively over her king's rook.

"You may not castle to move your king out of check," he reminded her drily.

"Oh, no, of course not, I forgot." Her hovering hand dropped into her lap, and her frown deepened as she gazed at the pieces. Then she moved her king one space to the left, out of the queen's line of fire but by no means out of danger.

Peregrine closed his eyes briefly. *What the hell is she playing at?* Apart from playing him for a fool? He was always slow to anger, but he felt the first flicker of irritation burn brighter. He looked across the board at her, his blue eyes sharp as daggers. "That's not going to do you much good."

"Oh, dear." She covered her mouth in distress, her hand lifting to the king, then dropping once more. "Oh, but I can't change my move."

"No," he agreed. "You can't." He moved his bishop. "Check."

She cupped her mouth with both hands, looking wide-eyed at him across the board. "I think it's mate next move, whatever I do."

"So it would appear," he said, his voice cold, his eyes glacial. "You'd have impressed me more if you'd lost with a little more subtlety, ma'am."

Alex toppled her king and murmured, "Why would I wish to impress you, sir? I warned you I play a poor game of chess."

"You did . . . but you may not know, Mistress Alexandra Hathaway, that you have also thrown down the glove. And I can never resist a challenge." He pushed back his chair and rose from the board. "One day, we will play chess." He walked away.

Alex put the pieces back into the box, unable to dismiss the feeling that she'd overstepped the boundaries she had so carefully set for herself. Instead of boring him with inept play, she had merely offended him.

And in truth, she would have been offended herself, she reflected, if anyone had played down to her like that. *Damn.* Why couldn't Peregrine just accept that she was out of bounds, that she had nothing to offer him?

She flexed her shoulders wearily and felt the pad shift. A quick glance around those close to her reassured her that no one was looking at her. The Honorable Peregrine was deep in conversation with Marcus and several other men. She could slide from the salon without being accosted.

Peregrine was aware of her departure even though he didn't look at her. For some reason, as she slipped from the room, it seemed emptier.

"How about dice, my dear fellow?" Marcus shook a cup invitingly.

Peregrine shook his head. "No, you must excuse me, Marcus. I've a mind for an early bed."

Marcus shrugged easily. "As you wish, my friend. Don't look for me before noon tomorrow." He moved to join a rowdy group of dice players.

Peregrine moved to the door. His host was deep in a card game where the stakes seemed alarmingly high, and his hostess was playing loo in a lively group by the fire. No one would notice his departure. He slipped from the room and made his way down the drive. It was a glorious moonlit night. It would be autumn soon enough, but tonight summer still lingered in the soft, almost balmy breeze from the sea.

He walked past the Dower House and veered across the lawn towards the cliff top, enjoying the cool sea breeze on his cheek. His easygoing temper was badly disturbed. Mistress Alexandra Hathaway had heated his generally humorous acceptance of life's quirks into a bonfire of indignation. *How dare she pretend to be such a simpleton?* Whatever her reasons for the charade— and he was willing to accept that they could have a vitally important basis—she had no right to treat him like an idiot.

⸙

Alexandra sighed with relief when she reached the safety of her own bedchamber and locked the door behind her. Carefully, she removed all traces of her disguise, put on her nightgown, and sat down on the window seat with her glass of Madeira—the last of her now-discarded bottle—waiting to feel sleepy. But she couldn't rid herself of unease. She should not have treated Peregrine to such a display of inanity. It was playing with fire. He was no fool, he'd known what she was doing, and it had angered him. Would it, as she hoped, give him a disgust of her, ensure that he stopped probing? Or would it do the opposite? Had she overplayed her hand?

Oh, why did Peregrine Sullivan have to come to Combe Abbey? Couldn't the fates just once have left her with an untrammeled path? It was difficult enough to follow as it was. She didn't ordinarily indulge in self-pity, but for a few moments, Alexandra raged at fate and its injustice to her heart's content. But then she dashed the tears from her eyes, blew her nose, and faced the realities of her situation once again. All she had to do was keep Mr. Sullivan at arm's length until he left Combe Abbey, which he would do eventually. He must have another life to go to. A London life of dandified dissipation.

The reflection brought a reluctant chuckle to her lips. Such a description of Peregrine Sullivan was absurd. He was certainly a beautifully dressed, impeccably mannered aristocrat, but dandified and dissipated? Definitely not. He had the mind and education of a scholar. And therein lay her problem. An aristocratic man-about-town would have no appeal for her at all. She despised them as a group and always had done. But the combination of a keen mind and a powerful physical presence was irresistible. She wanted nothing more than to be in his company, talking with him, exchanging views and pieces of knowledge. There was so much she wanted to know about how he thought, what he liked, what he disliked . . .

Moonlight flooded the lawns below, and a blackbird burst into full-throated song, as they so often did on a beautiful night at Combe Abbey. It was no wonder they were often mistaken for nightingales, she thought, remembering how she and Sylvia as children had always insisted that the glorious sound could only come from a more exotic creature than a blackbird. They had woven their own *Arabian Nights* stories lying in bed, imagining flights of fancy to the background music of the songbird beyond their window.

Voices rose from below as the evening's guests began to leave, noisily as usual after Stephen's generous hand with the wine bottles. For all his avarice and penny pinching, he never stinted on his hospitality, and his guests were generally loud and reeling when they finally departed.

Alexandra listened until the last voice had died away, the last rattle of coach wheels on the driveway had ceased, and the house had fallen silent. Restless, she got up from the window seat. Sleep seemed even further away, and the urge to go out, to walk in the moonlight, was suddenly irresistible. No one was around, the house slept, and she could go down by the backstairs and let herself out through the kitchen door.

The thought was father to action, and she picked up her cloak, pushed her feet into her slippers, and crept on tiptoe from her chamber.

The only sounds as she went down the backstairs were the creak of a floorboard and the rustle of mice in the wainscot. The kitchen was in darkness save for the glow from the banked range. The boot boy slept in a blanket roll under the settle alongside the range, but he didn't stir as Alex trod silently to the kitchen door. She opened it just far enough to let herself out and closed it behind her, hearing only the faint click of the latch. Moonlight flooded the kitchen garden, and she kept in the shadows against the house wall as she made for the gate that would lead to the side path. It was unlikely that anyone was watching from an upstairs window, but she couldn't afford to take any chances.

Once on the path, Alex breathed more easily. From the house, she would be no more than a vague moving shadow beneath the trees, and once in the shelter of the orchard, she was free and clear. The soft air was faintly tinged with salt, and she could hear the waves breaking on the shore of the cove.

Once on the cliff top, she made her way to where a narrow sandy path snaked down the cliff to the beach below. The silver sea rolled through the horseshoe-shaped entrance to the cove, and the cliffs glimmered white. It was a deceptively gentle coastline, but Alex knew that out in the Channel, many an inexperienced sailor had come to grief in the fierce races that ran parallel to the shore.

She slipped on the rough path but grabbed onto a scrub bush clinging to the sandy soil and regained her footing easily. It was a route down the cliff that she had taken countless times in the past. Once she reached the sand, she kicked off her slippers and walked barefoot to a rocky outcrop at the far side of the cove, curling her toes into the sand with a deep sensual pleasure. She was herself now, and the strain of the pretense slid away from her. She tossed her head, reveling in the freedom of her hair flowing around her face, and she flexed her shoulder blades, feeling the cricks and aches that her daytime posture forced upon her spine melt away as her back straightened. With a light laugh, she dropped her cloak to the sand, caught up the hem of her night-gown, and began to run through the foaming, curling ripples at the water's edge. She wanted to shout aloud with the sheer freedom of these moments of solitude while the world around her slept.

So this is what lies beneath the poor, twisted body of the dowdy spinster librarian. Peregrine stood above on the cliff top, watching, transfixed by the sheer joyousness of the figure on the sand below. She was like some newly liberated sprite, he thought with a rush of pleasure. The moonlight caught the tawny and gold shades in the fall of chestnut hair, and her lithe body in its flowing white gown danced through the wavelets with the agility of a fawn.

Dear God! He'd imagined all sorts of incarnations under the carapace but never anything as strikingly beautiful and alive as this dancing sprite. He had known immediately who she was the moment he had glimpsed the figure slipping and sliding down the cliff on the sandy path. It had been an instinctive leap of recognition, as if he should have known her all along. As he watched, almost breathless with the sheer joy of watching her, a sudden gust of wind from the Chan-nel flattened the thin gown against her body, and for a tantalizing instant, he could make out the outline of her figure, the swell of her breasts, the curve of her hips, the roundness of her backside, the length of her thighs.

It was only an instant, but his body stirred in response. He stepped back swiftly from the cliff. He didn't want her to know she was being watched; it would spoil her delight in the liberation of her body and her spirit. How difficult must it be to curb that energy day after day, to restrain the bubble of high spirits that seemed to glow around her like an aura? No, he would not interrupt these moments of her freedom. He would wait until she had had her fill.

He walked along until he reached the head of the path she had taken down to the beach. He sat down on the rough grass and waited, reasoning that she would ascend by the same route she had descended.

After a while, Alexandra walked out of the water and sat down on the rock outcrop at the edge of the beach, wriggling her toes as they dried. The breeze had freshened as it often did before the false dawn, and she shivered suddenly. It was time she sought her bed, if she was to be fully in control of herself in the morning, when Mistress Hathaway must take her place on the world's stage.

She got up off the rock and began to walk back along the beach to where her discarded cloak and shoes lay. She draped the cloak around her shoulders but carried her shoes. Her sandy feet would only make them uncomfortable. She could clean off the sand when she reached the grass of the cliff top.

She began the climb up the steep path, pausing now and again to look over her shoulder across at the widening vista of the Channel beyond the horseshoe. The breeze was strengthening by the minute, and she thought she could catch the faintest lightening on the horizon. Maybe she could plead a headache and keep to her room until later in the morning. It was a tempting thought.

The chestnut head popped up above the edge of the cliff first, and Perry leaned back on his elbows waiting for the rest of her to follow. She clambered up onto the grass, straightened, her hands pressed to the small of her back for a moment, then looked around.

She stared, dumbfounded, at the figure on the grass a few feet away.

"Good evening again, Mistress Hathaway . . . but no, I'm certain that can't be right." Peregrine stood up in one easy movement, dusting off his breeches with his hat. "'Tis not Mistress Hathaway, is it?" He raised his eyebrows with a smile that was filled with the warmth of his earlier delight in her dance upon the beach.

But Alex saw none of that. With cold clarity, she thought simply, *It's over*. All over. All the work, the misery of the charade, the desperation, all for nothing. This man, this complete stranger, had ruined everything. There was nothing left now, nothing she and Sylvia could salvage from the wreck of their lives, and all because this man decided to poke and pry where he had no business. Blind rage filled her.

She took a step towards him. "Do you have the first idea what you've done? You come here cocooned in your own perfect little world where nothing could ever go wrong, where no one would dare to make you uncomfortable, and you decide to amuse yourself, playing with some insignificant creature who couldn't possibly have a life or feelings of her own." Without thought, she raised her hand, and her palm cracked against his cheek.

Peregrine reared back, shocked at the violence of her reaction. He grabbed her wrist as her hand lifted to strike him again. "*No.*" He forced her hand down, his eyes locked with hers. "No, you won't do that again."

Slowly, under the steady blue gaze, Alex felt the rage die down, leaving only a dull resignation in its place. She pulled at her captive wrist, but his fingers only tightened. "You've ruined *everything*," she said in a low voice.

"How?" he demanded. "I certainly haven't the first idea why you're deceiving everyone in Dorset, but I haven't done anything to spoil your game, and I don't intend to." He caught her other wrist as her free hand came up, with what intention he didn't wait to discover. "No . . . just take a hold of yourself. I'm only curious."

"You have no right to be curious," Alex said dully. She tried again to free her hands, but he wouldn't release his grip.

"Of course I do. I have every right. I admit I don't have the right to ruin whatever 'tis that you're up to, unless, of course, it has some nefarious purpose and as a good citizen I should do so—Does it?" he asked abruptly.

Alex, to her chagrin, felt her cheeks grow hot. "Of course not," she muttered.

Peregrine regarded her thoughtfully. So much for imagining that she would find his presence on the cliff top as pleasant a surprise as he had found hers on the beach. He'd certainly been deluding himself. "So, are you going to tell me what you're up to, or must I march you to the nearest Justice of the Peace, whom I assume is Sir Stephen?"

"You would not." She pulled at her captive hands, a flash of desperation in the gray eyes.

"No, I would not," he agreed, regretting his threat. He had no wish to hurt her—quite the opposite. "Will you take a deep breath and tell me your first name, at least?"

"Alexandra. Let go my hands, *please*."

"You promise not to run?"

She shook her head impatiently. "Where the hell would I run to?"

That made him smile again, dissipating the tension. "Much better. Now I feel I'm in the company of the real Alexandra . . . whoever she may be." He released her wrists.

Alex rubbed them accusingly, but while his grip had been firm, it had been in no way hurtful, and the gesture failed to have the desired effect.

"So, how can I be of help?" Peregrine asked.

"You can pretend this never happened and let me go back to my bed before I have to start all over again," she stated. Maybe it was an option, or maybe she was clutching at straws.

"Oh, no, I'm afraid I can't do that." He shook his head, but the smile lingered. "I could certainly never pretend I didn't see you frolicking on the beach, with your hair flying in the breeze." He reached out and lifted a rich chestnut strand from her shoulder, twisting it around his finger. "Beautiful," he murmured.

For a moment, Alexandra was transfixed by the look in his eyes as he trailed his fingers through the cascade of hair. Then his hands moved up to cup her face, and his gaze became even more searching.

"You are lovely," he said softly. "Do you know that?" The mystery of Alexandra Hathaway suddenly lost its importance. Her gray eyes seemed to reflect the moonlight, giving them a silvery sheen.

His mouth hovered over hers, his breath brushing against her cheek. She inhaled his scent, felt her surroundings slipping away, her eyes locked with his, watching his mouth come ever closer, felt herself leaning into him, lifting her face for the touch of his lips. Then she jumped back, as if she was too close to a raging fire, and his hands fell to his sides. Her breath was coming fast, and her body felt very strange, her legs quivering as if she'd been running for a very long time.

"No . . . no, I can't . . . mustn't," she murmured

He shook his head, the glow in his eyes undiminished. "Can't, mustn't . . . why not, Alexandra? You want to . . . I want to kiss you more than anything in the world right now. You are so very lovely, and I want to know you. Won't you tell me *why* you're practicing this insane deception?"

"There's nothing insane about it." The defense was automatic, but she looked at him uncertainly for a moment, before saying hesitantly, "Will you leave me alone, let me do what I have to do?"

"And if I agree to do so, will you tell me the truth?"

Alexandra shook her head. "I cannot . . . please, you have to believe me. Leave me be, *please.*"

He could not resist the plea in her eyes, which seemed now haunted. He raised a hand and lightly traced the curve of her cheek with his fingertip. "If you insist. For the moment, anyway."

Her skin seemed to vibrate under his touch, and she felt strangely breathless. She managed a low "Thank you," then walked quickly away across the cliff top, almost praying that she had imagined the whole encounter. Maybe she'd open her eyes and find herself in her bed, and it had only been a dream.

Chapter Six

Alexandra drew the hood of the cloak over her hair and pushed her still-sandy feet back into her slippers before letting herself back into the kitchen. The household would be up at six, but it was always possible that a scullery maid or the boot boy would already be raking the ashes in the range. But the kitchen was as quiet as when she'd left it, and the boy under the settle still slept.

She locked the door again, sped across the kitchen to the backstairs, and raced up them to the safety of her own bedchamber. She closed and locked the door and stood leaning against it, catching her breath. It seemed she had been holding it since the moment she had seen Peregrine on the cliff top.

That had been no dream. None of it. Wonderingly, she touched her cheek, almost as if she could still feel the light brush of his fingertip on her cheek. She hadn't dreamt her own feelings, that sweep of desire when he'd been about to kiss her, the moment when the world seemed to dissolve and it was just the two of them in the moonlight.

Dear God, how did it happen? It was a disaster. The ruins of her plan lay heaped about her. All it had needed was one person to suspect, and it was over. She could not maintain such a monumental deception when she knew that one single person other than her sister knew the truth.

Feeling sick, Alexandra sat down on the window seat and stared out at the coming dawn. Should she make her escape now, before the house was up? Should she plead sickness, keep to her chamber, and wait until tonight to flee, when she was once more certain everyone was asleep?

But to give up was to give up everything. Her clever diversion of Stephen's gains on 'Change were not yet sufficient for Sylvia's trouble-free future, let alone her own. And the library catalogue, while almost complete, still needed more work to be ready to present to the market. If she abandoned her task in the middle, she might as well never have bothered to start it in the first place.

Can Peregrine Sullivan be trusted? Her mind shifted to what had been unthinkable a moment ago. If he could be trusted to say nothing, then she could keep on with her work. She didn't have to run immediately.

Alexandra got up from the window seat and began pacing her chamber, frowning in thought. If she could trust the Honorable Peregrine to keep his word, then she didn't need to panic. And there was no reason for the Honorable Peregrine not to *honor* his word.

But could she trust herself? After those tumultuous moments on the cliff top, she had no confidence that she would run away in time again. It had taken every ounce of willpower to turn from him at the last moment. She had wanted that kiss. There was no point in denying it. Tearing herself away like that had been like tearing away a piece of skin. So if she didn't abandon her plan, there was really only one option. She would have to find ways to avoid him for as long as he was at the Dower House. He couldn't stay in Dorset indefinitely. Marcus never stayed in the country for more than a week, and soon he would be ready to return to London and his own pursuits, and his guest, perforce, would accompany him. And she would be left to finish what she'd started. If she could only keep out of danger until then.

Resolution hardened as she watched the sky grow pink and then glow deepest orange as the sun rose over the sea. She was too close to give it all up now, just for want of courage.

A wave of exhaustion washed over her, and she knew she had to sleep for a few hours before she could resume the game. She wrote a hasty message on a sheet of parchment explaining that she had a severe headache and hoped to attend to her duties in the library that afternoon.

Stealthily, she opened her door and put her head outside. Sounds of the servants beginning their day came from belowstairs as she fixed the note to the door latch.

She closed and relocked the door, then crawled into bed. When she didn't appear at the breakfast table, a servant would be sent to find her and would find the note.

Peregrine returned to the Dower House, his mind whirling. Of course, he had no intention of betraying Alexandra's secret, but now he was even more resolved to discover what lay behind it. It was such an extraordinary deception, such an effective disguise, it was hard to believe the evidence of his own eyes. But he *had* seen a radiant, chestnut-haired young woman dancing barefoot through the wavelets on the beach, the very same woman with whom, just a few hours ago, he'd been playing chess. A hunched drab of a woman of indeterminate age.

She had been terrified when she'd seen him there and knew that she was discovered. Terror had fueled the anger she had unleashed upon him in those furious moments. What had happened to her? What dreadful event in her life had caused her to adopt this appallingly dangerous deception? His intense curiosity now was informed by a need to help her. He didn't trouble to question why he was so drawn to her, it wasn't necessary to analyze it. Beneath that prickly, courageous exterior lay a vulnerable young woman. A beautiful young woman with a mind to match. And he had certainly never met her like before. She was quite possibly unique, a thought that gave him exquisite pleasure.

Marcus had told him that the side door to the Dower House was always unlocked when he was in residence, and Perry was relieved to find it still so. Dawn was just breaking, and a sleepy servant with a scuttle of coals blinked at him as he appeared in the hall.

"Mornin', sir."

"Good morning." Perry nodded pleasantly and made his way upstairs to his own chamber. What could possibly have happened to force Alexandra into such an extreme charade? There had to be something suspect about the entire business. She couldn't possibly have an aboveboard reason for such an astounding lie. And it was a blatant lie—there was no way of softening that basic fact.

And Perry's soul had always shriveled at the thought of anything underhanded and deceitful. Would he regret discovering the truth if it showed her to be an irredeemable liar with no good reason for her deception? Was she a cheat . . . a thief? A criminal running from prosecution? Not a murderess, he was fairly certain of that. But a mountebank of some kind?

He lay back on the bed, still dressed, linking his hands behind his head, staring up at the embroidered tester. A rather intricate pattern of garlands in a riot of color made his eyes ache after a minute, and he closed them.

When next he opened them, Marcus was standing beside the bed, a coffee cup in his hand, laughing down at him. "Well, well, where did you get to, my friend? I looked for you when the party broke up, but you'd disappeared. I assumed you'd come home, but you were not sleeping the sleep of the just when I got back. And now it looks as if you're recovering somewhat inadequately from a night on the tiles." He set the cup on the table by the bed. "Where were the tiles? I've never managed to find any in this backwater."

Peregrine rolled onto his elbow. "There aren't any to speak of, Marcus." He reached for the coffee and took a scalding sip. "I felt like a walk along the beach. And by chance fell in with a wench on her way home from a fruitless night plying her trade in the village."

Marcus gave a ribald chuckle. "And you felt sorry for the poor creature and made up for her lack of fortune . . ."

"Just so, dear boy, just so." Perry yawned. "You'll have to excuse me from any pursuits this morning, Marcus. I've need of a shave and a change of clothes before I can face the day."

"By all means. A ride to Durdle Door is not the most exciting excursion. Take your time." He went to the door, saying over his shoulder, " 'Tis to be hoped you didn't take a dose of the clap last night."

"Devoutly to be hoped," Perry agreed with a quiet smile as the door closed on his friend.

❧

Alexandra awoke at noon, her sleep undisturbed by inquisitive servants. She splashed cold water on her face and then began the careful process of turning herself into Mistress Hathaway. An hour later, she was ready and left her bedchamber to make her way to the library. She was hungry and in need of coffee, and once ensconced behind the desk, she rang a bell. She almost never asked the servants for anything, and the footman who answered her bell looked surprised.

"Yes, ma'am?"

"Could you bring me coffee and perhaps a little bread and cheese?" she asked with the quick nervous smile she had perfected. "I'm sorry to trouble you."

"No trouble, ma'am." The man bowed, managing to convey a degree of superiority in the gesture. Mistress Hathaway, after all, was little more than a servant herself.

It was a shame she'd never have the opportunity to show these disdainful, presumptuous servants whom they were really dealing with, Alex reflected. She hadn't expected to find it as irksome as she did to have to endure the slights of the household staff in her own family's home, where she had grown up as the indulged daughter of the house. But it was a minor irritation, and mortification was probably good for her immortal soul, she told herself without too much conviction.

She began to go through the catalogue she had assembled thus far. But for once, she found it hard to concentrate on her task. She found herself staring into the middle distance, castigating herself for the unutterable stupidity in venturing outside her bedchamber without her disguise intact. What had possessed her to take such a pointless risk?

And in the hard light of day, she was forced to accept the fact that she couldn't possibly avoid Peregrine when he came up to the Abbey, as he was bound to. She was expected to appear in the public rooms at certain times, and she couldn't take to her bed indefinitely. But even if he was willing to keep his distance, how could she keep up the charade in his presence, knowing that he knew that Mistress Hathaway didn't exist? How could she still be convincing in front of someone who knew the truth? She'd be second-guessing herself at every moment.

She jumped, startled, as the door opened. "Ah, there you are, Mistress Hathaway. Feeling better, I trust." Stephen came into the library, flicking his boots with his riding crop.

"Yes, thank you, sir." She gave him a rather strained smile. "Did you enjoy your ride to Durdle Door?"

"Well enough, I suppose." He perched on the edge of the desk, still flicking at the dust on his boots. "Not one for scenery, really, but the ladies like it." He leaned sideways to look at the paper Alex was working on. "Getting on with the catalogue, I see."

"Yes," Alex said, wondering where this was leading.

"Well, good . . . good." He frowned down at his boots, as if something about them displeased him. "Fact is, Lady Maude thinks, and I do, too, that 'tis time for this book business to be finished."

Alexandra bristled involuntarily. Stephen had never pressed her about time before, so presumably his wife had put him up to it. And what did Lady Maude know of the complexity of the work?

" 'Tis a considerable task, Sir Stephen. There are many volumes to itemize and categorize. And they all have to be cross-referenced as well. Prospective buyers will have different interests, and as many of the books come into several different classifications, they will appeal to several different buyers. A healthy competition can only increase their value."

She stroked her cheek with the feather end of her quill, continuing without expression, "You do, I assume, sir, wish the library to fetch its true worth? In which case, 'tis necessary to attract the widest pool of possible buyers."

It was a master stroke, as she had known, and her employer puffed out his cheeks, nodding vigorously. "Of course, of course. 'Tis up to you to know the right time. Well, I'll leave you to it, then." Still nodding, he got up and left her alone.

Alexandra closed her eyes for a moment. *Maude again.* She seemed determined to make trouble for her. Did she sense some threat in her presence at the Abbey? No, that was ridiculous. How could a downtrodden, impoverished, unregarded spinster offer a threat to Lady Maude, wife of Sir Stephen Douglas, lord of the manor and all he surveyed? But Maude was a bully by nature, and like all bullies, she chose the most vulnerable victims. Mistress Hathaway was dependent upon her employer's goodwill, and Stephen's patronage probably infuriated his wife. She didn't seem to enjoy her husband's company that much herself, but she could resent his spending so much time with the librarian. And of course, when Stephen defended her against his wife's criticisms, that would merely incite increased resentment.

As far as Maude was aware, Mistress Hathaway had no other means of earning her bread and the roof over her head. Cast out of the Abbey, she could well end up in the work house. Maude would relish that prospect, Alex thought with a grim smile. But even more would she relish seeing Alex languishing in a jail cell awaiting the assizes. And that would happen if anyone ever penetrated her disguise. *Anyone other than Peregrine Sullivan.*

The library, a room she had loved all her life, became suddenly oppressive. The house itself seemed to be closing in on her, and for the first time, she felt the strain of her self-imposed task to be unendurable. How much longer could she keep it up? How many more mornings could she go through the business of turning herself into someone else? How much longer could she go on without any real contact with anyone outside this theatre where she put on her performance?

She had to get away from the house for a while, had to drop the performance just for a little bit. If she could put some distance between herself and Maude for a while, maybe the lady would find someone else to torment. But how to manage it? What excuse could she have for leaving Combe Abbey for a day or two?

And then it came to her. In that conversation with Stephen, she had just given herself the perfect pretext to escape for a few days. It would remove her temporarily from Maude's attention and free her from Peregrine Sullivan. He would be long gone by the time she returned to Combe Abbey. And if she couldn't manage to finagle a quick visit to Barton to see Sylvia while she was away, then she was not as resourceful as she liked to believe.

Her spirits lifted, and she felt a surge of exhilaration at the prospect of freedom, for however short a time. Swiftly, she left the library and went in search of Sir Stephen.

She found him with his wife and some of his houseguests in the salon. The French doors were open to the long terrace that stretched the width of the house, giving access to the lawn and from there down to the cliff top. Lady Maude was sitting with her tambour frame amidst a small circle of similarly occupied ladies. She glanced up as the librarian entered timidly, as was Mistress Hathaway's wont. She did not ordinarily leave the library during the daytime hours, and Maude frowned at her, as if, thought Alexandra, she was a rather unpleasant form of insect. She crooked an imperative summoning finger.

"I do beg your pardon, ma'am." Alexandra approached with a curtsy. "But I would like to talk with Sir Stephen about the library."

"'Tis about time you finished that task," Maude declared with a wrinkle of her nose. "I cannot imagine how making a list of a few books could possibly take so many weeks."

"Indeed, ma'am, 'tis a little more complex than that," Alexandra demurred, hating the woman for her smug complacence and malicious eyes, for the fact that she was upbraiding her in front of her guests, who had abandoned their tambour frames and appeared eager for a show. "But I have an idea for speeding the process a little, since it seems to irk you so much."

Maude's small eyes sharpened. There was something in the librarian's tone of voice that could almost be called impertinent. Alexandra hastily dropped a curtsy, her head lowered, her heart beating fast as she felt the other woman's hostility. Her wretched temper would bring this adventure to a bad end before any of her other mistakes did.

Maude sniffed and pointedly turned to her neighbor, ignoring the subservient librarian. "I wonder which silk to use for these bushes. The dark or the light green . . . would you favor me with your opinion, Lady Stella?"

Alexandra stepped backwards out of Maude's circle and took a deep steadying breath. She glanced around the salon and saw Sir Stephen, who was engrossed in a game of dice and didn't appear to have noticed her arrival. She went over to him, a diffident smile on her lips. "Sir Stephen, I wonder if you could spare me a few minutes." She dropped a curtsy beside his chair.

He looked up with a flicker of annoyance. "Just let

me finish this game, Mistress Hathaway. I'm a throw of the dice away from winning."

"Of course, sir. I didn't wish to disturb you. Whenever you are able to spare me a moment." She curtsied again and backed away, as one of the dice players threw the dice and gave a shout of triumph. "Too confident by half, Stephen, m'boy. A pair of sixes. You can't beat that."

Alexandra was feeling the first rush of exhilaration die down. Maybe she had been too impetuous. It was never wise to hurry these things, she knew that, but in the full flush of her excitement at seeing a way out of this prison for a while, she hadn't stopped to consider a moderate approach to her employer. She seemed to be making mistakes left, right, and center these days. It was not a comforting thought.

She went to the open French door and through onto the terrace, wondering whether to wait for Stephen to be free or return to the library and hope he would remember to come to her. She glanced across the lawn and then froze. Peregrine and Marcus were walking up from the Dower House, each carrying a brace of pheasants.

She was about to duck back into the salon when Peregrine raised his free hand and called, "I give you good day, Mistress Hathaway." His pace increased, and he reached the terrace before she could fade back into the salon and from there to the sanctuary of the library.

"Mr. Sullivan." She curtsied with the murmured greeting. "You must forgive me, I must return to the library."

"By all means," he said cheerfully. "I'll join you shortly, when I've made my offering to Lady Douglas." He waved the pheasants in illustration. "I'd dearly like to take another look at the *Canterbury Tales*."

She could not refuse to show him the volume, so she managed a tight smile of agreement and slipped from the room, crossing the hall swiftly back to the library.

Now not only was she balked of her opportunity to speak with Stephen, but she was going to have to fence with the Honorable Peregrine. How could she avoid seeing him alone? In public, she would find distractions, but alone in the library, examining together the most precious volume in the library, at least for her . . . how could she possibly stick to her resolution?

She sat down at the desk and picked up her quill, twisting it between her fingers until it snapped, sending a splatter of ink drops over her sheet of calculations.

Crossly, she blotted the mess and was still muttering under her breath when the door opened softly and her nemesis entered, smiling. "Oh, dear," he said. "Did you spill ink? Can I help?"

"The quill broke. And no, you can't . . . thank you," she added belatedly. "The Chaucer is where it was before, on the last-to-top shelf in the corner. I'm sure you can reach it."

"I'm sure I can," he agreed amiably, making no attempt to do so, instead perching on the arm of a chair and regarding her with a quizzical smile. "How long does it take you every morning to achieve this hideous miracle?"

" 'Tis none of your business," she retorted.

"As you've already told me more times than I care to hear. But I'm curious about the mechanics of the disguise." He glanced around the room with exaggerated caution. "I don't believe there are any eyes or ears in the walls."

"Maybe not." Alexandra looked at him in frustration. "Don't you understand, the only way I can remain convincing is by not letting it slip for a minute when I'm out of my bedchamber? If you keep pressing me and reminding me that you know the truth, then I will make a mistake, and it will be a disaster. A catastrophe . . . you couldn't begin to understand the magnitude of it."

"No, I believe that," Perry declared. "Only something of magnitude could lie behind this charade." He smiled that devastating smile that seemed to draw her soul into her eyes. "You're frightened, my dear. Won't you let me in . . . let me help in some way?"

Warmth, compassion, sympathy . . . there were no more insidious weapons in any arsenal. And he knew it, too. He knew exactly how his words could wriggle beneath her defenses.

"I don't need your help," she said with the soft ferocity of determination. "Would you please go away? Or look at the Chaucer, if you must. I have work to do, and you promised you wouldn't torment me with questions."

"The last thing I want to do is torment you, Alexandra." A note of impatience had crept into his voice now. "Can't you see that?" He glanced over his shoulder as the door opened.

Alex began to feel trapped as Stephen came into the room. She didn't want Peregrine to know what she was planning, but she couldn't see how to get rid of him if he wouldn't remove himself. He showed no sign of doing so, merely nodded at his host and strolled to the bookshelves.

"I'm just admiring this wonderful volume of Chaucer, Sir Stephen. What treasures you have here."

"Yes, I suppose so," the other man agreed with a vaguely dismissive hand. "Don't see much to 'em myself, but I'm told they'll fetch a pretty penny. So Mistress Hathaway, you wanted to speak to me, and here I am."

Alexandra could see no alternative. She didn't wish to postpone the conversation, so it would have to take place in Peregrine's hearing. "Well, after our earlier discussion, sir, about the need to hurry with the cataloguing, I was wondering if perhaps it would be wise to make some preliminary inquiries in London, among those who would make up this pool of potential buyers. I could stir up some interest by informing certain people that the collection will be for sale."

Stephen regarded her doubtfully. "Are you positive you know the right people, Mistress Hathaway? Are you able to make those contacts?"

"Yes, indeed, sir." She glanced at Peregrine, but his averted back told her nothing. She plowed on, knowing that he was listening and that his agile brain would be assessing every word. "My father had a wonderful library, and many fellow collectors would visit it. There was nothing he liked better than to share his treasure, and since I had grown up to be utterly familiar with his collection, I was always welcome to take part in the conversations. I know many dedicated bibliophiles, and my father's name will give me an entrée into an even wider circle. A few letters to a select company, explaining that the Combe Abbey collection will shortly be for sale, will generate immediate interest."

She could almost see Peregrine's ears pricking, almost hear his brain turning over her words, looking for facts that would lead him somewhere.

"Yes, yes . . . yes, of course. Competition, as you said earlier. That's what we need." Stephen nodded.

Perry kept his eyes on the Chaucer, listening with incredulity as this extraordinary latest scene in the play unfolded. Alexandra was proposing to go to London. Alone, it seemed. Had she spoken the truth about her father, or was it a farrago of invention like so much else about her? He had the feeling that this trip to London would encompass more than her obligations to Stephen and the library. Why else had she come up with it out of the blue? The proposal certainly seemed to have surprised Stephen.

Stephen was frowning, tapping his mouth with his fingertips. "So, you would propose to go yourself to London?"

"Certainly," she said with a brisk, confident nod. "I am no debutante, Sir Stephen. A woman of my age has no need of a chaperone. I will find a respectable hotel from which I will send out the necessary communications and interview prospective buyers."

A woman of your *age*. Peregrine bit back the urge to laugh and waited with interest to hear what new and outrageous twist she was about to come up with.

"Well, I suppose that's true. You know your own situation best," Stephen said thoughtfully. "But how do you propose traveling to London? On the public stage?"

Alexandra knew her penny-pinching employer well. She chose her words carefully. "Of course, I would be perfectly happy to do that, Sir Stephen. If the gig could take me to Dorchester, I could catch the London stage at the Red Fox, but . . ." She frowned down at the desk, chewing her lip as if in puzzlement. "There is one thing . . ."

"One thing?" he prompted when she didn't immediately continue.

"Well, there is a difficulty, sir." She looked up with a diffident smile. "I would need to take a few of these volumes with me, to show prospective buyers . . . to whet their appetites, so to speak. And they are so valuable, I would hesitate to trust them to the public stage."

Stephen's frown deepened. "Oh . . . yes, I suppose so." He glanced around at the bookshelves. "You really think there might be thieves interested in something as unlikely as a book?"

"They are immensely valuable, sir," she responded simply. "The possibility of damage on the stage cannot be discounted."

"Mmm." He looked around again. "So, you're suggesting a hired post chaise, then?"

"I see no other way, sir. Should you wish me to make the journey." The same diffident smile accompanied her words.

Peregrine held back his laughter once more. She was a consummate little actress and an utterly manipulative minx. It had occurred to him fleetingly, and reluctantly, at the beginning of this extraordinary conversation that she intended to steal the books herself, but for that, the public stage would be the obvious option. She could disappear into the maw of London without a trace or even take the stage in the opposite direction away from London. No one would ever find her. A private vehicle was always traceable.

"Mmm." Still, Stephen hesitated, calculating the cost of such a conveyance. "With a post chaise, there'd have to be postilions, outriders . . ."

Peregrine coughed. He had offered to help, and here was his opportunity. "I would be delighted to escort Mistress Hathaway to London, Sir Stephen. I'll be happy to ride beside her chaise, which will do away with the need for outriders."

"Indeed, sir, I have no need of your escort," Alexandra spoke sharply. "And I see no need for outriders, Sir Stephen. Just the coachman and a postilion."

"I think that with such a valuable cargo, ma'am, you should take all precautions," Peregrine said with a smooth smile. "I am considered quite handy with both pistols and a small sword. I believe I can be of service in the event of any unpleasantness. Besides," he added with a glint in his eye, "it will be no trouble to me. I am returning to London in the next day or so and will be entirely at your disposal."

"Well, I think that's a splendid solution, sir," Stephen declared, looking relieved. "Very good of you, sir, very good, indeed. Mistress Hathaway will be delighted to accept your escort."

We'll see, Peregrine thought. Those clear gray eyes were regarding him now rather speculatively, and he couldn't read the speculation.

Alexandra was thinking quickly. Accepting Peregrine's escort ensured her escape from Combe Abbey. But it would play the very devil with her plan to see Sylvia. But she was adept at adaptation. A solution would present itself, for now her escape was assured. She offered a grateful smile. "That is so very kind of you, sir. I own I will find the protection of a male escort most reassuring."

Peregrine bowed. "It will be my pleasure to serve you, ma'am."

Chapter Seven

"Here's a letter for you, m'dear. Looks like Mistress Alex's writing." A round-faced woman bustled out of the back door of the thatched cottage and hurried towards the garden chair beneath a spreading copper beech, where a young woman sat wrapped in a blanket.

"Oh, give it to me, Matty. She hasn't written in over a week." The young woman turned eagerly, hand outstretched. Sylvia was a pale version of her sister, frail where Alexandra was lithe and strong, her brown hair a shade lighter than her sister's rich chestnut, but the gray eyes were the same, clear and sharp with intelligence. The hand that took the letter was rather thin but elegant nevertheless.

"Now, now, m'dear, you mustn't catch cold." Matty tucked the blanket in more closely. " 'Tis growing chillier these afternoons."

" 'Tis still a beautiful autumn, Matty." Sylvia slit the wafer with her fingernail. "I would stay out for as long as possible. The sun makes me feel stronger."

"Well, maybe just for another half hour." Matty

glanced up at the sun, which was getting low in the sky. "Now, read the letter. How is the child?" She tutted. "I do worry about her. Whatever she's up to . . . but then, Mistress Alex was always up to something."

Sylvia was too immersed in the letter to do more than murmur in vague response as her eyes devoured Alex's crisp, bold script. Her handwriting was like everything else about her—clear, straightforward, without flourishes.

Darling,

I think I have managed to find a way to visit you. Only for a night, probably, but I ache to see you. Are you well? Do you have everything you need? Oh, I can't begin to describe how much I miss you. I need to talk to someone properly again. I never realized how difficult it would be to keep up the pretense. Or at least for such a long time. Everything is going as we planned it. Except . . . well, something unplanned has happened. A certain guest of our stepbrother's has found me out. Now, don't panic, darling. I think 'tis going to be all right. He doesn't know who I am and has promised to keep silent about what he does know, and anyway, he will be leaving Dorset in a day or two. I am going on a pretext to London, to test the market for Papa's library. Oh, it breaks my heart to think of these wonderful volumes being scattered into libraries across the country or even abroad. But they don't belong to us, so my duty to Papa is to find good homes for them. I have told Cousin Stephen that I need to go to London to encourage the competition. He's only interested in getting the best price, so it was quite easy to persuade him that this was the way to do it. Unfortunately, I must accept the escort of the certain guest in order to save our dear cousin a few guineas in payment to outriders, but I shall give him his congé when we are well away from Combe Abbey, when I will instruct the coachman to take the detour to Barton. Look for me within the week. Give Matty a kiss for me.

Your loving sister,

A.

Sylvia gazed down at the letter in her lap. Alex sounded too insouciant, and Sylvia could read between the lines. Her sister was scared. And with good reason. If someone had discovered her true identity, then she needed to leave Combe Abbey immediately. Except that it didn't appear from this letter that Alex had any intention of bringing the game to a permanent close.

"What is it, dearie? Is everything all right? Mistress Alex . . . she's not sick?" Matty's worried voice broke into Sylvia's anxious musing.

"No . . . no, quite the opposite." Sylvia looked up with a bright, reassuring smile that did not reflect her true feelings. "She's coming for a visit. Within the week, she writes. Won't that be splendid?"

"Oh, my goodness, yes. To see the dear child again. I must get baking. One of those elderflower cheese tarts that she loves so much . . . oh, and a batch of gingerbread and some almond cakes . . ." Matty hurried off, still going through her repertoire of delicacies.

Sylvia smiled, but her smile faded quickly as she re-read her sister's letter. Who was this mysterious guest of their stepbrother's? And why hadn't Alex written his name in the letter? Was he old, young, married? Of course, if he was a friend of Marcus Crofton, it was to be assumed that he was relatively young, but he didn't have to be single.

Alex had first met their stepbrother very briefly soon after arriving at Combe Abbey to take up her employment with the new incumbent. She had told her sister only that Marcus was probably in his mid-twenties and seemed personable and pleasant enough at dinner, but he hadn't paid her much attention, which was exactly as it should be. So, how had it happened that a friend of his managed to penetrate Alexandra's disguise?

Sylvia sighed and refolded the letter. She would know soon enough, if Alex managed to make the visit. And knowing Alex, she would manage it. She was not one to be diverted from a set path, as Sylvia knew well. The present charade had been entirely Alexandra's idea. Sylvia had been against it, seeing all the risks, terrified of letting her sister go alone into such a lion's den, but Alex had been adamant. It was the only way to gain justice and secure their future.

In the end, Sylvia had accepted that all she could do was help her sister perfect her part and let her go. They had rehearsed for hours until Alex was letter-perfect in her story, and her disguise was impenetrable.

Or at least, that was what they had thought.

Sylvia scooped the blanket from her knees and stood up. *What could have gone wrong?* Hitherto her main comfort had lain in her knowledge of Alex's talent for charades. They had played so many games in their childhood, and Alex in particular had always delighted in the art of disguise, dressing herself in a different persona, both physically and mentally. How had she slipped up this time?

Sylvia shivered suddenly. The air was growing chill as the sun dipped behind the trees. With a shake of her head, she made her way back up the path to the cottage. Alex would be here soon enough, and she would know everything then.

"Well, I don't know why you have to go to the expense of a post chaise for a mere servant," Maude muttered to her husband in the hall. It was just after dawn, and the carriage was already at the door, coachman and postilion holding the horses.

Stephen sighed. "I've explained, ma'am. The books are too precious to entrust to the public stage."

Maude sniffed. "That's as may be. I still consider it an unnecessary expense. Why didn't you send the woman and the books up to London in the old carriage? We could have used our own grooms and the second coachman."

"I did consider that, ma'am. But the second coachman is not skilled with such a cumbersome vehicle, and I felt sure you would not wish to do without Benjamin's services for your barouche. Besides, the front axle of the carriage is in need of repair, and if it broke down on the road, the expense would be even greater than that of a post chaise with one postilion." Stephen's voice was impatient. He was no happier than his wife about this expense, but he'd looked at every alternative, and none seemed to fit the bill.

"Besides," he added, "the profit Mistress Hathaway will ensure from the sale of the books will more than compensate for an entire fleet of hired chaises . . . And there is Mr. Sullivan, on time to offer his escort." He moved to the open front door to greet Peregrine, who rode up on his big gray and doffed his hat.

"Sir Stephen. Beautiful morning, isn't it?"

"Perfect for a journey," Stephen declared with a genial smile. "It really is very good of you to keep an eye on the books, dear fellow. I won't know a moment's peace until they are safe under lock and key in Douglas House."

"Douglas House?" Peregrine raised his eyebrows in question. "I understood Mistress Hathaway was to stay in a hotel."

"No, no . . . no need for that expense," Stephen said.

"As m'lady wife pointed out, the house is sitting there under dust covers, and the staff are eating their heads off with no employment. They can open up one or two rooms, a bedchamber and a small parlor for Mistress Hathaway. Much the better solution."

Peregrine could only imagine the dusty, chilly reception Mistress Alexandra would receive from the skeleton staff of a shut-up mausoleum on Berkeley Square. He inclined his head faintly. "Is the lady ready?"

"Oh, she's just supervising the final packing of the books. 'Tis very important they're protected from light and dust on the journey." Stephen turned back to the door, calling to a manservant. "John, have you secured Mistress Hathaway's portmanteau?"

"On the roof, sir."

"Good. Then go and inquire if Mistress Hathaway is ready to leave."

"Sir." The man bowed and disappeared into the shadows of the hall.

Alexandra watched critically as the last nail was hammered into the tea chest containing the selection of books she had picked. Much as she hated to do it, she would honor this commitment to Stephen, but her real commitment was to her father's books. They would go to the buyer she considered most worthy, regardless of whether his bid was the highest, but she would keep that little proviso to herself. And she intended to vet every potential customer for the library through her father's eyes.

"That will do," she said. "Have the chest put inside the chaise. It mustn't be exposed to the weather."

Drawing on her gloves, she followed the man who had shouldered the heavy chest. Her spirits were absurdly buoyant, and she caught herself fancying that the square of early sunlight framed in the open front door was a shining path to freedom. Ridiculous, of course, but she had to work to keep her footsteps to the sedate pace appropriate for the librarian as she crossed the hall to the door.

Maude was standing in a dressing robe at the foot of the stairs. Alexandra curtsied. "Good morning, ma'am."

"Sir Stephen and I have decided there's no need to waste money on a hotel for you," Maude stated. "A message was sent yesterday to the caretaking staff at Douglas House to expect you. I daresay you'll do well enough there. The house has been standing empty for a year, but we intend to open it properly this November for the Season."

This was the first Alexandra had heard of the change of plan, and her heart lurched. What if the caretaking staff at the London house were part of her father's establishment? All of the senior retainers from her childhood at Combe Abbey had left their employment on her father's death, provided with small pensions in Sir Arthur's will, so she had been in no danger of recognition here, but she didn't know about the London house. All of the old servants in Berkeley Square knew her . . . *had* known her, she reminded herself sharply. She had been fifteen when she had last seen any of them, and in her present guise, she bore no resemblance to that exuberant young girl. No, of course they wouldn't recognize her.

She curtsied again, murmured something, and made her escape into the pale, cool sunlight, where her high spirits received another dousing of cold water. She had tried to forget her escort, but there was Peregrine Sullivan, atop a big gray gelding, doffing his hat and smiling at her with that warmth that made her stomach plunge.

Peregrine swung down, bowing as she came down the short flight of steps to the gravel sweep. "Mistress Hathaway, your escort reporting for duty, ma'am."

She gave him a brief nod and a murmured "Good morning, sir," before busying herself with seeing to the disposal of the tea chest against the farthest door of the chaise. Then she turned to Sir Stephen. "All is in order, Sir Stephen. I will send word from London as soon as I discover how much interest there is in the collection."

"Yes, do that . . . do that. But don't be gone more than a week, mind. I have need of you here, too, you know. Business matters won't just take care of themselves."

She inclined her head. "No, indeed, sir. I will make all haste to conclude the business." Peregrine was holding the door of the chaise for her, and she stepped up inside, settling on the worn leather squabs. It was not the most commodious of vehicles and by no means in the first flush of youth, but she guessed it had been the cheapest the Red Fox in Dorchester had available.

"Are you comfortable, ma'am?" Peregrine's head was in the doorway.

"Quite, thank you," she returned stiffly, and turned her head to look out of the other window. If she tried hard enough, at least she could avoid eye contact for the part of this journey that they must perforce spend together.

So, that is how it is to be. Peregrine pursed his lips and closed the door, the coachman's whip cracked, and the carriage moved away from Combe Abbey.

Only then did Alexandra lean back against the squabs and breathe deeply. She was free . . . not for long but long enough to refocus, recover her strength of mind, and return to the fray with all the purpose and determination of before.

Except that before she could truly relax into this freedom, she had to dispense with the Honorable Peregrine Sullivan. She could do nothing about what he knew of herself at this point, but as long as he didn't take up permanent residence in the Dower House, she thought she could continue with her plan without fear of discovery. But under no circumstances could he know of Sylvia's existence. Sylvia must not be associated with her sister's deception, must not in any way be touched by the fraud that could bring her sister to the gallows. So, sooner rather than later on this journey, she would have to dispense with her escort. She could hear him whistling as if he had not a care in the world as he rode beside the carriage, and she found the sound supremely irritating. She couldn't remember when she'd last felt like whistling herself.

It was about twenty miles to Christchurch, Alexandra calculated, where they would have to change horses. They should reach there in about three hours. They would presumably break to refresh themselves while the horses were being changed, and she would tell Peregrine then that she was not continuing to London. He could have no justification for continuing with his escort unless he wanted to make mischief. He had offered to help her; if she explained that this was the only way he could do that, then he would surely continue on the road to London, and she would be free to enjoy Sylvia's company for tonight and tomorrow.

She would instruct the coachman to take the coastal detour that would bring them to the little hamlet of Barton just a few miles along the coast from Lymington. She had sufficient funds of her own to pay the coachman for such a short delay, and he and his horses could put up at the Angel Inn in Lymington. A different chaise and coachman would return her to Combe Abbey from London, so there was no possible reason for Cousin Stephen to hear of the detour, and if he heard of her delayed arrival in Berkeley Square, there were any number of travelers' tales she could use to explain it.

It should all work beautifully. So, why did she have this nagging doubt?

Peregrine continued whistling cheerfully as he rode beside the carriage. This offer to escort Alexandra had been pure impulse, a way to spend time alone with her in a noncompromising situation. He was hoping she would take him into her confidence in private, away from prying eyes. Of course, her present rather frigid attitude made that hope seem optimistic, but he had not expected it to be easy.

She would resist, and he would push back. He would not betray her, and she had to know that now. Eventually, she would come to trust him fully if he persisted. She was by no means indifferent to him; even though she had run from him in the end, her response to him on the cliff top had made that clear enough. He had not mistaken the deep sensual glow in her eyes, the soft yearning of her body as she'd leaned into him.

A smile quirked his mouth as he thought how much he wanted to see the moonlight in her gray eyes once more, the straight and slender body, the true and vulnerable self revealed beneath the disfiguring marks on her smooth complexion. And most of all, he wanted to hear her talk, see her smile, her true smile, enjoy fencing with that rapier wit.

He moved Sam closer to the chaise. Leaning down, he used his crop to push aside the leather curtain that closed the window aperture. "Is all well in there?"

Alexandra jumped, startled from her musing. She looked at Peregrine, who was smiling that inviting smile. Resistance was easier with rudeness. "It was," she said pointedly. "Now 'tis drafty with the window open."

An eyebrow lifted. "My apologies, ma'am. I wished only to ensure you were comfortable and needed nothing. We could stop for a short while any time you wish."

"I have no need and no wish to stop before we reach Christchurch." She leaned back against the squabs and closed her eyes, hoping it was enough.

Peregrine let the curtain fall. He would have settled for a polite response to his solicitous inquiry, but he'd never been averse to a challenge.

Alexandra kept her eyes studiously closed in case her escort took it into his head to peek in at her again. The less they spoke, the safer she would feel. Soon they would reach Christchurch, and she would send him on his way.

The Norman tower of Christchurch Priory dominated the skyline as they approached the town. Alexandra sat up, moving aside the leather curtain on the far side of the chaise, away from Peregrine, and looked out at Christchurch Harbor protected by the cliff at Hengistbury Head. The chaise turned up the High Street from the harbor and drew up in the yard of the George Inn. The George was the only coaching inn in town, and ostlers ran from the stables to remove the horses from their traces.

Peregrine dismounted and opened the door, asking politely, "Will you step into the inn, ma'am? You'll welcome some refreshment, I daresay."

"Thank you." She ignored his proffered hand and stepped down onto the cobbles. She approached the coachman, who was talking with one of the ostlers. "How long to make the change?"

"Ten minutes, ma'am. We'll leave when you're ready."

"Fifteen minutes will suffice." She gave him a nod and crossed the yard to the inn door, where the landlord stood attentively. His expression was somewhat dour as he realized that this drab passenger was unlikely to request a private parlor or any of his more expensive amenities.

"Ma'am. Welcome to the George."

"Thank you. I'll take coffee in the taproom."

The man bowed his acknowledgment and then bowed rather more deeply to the gentleman who was following the lady. His blue wool coat was that of a gentleman of fashion, even if it was rather plain, and he carried himself with all the natural authority that the landlord considered necessary to a gentleman of Quality. He rubbed his hands again, saying with an obsequious smile, "Sir, I've a fine strong ale, a local brew, if you'd care to try it."

Perry nodded, stripping off his gloves. "Yes, bring it with the coffee. We'll find a quiet corner in the taproom." He placed a proprietorial hand under Alexandra's elbow and eased her into the dim hallway.

She would have resisted the hand if they were not being observed by the landlord and a bobbing maidservant, who stood at the door to the taproom. She walked into the room, which smelled of ale and wood smoke from the fire in the hearth.

"Over there, I think. 'Tis secluded." Peregrine steered her to a settle in a shadowy corner by the fire. "May I take your cloak?"

"No, thank you," she said stiffly, sitting down. "I'm not staying very long."

"Maybe not, but that's no reason to sit swaddled in that hideous garment." He sat on the settle opposite her, laying his whip and gloves on the table between them.

Alexandra ignored this. "Mr. Sullivan," she began, "this is where we part company."

"Oh? How so?" He looked only mildly interested in the statement, leaning back as the maidservant set a pot of coffee and a foaming tankard on the table. He picked up the tankard and drank deeply.

Alex poured coffee and marshaled her forces. "As it happens, I am not traveling immediately to London. So you will wish to continue your journey, while I continue mine in a different direction."

His eyes sharpened. "What different direction?"

"That, sir, is none of your business." She sipped her coffee.

He sighed. "No, I'm sure that's true. However, I seem to have made *you* my business. So, where are we going if not to London?"

"*I* am going my own way." She began to feel like Sisyphus pushing his boulder up the mountainside. "*You* are going *yours*."

Peregrine stroked his chin, regarding her thoughtfully. "Well, there's a certain difficulty there. You see, I agreed to watch over Sir Stephen's precious books and see them safely delivered to Douglas House. So, wherever you're going, I'm afraid you'll have to accept my escort."

"Oh, don't be ridiculous," she said. "You have no obligation to Sir Stephen at all. Believe me, I will take very good care of the books." She set down her cup with an air of finality. "Now, if you'll excuse me, I must be on my way." She got up from the settle and marched out of the taproom.

Peregrine drained his tankard, put a coin on the table, and followed her out. The chaise was still in the yard, fresh horses in the traces, and the coachman and postilion were finishing their own ale tankards. There was no sign of Alexandra.

He went up to Sam, who had been watered and rubbed down, and stroked his neck. The horse had another five or six hours left in him if they took it easily. After a few minutes, Alexandra appeared in the yard again, coming from the direction of the outhouse at the rear of the inn. He went to open the chaise door for her.

"So, where to, ma'am?"

She looked at him in frustration. "Why? Why are you insisting on this? My plans have nothing to do

with you. You have your own life to get back to in
London. Why can't you accept that?"

He shrugged. "Perhaps because you interest me beyond reason. Perhaps because I think you are in trouble, and I don't seem able to stand aside if I can help in
any way." He looked at her closely. "Are you intending
to steal the books in the chaise?"

"Oh, that's just insulting," she responded. "Why on
earth would I do that?"

"Because they're valuable?"

"I am not a thief."

"No, I didn't think so. So, what *are* you?"

She didn't answer him, merely turned on her heel
and approached the coachman. "I'm taking a detour.
Take the coastal road to Lymington, if you please."

"Lymington, ma'am?" He looked astonished, glancing at Peregrine for confirmation.

"Do as the lady says," Peregrine instructed. "Ma'am,
will you get in?" He indicated the interior of the chaise.

For a moment, she stood, nonplussed. Very rarely
had Alexandra experienced this sense of total helplessness. Short of putting a bullet in him, she could not
compel him to leave her alone, and she couldn't outrun
him.

"Come now," he said softly. "I mean you no harm,
Alexandra. But I am coming with you."

Maybe she should give in and simply tell the coachman she'd changed her mind and he should continue
to London. But now the need to see her sister was all-

consuming. She was so close, and there was no knowing when another opportunity would arise. What difference did it make if Peregrine came with her as far as Lymington? She could give him the slip there. They would reach Lymington, she would pretend that was her final destination and take a chamber overnight in the Angel, and at some point in the evening, she would make her escape. She could hire a pony from the inn and ride over to Barton—it was a mere five miles over the heath. Peregrine would never know how to find her.

Chapter Eight

It was less than twenty miles to Lymington, but the coastal road was rough, and the chaise could make little more than six miles an hour. Sam picked his way carefully through the ruts in the narrow lanes, and Peregrine allowed his mind to roam. The gray-green waters of the Solent stretched to the green humpbacked-whale shape of the Isle of Wight and the sharp danger of the Needles rocks off St. Catherine's Point at the entrance to the English Channel. The salt-smelling air was fresh, and it felt good to be alive.

Every once in a while, he would draw closer to the chaise, but its occupant never showed her face at the window. It must be an uncomfortable ride, he reflected. The chaise was ill sprung and the lanes uneven, but one thing he had gathered about Mistress Alexandra, she had the dedication of a stoic. *And the determination of the desperate.*

Alex was thoroughly miserable and thought enviously of her companion enjoying the air on horseback. She would have given anything to ride. After two hours of misery, she knocked on the roof of the chaise, and the coachman drew rein. The door opened quickly, and her escort leaned in.

"Is something amiss?"

She ignored the question. She opened her own door and stepped carefully over the tea chest to step out onto the lane on the opposite side of her escort. It was a childish gesture of defiance, she knew, but it gave her some satisfaction. He might force his company upon her, but she didn't have to acknowledge it.

"I'll walk for a while," she called up to the coachman. "The going's so slow, anyway, it won't hold us up."

"Right y'are, ma'am." He touched his forelock and set the team into motion again at a slow amble while she strolled beside the chaise, her stride lengthening as her cramped muscles loosened.

Peregrine dismounted and led Sam around the back of the chaise to the same side. "I don't blame you," he remarked cheerfully. "'Tis a beautiful day. A little nip in the air, but all the fresher for it."

Studiously, she ignored him and increased her pace. He persevered. "The coachman says it should take another two hours at this speed. I gather the Angel is the best coaching inn. I'm looking forward to a good dinner, I must say."

Alex was famished herself—it was early afternoon now, and it had been many hours since she had broken her fast before dawn—but she maintained her resolute silence. If he had not forced himself upon her, she would have continued the last few miles to Barton and been there in time for one of Matty's splendid dinners. Instead, she was going to have to kick her heels at the Angel and waste good money on dinner there, until she could give him the slip.

"Did you bring other clothes in your portmanteau?" he continued as if he hadn't noticed her silence. "Surely you don't intend to show yourself on the streets of London in your present guise."

Alexandra bent and picked up a pebble from the lane. She spun away from him and hurled it off the cliff and into the sea. The furious force of her throw almost upset her balance, and he pulled her back as she teetered precariously close to the cliff edge. "Steady, now. Why am I making you so angry?"

"How could you possibly need to ask such a question?" she snapped, pushing against his chest. "Let go of me."

Her cloak was hanging loosely from her shoulders, and his hands were on her waist. Not even the coarse folds of her gown could hide the slimness of her body, the tensile strength as she tried to thrust him away from her. He was aware of that same powerful sensual current that had swept through him on the cliff top and saw in the sudden arrested flash in her gray eyes that she felt it, too. Reluctantly, he decided to take the high road, dropped his hands, and stepped back from her. It was a sacrifice, but it was her trust he wanted, not a surrender that she would bitterly regret.

"I think in your present frame of mind, it would be safer to walk away from the edge of the cliff," he commented, his voice dry.

"I'm getting back into the chaise." She raised a hand to the coachman, who drew rein, waiting until she was back inside and the door firmly closed.

Alexandra felt hot, and her heart was racing. If he hadn't done the gentlemanly thing, would she have resisted him this time? She would never know. Oh, *why* was this happening to her? If she hadn't been so angry at the perversities of fate embodied in the person of Peregrine Sullivan, she would have burst into tears.

It was mid-afternoon by the time they turned under the arched entrance to the Angel's coaching yard. Alex was by now stiff and heartily sick of the whole business. She knew that without her persistent escort, her excitement at the prospect of being so close to journey's end would have made nothing of her ills, but now she could only see hours of anxiety ahead of her until she could rid herself of the Honorable Peregrine.

Peregrine handed Sam over to a groom with the instruction to give him a good rubdown and a bran mash. The coachman, with much the same relief, relinquished his team to the ostlers. "You'll be restin' 'ere, then, ma'am?" he inquired as Alex stepped out of the chaise.

"For the night, yes," she responded. She walked into the inn, where Peregrine was already talking with the landlord.

"There's a chamber available abovestairs on the side and another, rather larger, at the front. I think you'll be more comfortable on the side. It'll be quieter than facing the street, so if you're agreeable, I will take the one at the front."

It wasn't worth telling him she was quite capable of making her own decisions when it came to her own accommodations. He was right that she would prefer the quieter room, so she merely gave him a curt nod and addressed the landlord. "Would you have the tea chest and my portmanteau brought up from the chaise to my chamber? And I would like hot water immediately, and then I will dine in my chamber in half an hour."

For such a timid-seeming mouse, Mistress Alexandra, once away from Combe Abbey, had a very commanding way with her, Peregrine reflected. "I'll see to your things." He beckoned to a man in a leather apron. "Come with me."

"If you'll follow me, ma'am." The landlord went to the stairs, and Alex followed him up to a small but fairly comfortable chamber at the side of the building. "Will you wish to keep the bed to yourself, ma'am?" the man asked. "If so, it'll be three shillings a night. If you don't mind bundling, then I can let you 'ave it for two."

"I'll pay the extra," she said, tossing her hat and cloak onto a bench at the foot of the poster bed. She had no choice, since she would have to leave the tea chest locked in here overnight when she went to Barton, instead of taking it with her as she'd intended. Her original plan, before Peregrine had intruded, had been that the coachman would drive her to Barton, where she could unload the chest, and then he'd drive back to collect her and her possessions the following day. Now she was obliged to spend money she didn't have to waste simply because the Honorable Peregrine felt a perverse need to help her with something she could manage perfectly well herself.

The man bowed and backed out, and a few minutes later, Peregrine appeared with the servant, who was struggling under the weight of the tea chest. Peregrine put her portmanteau on the bed and glanced around as the servant set the chest in the corner of the room. "This seems adequate."

"Yes," she agreed shortly. She opened her coin purse for something to give the servant, but Peregrine forestalled her, tossing the man a sixpence.

"I've bespoken a private parlor where our dinner will be served in half an hour," Peregrine informed her. "The landlord tells me that he has a leg of mutton with red currant jelly and a halfway decent burgundy in his cellars."

"I prefer to dine alone up here," she stated.

"Why?" he asked simply.

She stared at him in astonishment. "*Why?* You would ask that. Sweet heaven, you have windmills in your head."

"Not so," he denied. "But I cannot see the virtue in dining alone shut in this chamber when you can sit at a proper table in what I trust will be good company. I am considered good company, in general," he added on an almost plaintive note, but his eyes were dancing.

It was no good. She was standing like Sisyphus watching the immense boulder roll back down the mountain. And maybe it would be wise to yield on this one issue. She needed to ensure that he didn't suspect her intention, and what better way to do that than to appear to accept defeat, lull him into thinking that he had won. After dinner, she would plead fatigue and retreat to her chamber. It would be simple enough to slip away. There was a livery stable at the bottom of the High Street where she could hire a horse. With any luck, she would be with Sylvia before nightfall.

"Oh, have it your own way," she said with a gesture of resignation. "I'll join you in half an hour."

"I look forward to it, ma'am." He bowed his way out of the chamber, moving aside to give entrance to a serving girl with a jug of hot water.

"'Ere y'are, ma'am." The girl set it on the marble-topped washstand. "Will there be anythin' else?"

"No, thank you. That'll be all." The girl bobbed a curtsy and disappeared, and Alex swiftly turned the key in the lock. She went to the small casement, which opened onto a narrow side street. She leaned out, listening to the bustle from the High Street at the front and the shouts from the coaching yard at the rear. But the lane below was deserted. She couldn't escape that way, though. There was no drainpipe and no ivy or wisteria, either. It would have to be the inn's back door into the yard.

She left the window and went over to the bed, where she opened her portmanteau. She had a second string to her disguise buried at the bottom, beneath the dowdy gowns and limp petticoats appropriate for Mistress Hathaway. It was her swift-escape costume, something that she and Sylvia had concocted in case Alex had to beat a hasty retreat and couldn't risk appearing either as herself or as the drab librarian. It wouldn't pass muster at close quarters but from a distance would draw no remark.

She made sure everything was still there, then went to the washstand, dipping a cloth in hot water and applying it to her throat and neck. She couldn't wash her face without ruining her makeup, but she felt fresher. She looked at herself in the beaten-copper mirror and grimaced. What a hag. In truth, she couldn't really blame Peregrine for his curiosity once he'd actually laid eyes on the true face of Alexandra Douglas. She pinned up her hair again, pulling it tight against her scalp. It made her look even worse, but that was all to the good. She wanted everyone in the inn to have her present image indelibly printed in their minds.

However, she could do without the humpback, she decided, swiftly unbuttoning her gown, pushing it to her waist so that she could untie the pad. She flexed her shoulders with relief, then thrust her arms back into the sleeves and refastened the bodice.

The clock on the mantel struck the half hour, and she cast a last glance around the chamber before leaving it, locking the door behind her and slipping the key into the pocket of her kersey apron. Then she made her way downstairs. The serving girl showed her into the private parlor, where Peregrine awaited her, standing before the fire, cradling a glass of wine. He shook his head when she came in.

"I found myself hoping I would see someone else, but I suppose 'tis something that you've got rid of the dowager's hump," he observed. "Is it necessary to maintain the rest of that disguise here, where no one knows you?"

"If I appeared as myself, sir, I would draw instant remark. Young women traveling unchaperoned are certain to cause talk. Particularly a young woman traveling in the company, however unwelcome, of a strange man."

"I could pretend to be your brother," he suggested, filling a glass from the wine decanter. "A perfectly suitable escort."

"You could also not be here at all," she retorted, taking the glass he proffered. "Thank you."

"'Tis a fine burgundy, as mine host promised," Perry said. "Will you come to the table? There's some excellent smoked trout to keep us busy until the mutton is ready."

Alex was too hungry to fence further. She sat down and helped herself to the smoked fish and a hunk of barley bread. A salad of watercress and tender herbs accompanied the fish.

"So, I'm assuming there's a good reason for us to be in this town," Perry observed. "May I know what it is?"

"No." She buttered her bread liberally. "At the risk of repeating myself into tedium, 'tis none of your business, sir."

"I fear you crossed the line into tedium quite some time ago," he commented, filleting his trout. "But I keep hoping you'll change your tune. I've always been an optimist, you see." He smiled amiably as he leaned forward to refill her glass.

Alexandra helped herself to a little of the salad, observing, "You must be doomed to disappointment much of the time, then."

"Oh, no. Very rarely, as it happens." He leaned back in his chair. "Optimism runs in my family. We Blackwaters are seldom downhearted."

"How many of you are there?" Despite herself, she was curious.

"Three brothers. I have a twin, Sebastian, and we have an older brother, Jasper, the fifth Earl." He sipped his wine. "How about your family? I know you have an invalid cousin, but do you also have siblings?"

"One." And then she caught herself. She had pretended she had an invalid cousin in her conversation with her stepmother. Why on earth couldn't she have kept to that fabrication now? Even though it seemed a harmless enough conversation, one that it would be all too easy to allow to continue under the relaxing influence of wine and good food, it was far too dangerous to drop her guard for so much as a syllable.

"Brother or sister?" he prompted.

She shook her head. "I have no interest in this conversation."

"Probably because you know all the answers. I, on the other hand, am very interested in learning the answers."

She put down her fork. "You are incorrigible, Mr. Sullivan. You're like a runaway horse. Tell me what it's like to have a twin." If she could keep the conversation on him, they might manage to brush through dinner without mishap.

"I can't imagine what it would be like not to have Sebastian," he said seriously. "As a small boy, I always felt sorry for people who didn't have a twin." He laughed. "I couldn't understand how they managed to live alone, without that special connection . . . it's hard to describe, really."

Alex found herself drawn into the topic without even being aware of it. "I think I know what you mean, though. Sy—" She bit her tongue. But it was too late now to draw back completely. "My sister and I are only eleven months apart. I don't really remember a time when she wasn't there."

Peregrine gave no indication that he had noticed her slip. He buttered bread, observing, "Our father died when we were very young, and our mother, to all intents and purposes, abandoned her children and retreated into her own private world. The three of us had only one another to rely on."

"Of course, you have an older brother, the earl." Alex sipped her wine. "Are you as close to him as to your twin?"

"In a different way. Sebastian and I share more than our physical features." He laughed lightly. "We always know what the other's thinking. That doesn't happen with Jasper, but without him, I don't know what would have happened to us."

"Tell me."

He began to talk of his childhood, the miseries of their school days, the protection Jasper had given his brothers, and the glorious delights of vacations in the wild countryside of Northumberland. He said little about his mother, but it was enough for Alex to know that maternal estrangement had been as much a part of his life as it had been of hers.

He was different talking so personally like this, she thought. His expression was both reflective and soft, and she felt drawn to him in a different way, as if she could understand so much of the childhood that had produced the man because in so many ways it mirrored her own.

Then, suddenly, he stopped and smiled at her. "You certainly managed to divert the conversation, Mistress Alexandra. But let us talk of something else altogether. Your chess game, for instance. How old were you when you first learned to play? And don't think to hoodwink me again. I know perfectly well that you play a first-rate game."

"How could you know that?"

"What kind of gull do you take me for?" He leaned over to refill her glass. "I know your mind, ma'am. And I know how competitive you are. You decided to play me for a fool, and you succeeded, I grant you that. But not to the extent you may think. I knew what you were doing. So, how old were you?"

She inclined her head in acknowledgment. She could hardly deny what he so obviously knew. "I don't really remember a time when I didn't know how to play. My father played a great deal, and I think I learned just watching him when I was very small."

"This would be in the vicarage, then."

Careful, Alex told herself. For an instant, she had forgotten the narrative. "Yes," she said blandly. "In the vicarage, of course."

Peregrine's smile was as bland as her tone. *I don't believe you've been inside a vicarage in your life.* "Of course, your father was a considerable scholar."

She nodded.

He took another sip of wine. "It seems very unusual for an impoverished country vicar to have the means of such considerable scholarship, not to mention the acquisition of the books you were telling Sir Stephen about."

"My father was the youngest son of seven," she

stated firmly. "He was well educated, and he inherited the family library. It was all he inherited, apart from a small country living. Does that satisfy your curiosity, sir?"

"Not in the least," he said amiably. "But I'll live with it for the time being."

Silence fell, and it was with relief that Alex welcomed the arrival of the maidservant with the mutton and the red currant jelly. "There's a nice onion sauce to go with the mutton, sir . . . ma'am. And a dish of roast spuds. Very good they are." The girl set the dishes on the table. "Will that be all for the moment, sir . . . ma'am?"

"Yes, thank you." Peregrine nodded dismissal and took up the carving knife. "May I serve you some meat, ma'am?" He carved several thick slices, laid them on a plate, and passed it across to her.

"Thank you." She poured onion sauce on the meat and took a spoonful of potatoes, her mouth watering at the rich scents. And for the next fifteen minutes, Peregrine left her in peace to enjoy her dinner; he was too hungry himself to continue with his catechism, and the companionable silence continued apart from his asking her to pass the red currant jelly and the soft sound of pouring wine as he refilled their glasses.

At last, Alex put down her fork and sighed with pleasure. "That was the most delicious meal I can remember in ages."

"Really? I didn't find Sir Stephen's table particularly

unsatisfying." He wiped his mouth and took up his wine glass.

It wasn't that, Alex reflected, it had just been impossible for her to enjoy eating while maintaining her charade. One instant of relaxation, and there was no knowing what she might let slip.

"It was adequate," she said vaguely. "But I didn't particularly enjoy the company."

He nodded. "I can understand that. Lady Douglas has a most unpleasant tongue." He looked at her thoughtfully. "I have been wondering why she dislikes you so much."

Alexandra flushed uncomfortably. "She dislikes most people," she muttered.

He shrugged. "I grant you she's not the friendliest of souls, but she seems to reserve a particular vitriol for you. I wonder why."

"I daresay she resents the money Sir Stephen pays for my employment," she said. "They are both pennypinchers, but at least Sir Stephen can see the advantage in a certain outlay that will produce profit in the end. Lady Maude doesn't have the wit to see that."

Perry chuckled. "I can see you have no more love for the lady than she has for you."

"Why should I have?" Alex challenged.

"No reason at all."

The door opened again, and the maid came back with another tray. "A nice piece of cheese, sir . . . ma'am, and Mistress Hoxforth's plum tart. She says, would you like a slice? An' there's cream fresh from the cow."

"Well, I would certainly," Peregrine declared. "Mistress Hathaway?"

"Please." Alex smiled at the girl, who set pie and cheese on the table with a jug of thick golden cream, scooped up the dirty plates, and disappeared.

"This is indeed a feast." Peregrine passed his plate as Alex cut into the pie. She laid a large slice on his plate and took a smaller piece for herself.

"I shall retire very early," she said when she had eaten the last crumb. "The day has been very tiring, and I need to seek my bed. So, if you'll excuse me, sir."

He rose immediately. "Of course, but I trust you don't have bad dreams. 'Tis not wise to sleep on a full stomach."

"That's an old wives' tale," she retorted. "I give you good night, Mr. Sullivan."

He bowed to her back as she left the chamber, then sat down again, cut himself a chunk of cheese, refilled his glass, and continued his repast, a very thoughtful look in his eye.

Alex unlocked the door to her chamber and locked it again behind her. She was not in the least tired but was instead filled with a renewed energy at the thought that she would be with Sylvia in little more than an hour. The church clock chimed five as she went to the bed.

She shook out the unremarkable woolen breeches, leather jerkin, and linen shirt of a young working man.

A woolen cap, woolen stockings, and shoes with paste buckles completed the costume. She had practiced putting her hair up under the cap so that no chestnut wisps escaped. But she had to do something else with her face. Mistress Hathaway's visage was all too remarkable and not at all appropriate for a youth.

She soaked a cloth in the now tepid water in the ewer and wiped away one face before starting on another. A smudge of charcoal on her upper lip gave the impression of a youthful moustache, and a shadow under the cheekbones made her cheeks seem thinner, slightly sunken. She examined her reflection with a critical frown. She didn't want to overdo it, and the shadows were lengthening outside; she would not be in harsh light when she was doing business at the livery stables. It would pass muster, she decided, and began to remove the drab-lady garments.

The breeches and jerkin were wonderfully liberating. She pinned her hair securely on top of her head and adjusted the wool cap, pulling the brim low to leave her face in shadow. A kerchief around her neck was the final touch, and for a few moments, she practiced walking up and down the chamber until she felt comfortable with the unladylike stride.

She let herself out of the chamber, closing the door softly behind her. Where was Peregrine? Still in the parlor, perhaps, or perhaps he'd retired to his chamber. She remembered that his chamber was at the front of the inn looking over the High Street. He might be looking out of the window as she emerged from the inn. She didn't think he would see anything untoward even if he did notice her on the street, but as she knew to her cost, Peregrine saw all too much. To be on the safe side, she would slip from the inn through the kitchen door into the yard and reach the street through the arched side entrance to the yard.

She found the backstairs at the end of the side corridor and hurried down them. The thronged kitchen was a melee of cooks and servants rushing from the pantry to stir the huge cauldrons steaming on the range. Clouds of flour rose from the massive pine table in the center of the stone-flagged, low-beamed room, where three kitchen maids were rolling out pastry. A red-faced woman wielding a ladle was yelling at the pot boy, who was turning legs of mutton over three spits in the massive fireplace. No one took any notice of the youth flitting across the kitchen to the back door that stood open to let out the steaming heat.

Alex breathed a sigh of relief in the fresh air, wondering how anyone could work in such frenzied heat. But despite that, they could certainly produce an excellent dinner, she reflected, threading her way across the yard. A carriage had just entered through the archway, and the ostlers and grooms were occupied with the team, so again she slipped unnoticed under the arch and out into the High Street. It was almost six o'clock, but there were still plenty of folk on the street as she made her way to the livery stable situated at the bottom of the street before it descended in steep cobbles to the quay.

In her time at St. Catherine's, Lymington had been the closest town of any size, and its weekly market was a focal point for the surrounding hamlets, so Alex was very familiar with the town's businesses. On occasion, she had stabled her own horse, or St. Catherine's pony and trap, in the livery stables while she and Helene had done whatever business they had to undertake in the market, but she was confident that the owner of the livery stable would not see in this workmanlike youth the lively young woman who had accompanied Mistress Simmons from the young ladies' seminary so many months earlier.

The owner of the livery stable was sitting on an upturned water butt in the yard, smoking a corncob pipe. He regarded his visitor with only mild interest as the youth came over the cobbles to talk to him.

"I need to hire a pony until tomorrow afternoon," Alex said without preamble.

He nodded, looking her over with an assessing eye. "Reckon Sally'll do ye. Ye're not carryin' much weight, lad." He heaved himself off the barrel. "Where're you takin' 'er?"

"Not far. Just to Barton. I'm looking for work there. I'll bring her back tomorrow afternoon."

"Oh, aye." He nodded. "Let's see yer coin, then?"

Alex drew a gold sovereign from her coin purse. Stephen paid her a pound a week for her toils in the library and her money-making efforts with his financial investments. Much of her original fifty pounds had gone to creating the charade itself, but she spent very little at Combe Abbey and managed to keep her coin purse relatively plump. She hated wasting funds, but she could certainly afford to hire a pony for a day and a half.

The man took it, bit it, and nodded again. "Aye, reckon that'll do it." He started walking to the stables behind him. "I'll see 'er back 'ere before sundown tomorrow."

"Of course." Alex followed him into the low building. It was almost dark inside and smelled of straw and the rich scent of horseflesh.

"So, who's lookin' fer hired help in Barton, then?" he inquired pleasantly. "'Tis a small place. We know most of the folk hereabouts." He led a piebald pony from a stall.

"Oh, I don't know the name," she said hastily. "But I met someone in town who told me there might be work at the dairy farm there. Said they'd give me a bed in the barn. So I thought I'd go and see."

"That'll be Edgar. He has the biggest dairy farm in these parts," the liveryman said. "He'll give you a bed overnight, even if there's no work for you. Got a good 'eart, has our Edgar." He led the pony out into the yard. "Saddle's in the tack room. You'll have to do it yourself, all my lads 'ave gone 'ome fer the night."

"Yes, of course." She let herself into the tack room

and selected a saddle and bridle that looked suitable for the pony's size. The liveryman returned to his water barrel and watched her sleepily as she saddled the little mare. For a hired hack from a livery stable, the pony was quite lively, well shod and groomed, and Alex could detect no saddle sores or swollen fetlocks. Her mouth was soft as she took the bit, and she whinnied when Alex stroked her neck before putting her foot in the stirrup and hauling herself up with the pommel.

She raised a hand in farewell and walked the mare out onto the High Street.

Chapter Nine

Peregrine stood in the doorway of a milliner's opposite the entrance to the livery stable and watched the piebald pony and its rider take the left turn at the bottom of the High Street. When they were out of sight, he crossed the street and entered the yard of the livery stable.

After Alexandra had ostensibly retired early from the dinner table, he had strolled out into the town, too full of his own thoughts to settle quietly in his own chamber. It was a pretty little town, with a lively quayside, and if he had known why he was there in the first place, he might have enjoyed it more than he did. After half an hour, he returned to the High Street and went into a tavern opposite the Angel. It was a pleasant evening, and he had decided to take his ale to the ale bench outside, where a crowd of locals were already gathered.

At first, he had barely registered the youth who emerged from the archway at the side of the Angel, and then something had brought him up sharply. He walked forward, watching the figure striding briskly down the hilly street. There was something familiar in the way the young man walked, the swing from his hips, the bounce in his step. And there was something very familiar about the physique. The jerkin and breeches were a close fit, and his gaze was riveted to the shape they revealed.

What in the name of the devil is she doing now?

He had known instinctively that it was Alexandra, known it in the marrow of his bones, just as he had known the sprite dancing on the beach at Lulworth Cove. He set his tankard on the bench behind him and set off down the street, keeping just behind her on the opposite side. She had turned aside into a livery stable, and he had stepped back into the doorway of the milliner's and waited until she and the pony had turned the corner at the bottom of the street.

A man was sitting on an upturned water butt in the yard of the livery stable as Perry entered the yard. He got off his perch as the visitor approached. "What can I do ye fer, good sir? We're about closed up for the day."

"No need to disturb yourself," Perry said with an easy smile. "The young man who just hired a horse from you, did he say where he was going?"

The liveryman looked a little suspiciously at his visitor. "Why? Is he wanted fer summat?"

Perry shook his head. "No . . . not that I know of. But he reminds me of a stable boy who worked for me some months ago. I think he came from these parts."

The man's eyes narrowed. "Said he was lookin' fer work, sir. He's gone to try Edgar's dairy farm out Barton way. Said he'd be bringin' the 'orse back tomorrow afore sundown."

"I see. Thank you. It can't have been the same youth. I don't think the one who worked for me knew one end of a cow from the other."

The liveryman chuckled and spat a stream of tobacco juice onto the cobbles at his feet. "Long as he knew one end of a 'orse from t'other, right?"

"Right." Perry gave the man a civil nod and left the yard. *Now what?* It was clear that this new incarnation of Mistress Alexandra had everything to do with why they were in this sleepy market town in the heart of Hampshire. *Barton.* What was the significance of that?

Well, he wasn't going to discover it while pondering the mystery on Lymington High Street. On impulse, he turned back to the livery stable. The owner was preparing to leave his perch when Peregrine came back.

"How far away is this Barton?"

The man frowned. "Five miles, mebbe."

Less than an hour on a fresh horse. "D'you have a horse I could hire for the evening? My own mount has been well ridden today."

"You goin' to Barton, too, then, sir?" The man looked very curious.

"'Tis as good a destination as any," Perry said easily. "I've a mind to take a look at the countryside, but I'll return this evening. I'm staying at the Angel. I'll stable the horse there overnight, and you may collect it in the morning."

The man looked up at the setting sun. "'Tis late to ride five miles there and five miles back, sir, though there'll be a good moonlight, 'tis almost full. But the lanes are rough goin'. O' course, there's always 'cross the fields. 'Tis quicker, if ye knows it."

Which he didn't. But Alexandra surely would. She'd hardly have made such an elaborate scheme to engineer this detour if she didn't know what she was doing.

"How large is this village of Barton?"

The liveryman shrugged. "'Tis little more than a 'amlet, really, just a few cottages, a farm or two . . . St. Catherine's Seminary for Young Ladies is the largest building thereabouts. 'Tis half a mile outside the village."

A seminary where a young lady might just gain a wider education than most. Peregrine smiled. Could she be going there?

"If you've a mount, I'll take my chance."

The man gave him the same assessing look he'd given Alexandra. "Reckon Dusty'll suit. I'll fetch 'im." A few minutes later, he emerged from the stable leading a broad-backed brown gelding. "I'll saddle 'im up fer you, sir. Stable lads've all gone 'ome."

Perry gave him an impatient nod. It was harebrained to go charging off on a strange horse in strange territory in the twilight, but what else was he to do if he was to solve this mystery? And he could already taste the satisfaction of solving the mystery of Mistress Alexandra.

Five minutes later, he was on his way, the liveryman's directions etched in his memory. Left at the bottom of High Street, right at the top of the hill, and straight for about three miles onto the gorse-covered heath that constituted large tracts of the New Forest. At the gibbet at the crossroads, he was to go right, and the lane would take him into the village of Barton.

Alex left the road and took the pony across the heath, urging her into a gallop under the rising full moon. She was close now, the last mile seemed interminable, but she finally crested a small hill on the heath and looked down on the cluster of cottages that made up the village of Barton.

"Come on, Sally. Almost home." She nudged the pony's flanks, and Sally trotted down the hill onto the lane that ran between the cottages and their candlelit windows. At the end of the village, a cottage slightly larger than the rest occupied a larger piece of land. Smoke curled from the chimney, and the two windows on either side of the front door were lamplit.

Alex heaved a sigh of relief. She had been half afraid that Sylvia and Matty would have already retired for the night, although it was barely seven. They tended to keep the same country hours as other folk in the village, following the sun's path. She rode around to the back of the cottage and tethered Sally in a lean-to at the bottom of the kitchen garden. She stroked the pony's nose. "I'll bed you down in a little while, Sally." Then she set off up the path.

The kitchen door was unlocked, as it always was. No one feared intruders in this out-of-the-way spot. She pushed it open and stepped into the kitchen, listening, torn between the desire to surprise her sister and the fear that such a surprise might startle Sylvia too much.

She called softly, "Anyone at home?"

The door to the front hall flew open. "Lord-a-mercy, Mistress Alex." Matty threw up her hands, her plump face wreathed in smiles. "Oh, dearie me, what are you doing in those clothes? What do you look like? Your poor mother would have an attack of the vapors."

"No she wouldn't, Matty. Mama has never had an attack of the vapors in her life," Alex declared, flinging her arms around her erstwhile nurse.

"Alex, dearest, 'tis really you. Oh, I've missed you so much." Sylvia flew across the kitchen, arms outstretched, and hugged her sister tightly. Then she stood back, gazing at Alex's costume with a worried frown. It had been agreed between them that Alex would only wear the boy's costume if she had to run from an untenable situation. "What has happened, Alex? Why are you wearing the escape disguise?"

"Because I needed to escape from my escort," Alex told her. "Now, don't look so alarmed, Sylvia. 'Tis nothing serious, but I needed to give him the slip. He's taken on the role of jailer, for some reason."

"Jailer?" Sylvia shook her head. "Come, you must tell me everything." She seized Alex's hand and dragged her into the sitting room next door. "Who *is* this man?

Why didn't you give me his name in your letter? D'you know how frustrating it is for me, just sitting on the sidelines trying to read between the lines of your letters?"

"Oh, don't scold, darling. I will tell everything I can up to this moment." Alex sat down beside her sister on the broad seat in the lighted front window, their arms intertwined, and began her tale.

Peregrine's livery hack was fresh and trotted along without complaint as the evening shadows drew in. He had hoped that perhaps he would catch up with Alexandra, but he saw no sign of her on the lanes and guessed that she had indeed headed cross-country. The wide, open heath studded with gorse bushes and lush ferns stretched on either side as he reached the gibbet crossroads. The gibbet hung still and empty as the moon rose, casting a bright light across the heath. A hunting owl swooped low over the ground and dived suddenly, rising again with a small rabbit in its talons.

There was no sign at all of human habitation, and Peregrine began to regret his impulse until the lane took him at last into a small hamlet, cottages on either side of the lane.

The cottages all had small, well-cultivated gardens, giving the hamlet a prosperous air. The buildings, most with thatched roofs, seemed in good repair.

He rode the length of the village, looking for some

sign of Alexandra's arrival. What he expected to find he didn't know, until he reached the last cottage, almost on the outskirts of the village and slightly larger than the others. Two figures were outlined in one of the front windows, heads bent, arms encircling each other. One of them was Alexandra. She no longer wore the woolen cap, and the rich, glowing chestnut of her hair pinned in a topknot was unmistakable in the lamplight. He drew back out of sight of the window. Now was not the moment to announce his presence.

He took a lane that led him around the back of the cottage, where he found the piebald pony she had hired from the livery stable, tethered beneath a lean-to at the rear of a small kitchen garden.

Peregrine nodded to himself and continued along the lane that would lead him back to the beginning of the village and the road back to Lymington. He would return in the morning.

∽∾

Sylvia listened to her sister's tale in a mixture of outrage and disbelief. "This Sullivan man has really taken it upon himself to force himself upon you? How dare he? What possible justification does he have for it?"

"Simple curiosity, I suspect," Alex said with a wry headshake. She couldn't bring herself to confess, even to Sylvia, the powerful but mortifying muddle of feelings she had for Peregrine or the fact that they were clearly reciprocated. "The man has an inquiring mind, and he doesn't care for puzzles. Unfortunately, I showed him one, and he can't let it go unsolved."

Sylvia frowned. "That's no excuse."

Alex sighed. "Maybe not, but the fault is mine in the first place. I can't think why I would jeopardize everything so stupidly."

"Alex, you cannot blame yourself. The strain of keeping up the charade day after day must be unendurable. I don't blame you in the least. And it was the middle of the night, after all."

"Mmm," she agreed, but without much conviction.

"Now, girls, I've made you both a nice hot posset, with plenty of nutmeg, as I know you like." Matty interrupted their tête-à-tête, setting two fragrantly steaming pewter tankards down on the hearth. "'Tis time you were in bed. I've bedded down that pony, given 'er a good feed of hay. You look dead on your feet, Mistress Alex, and what you're doin' in those dreadful clothes I can't imagine. You'll put on your own good dress in the morning. Your clothes are all in the linen press, and I fetched a nice muslin down to the kitchen fire to air. I'll bring it up to you in the morning."

"Thank you, Matty. I own it will be good to look like myself, even if 'tis only for a few hours." Alex slid off the window seat and curled up on the rag rug in front of the fire, taking up her tankard of brandy-spiced milk. "It smells good, Matty. Have the Gentlemen made a delivery recently?"

Matty put a finger to her lips and shook her head.

"Now, now, Mistress Alex, you know we don't talk of such things."

Alex chuckled and sipped her drink. The smuggling trade was a lively one in the villages and towns along the south coast. Christchurch was a particular stronghold, as the entrance to the harbor was narrow, guarded by Hengistbury Head, and difficult for the coast-guard cutters to penetrate. The locals enjoyed the fruits of the trade and kept their mouths shut. Bottles of wine and brandy, bales of delicate lace and French muslins appeared mysteriously in barns overnight, and not a word was spoken.

Sylvia was sitting on a low cushioned stool beside Alex and sipped her own posset appreciatively. "I did see them pass one night, when I couldn't sleep. But I hid behind the curtain. You always said 'twas bad luck to see the Gentlemen, Matty."

"Aye, and so 'tis." Matty tutted. "But I should have spared my breath to cool my porridge, all the notice you girls ever took."

Alex felt the last threads of tension leave her. If she closed her eyes, she could be back in the nursery, which Matty had continued to occupy even when her charges had graduated to their own bedchambers downstairs. Alex and Sylvia would spend many hours there, particularly when their mother was away on one of her frolics and Sir Arthur had retreated to his library. The atmosphere in the house then was so oppressive, and Matty's domain was one spot of warmth in a frigid land, where the servants crept around, whispering behind their hands. Matty would have no gossip in her haven, and whatever she thought of her employer's errant wife, no one ever discovered.

Sylvia yawned and drank the last drop of her posset. "Come to bed, Alex. You've been on the road since dawn. Matty's right, you look dead on your feet."

Alex couldn't remember when she had last been able to sleep without anxiety. The prospect of the morning had haunted her nights, so that she frequently woke at Combe Abbey feeling as if she hadn't closed her eyes at all. But the wonderful relaxation she felt now was going to ensure that she fell into a black pit of unconsciousness.

Her own nightgown lay on the bed that she and Sylvia would share, and she picked it up, inhaling the scent of lavender in the soft cambric folds. Her nightgowns at Combe Abbey these days were of thick linen, all stiff, voluminous folds. The laundry maids would consider soft silks and lace-edged cambrics inappropriate for an impoverished librarian of indeterminate age.

She undressed quickly, dropped the nightgown over her head, and climbed into the high feather bed beside her sister. "Oh, what bliss." She slipped down in the bed and turned on her side, pillowing her cheek on her hand. "Good night, Sylvia."

"Good night, dearest." Sylvia tucked the sheet around her sister's shoulders and smiled as she realized that Alex was already asleep. She lay back against the pillows in the flickering candlelight, wishing there was some way she could relieve Alex of some of the heavy burden she carried for them both.

⁓

Peregrine awoke in the Angel soon after dawn. He rang for hot water and coffee and dressed rapidly, filled with a sense of urgency and anticipation. He consumed a large breakfast in the private parlor, served by a rather sleepy maid, then went to the yard to fetch the livery's hack, who had spent the night in one of the inn's stalls. He decided to take the horse back to the livery stable himself, where the man he had spoken to the previous evening took his money with a laconic nod and led the horse away.

"A question for you?" Perry called after the man. "In the village, Barton, that is, d'you know who lives in the end cottage? 'Tis a little larger than the rest."

"Reckon so." The man nodded, still holding the horse's bridle above the bit. "That'll be Mistress Matty. Been 'ere for close on six years now, wi' that poor invalid lady she takes care of. Mistress Sylvia, I believe. We don't see much of 'er out an' about. Weak 'eart, they say. But Mistress Matty's a good woman. One of us, she is." He nodded in decisive punctuation and led the horse into the stall.

Sylvia? Peregrine remembered Alexandra's slip the previous evening. She had started a word but cut herself off. Perhaps this Sylvia was the sister she didn't want to name. He returned to the Angel to collect Sam.

Taking the road to Barton in broad daylight was rather different from his previous journey. The heath didn't seem so menacing when bathed in sunlight, and he passed donkey carts, riders, and men carrying pitchforks on the lane. The village itself was quiet. He passed a woman hanging washing under an apple tree in one of the front gardens and a group of small children carrying buckets from the well in the center of the village. The children stared in wide-eyed curiosity at the stranger on his handsome gray horse, rather as if he were some circus freak, Peregrine thought, smiling at them with what he hoped was reassurance. He doffed his hat to the woman hanging washing and pressed on down the lane to the last house.

A young woman was cutting big orange and yellow chrysanthemums in the front garden, laying them carefully in the trug she carried over her arm. When Peregrine drew rein at the gate, she straightened and turned, shading her eyes, although the sun was not that bright. A frown crossed her pale, pretty face, and she walked up the path towards him.

Peregrine decided on the direct approach. "Ma'am." He bowed from the saddle, holding his hat to his chest. "Is Mistress Alexandra still abed?"

The young woman looked him over with an air of disdain. "The Honorable Peregrine Sullivan, I assume." Her voice was cold.

"You have the advantage of me, ma'am."

"Indeed?" She raised her eyebrows. "An unusual experience, I daresay."

"You're as sharp-tongued as your sister," he observed. Even without his earlier suspicion, the family resemblance was unmistakable, although this young woman somehow lacked Alexandra's rich vibrancy; everything about her was a shade paler, it seemed. But nevertheless, they could almost be twins.

The eyebrows remained raised. "Do you have business in the village, sir?" The question conveyed a degree of incredulity.

Peregrine grimaced. "My business lies with Mistress Alexandra, ma'am."

"Does it, indeed? Well, I doubt she would agree with you."

Perry sighed. "I am paying a courtesy call, ma'am, on a lady to whom I have already been presented. I fail to see what is objectionable in that."

Sylvia laughed with genuine amusement. "Alex was right, you really are incorrigible. Well, sir, since the lady in question has decided she is not at home for your call, I fear you must take your leave. Perhaps you would like to leave your card?"

"No, ma'am, I would not." Peregrine dismounted and laid a hand on the gate. "Would you be good enough to inform Mistress Alexandra that I await without?"

"I'm sure she knows perfectly well that you're here, sir. I daresay she's been watching from the window."

Sylvia was intrigued, despite her indignation on behalf of her sister. There was something about the man that commanded attention. And for some reason, she didn't sense that his interest in Alexandra was threatening. He was in a position to do her a great deal of harm, but nothing in his manner gave the impression that he had such an intention. Indeed, it felt quite the opposite. There was a directness about his steady gaze and a most appealing touch of humor to his mouth.

"If you'll wait here, I'll ask her if she's willing to see you," she temporized, seeing that he had every intention of entering the garden, whether she barred the gate or not.

He bowed his acceptance. "I will await your return most eagerly, ma'am."

Sylvia turned and walked slowly into the house. Alex was hovering on the bottom step in the hall. "Has he gone?"

"No, he is a most persistent gentleman." Sylvia set her basket of chrysanthemums on the hall table, continuing thoughtfully, "I think you had better see him, Alex. I have a feeling it will be sensible to give him a little information, just enough to satisfy his curiosity. We don't have to tell him everything." She busied herself arranging the flowers in a copper jug, not looking at her sister. Alex had to come to the decision herself.

She considered. Sylvia had always been the practical one. She herself was much more impulsive, the one with the ideas, always the instigator and the planner, but she relied on Sylvia to point out the realities when she got carried away by her enthusiasms. Reluctantly, she came to the conclusion that Sylvia was probably right. The wolf was at the door, and he wasn't leaving without a morsel of something. *And we don't have to tell him everything.* She just needed a convincing enough version of the truth to send him on his way.

"Perhaps you're right. But I don't know what to tell him. We can't tell him who we really are, Sylvia."

"No, of course not," Sylvia agreed, inserting a yellow chrysanthemum into the jug.

Alex picked up a deep orange flower and thoughtfully set it in the jug. "I do love the rich lusciousness of these colors."

"Mmm," Sylvia agreed, standing back from the arrangement with a critical frown.

Alexandra pursed her lips, then declared, "Ah, I have it . . . I know exactly what to do. We need to keep it very simple."

"Are we still arranging flowers?" Sylvia inquired with a smile.

"No, we're arranging Sullivans," her sister responded. "Just follow my lead." Alex went to the door and walked up the path to Peregrine, who still stood by the gate. Sylvia followed a few steps behind, unabashedly curious to see these two meet.

Peregrine swept off his hat with a deep bow as he took in Alexandra's appearance. "Ma'am, my congratulations. Dare I imagine that this incarnation is the true image of Mistress Whoever-you-are?"

"My name, sir, is Alexandra Hathaway, as you know full well. Allow me to present my younger sister, Mistress Sylvia Hathaway."

"Mistress Sylvia and I have already met," he said with a smile. "The sisterly resemblance is quite striking."

"Yes, so we have been told," Alex responded rather briskly. "If you would care to tether Sam and step inside, I'm sure we can offer you some refreshment after your ride from Lymington." She couldn't resist adding, "Such an unnecessary journey, after all."

"Oh, far from it, ma'am," Peregrine returned, knotting Sam's reins and looping them over the gatepost, giving him sufficient leeway to crop the grass verge. "A most enlightening journey, I'm finding."

Alex exchanged a quick knowing glance with her sister, then preceded Perry into the house, showing him into the front parlor. "I'll just go and see what Matty can provide."

Sylvia forestalled her. "No, Alex, let me go." She whisked herself out of the parlor, leaving the door open so that she could hear their conversation.

"Pray, sit down, sir." Alex indicated a chair and herself sat on the window seat. "I suppose there's no point asking how you found me."

"That, my dear, was a matter of simplicity. I saw you in that ridiculous, although I must confess rather enticing, garb on the High Street last evening when you left the livery stable. A few inquiries of the liveryman told me your destination, and I followed you."

Enticing? What did he mean by that? Alex shied away from a question that could only prove a distraction. She said tartly, "I would have known if I was being followed. I came over the heath."

"I guessed as much. But I saw you with your sister in that window, where you're sitting now. And I found your pony tethered in the kitchen garden." He tapped his whip against his riding boots. "My dear girl, why won't you confide in me? I know you must be in some kind of trouble. Why else would a lovely young woman enter into such an elaborate charade? As I've told you before, I am willing to help, if you'll let me."

His voice was warm and sincere, and he got to his feet suddenly, coming over to her. Reaching down, he took her hands and drew her to her feet. "Alexandra, *trust* me."

She looked at him, her eyes meeting his, and the world seemed to swing off course. Always before, apart from that one moment on the cliff, she had had her disguise to protect her, to give her distance, but now there was nothing between them, no barrier to the strange confusion of sensations that swept through her once again. His hands were warm and firm around hers, and she could feel his breath warm on her cheek, lifting little tendrils of chestnut hair from her forehead. Her heart seemed to be beating very fast against the muslin bodice of her gown, and the air around them was redolent of his own particular scent, leather and horseflesh and lavender from his linen. His eyes had taken on an intensity that deepened the blue, and his mouth was both serious and smiling.

"*Trust* me," he repeated softly. "What has happened to force you into this?"

Sylvia stood listening in the hall, aware suddenly that she was holding her breath. She took a step to the open door. The pair were framed in the window, and the rush of emotion in the room was so powerful as to be almost palpable. She thought Alex looked confused, frightened almost, and then she abruptly pulled her hands free of Peregrine's and stepped to one side away from him. Her eye fell on Sylvia, standing in the doorway.

"Oh, Sylvia. Is Matty bringing refreshment?" Her voice sounded odd to both herself and her sister.

"Yes, a jug of cider. We press our own apples here, Mr. Sullivan," Sylvia said, perfectly composed as she entered the room. "But I should warn you, 'tis almost as strong as real Somerset scrumpy."

"Aye, that it is, sir," Matty affirmed as she followed Sylvia with a stone jug and a plate of apple cakes. "Don't often get gentlemen visitors around here," she observed, setting her burdens on a gate-legged table. She reached up to a shelf on an oak dresser against the far wall and took down three pewter tankards.

She filled the tankards, talking all the while. "Mistress Sylvia, you go easy, now. And you, too, Mistress Alex. Don't want it goin' to your heads. Such little bitty things you are." She handed a tankard to Peregrine. "Don't get much call for fine wines, I'm afraid, sir. Village life isn't as refined as I daresay you're used to. But I trust this'll hit the spot."

"I'm sure it will. Thank you." He took the tankard with a smile.

Matty nodded and glanced significantly at the girls. "Go easy, remember," and left them to it.

Sylvia took a small sip and set her tankard aside. She sat down in a low chair by the fire and took up a tambour frame, prepared to leave the conversation to her sister while she observed these two in her own time. There was more to this situation than met the eye. Much more.

"So," Peregrine invited. "Will you tell me your story?"

"Why, 'tis simple enough." Alex chose her words carefully. "Our father gambled away his fortune, and we were left almost destitute. One of us needed employment, and when I saw Sir Stephen's advertisement for a librarian to catalogue his collection, I applied. But I didn't think he would take me seriously as I am. So young and seemingly inexperienced." She opened her hands in an expressive gesture. "I don't look as if I would know one rare volume from another, do I?"

Peregrine inclined his head in acknowledgment. "I can see your point."

"So, Sylvia and I created my disguise, and it worked so well that Sir Stephen employed me on the spot. The rest you know." She shrugged and took a sip of cider.

"And where did St. Catherine's Seminary for Young Ladies come into it?" He hazarded the question, watching her closely.

She shot a startled look at her sister, who also looked up sharply from her tambour frame. "What do you know of St. Catherine's?"

"Nothing, really. The liveryman mentioned it, and I rather put two and two together. Did I make four?"

There was no point in prevaricating, Alexandra thought. And she had to keep him away from making inquiries at the seminary. The only way to do that was to give him some of the truth. "Yes, you did. I spent several years there, until there was no more money for the fees."

"You seem to have received a most unusual education," he commented. She was giving him something, but he was as sure that he was not getting the full truth as he was that dawn would break tomorrow.

"Only because I happened to enjoy it," she responded. "But it was fortunate, since it's now standing me in good stead."

"Why a librarian?" he asked. "Why such an elaborate charade? You could have earned your living as a governess, surely."

The look she gave him was so full of scorn he almost laughed aloud. "And waste my time and my brain in some schoolroom on spoiled, runny-nosed brats with no interest in learning anything . . . I would rather die."

He laughed then; he couldn't help it. "Oh, Alexandra, yes, indeed, you would make a dreadful governess. I wouldn't condemn the children of my worst enemy to your impatient mercies."

"Oh, that is unjust, sir." It was Sylvia who spoke indignantly. "Alexandra is wonderful with children."

"No, I'm not, darling. Although 'tis very sweet of you to defend me," Alex said, chuckling. "As it happens, I don't really have any experience with them. So, sir, have we satisfied your curiosity? Are you willing to leave me alone now?"

He smiled slowly, setting down his tankard. "I won't press for further information for the moment, but no, Alexandra, I will not leave you alone. I shall escort you and your precious books to London in the morning, and then we shall see. For now, I will take my leave, and I will expect to dine with *you*," he stressed with significance, "at the Angel this evening. Oh, and I took the liberty to inform mine host that you were keeping to your chamber today as you were feeling the effects of yesterday's long coach journey. The chambermaid didn't know what to make of your locked door."

He raised an eyebrow as he rose to his feet. "I confess I was surprised you hadn't thought to quell the inevitable curiosity yourself. It seemed unusually careless of you." He took up his hat, noting Alexandra's chagrin with a degree of satisfaction. "Mistress Sylvia . . . Mistress Hathaway." He bowed to them in turn. "I'll see myself out."

Sylvia looked at her sister. Alexandra was flushed, her gray eyes filled with thunderclouds. "Of all the pompous, arrogant, interfering . . . oh, there are no words, Sylvia. What am I to do?"

"Accept his escort with a good grace, I should say," Sylvia said calmly. "He is immovable, so I wouldn't waste your strength trying to move him." She gave her sister an assessing look. "You don't dislike him as much as you say, dearest. You can't fool me, even if you can fool yourself."

Alexandra's flush deepened. "Oh, don't be silly, Sylvia. Even if I did like him, against all reason and sense, what possible good would it do? Where could it lead? Nowhere, that's where."

"You may be right," Sylvia said, calmly plying her needle. "But how do you see your life once this wretched business is settled?" She set a stitch carefully. "Once we both have a sufficient independence, what do you think you will do? We've never really talked about it."

Alex frowned. "But of course we have. We will buy a cottage somewhere pretty and peaceful, and Matty and you and I will live our lives as we choose. We shall want for nothing, and no one will be able to dictate to us. Isn't that what we always agreed?"

"Did we?" her sister queried, knotting a thread and

snipping the end with her embroidery scissors. "I am not convinced that you, sister dear, are temperamentally suited to a life of rustic tranquility. Oh, it would suit me well enough, I daresay, I'm ill fitted for town excitement, but that is not true of you, Alex. You're not yet twenty-one. How could you possibly endure a life of country seclusion? You would be bored out of your mind within a year."

"What are you suggesting?" Alex looked suspiciously at her sister.

"Nothing in particular," Sylvia said airily. "But I think you should consider alternatives to the life of a recluse."

Alex's frown deepened, she opened her mouth to say something, and then she shook her head impatiently. "I'm going for a walk."

Sylvia smiled to herself as her sister left the parlor. She had the strangest sense that maybe a solution to all of their difficulties hovered on the horizon if Alex could be brought to see it.

Chapter Ten

Alexandra checked on the piebald pony, who seemed content to eat her head off in the lean-to in the kitchen garden. She let herself out into the lane at the rear and climbed up a little hill behind the houses onto the wide expanse of the heath. A cold wind was blowing, and her loosened hair blew around her face, but it cooled her blood and cleared her head.

Twice this strange thing had happened to her, this frightening sense of losing her bearings, as if her own personal compass needle had swung wildly off course. When Peregrine Sullivan stood so close to her, looked so deeply into her eyes, that full, sensual mouth hovering just above her own, she felt herself as malleable as a lump of clay on a potter's wheel.

It was absurd. She had never experienced such a feeling before. There had never been time or occasion in her life hitherto for such encounters with the male of the species. By the time she had gone to St. Catherine's, at an age when young women were beginning to venture into the social world, she had, to all intents and purposes, gone into an all-female seclusion as tight as that of a convent. Men had not visited the seminary unless they were servants or parents of the pupils. Oh, there had been an occasional brother, gangly, spotty, and awkward for the most part, and Alexandra had never had the slightest interest in cultivating them. Now she felt herself as innocent as the most naïve, sheltered, medieval maiden in a stone castle on the Welsh Marches. Probably more so, she reflected wryly, remembering the rather more barbaric aspects of medieval castle life.

So, what was she to do now? Peregrine had made it clear that she was not going to be rid of him in the short term, and the remainder of the journey to London lay ahead of them. She would, of course, revert to her librarian's costume as soon as she returned to her chamber at the Angel. That would help, of course. The danger only seemed to arise when she was herself, Alexandra Douglas. The costume gave her all the protection of a medieval chastity belt.

She took a deep breath of the chill air, standing with her hands on her hips, her muslin skirts flattened against her legs, and let the strength of will flow back. And across the flat expanse of the heath, by the gibbet at the crossroads, a man on a big gray horse watched the small figure with a half smile on his lips.

Alexandra looked across the gorse-strewn landscape, as if her eyes were magnetized. She saw the distant figure watching her. And the strength and confidence of a moment ago evaporated.

Peregrine rode back to Lymington, stabled Sam in the Angel yard, and went into the taproom. The landlord was polishing tankards at the bar counter, and a few men sat drinking at a long bench in the window, conversing in laconic bursts. Perry leaned on the bar counter. "A pint of porter."

"Aye, sir." The landlord filled the tankard and set it down before him. "D'you fancy a bite of summat, sir? 'Tis a time since you broke your fast."

"What are you offering?" Peregrine buried his nose in the tankard.

"A nice bit o' gammon, sir, and a slice o' meat pie. My Bertha makes the best meat pie this side o' Yorkshire."

"Then gladly, landlord." Perry leaned one elbow on the counter and swiveled to look at his fellow inhabitants of the taproom. "Local folk?"

"Aye. But you should be 'ere on a Sat'day, sir. 'Tis market day, an' folk can't move fer the press. You'd be 'ard pressed t' get close to the bar then." The landlord beamed his satisfaction at the prospect and set a hearty piece of meat pie and a thick slice of gammon in front of Perry. He sawed off a hunk of wheaten bread from a loaf at the end of the counter and passed it up on the point of the knife.

"My thanks." Perry took it off and set it on his plate. "So, I understand there's a seminary for young ladies around here."

"Oh, yes, sir. St. Catherine's that'll be." The man leaned comfortably on the counter, prepared to chat. "'Tis run by Mistress Simmons, a real lady she is. We see 'er on market day sometimes, but most times she comes in the week to do her business wi' Mr. Buxton, the lawyer, who does the bankin' for folks around 'ere. An' sometimes one of 'er girls is took sick, an' the doctor goes out there. Never misses a pay day, does Mistress Simmons."

"A veritable paragon," Peregrine murmured. "D'you remember a Mistress Hathaway, who was a pupil there for a few years?"

The landlord frowned and shook his head. "Don't know as I do, sir. But we didn't know the young ladies in the town. They came in once in a while to visit Mistress Collins, the milliner, but they never come in 'ere."

"No, of course not." Peregrine cut into his ham, debating his next question. He had the feeling that if his questions became too searching, too specific, then the landlord would clam up. Country folk were not generally happy to discuss their affairs with strangers. "I was talking with a Mistress Matty, over in Barton, earlier. She mentioned the seminary, and I was interested. 'Tis an out-of-the-way spot for such an institution."

"Oh, I don't know about that, sir. The air's good an' clean, we've the sea an' the forest. A little piece o' heaven, we think it."

The landlord moved away down the bar. Peregrine

finished his meal, drained his tankard, and left the tap-room.

Until Alexandra returned that evening, there was nothing he could do . . . unless he asked a few questions at the seminary. Mistress Simmons might throw some light on the mystery. If he was to help Alexandra, he would have to get to the bottom of it, with or without her consent. And just why was he so anxious to help such an obstructive, exasperating, perverse young woman? He didn't need to ask himself the question. He'd never met a woman like her, and she drew him like a lodestone. He wanted to know her in every facet. He found her company stimulating, and he couldn't imagine he would ever find it anything else. The glimpses he'd had of the woman beneath the subterfuge fascinated him, so much so that he had a feeling that they were somehow made to partner each other.

Perhaps it was irrational, and he was not in general an irrational man, and yet this compelling need to persist in his pursuit regardless of her opposition seemed absolutely the only possible thing he could do. He had a tidy mind, and this course he was pursuing seemed likely to lead only to chaos, and yet his heart sang and his spirit danced at the prospect of such chaos.

The groom brought Sam out into the yard, and he swung into the saddle. "Where will I find St. Catherine's Seminary?"

"Oh, 'tis out Barton way, sir, mebbe a mile outside the village. Take the coast road that-a-way"—the elderly groom gestured back up the High Street—"an' ye'll come to a bridle path on the left after about two miles. You'll see the 'ouse up on the cliff. Big gray 'ouse, can't miss it."

"Thank you." Perry turned Sam out of the yard and up the street away from the quay. The sandy road ran parallel to the cliff top and the gray-green waters of the Solent stretching to the Isle of Wight. The day was overcast, the wind was brisk, and the first intimations of autumn were in the air. The lane curved away from the cliff and wound down quite a steep hill between high hedges thick with blackberries. He came to the bridle path as the groom had said, and as soon as he turned onto it, he saw the house, set back from the cliff.

He turned through stone gateposts and rode up a well-kept driveway. A group of young girls came giggling down the drive, carrying baskets overflowing with blackberries. The youngest were still children, their mouths stained purple with the fruit they were eating as they walked. They all stopped and stared at the stranger.

He swept off his hat and bowed. "Good afternoon, ladies. I was hoping to speak with Mistress Simmons."

The tallest in the group came to her senses first. "Amelia, run up to the house and tell Mistress Simmons she has a visitor," she instructed, and one of the youngsters turned and raced up the drive to the house, berries spilling from her basket.

"Thank you." Perry bowed again, before setting his

hat back on his head and riding slowly on to the house to give the child time for her warning. He wondered if Alexandra had ever roamed the countryside picking blackberries, her mouth stained purple. Or had she preferred to stay indoors buried in her studies? The reflection brought a smile to his lips, and a warm glow seemed to settle behind his ribs.

The door stood open, and as he dismounted before the house, a woman appeared in the doorway. Her pale gray gown was plain, but the material was good. Her hair was banded in neat plaits around her head. She lifted a lorgnette and subjected her visitor to a careful scrutiny as he walked towards her.

Peregrine bowed low. "Do I have the honor of addressing Mistress Simmons?"

"You do," she said quietly.

"The Honorable Peregrine Sullivan at your service, ma'am." There was something about the woman that reminded him of Alexandra. The sharp eyes, the air of one who did not tolerate inanities, the air of one who took no prisoners.

"Indeed, sir. And to what do I owe the pleasure?"

Peregrine came straight to the point. The woman seemed to encourage directness. "I have recently made the acquaintance of Mistress Alexandra Hathaway, ma'am. I believe she was a pupil here."

The look of confusion that flashed across her eyes confirmed what he had long suspected. Hathaway was not Alexandra's name. But almost as quickly as it had appeared, the confusion vanished, and Mistress Simmons said simply, "That is so. But it has been many months since Mistress Hathaway was living here. She left to seek her own employment."

"As a librarian, I understand."

Helene had had only the sparsest communications from her protégée since she'd left the seminary, and her early disquiet had grown into a deep sense of foreboding that Alexandra, always impulsive and hotheaded, was involved in some madcap scheme. Her first thought now was that Alexandra was in trouble. "I'm not aware of the lady's employment," she said carefully. "I know nothing of what became of Mistress Alexandra when she left my roof."

"I see." Peregrine frowned. "Forgive me, ma'am. I am merely seeking confirmation that Mistress Hathaway has sufficient knowledge to carry out her duties as a librarian cataloguing some very rare and valuable volumes."

Helene breathed a little easier. Working as a librarian was an eminently respectable profession, although somewhat unusual for a woman, and most particularly one as young as Alexandra. But why had she changed her name? "Certainly she has, Mr. Sullivan. Alexandra was a very accomplished pupil. Indeed, I can safely say I have never known her like."

"I can believe that," Perry said. "Neither have I."

"I beg your pardon?"

He shook his head with a slight laugh. "Thank you

for your opinion, Mistress Simmons. It merely confirms my own, but I wished to be sure. How long was Mistress Hathaway a pupil here?"

"Five years . . . and they were five years well spent, I assure you." Helene, confident now that she was being asked to provide a reference for Alexandra, spoke without hesitation.

Peregrine smiled. "I would expect nothing else. I understand Mistress Hathaway has a sister?"

Helene's eyes narrowed. "I fail to see what that has to do with Alexandra's abilities as a librarian, sir."

Peregrine retreated. "No, of course, ma'am. Forgive my curiosity. I wish only to discover if Mistress Hathaway has any family members for whom she is perhaps responsible. Her work is so outstanding, I would wish to ensure that her remuneration is sufficient. I don't wish to lose her, you understand."

And just where had he managed to come up with such a tissue of lies? He hated lying. It seemed that association with Mistress Alexandra was very bad for a man's moral conduct.

But it seemed to have worked. Mistress Simmons was smiling now. "I believe her sister is well taken care of, Mr. Sullivan."

"Very well." He bowed. "I will take up no more of your time, ma'am."

She inclined her head in acknowledgment. "Pray, give Alexandra my warmest wishes when you see her next." She turned back to the house and then paused, saying over her shoulder, "Where did you say your house was, Mr. Sullivan . . . the library where Alexandra is working? Is it in London?"

"In Dorset, ma'am. In the village of Combe."

The look on her face brought him up short. Mistress Simmons looked horrified. Then, abruptly, her expression was wiped clear, and she merely nodded and took herself inside. Peregrine turned Sam back down the drive. So, there was some connection between Alexandra's charade and Combe Abbey. He felt a chill run down his spine. If this deception she was perpetrating on Sir Stephen and Lady Maude had some criminal purpose, she was in the gravest danger. How could she expect not to be discovered? He had found her out; someone else surely would. And they would not feel about her the way he did. Should he confront her with this new knowledge? Or would her understandable anger at his prying destroy their present all-too-tentative accord? For the moment, he could find no answer to the question.

The day went by too quickly for the sisters. There weren't sufficient hours to say all that had to be said between them, and when Alex finally donned her breeches again, tears stood out in both pairs of gray eyes.

"I can't bear the thought of your going back into that dreadful situation," Sylvia said, hugging her convulsively. "How much longer must you continue the charade?"

"Until I have finished what I started, dearest." Alex's jaw was set as she struggled with her own sense of dismay and dread at the prospect of stepping back into her part.

"We don't need so much money, Alex. We could live here together with Matty on very little."

Alex shook her head. "No, I will have justice, Sylvia. We will take what's owed us. Nothing more but not a penny less. Another couple of months should do it if my own investments prove as profitable as I expect them to. But I have to be careful not to siphon off too much at once into my own account. I don't think Stephen would notice, as long as he keeps seeing a profit for himself, but I can't take the risk."

Sylvia said no more, knowing it would be futile. "Well, at least you'll have a little freedom in London," she said. "Even though you must keep to your disguise, you won't have Stephen or Maude looking over your shoulder the whole time."

Alex nodded, trying to look more cheerful. "That's true, and I shall think only of that. If it weren't for the Honorable Peregrine, there would be no fly in the ointment at all."

"Why don't you simply enjoy his company, since you can't evade it?" Sylvia suggested, as she had been doing obliquely all day.

Alex's shrug was noncommittal. She put on the leather jerkin and looked at herself in the long glass. "This disguise is so much more comfortable."

"Yes, but much harder to maintain," her sister pointed out. "You look the part from a distance, but it won't stand scrutiny."

"No, you're right, as usual." Alex turned to hug her one last time. "I'll try to come again, love. Will you send Helene a little note for me? I feel so guilty that I haven't really written to her since I went to Combe Abbey, but I didn't want to lie to her, and I couldn't possibly tell her the truth."

"Well, what shall I tell her?"

"Just that you've heard from me, and everything is well, and I send her my love."

Sylvia nodded. "I'll do that." She glanced out the window. "You must go if you're to dine at the Angel. You'll need time to resume your disguise."

Alex grimaced but didn't argue. Peregrine, she remembered, had said he expected to dine with *her*. By which she assumed he meant her real self, but he would have to be disappointed. She had been seen too often on the streets of Lymington when she was at the seminary to risk appearing as herself in one of its major hostelries.

Sylvia came outside with her as she saddled the pony. She gave Alex a parcel, wrapped in silk and tied with blue ribbon. "Don't open this until you get to London, darling," she said, smiling as Alex looked at her askance. "Promise?"

Alex nodded. "Promise, but what is it?"

"Wait and see," Sylvia responded, her smile a little misty.

Alex tucked the parcel under her saddle bow and rode away, Matty waving from the kitchen door, Sylvia standing at the back gate, hugging her shawl around her, looking suddenly very frail and forlorn. Alex swallowed her tears and cantered up the hill onto the heath. She rode fast back to the town, left the pony in the livery stable, and walked back up the High Street to the Angel.

Peregrine was standing in the doorway, watching for her as he had been for most of the past hour. As she reached the inn, he stepped forward. "Wait here, while I make sure no one's around." He moved back into the hall. The taproom door was ajar, and the sound of voices came from within, but he could see no one in the hall or on the stairs. He beckoned to Alex, standing just outside the inn's front door, then stood himself in the doorway to the taproom, blocking the hall from view.

Alex darted forward and ran up the stairs, her heart beating fast as she fitted her key into the lock of her chamber door. It opened soundlessly, and she whisked herself inside, closing and locking it behind her. A quick glance around showed her that nothing had been disturbed, thanks to Peregrine. Once again, she cursed her own carelessness in not thinking to explain her seclusion to the landlord before she'd escaped. For all she knew, the landlord had a second key to the door and could well have used it if he thought something was amiss.

Well, it hadn't happened, she told herself, and

there was no point chastising herself further. She undressed swiftly, folded her costume and packed it at the bottom of her portmanteau together with Sylvia's silken parcel, then reluctantly began to dress herself again in Mistress Hathaway's dowdy gown. She had done away with the back pad last evening, so she could leave it off again, but her face was a different matter. She peered at her reflection in the mirror. What could she get away with?

Perhaps if she just shaded in the birthmark below her right cheekbone, she could forget for this evening the faint aging lines at the corners of her eyes and mouth. The gray streaks in her hair had vanished in the last couple of days. The paste she made of dampened chalk never lasted very long, but if she wore a cap this evening, she could also forget that. She had several matronly caps, although she rarely wore them, but one would hide her hair completely for tonight.

The mob cap had a full puffed crown and side lappets. She tied it under her chin in a neat bow and almost laughed aloud at her image. The clear glass pince-nez that she usually wore on a ribbon around her neck she now perched on her nose. The effect was perfect. She looked every inch the fussy spinster lady she purported to be.

She put on her black silk mittens and left her chamber, locking the door again behind her, and made her way to the private parlor. It was deserted when she entered, but the table was laid for dinner, and the fire was freshly made up. She poured herself sherry from the decanter on the side table and sat down beside the fire to await her dinner companion.

Peregrine came in after a very few minutes. He had changed into a red velvet coat with shining silver buttons, black velvet breeches, white stockings, and black shoes with silver buckles. Lace edged his shirt collar and cuffs, and his golden hair was fastened at his nape with a matching silver buckle.

"I give you good evening, Alexandra." He bowed, and then his eyes widened as he took in her appearance. "Dear God in heaven, what have you got on your head? Take it off, woman. It's revolting."

"But appropriate, don't you agree?" she returned with a demure smile. "I think it rather fetching."

"I thought we'd agreed you would appear as yourself this evening." He crossed the room to her chair, standing over her in a manner that she found rather intimidating.

"No, I agreed to no such thing, sir. I am known in these parts, and I might well be recognized."

"Be that as it may, this will not do. It'll put me off my dinner, and I happen to be rather hungry." He leaned over her and swiftly untied the ribbons beneath her chin, lifting the cap clear. "Give me those ludicrous pince-nez." He took them off the end of her nose and held them up, peering through them. "They're just plain glass."

"Well, of course they are," she retorted. "I don't need them to see with."

He tossed them together with the mob cap onto a

settle at the far side of the parlor, then stood looking down at her, his hands on his hips. "The maid who serves us is far too young to have known you before. You'll be quite safe in here."

"I don't care to take risks."

"Don't tell me you believe this charade is not a risk in itself," he declared sharply, turning aside to pour himself a glass of sherry. "Every moment you play this part, you are at risk. Are you going to maintain it in London?"

His tone shocked her with its vehemence. He was right, of course he was, but did he imagine that she wasn't aware of the risks every moment of every day? "I don't know what I'll do," she responded, trying to keep her tone moderate. She hadn't decided as yet, since it depended on whether the retainers in Berkeley Square were part of the establishment who had known her in her youth on her very rare visits to London. If Stephen and Maude had hired new servants, she could occasionally appear as herself.

"Well, I'm assuming that the people you intend to contact about the sale of the library are people from your previous existence. Friends of your father's, I believe you said. Won't they be expecting to see your father's daughter?"

"Not necessarily," she said, turning away from his questioning gaze.

"And how is that?"

"That is no concern of yours. Once we reach Berkeley Square, your self-imposed task for Sir Stephen will be completed, and you may go your way and leave me to go mine."

He looked at her in frustration. "For such an intelligent woman, you are being remarkably obtuse," he declared, sounding as exasperated as he felt. "You *know* that's not going to happen, so why don't you just accept it, and we can plot our next moves accordingly?"

"I am not in the least obtuse," she snapped. "*You* are, though. I don't want your help, and I don't want your company. Can't you get that through your head?" Even as she spoke, she knew she was lying to both of them. Angry tears pricked behind her eyes, and she blinked them away furiously. *Why do I want to cry all of a sudden?*

Peregrine set down his glass and came back to her chair. He bent and took her own glass, setting it aside, then lifted her to her feet, pushing up her chin with his thumbs. The sheen of tears in the gray eyes increased his exasperation. She didn't mean what she was saying; she wanted to be with him as much as he wanted to be with her. "Listen to me, Alexandra. I find you irresistible, God help me. I don't know what sin I've committed to deserve it, but 'tis a fact, and I am learning to live with it. And you must, too."

The outrageous statement, the roughness of his tone, winded her, and before she could draw breath again, he had brought his mouth down to hers, and she felt as if she were losing all contact with her self.

The boundaries of her body were melting, merging into his, and her legs no longer seemed capable of supporting her. The only kisses she had ever experienced had been chaste and familial, and she seemed now to be entering some world of sensation for which she had no name. And then he raised his head and stepped away, just as the door opened behind them to admit the maid with a tray of covered dishes.

Alexandra spun away towards the fire, pressing her fingers to her lips, which seemed twice their usual size. Her cheeks were burning, and her legs were still quivering in the most ridiculous fashion. Behind her, Peregrine was talking to the maid in his own perfectly normal, perfectly composed voice, and when the door finally closed on the girl, he said calmly, "Won't you come to the table, ma'am?"

She turned slowly. He was smiling, and it was not his usual smile; it held some knowledge that he was inviting her to share. That intensity was in his eyes again, seeming to penetrate her very soul. She moistened her lips and moved to the table as if in a trance.

He held out her chair for her, pushed it in, and passed her a napkin. Then he filled their wine glasses and took his own seat opposite her. "May I serve you some soup?"

"Thank you." She stared down at the white tablecloth for a moment. *Could he possibly have meant it?* No, it was absurd; either he was playing with her, or he was quite mad. She took refuge in renewed anger, demanding fiercely, "Why would you take advantage of me in that fashion? I thought you a gentleman, at the very least, but you're a cad. I'm a lone woman, unprotected, and you think I'm fair game. Well, you are mistaken, sir."

Peregrine gave her an incredulous look. "Take advantage of you? Sweet heaven, that's rich, coming from one who's taking advantage of everyone she comes across by perpetrating this massive hoax for some nefarious purpose that I can't begin to imagine."

He shook his head vigorously. "No, I most definitely don't think you're fair game, and I most certainly didn't take advantage of you." He passed her a bowl of soup. "You enjoyed that kiss every bit as much as I did, so don't pretend, Alexandra. I don't know why I find you so bewitching. God knows you do everything in your power to make yourself as unalluring as possible, and you're thoroughly obstreperous, and your tongue's so sharp I'm amazed you haven't cut yourself, but somehow none of that matters. I'm in love with you." He shrugged, shaking his head with a degree of bewilderment. "'Tis thoroughly inconvenient."

Alexandra listened in astonishment to this most unlover-like declaration, and all she could manage was a murmured "Oh."

Peregrine picked up his spoon and began to eat his soup, his expression still one of mingled annoyance and bewilderment. After a moment, aware that she was sitting stock-still, staring down at her bowl, he said, "Is there something the matter with the soup? I find it quite tasty. D'you not care for mushrooms?"

"Oddly, I find you've killed my appetite," she stated, finding her voice at last. "I can't imagine why that should be. I am, of course, quite accustomed to receiving declarations of love from someone who also finds me unlovable."

Peregrine laughed. "Absurd creature, I don't find you in the least unlovable, even though I'm certain I should. Eat your soup, now."

Alexandra took up her spoon. Her thoughts were so confused that she took refuge in the plain pedestrian activity of eating her dinner. The automatic motions of hand to bowl to mouth were somehow soothing. He had to be playing with her. Teasing her. Nothing he said made any sense, and she wouldn't dignify it with an attempt to understand it.

After a few minutes, Perry remarked conversationally, "I seem to have effected a miracle. I appear to have rendered Mistress Alexandra speechless."

"Far from it, sir," she stated without expression. "I merely see little point in conducting a conversation with someone who insults my intelligence."

He shook his head, buttering a piece of bread. "No, no, Alexandra. I would never do that. I have far too much respect for your intelligence. However, I do find myself somewhat apprehensive about the purpose to which you are at present devoting that intelligence."

This topic was a lot safer than declarations of love. "Why would you assume 'tis a nefarious purpose?" She finished her soup and took a sip of wine, her composure somewhat restored.

"Well, tell me 'tis not, and I'll accept your word," he challenged, watching her expression.

And how could she do that with any honesty? Alex fiddled with the salt cellar as she contemplated her answer. In truth, she could understand his assumption. What possible legitimate reason could she have for this elaborate masquerade? But in her heart, she didn't consider her reason to be anything but just.

Finally, she said firmly, "I do not consider my reasons to be reprehensible. Quite the opposite."

The maid's return with the second course prevented Perry's responding, and when she had left them with roast chicken and buttered parsnips, he turned the conversation. "We should leave soon after dawn in the morning, if you wish to reach Basingstoke by nightfall."

"Of course." She toyed with her chicken and then put down her fork, pushing back her chair. She felt mangled, twisted and knotted inside. "I'm going to bed."

He made no attempt to stop her, merely rose with her and went to open the door. Before lifting the latch, he laid a hand on her arm. "I meant what I said, Alexandra. I love you. For better or worse." His smile was a little rueful. "I won't press you for a response, but I'd appreciate it if you gave it some thought." He lightly kissed her brow and opened the door. "Good night."

"Good night." The automatic response was little more than a whisper, and she hurried for the stairs and the sanctuary of her own chamber.

Chapter Eleven

❧

Peregrine made no further mention of his inconvenient feelings the next day or during their overnight stay at the Hare and Hounds in Basingstoke. He was a charming and attentive companion, and Alexandra at first found this more bewildering than his extraordinary declaration . . . a declaration that had terrified her and thrilled her in equal parts. She had lain awake wondering how she should respond. She was still confused by her own feelings towards him. She couldn't think clearly about anything but the next step in her plan, and the emotional upheaval Peregrine had brought into her life didn't help at all. Every time she thought she had managed to push it to the background, the question would creep back into the forefront of her mind, obscuring the clarity of her mission: *Do I feel the same way about him?* Even if she did, what could she do about it? It wasn't practical to be in love with anyone, let alone with the Honorable Peregrine Sullivan.

His demeanor didn't change at all throughout the remainder of the journey, and when they arrived in

Berkeley Square in the late afternoon of the second day, Alex was no closer to unraveling the impossible tangle of needs, desires, and hard reality.

The double-fronted mansion was just as she remembered it, although she had not visited it in six years. Peregrine lifted the brass lion's-head door knocker and let it fall with a resounding clang, while the postilion carried the tea chest of books up the steps. A few minutes later, the door was opened, and an elderly man in a baize apron peered myopically at Peregrine.

Alexandra, who was still sitting in the chaise waiting to see who would welcome her, felt a rush of relief. This man was unknown to her. Her father's London steward had been a vigorous gentleman in his middle years, ably assisted by his equally brisk and energetic wife.

Peregrine nodded to the man and came back to the chaise. He opened the door. "They are expecting you, it seems. But I wouldn't give much for the quality of the hospitality. The old man tells me the house is still in dust covers, and there's only himself and a Mistress Dougherty to keep things ticking over."

"I will need little enough hospitality," Alex said, stepping down to the street. "I'm quite capable of looking after myself."

"I don't doubt it," Perry agreed with a half smile. Mistress Alexandra was one of the most competent young women he'd ever had dealings with. He escorted her into the hall where the caretaker waited.

"Name's Billings, mistress." The old man introduced himself with a somewhat creaky bow. "Mistress Dougherty is still airing out the yellow bedchamber, but we've a fire goin' in the breakfast parlor. Reckon that'll do ye for sittin' and the like." He gestured to a door at the rear of the hall.

Alex looked around the large hall. It smelled musty, and the surfaces were thick with dust. Her father would have been outraged. The yellow bedchamber was at the back of the house, away from the street, she remembered. It was one of the smallest chambers but easier to air and to warm. It would certainly do, and the prospect of having the house almost to herself filled her with a sublime sense of liberation. There was no one she had to pretend to. If Mistress Dougherty was as ancient and creaky as Billings, then they'd barely notice her comings and goings. She could manage a whole week of peace and quiet apart from conducting her necessary business, and that she could do mostly by correspondence.

Peregrine was watching her, and he could almost see her slough the tension like a snake shedding its skin. She stood straighter, lifted her chin, and smiled the genuine smile that had captivated him on the rare occasions he'd seen it.

"So, I will leave you to settle in, and I will come for you at six o'clock this evening," he informed her.

She looked at him, startled. "I beg your pardon?"

"You heard me. I will come at six, and we shall dine

in the Piazza. No one will know you there, so I trust you won't condemn me to an evening in the company of the librarian?" He raised an eyebrow in question.

"I don't wish to dine abroad."

"Nonsense, of course you do. I can feel what you're feeling, Alexandra. You're free for the moment from whatever is chaining you, and you may as well enjoy it to the full. I'll be here at six." On which statement, he bowed and took his leave.

Alex stood still in the dusty hall, staring after him. The door closed, and she shook her head, trying to dispel the increasingly frequent sensation of being adrift on a sea of confusion.

"What d'ye want doin' wi' that chest, then, ma'am?"

The retainer's question brought her back to her surroundings. "Would you take it into the breakfast parlor, please, Billings?"

He looked at it doubtfully, and she said swiftly, "I daresay 'tis too heavy for you. Is there anyone to help?"

"Aye, there's the lad." He turned and shuffled towards the door to the back regions, leaving Alex where she was. She made her way to the breakfast parlor. It was a small room that she remembered as being warm and cheerful. The fire in the grate was sullen, and a gust of smoke blew into the room from a chimney that clearly needed sweeping. She picked up a cushion from the sofa and pummeled it, averting her head from the cloud of dust.

She was too much of a Douglas to let this pass, and

when a strapping lad appeared with the tea chest on his shoulder, she said briskly, "The chimney needs sweeping. There's probably a bird's nest up there. Let the fire go out in here, and put a broom up it before morning. Also, ask Mistress Dougherty to bring me tea. I wish to talk with her without delay."

The lad looked at her with a flicker of respect. From what he'd heard of the talk between the caretakers, Lady Douglas had told them to expect someone of the status of an upper servant, but this lady had a very different air, even though she was hardly dressed like a lady of means. "Right y'are, ma'am." He set the chest down and vanished

Alex discarded her cloak and walked around the chamber, noting what needed to be done to make it as welcoming as it once was. She turned from wiping a gloved finger down the grimy windowpane as the door opened to admit an elderly woman with a tea tray. "Not got much in the way of tea, mistress," she said. "Just a bit o' dust left in the caddy. But I reckon it'll do." She set the tray down with a somewhat doubtful air.

"I very much doubt that it will, Mistress Dougherty," Alex said with a frown. "Where do you normally order your supplies?"

The woman looked a little surprised. "Well, Billings 'n' me, we don't need much, just a loaf o' bread, a pig's cheek now an' again, an' a drop o' milk, and Billings's ale, o' course. I usually gets the necessaries from the barrow boys what comes by every day or so. But they don't 'ave the likes of tea." She shook her head. "A bit too refined, that."

"Well, we'll have to do better than that." Alex poured the thin liquid into a cup. It was so pale as to retain almost none of the deep brown she would have expected. "I'll be here for a week, and I expect a decent cup of tea, Mistress Dougherty, and fresh milk and eggs. We'll discuss the day's supplies every morning while I take breakfast."

"Well, who's to pay fer this, then?" the woman asked, blinking rapidly.

"Does Sir Stephen not provide you with funds to keep the house running?" Alex knew well that for Stephen, the general management of his estate and tenants' affairs were of very low priority, but it was hard to believe that he'd leave this couple in charge of such a large house without any funds for essential maintenance.

"Well, now, that Master Riley comes by now an' again to look the 'ouse over, an' if there's summat that needs doin', then he gives Billings a few shillings. We get by well enough."

Alexandra knew Master Riley, who had been her father's agent and estate manager, and Stephen kept him on because he had no idea how to do the job himself. As long as his revenues kept coming in, he never questioned the agent's business, except when he was required to fund a new roof for a tenant or make repairs to the water mill. Then he moaned and grumbled for days, complaining that his agent was robbing him blind.

No provision had been made for Alexandra's sojourn in Berkeley Square, so it rather looked as if she was going to have to provide for herself, she reflected grimly.

"I will pay for my own food," she said. "We'll discuss the day's needs every morning, and I will give you the necessary funds." She set down her teacup with a grimace, looking around at her surroundings again. The neglect was Stephen's responsibility. If he didn't provide for the house's upkeep, then this old couple couldn't be expected to care for it in any but the most basic fashion. But still, it was upsetting to see what had once been such an elegant and welcoming abode in such a condition.

"I am sure we can do something about this room, Mistress Dougherty. It will cost not a sou to put it to rights. It needs dusting, airing, and the windows cleaned. Would you ensure that's done before the morning?" She didn't wait for a response, rising from her chair, continuing with the same brisk determination, "And now I'll go to my chamber. Would you show me up?"

She knew the way perfectly well, but the housekeeper was not to know that. She followed the woman up the stairs to the small back bedchamber. At least, the fire was not smoking, and an inspection of the bed showed the linen to be freshly laundered. "Bring me some hot water, if you please." She nodded a pleasant dismissal to the housekeeper, who was not looking best pleased at this disruption to her usual day.

"An' what'll you be wantin' fer your dinner, then?" the woman asked as she turned to leave.

Alexandra thought swiftly. Dinner with Peregrine in the Piazza . . . the very prospect made her toes tap, even though every self-preserving instinct shrieked danger. But it was that or a safe, dreary, and inevitably inadequate meal by the smoking fire in the breakfast parlor. "I shall be dining out this evening. So you need make no preparations," she said. "We will start afresh in the morning."

The housekeeper bobbed her head and vanished, reappearing with a jug of tepid water a few minutes later. "Anythin' else, ma'am?"

Alex shook her head, opening her portmanteau on the bench at the foot of the bed. "No, thank you."

She examined the contents as the bedchamber door closed on Mistress Dougherty, shaking out the dowdy garments of her charade with a sense of gloom. And then she stopped. Sylvia's silken parcel lay beneath the hideous bombazine. She untied the ribbons and took out a pale lavender silk saque gown with a small train and a modest décolletage. The lace fichu that had accompanied it was tucked into the folds with a sprig of lavender. She lifted it out, inhaling the delicate fragrance, holding the soft silk against her cheek. It somehow encapsulated her previous life.

Sylvia must have looked through her sister's wardrobe in the cottage, which held all of her clothes from her life as Alexandra Douglas. And she had not forgotten silk stockings or the stiffened cambric petticoat that would allow the gown to flow from the hips. She had even remembered the dainty lavender kid slippers that went with the gown. *What was Sylvia thinking?*

But Alexandra knew quite well. Her sister had been thinking about the Honorable Peregrine Sullivan. Alex laid the gown upon the bed, smoothing the silk, a frown corrugating her brow. From earliest childhood, Sylvia's physical frailty had condemned her to exist on the periphery of other people's lives. Her only way of participating in those lives was with her eyes and the sharp focus of her intelligence. She saw things below the surface that those who were in the midst of events failed to see. Alex had long respected the accuracy of her sister's vision. Sylvia had not been a party to Peregrine's declaration, but she had seen something in the man that her busy sister had missed. *Or perhaps had been too scared to acknowledge.*

She sank down on the bed, gazing sightlessly at the fire, finally allowing herself to look clearly at everything that had happened since Peregrine Sullivan had walked into Combe Abbey on that first evening. It had been so much simpler to ignore her confusion, to rely on anger at his persistence, rather than attempt to understand what prompted it. Or to attempt to understand why, despite the danger of allowing herself to get close to someone, she was drawn to him in ways that she could not explain.

What if Peregrine's declaration of love had been sincere? What did that mean? How was she to respond? How did she want to respond? The answer to that last question brought a tantalizing thrill of pleasure, but it was impossible. She could not countenance such a response. Not in the midst of this imbroglio. And if he knew the truth about the whole elaborate fraud she had concocted, then he would fall out of love as quickly as he'd fallen into it.

She looked at the gown, the incredible soft silkiness on the bed. It was singing a siren's song. Surely, she could permit herself one evening away from the charade. Peregrine would only see what he already knew lay beneath her disguise. She was not revealing anything new to him. But did she dare wear the gown in public?

Of course she did. No one would recognize her. No one had seen her for almost six years, and she looked very different now, even as herself, from the fifteen-year-old she had been on her last visit to London.

With a surge of excitement, she unbuttoned her gown and stripped to her chemise. She washed her face and neck, removing all traces of her charade, and then, her fingers trembling slightly, drew on the silk stockings, tying the garters above her knees. She fastened the petticoat at her waist, flicking the stiff folds into position, before stepping into the delicate gown. She hooked the stiffened bodice, which lifted her breasts in a smooth swell above the décolletage, and patted the skirts into place. They flowed over the petticoat just as they should, giving a pleasing curve to her hips and accentuating the narrowness of her waist. She fastened the fichu just above her breasts with the small enameled brooch that was the only piece of jewelry from her past life that she had permitted the librarian.

The mirror was spotted and discolored, but she could still make out the reflection of a young woman in an elegant gown. She pointed a toe, admiring the dainty kid slippers. Her feet were as small-boned as the rest of her, and there had been a time when she'd been rather proud of them. There'd been no place for vanity in the last few months.

She sat down at the dresser and unpinned her hair. Maybe she would wear it loose. It would be such a relief not to have those tight braids or the prim bun at her neck. She brushed out her hair until it shone in a cluster of curling waves on her shoulders. The transformation was complete.

The tall clock in the hall chimed six just as she came downstairs, and in synchrony, the door knocker sounded. Billings shuffled out from the kitchen regions, wiping his mouth on a checkered handkerchief. "I'll get it, ma'am." He wrestled with the heavy bolt and pulled the door open. "Oh, 'tis that gennelman what came with you this a'ternoon," he informed her unnecessarily.

"Thank you, Billings." She took a step to the door. "Good evening, sir."

Peregrine's reaction as he stepped into the hall was everything she had hoped it would be. He looked her over, a sweeping gaze from the glowing rich chestnut head to the toes of her dainty slippers. His eyes widened, and slowly he smiled appreciatively.

"Well, well. Your most obedient servant, ma'am." He doffed his hat and made a flourishing bow. "I hoped only to escort a sharp-tongued young woman in a pretty, if simple and rather countrified, muslin gown. Instead, I find myself keeping company with an exquisite diamond of the first water."

Alexandra returned the bow with a deep curtsy of equal formality. Despite her misgivings, her eyes were sparkling with pleasure at the extravagant compliment and, she had to admit, with the delightful feeling that, extravagant or not, it was entirely justified. If her life had proceeded as it should have done, she would have had her debutante season two years earlier, and this lovely sense of pride in knowing that she looked every inch the Society lady would be so familiar as to be barely worth remarking. As it was, it was really the first time that full-grown Alexandra Douglas had experienced herself as the woman she had become, even, if she was permitted a little vanity, the rather attractive grown woman she should always have been if the fates had dealt her another hand. And for the moment, under the appreciative gaze of the Honorable Peregrine Sullivan, she could revel in it.

"You are too kind, sir. I must protest such fulsome compliments."

He laughed, shaking his head. "Not a bit of it. Come, let us go out upon the town, Mistress Alexandra, and show the world this entrancing new face." He offered his velvet-clad arm.

Alex laid her hand upon his arm, turning to Billings as she gathered up her skirts in her free hand. "Do not wait up for me, Billings. Leave the key to the side door on the ledge above the doorframe." She didn't stop to see the retainer's reaction to this instruction and stepped out into the cool air of evening, filled with a buoyant sense of promise.

"You seem very familiar with the side entrance to a house you've never visited before," Perry observed.

"No, but I know there must be a side door, and all doors have ledges above the frame," she responded. It seemed plausible enough, she thought, and Peregrine offered no other comment.

The evening bustle had already begun. Link boys ran up and down the street with their torches, sedan chairmen plied their trade on every corner, carriages with arms emblazoned upon the panels clattered over the cobbles. Alexandra was aware of a surge of excitement. This was all so new, so thrilling, that for a short while, she could forget the trials and tribulations of her present existence.

Perry raised a hand to a hovering hackney, and the jarvey brought the vehicle over. "The Piazza," Perry instructed as he opened the door, assisting Alex inside with a hand under her elbow. She settled on the bench, turning to look through the window as the carriage started forward. It was a novel experience, being carried through the streets of London in a common hackney, and the streets themselves fascinated her as she gazed out at the passing scene. On the infrequent visits she and Sylvia had paid to Berkeley Square, they had never been permitted to leave the house after dusk, and when they left in the daytime, it was always closely chaperoned in the family carriage.

Peregrine sat opposite, watching her face in the flickering lights of the link boys' torches. Her expression was one of fascination, as if a whole new world was opening up before her eyes. *So, what is she?* Her present dress indicated that at some point in her past, it had been intended that she should be a part of this world, and her manner, her speech, her unusual education, and the natural assurance that, as Mistress Hathaway, she worked so hard to conceal under a façade of intimidated diffidence all pointed to a destiny very different from the one she presently inhabited.

Not that this told him anything he didn't already know. It merely added fuel to the fire. As they approached Drury Lane, he said casually, "Maybe you should have another alias for this kind of excursion."

Alex looked at him, startled. "What do you mean?"

"Well, merely that Mistress Hathaway is a spinster lady of a certain age, devoted to her books, and in the employ of Sir Stephen Douglas. You've made it clear that you're not prepared to reveal your true identity, an identity that might go some way to explaining your present guise, so it seems logical that for this third identity, you should probably have a different name. If we happen to meet anyone I know, I will have to introduce you, and I find myself at something of a loss." He smiled a deprecating smile that didn't fool her for a moment.

"A third identity seems unnecessarily complicated," she returned.

He shrugged. "If you'll forgive me, ma'am, the complication is entirely of your own making."

"It most certainly is not, sir. You were the one who insisted upon this public evening," she retorted.

He smiled again. "But you, my dear girl, were the one who agreed to it."

There was no answer to that. Alex regarded him across the narrow space between them with a mixture of resignation and irritation. "I don't know why you so enjoy putting me at a disadvantage."

He held up his hands in a gesture of defense. "But that is never my intention, Alexandra, believe me. I'm trying to part an opaque veil of confusion, and you won't tear aside a single thread to lighten my darkness."

Alexandra leaned an elbow on the windowsill, staring out at the crowds thronging the streets around Covent Garden's Great Piazza. Her sensible, rational self told her that Peregrine was quite right. And she probably had no right to expect this level of accommodation from him. So far, he had shown himself willing to go along with whatever charade she was enacting, but how long could she expect him to continue doing so when she refused to give him anything to help him understand why it was necessary?

But then, she reflected, he had pushed himself into this hornet's nest without an invitation. Why should she compromise the play to reward him for his interference?

Except . . . and it was a big except. His presence was becoming indispensable to her comfort. As she threaded her way through the maze of her deception, Peregrine's physical presence gave her strength, brought her reassurance and comfort.

The realization shocked her even as she knew it was telling her nothing she hadn't already tacitly accepted. She had been so dreadfully alone navigating the rocky channels of her charade that having just one person she could be herself with had somehow become essential to her comfort. She had come to rely upon his presence, even as she raged against his interference. And with this realization came the acknowledgment that the emotional confusion of the last few days was of her own making, and only she could untangle its strands.

She turned to look at him again, feeling the warm concern in his gaze, contrasting with the quizzical gleam in the blue eyes. "Can you think of a suitable alias? I confess my imagination has run dry."

"I doubt that," he responded with a flicker of a

smile. "But why don't we take the path of mystery? What d'you think of Mistress Player?"

"It sounds contrived."

"But of course. 'Tis the beauty of it. For obvious reasons, you cannot belong to the social world you so clearly *do* belong to, so try another role. As Mistress Player, you could be a courtesan, an actor . . . any one of the dozens of beautiful women who must earn their bread in a certain stratum of London Society. No one will question it. And most will simply assume that you are my mistress."

"Oh?" Alex began to see the appeal in this. In this unrestricted aspect of London Society, she could have all the freedom of one who had no constraints on her behavior. She could let the inner, playful Alex, whom she barely remembered, run free. And in Berkeley Square, she could be the solemn purveyor of rare volumes. Until she was obliged to return to Combe Abbey, she was free to play on whatever stage she chose, with Peregrine as her opposite.

And then she took in the import of his last words. *His mistress. How does one playact a mistress?*

"You don't care for the idea?"

"I'm not sure I'm capable of playing the part."

Peregrine laughed. "My dear girl, I doubt there's a part on any stage in the world that you could not play to perfection . . . Ah, we are here." He opened the door as the hackney drew to a halt on the corner of Long

Acre and James Street. "Let us alight here. We'll stroll to the Shakespeare Head. They have a pleasant coffee room where we won't encounter any of the town bucks, and we'll get a good dinner."

He jumped down and offered his hand. Alex took it and stepped to the street, instantly overwhelmed by the sounds and smells of Covent Garden, the biggest flesh market in the city and the playground of the licentious rich.

As they walked down James Street, she couldn't take her eyes from the parading courtesans, the hasty fumblings of lesser whores and their clients behind the pillars of the Piazza, and the kiosks selling pornographic texts and drawings. This didn't seem the kind of place that the Honorable Peregrine Sullivan would frequent. But he seemed completely at home, guiding her with a proprietorial hand under her elbow, shielding her from passing sedan chairs and boisterous pedestrians, and all the time, she was conscious of his gaze on her, watching her every reaction.

"Here we are." Peregrine stopped outside a tavern, whose sign bore the face of William Shakespeare. He opened the door and ushered her inside. The taproom was hot and noisy, laughter and smoke curling to the blackened rafters, a log fire blazing in the massive inglenook fireplace. He steered Alexandra through the crowd and into a quieter chamber beyond the taproom and under the narrow staircase.

Several gentlemen with their female companions sat at dinner, and Perry moved unerringly to a small table and benches in the window nook at the far end. "We will be more private here." He moved the table to allow Alexandra easy access to the bench in the window and leaned back to wave at the tavern wench who was moving among the tables with laden plates and flagons of wine.

She came over quickly. "Sir?"

"Tansy cakes, a pigeon pie, and a flagon of Rhenish, if you please."

"Aye, sir." She bobbed her head and vanished, her now-empty tray held high over her head.

Alex leaned back into the window embrasure. "So, tell me, sir, how does a mistress act in public?"

She ought to have been shocked at herself for asking the question, she thought with an inner chuckle, but it seemed entirely in keeping with the present situation.

"I have no idea," Peregrine answered.

"Have you never had a mistress, then?" She forgot the game for a moment.

He chuckled. "Such indelicacy, my dear."

"That's a trifle hypocritical, since it was your suggestion that I play the part," she retorted.

"So it was. Well, to answer truthfully, I have never kept a mistress. Have I explored the regions where flesh is for sale? Well, yes, within limits."

Alexandra absorbed this. It seemed rather deliciously dangerous waters to enter. "So," she said, "if I were to be truly your mistress, would you set me up with a house?"

"That would be customary." He turned as the serving wench came up with a flagon of golden wine and two goblets. "Thank you." The girl set down her burdens and disappeared again.

Perry filled the goblets, raising his in a toast. "To a new charade, Mistress Player."

"A new charade," she murmured, taking a sip of wine. "Where do gentlemen such as yourself ordinarily set up their mistresses?"

Peregrine looked at her askance. "Are you interested in such a position, ma'am?"

Her eyes danced. She was happy to play this game; it was a welcome change from the usual one. "I don't know yet. I have to try it out first. But if I'm to play this part, then I need to know the narrative."

"Of course you do." Irrationally, he now found himself unwilling to enter into the spirit of the game as readily as Alexandra. "Such a consummate actor must, of course, be fully prepared."

Alex felt the sting in the words and was silent for a moment. The serving girl returned with a tray balanced on her shoulder. She set a dish of thin, crisp green fritters on the table, then the golden-crusted pie, a loaf of wheaten bread, and two platters, with barely a break in the rhythm of her movements, and then moved away in answer to another call from across the room.

"Ma'am?" Peregrine gestured to the pie. "Will you do the honors?"

Alex sliced into the pie and spooned a large helping onto her companion's platter, then helped herself more moderately. Succulent steam rose from the dish, and despite the sudden coolness of the conversation, her appetite was stimulated, and she remembered that it had been many hours since she'd last eaten.

She took one of the fritters and bit into it, observing, " 'Tis been an age since I had a true tansy cake."

"And when would that have been, exactly?" he inquired, taking one for himself, his eyes on her countenance. "In the young ladies' seminary, perhaps? Or in your father's parsonage?"

Damn the man. He never missed a trick. "At home," she said firmly. "My father's cook made them very well. She used sorrel and spinach, I believe."

"Ah." He nodded and took up his fork. "Nicely dodged, my dear." He forked a mouthful of pigeon pie. He hadn't missed the flash of chagrin in those gray eyes.

They ate in silence for a while, Peregrine watching her expression. He had touched a nerve. Alexandra played her various parts to perfection, but she—the real Alexandra—wasn't really comfortable with the charade. It reassured him a little. If she was a consummate actor, if the deceptions were somehow essential to who she was, then he was in love with an anathema.

He was in love with her. But if this woman were finally revealed as someone he could not begin to love, as against being *in* love *with,* then it would be time he withdrew and started to protect himself. But the enigma persisted. He felt now that he was beginning to know the true Alexandra, even through the veil she drew over her identity. But until she was prepared to open herself to him, to seek his help in whatever dreadful situation held her fast, he could only hover, probe, and persist.

Chapter Twelve

Alexandra was acutely aware of her companion's watchful and questioning gaze throughout the meal, although he said nothing and seemed to be eating with enjoyment. Around them, the voices of their fellow diners rose and fell, masking the silence at their own table. The serving wench set down a basket of custard tarts, and Peregrine refilled their glasses as she took away the detritus of the first course.

He leaned back in his chair and smiled at Alex over his goblet. "So, I bethought me of our postprandial entertainment. You owe me a game of chess."

Alex looked startled. "Do they have a chessboard here?"

"I don't know. Quite possibly. But I came prepared." He reached into the deep pocket of his coat and drew out a delicate enameled case embedded with lapis lazuli. He flicked open the little silver clasp with a fingertip and lifted the lid, which revealed a miniature chessboard of black and white ivory.

"Oh, 'tis beautiful," Alex exclaimed. "May I see?"

The chess pieces were already in place, held onto the board with magnetized bases. "I am very fond of it," he said. "It belonged to my uncle, Viscount Bradley. He's something of a collector, although in general, his collection is representative of rather less socially acceptable art forms." A rather sardonic smile touched his mouth. "But in a most extraordinary fit of generosity, on one occasion, he gave me this."

Alex lifted the delicately carved pieces reverently. "They're jade."

"Yes. Chinese jade. My uncle acquired it on one of his trips to China."

"A very well-traveled gentleman," Alex observed, all their previous constraint forgotten as she examined each piece in turn.

Perry chuckled. "He's certainly that. He's traded in India, China, and Japan and amassed a vast fortune in the process."

Alex looked up from the king she was holding and shot him a shrewd glance. "You don't sound as if you care for him very much . . . or approve of him."

"That would be an accurate observation," he said. "But unfortunately, he holds the family fortunes in the palm of his hand."

"Oh? How so?" She set down the king on its black square.

"He has made some rather eccentric conditions in his will. My brothers and I, if we're to inherit his fortune, must dance to a distinctly deviant tune." Perry took a custard tart from the basket and bit into it with pleasure. "Something you might find some sympathy with, I imagine."

Alex bit her lip. "There is nothing deviant about what I'm doing." Which, of course, wasn't strictly true. She was, after all, engaged in something that could be called thievery if you chose to look at it in that light. She quashed that reflection and met his gaze directly.

"Well, I won't argue with you," he said easily. "Since I have no idea what it is you're up to, I'm not in a position to judge."

"No," she agreed, setting the pieces up properly on the board. "If this is to be a rematch, I play white this time."

He shook his head and took two pawns from the board. "This is not a rematch, my dear. You and I have never played a game of chess." He put his hands behind his back, moved the pieces between them several times, and brought them out. "Take your pick."

Alex had to admit he was right. She certainly hadn't given him a game. She picked his right hand, which revealed the white pawn. "Well, it comes to the same thing," she observed, playing the queen's gambit, pawn to queen four. She helped herself to a tart, settling comfortably into the window seat. Would he decline or accept the gambit?

Peregrine chose to decline it, and Alex smiled. Much more interesting that way. Peregrine decided he didn't like that smile. His opponent seemed far too sure of herself for comfort. And as the game played out, he saw it slipping from him with an inexorable momentum that he could not begin to arrest.

"You are the very devil, Alexandra," he exclaimed as she forced him to move his king's bishop so that her pawn had an unimpeded path to his back line. She merely smiled that smile again and moved the pawn, dusting off her hands in a symbolic gesture. "My pawn is queened."

"Nicely played, ma'am." A voice spoke suddenly over her shoulder. "Sullivan, m'dear fellow, you appear to be facing checkmate in three."

Alexandra looked up, startled. A tall gentleman in a white wig, wearing a somewhat threadbare brown coat, stood behind her, looking down at the board through a quizzing glass.

"I didn't expect to run into you here, Maskelyne." Peregrine rose to his feet. "I'd assumed you'd be dining as usual at the Royal Society."

"Oh, you know what they say about change," the newcomer declared. "'Tis as good as a rest. Besides, on Fridays, the kitchen serves tripe, and 'tis a dish I abominate."

Peregrine turned to Alex, who was still sitting at the board, gazing at their new arrival with an air of almost wonderment. "Mistress Player, may I introduce the Reverend Nevil Maskelyne. Maskelyne, Mistress Player."

"An honor, Mistress Player." The gentleman bowed low.

Alexandra found her tongue. "Indeed, sir, the honor must be all mine. You are Reverend Maskelyne, the astronomer, are you not? I followed your writings when the Royal Society sent you to St. Helena last year to observe the transit of Venus. I am most fascinated by the principle of parallax, sir. If 'tis possible to measure the distance from the earth to the sun, then all knowledge of the size of the solar system will be laid open for us."

Her face was flushed with excitement, her eyes aglow as she continued in a rush, "And I understand you are at present working on a book about your research on the voyage to use the lunar position to determine longitude."

"You are very well informed, ma'am," the Reverend Maskelyne said with a rather gratified smile.

"Amazingly so," Peregrine concurred. "You never cease to amaze me, Mistress Player. Where, I wonder, did you have access to my friend's research?"

Alexandra said stiffly, "Scientific papers, particularly those from the Royal Society, were of particular interest to my father." Which was true, she reflected. Her father had stimulated her interest in mathematics, science in general and astronomy in particular, and had once shown her a letter from the Reverend Maskelyne in answer to a research query of his own, but it was Helene Simmons, who had a connection with a member of the Royal Society, who had provided her with much more detailed information on much of the research of its members. She had shared this knowledge with her pupil, and the two of them had spent many long nights happily studying the skies from the Barton cliff top through Helene's telescope.

Perry wondered if he believed her and then decided it didn't matter. She had the knowledge, however it was acquired.

"Indeed, ma'am, I wonder if I was acquainted with your father," Nevil Maskelyne said. "I correspond regularly with gentlemen who have an amateur interest in astronomy. But a Master Player . . ." He shook his head. "I confess, the name does not ring a bell."

Get yourself out of that one, Mistress Alexandra. Peregrine waited with interest to see how she would respond.

"I doubt you would have corresponded with him, sir. He was very much a recluse," Alex prevaricated. The urge to expand the lie was difficult to resist, but she had learned to keep the untruths as brief and simple as possible. Sir Arthur Douglas had, indeed, corresponded with Master Maskelyne on at least one occasion to her knowledge. He had many friends who were members of the Royal Society and corresponded with them regularly.

Fortunately, Reverend Maskelyne showed no interest in pursuing the subject. He returned his attention to the miniature board. "I wonder, ma'am, if, in my friend's shoes, I were to move my bishop to queen three, like so, it might avert mate by exposing your king in four moves to a threat of check from my king's rook, thus forcing a draw."

Alexandra frowned at the board for a few moments, then, without saying anything, moved her knight. Both Peregrine and the astronomer examined the board anew. "I don't see how that move . . . Oh, yes, of course." Peregrine shook his head. "No." He held up an arresting hand as Alex moved. "Let me play this through." He moved a piece and glanced at the astronomer, who gave a rueful nod.

"Aye," he said. "If the lady plays the knight, then 'tis inevitable. You must bring the last two pawns into play, my friend, like so, and the lady will play her bishop, like so."

"And she will have my king, like so," Perry said, laying the king on its side. "One of these days, we must play a game I can win. How's your piquet?"

She shrugged. "I enjoy the game, sir."

Maskelyne laughed. "Well, I'm for my dinner. I'll leave you to your inevitable defeats, my friend." He laid a hand on Perry's shoulder before bowing to Alexandra. "Your most obedient servant, Mistress Player. 'Tis a great shame the Royal Society do not permit ladies on the premises, because I feel sure you would hold your own amongst what we like to consider our august company."

"You are too kind, sir." Alex bowed from her seated position and began to put the chess pieces on their correct squares once more as Maskelyne departed.

Perry's hand closed over hers as she lowered the delicate lid of the box. Her hand stilled beneath the warm pressure of his, and she felt her breath suspended, as if she were waiting for something unknown but of vital importance to happen. Around them, the cheerful noise of the coffee room continued, but she heard it now as if from a distant plane.

Peregrine moved his free hand to cup her chin, lifting her face so that her gray eyes met his penetrating gaze. "Your father corresponded with the Reverend Maskelyne, didn't he, Alexandra?"

"Yes," she murmured. Suddenly, the lies overwhelmed her. She couldn't keep them up any longer, or at least, not tonight.

"So, who was he?"

She jerked her chin out of his hold and stood up abruptly. "I have to go home." She slid her hand out from his on the chess box, and he merely inclined his head in acknowledgment, although his mouth had thinned and his eyes showed clear disappointment.

"Come." He put a hand under her elbow and ushered her out of the coffee room, through the raucous crowd in the taproom, and out into the equally raucous Piazza. He ushered her along the colonnade to Russell Street, where a line of hackneys waited. "Berkeley Square," he called up to the jarvey as he handed Alexandra inside.

He climbed in after her, closed the door, and settled on the opposite bench, regarding her gravely. "I would like you to agree to something, Alexandra."

A little quiver of apprehension crept up her spine. "Agree to what?"

"That you will tell me no more lies. They do neither of us any good. I know when you're lying, so 'tis pointless for you to make the effort. And they make me very angry. I don't care to be angry; I find it a tiresome and wasteful emotion."

Alex closed her eyes for a moment against the light flickering from the torches in the street outside. "I cannot tell you the truth," she said, her voice sounding to her ears as if it were coming from some distance. "If you press me to do so, I cannot see you again."

"And do you wish to see me again?" He didn't move from his seemingly relaxed position against the seat back.

"Yes," she said softly. In her present state, she couldn't have lied about that if she'd been told that the headsman awaited her on Tower Hill if she told the truth.

Slowly, Peregrine smiled, and the grimness left his mouth. "Good," he said softly. "Because I most certainly wish to see you, Alexandra." He leaned forward, took her arms, and pulled her across the small space separating them. He drew her down beside him and then knocked with his fist on the roof of the hackney. The coachman slowed his horses and leaned down from the box, and Perry pushed his head out through the window.

"Take us to Stratton Street," he instructed.

"Stratton Street?" Alex exclaimed as the carriage started moving more quickly. "Where's that? What is there?"

"My house," he responded. "We are going somewhere completely private where we may establish some rules for the next stage of our play."

"But I wish to go home." She moved swiftly back to the seat opposite.

"And where is home?"

"Berkeley Square," she said with all the confidence of the truth teller. It had certainly been the truth not so long ago.

"Well, be that as it may, we are going now to my home, where I can guarantee no one will disturb us. When we have had our talk, I will take you home."

"So, you are abducting me?" she inquired.

"Don't be absurd."

"Not everyone would consider it absurd."

"Anyone who knew you would know it to be so," he retorted. "No one in their right minds would attempt to force something on you, Mistress Alexandra. And believe me, I am in my right mind."

Alex couldn't help herself. She felt her mouth curve and a little bubble of laughter building in her chest. Her earlier fatigue had vanished. What could it possibly matter if Mistress Player went to a single gentleman's house unchaperoned in the middle of the night? Mistress Player did not exist for anyone from her real world. A frisson of excitement coursed through her, and she felt her heart beat a little quicker.

"Stratton Street, yer 'onor," the jarvey called down as he drew up on the quiet street.

Perry jumped down and handed a coin up to the driver. He helped Alexandra to the street. She looked around with interest. For the most part, the single-fronted town houses lining the street on either side showed no lights in their front windows, but the star-light was bright enough to take note of their honed steps, well-polished brass railings and knockers, and well-tended window boxes. It was clearly an affluent street, but then, she would not have expected anything else from her companion, who was fitting a key into the lock of one of the anonymous front doors.

"Come in, Mistress Player." He held the door open, sweeping her inside with an encircling arm.

She stepped into a narrow hall, with a staircase rising from the rear. A single candle burned on a table beside the front door.

Peregrine opened a door to the left of the hall. "Pray, come into my parlor, ma'am."

She walked past him into a small sitting room, lit only by the glow of a fire burning in the grate. A fresh scuttle of coals stood on the hearth beside it. Peregrine took a taper from a wooden box and lit it at the fire. He lit the two-branched candlestick on the mantel and carried the taper to another on the sideboard. Golden light flared, showing the room to be as comfortable as it felt. The curtains were drawn at the windows, the cushions were plumped, and a covered tray stood on a sideboard beside a punch bowl and glasses.

"What a pleasant room." She wanted to laugh at how easy it was to make polite conversation in a situation that was the antithesis of polite convention.

"We think so," Perry said, taking her gloves and cloak. "Sit down, and I'll make us a brandy punch." He went to the sideboard and uncovered the tray. "Good, we have oranges and lemons, cinnamon and nutmeg."

"If I drink punch, I will not be able to move," Alexandra protested, taking a seat in the corner of a sofa.

Peregrine raised an eyebrow. "We'll take our chances on that." He leaned over and poked the fire into a renewed blaze, setting a kettle of water on the trivet, before beginning to mix his ingredients in the silver punch bowl.

Alex watched, feeling the warmth of the fire seep into her bones, almost as powerful as the deep sense of release she felt in this small private haven where she could let the strain of the charade slide from her.

"We? Do you share this house with your brother?"

"Yes, usually. But he and his wife are on the Continent taking an extended honeymoon." He poured hot water into the punch bowl and stirred with the ladle, tasting before adjusting the spices and adding more brandy. "There, now. See what you think of that." He ladled the steaming, fragrant liquid into a goblet and brought it over to her. Then he fetched one for himself and sat beside her on the sofa.

"So, Alexandra, let me go through the few actual facts about you that I know are true."

"Please, don't," she said softly.

He turned his head along the back of the sofa, looking at her profile. The relaxation he had seen a moment before was now replaced by a look of distress, a tautness to her jaw, and he realized that, however angry she made him, he was not capable of doing anything that would cause her pain.

He sipped his punch and set down his goblet. "Let us see if we can reach another kind of truth, then." He took her goblet from her suddenly slackened grip and placed it down beside his own. He caught her chin and turned her face towards his. "Let us see what this will tell me." It was such a soft murmur that she barely heard his words, but when his mouth came down on hers, she knew she had been expecting it from the moment he had told the jarvey to drive to Stratton Street. And she knew, too, that she had been wanting it from long before that moment.

Her mouth opened beneath the insistent pressure of his lips and the delicious sensation of his tongue, sweet with brandy and spice, moving around her mouth, dancing with her own tongue, transporting her to a different place, so that she seemed to inhabit only the warm, glowing place behind her closed eyes. His fingers plucked at the fichu at her neck, and she felt his hand slide inside her bodice, the fingers delicately moving over the upper swell of her breasts as his tongue, hot and muscular, continued its exploration of her mouth. She felt as if she were losing herself, losing the last ties to the hard lines of the real world, and it was the most wonderful feeling.

The crowns of her breasts hardened against the fine silk of her chemise as his fingers moved lower, finding the nipples, circling them with delicate fingertips. There was a strange, quivering weakness in her lower belly, even as her thighs tightened involuntarily under a wave of pure sensual urgency.

His hand lifted from her breast, leaving her feeling momentarily bereft, but then it was sliding beneath her skirt, his flattened palm moving up over her calf, stroking her silk-clad knee, moving upwards across her thighs.

Her belly tightened with a mixture of alarm and desire. She wanted those fingers to continue their magic, moving ever upwards, closer to her center, and yet she was terrified of what would happen if they did. She felt she was losing control, and yet the feeling was wonderful. Her body shifted against the cushions as he moved above her and over her. Somehow, she was now lying full length on the sofa, her head propped against the arm, and his body was long against hers. She could feel the hard line of his thighs against her own and the urgent jut of his penis pressing into her belly.

A little moan escaped her, a mere breath against his

mouth, which was still on hers, and she tried feebly to slide out from under him, but there was no conviction in her efforts. Perry raised his head, leaving his hand where it was. "Must I stop?" His voice was soft, but his eyes burned.

Alex shook her head, murmured, "Yes . . . no . . . I don't know." She shifted beneath him, her hips lifting without volition. She reached a hand up to his face and lifted her own head to meet his lips again. She didn't want him to stop. On the periphery of her rational mind, which seemed to be taking a holiday, she knew exactly what was going to happen, and she knew that she wanted it. It seemed inevitable, something she could not prevent even if she wished to. Her hands went to his backside, pressing into the hard-muscled contours with a surge of wicked delight. She pushed her hand up under his shirt, reveling in the feel of his skin, hot to her touch.

He pressed his lips to the fast-beating pulse in the hollow of her throat, inhaling her scent, before moving his lips down to the cleft of her breasts. His tongue moistened the heated valley before he lifted his face and with impatient fingers unlaced her bodice, revealing the creamy softness of her breasts. His tongue stroked the hard, erect nipples, lifting them for his kiss.

Alex slid her hand around his body to his belly beneath his shirt and felt with a little shock the moist tip of his penis pressing upwards. He pushed his hips up so that she could slide her hand down farther, enclosing the pulsing shaft in her palm against the constraint of his breeches.

Peregrine took his mouth from her breast and pushed back onto his heels, shrugging out of his coat. "This won't do. 'Tis most inelegant." Swiftly, he unlaced his breeches and as swiftly lifted Alex against him, pushing her gown off her shoulders, then easing it over her hips, tossing it to the floor. Her petticoat followed and then her chemise, and when finally she lay white and soft, naked in the candlelight except for her silk stockings and garters, he stroked down the length of her body with both hands, her breasts, the indentation of her waist, the dip of her navel, the creamy length of her thighs.

She lifted her own hands to the buttons of his shirt, her fingers fumbling a little in their haste, but it was done at last, and she passed her hands over his chest, through the dusting of silky fair hair, touching the dark nipples. A line of darker hair ran from his navel down into the luxuriant mass at the apex of his thighs, from which rose the hooded shaft of his sex.

She raised her eyes to his and saw the naked lust in their bright depths and knew it was mirrored in her own. Finally, she gave up the fight and yielded to the turbulent muddle of sensations, of wanting, of fearing, of needing, which had plagued her since his first kiss. "Now?" she asked. "Should it be now?"

He smiled and touched her red and swollen lips with his fingertips. "I would wish it to be now."

She let her head fall back on the arm of the sofa again in tacit invitation. Peregrine lightly slid a hand between her thighs and touched the hot, damp center of her body. She moaned softly, and her hips lifted instinctively. He rubbed the erect little nub of flesh, slipping a finger of his free hand within her. She made a soft, almost protesting sound as he moved deeper, but her body moistened around his exploring finger, and when he felt that she was ready, her body poised on the brink, he moved his hand, slid both hands under her bottom, and lifted her as he entered her in one deep thrust, tearing the thin membrane of her virginity so swiftly that she felt only an instant of pain, and her already prepared body opened to encase him.

He moved rhythmically within her, watching her face. Her eyes were closed, her lips slightly parted. When he could hold back his own need no longer, he increased his speed, and her eyes flew open. She looked, unflinching, up at him as his climax engulfed him. He disengaged from her the instant before he was lost and gathered her against him, holding her tightly until the paroxysms of fulfillment finally ceased.

He let her fall back onto the sofa and slid sideways down beside her, brushing a damp strand of chestnut hair from her cheek. Alexandra let her hand rest on his turned hip for a moment and then said, "I feel I missed something. But I don't know what."

Perry laughed weakly. "My sweet, you came very

close, amazingly close for a first time. Next time, I promise, I will take you with me all the way."

She wriggled up against the seat arm until she was half sitting and his head was resting on her bosom, and said conversationally, "I would certainly like to do that again, and do it even better next time."

Perry laughed again and sat up beside her. "You are the most extraordinary creature, Alexandra." He turned her face again to look into her eyes, and his expression now was deeply serious. "But tell me the truth, do you have any regrets? Any at all?"

"No, not a single one." The answer was immediate. She didn't have a single iota of regret. If someone had told her that morning that she would happily end the day a deflowered virgin, she would never have believed them, but in some strange way, all the turmoil of her life was for the moment straightened out. It was as if some deity had passed a hand over a tumultuous whirlpool and smoothed the violent waters into a placid pool.

Perry nodded. "Well, that is one truth I do not doubt. Shall we go to bed?"

"Where?"

"I have a very comfortable bed upstairs. I'll take you back to Berkeley Square after breakfast."

And there was no one to know or to care what she did at present. She was her own mistress, sailing her own ship. And it was the most wonderful feeling in the world.

"I have no nightgown," she demurred.

"You'll have no need of one," he responded, pulling her to her feet. "You'll have me to keep you warm in a good feather bed."

And much later, in the depths of that good feather bed, Alexandra understood what it was that she had missed earlier.

Chapter Thirteen

Alexandra awoke from a deep sleep that had been filled with strange but delightful dreams. As she lay in the warm hollow of the deep feather bed, her befuddled mind assumed that she was still on the road from Combe Abbey to London. She blinked up at the unfamiliar tester, wondering which hostelry she was in.

And then the mists of sleep cleared. Those had been no dreams. Her body told her so. She passed her hands over her nakedness, smiling to herself with what she was sure must be a fatuous smile of satisfaction. Indolently, she turned her head on the pillow, but the one beside her was empty. She stretched a leg across the bed, and the other side was cold.

Where is Peregrine? Had he abandoned her, awoken, got up, and left her to go about his daily business as if she were no more than a whore he'd hired for the night? Perhaps he'd left money on the dresser?

Her sense of well-being fled. She struggled up against the pillows and looked towards the dresser, half expecting to see a handful of coins there. There was none, only the painted jug and ewer she remembered. The fire was burning, so someone had put fresh coals on, and the curtains were drawn back, letting in a pale sun. She swung her legs over the side of the bed and sat groggily looking around. Her clothes were neatly laid across the bench at the end of the bed.

The door opened. "Ah, you're awake at last. I thought you were going to sleep the morning away." Peregrine's cheerful voice preceded his entrance with a laden tray. "I have brought you breakfast. I thought you might prefer the privacy of the bedchamber. Besides, Mistress Croft is putting the parlor to rights, and 'tis all lost under clouds of dust." He set his tray on a leather ottoman in front of the fire and came over to the bed, smiling. But his smile faded as he looked at her.

"Whatever is the matter, my dear? You look stricken."

She shook her head, trying to smile. "I thought . . . oh, I woke up, and you weren't here, and I thought you'd just left me."

He folded his arms and looked at her with a degree of exasperation. "Now, what on earth have I ever done to make you think I would do that? 'Tis a monstrous insult, Alexandra."

"Forgive me." She held out her hands to him. "I was sleeping so deeply, and when I awoke, I thought I had dreamt everything, and then, when I realized I hadn't and you weren't here . . . oh, 'tis so hard to explain."

He took her hands and bent to kiss the corner of her

mouth. That little speech had told him more than she had ever told him intentionally. It revealed the loneliness and the fear in a way that he had only sensed before. She *was* abandoned. Someone had left her to fend for herself and, if his instincts were right, for her sister, too. But who, and why?

"You're forgiven," he said easily. "Now, come to the fire and break your fast." He went to the linen press and took out a nightshirt. "Put this on; it should cover you adequately." He tossed it into her lap and turned back to the breakfast tray, sensing her need to gather herself together without scrutiny.

Alex dropped the nightshirt over her head and thrust her arms into the sleeves. She stood up, letting the folds fall around her to her ankles. She rolled up the ruffled sleeves as far as her elbows and flicked the collar straight. "I think I'm respectable," she said rather doubtfully as she came to the fire. The ease with which he'd accepted her garbled explanation had reassured her, and yet she had the feeling that it hadn't really satisfied him.

"Oh, eminently respectable," he agreed, pouring coffee. "We have a fricassee of kidneys and mushrooms and fried eggs." He gestured to the dishes on the tray.

Alexandra sat on the rug in front of the ottoman and sniffed hungrily. "I could eat an ox." She spooned the fricassee onto her platter and slid an egg on top, then took up her fork.

He smiled and helped himself. "So, what are your plans for today?"

Alex, her mouth full, glanced up at the clock on the dresser. Her eyes widened, and she swallowed her mouthful. "'Tis already ten o'clock."

"Yes, I told you I was afraid you were going to sleep the morning away."

How was she to explain to the caretakers in Berkeley Square why she had not come home last night? And then she thought, *why* did she need to? It was no business of theirs what the visitor did.

Perry watched her face with amused understanding. She had lived for so long in fear of being found out, and now she was beginning to see that, for the moment at least, she had no need for such fear. "So?" he prompted. "What are your plans?"

Alex took another forkful of kidneys and mushrooms. "Correspondence," she said. "I must send out some letters about the collection to some people who might be interested."

He nodded. "How long will that take you?"

"I'm not sure. Why?"

"Only that I was thinking we might take a ride in the park a little later."

"I don't have a horse or a riding habit," she pointed out.

"Hiring horses is no problem. As for a riding habit, you presumably still have those breeches. Just wear those underneath your regular gown." He buttered a piece of toasted bread.

"Where would we ride?"

"Well, 'tis customary for Society folk to take the air in Hyde Park in the late afternoon."

"And I, as you very well know, do not come into that category," she declared. "Besides, I can't possibly draw attention to myself in such fashion. People are bound to wonder who I am."

His eyes narrowed. "Are you perhaps concerned that someone might recognize you?"

"Since they will only see a crookbacked lady of uncertain years, with an unsightly birthmark, slumped upon the back of a jobbing horse, I think 'tis highly unlikely," she retorted.

He shook his head in frustration. "Very well. You have made your point. We will ride in Richmond Park instead. There are enough wooded rides there to avoid running into anyone else. And besides, one may gallop there without censure. What d'you say?"

It was an immensely appealing idea. An unfettered ride, a forest gallop with someone who posed no threat to her plans. She nodded. "Yes, please, I would like that."

"Good. Then finish your breakfast and get dressed. The sooner you get back to Berkeley Square, the sooner you will finish your tasks and we can enjoy ourselves again."

Alex swallowed her last mouthful of coffee and uncurled herself from the floor. "I'll be ready in ten minutes."

"Come down when you are." He gathered up the dishes on the tray and carried them out.

Alex dressed swiftly. The lavender silk gown was more appropriate for evening wear than a brisk autumn morning, but there was little she could do about that. She found an ivory comb on the washstand and tugged it through her tangled locks with limited success, then made her way downstairs, hoping that she would not meet anyone except for Perry.

He was awaiting her in the hall, her cloak over his arm. "Good, I've sent Bart to summon a chair for you. It would probably be more discreet if you returned home alone." He draped the cloak over her shoulders.

" 'Tis unlike you to concern yourself with discretion," she remarked, drawing the cloak tightly around her.

"No, 'tis not in the least unlike me," he retorted. "When have I exposed you to unwelcome public scrutiny?"

She frowned. "Well, never, I suppose. But I'm always on tenterhooks in case you do."

"Well, there's no need to be. One day, you'll tell me what's going on, and until then, I'll play your game. Should I ever decide not to, then I'll give you fair warning." He opened the door and peered out. "Ah, here's Bart with the chair."

He accompanied her out to the street and saw her into the chair. "I'll come for you at three o'clock." He raised a hand, kissing his fingers to her.

Alex sat back in the dim interior as the chairmen trotted down Stratton Street. She should have felt reassured by his promise, but his confident statement that one day she would tell him the truth made her uneasy. And she knew why. Because she was afraid he was right. How could this wonderful intimacy continue between them if she persisted in holding such an essential part of herself apart from him?

But if she told him, he would want nothing more to do with her. How could a man of Peregrine Sullivan's stature and integrity contemplate a relationship with a fraudulent bastard, intent on swindling a relative out of twenty thousand pounds?

When she put it as bluntly as that, she was flooded with a wash of depression, banishing the night's delightful memories. The whole situation was impossible, and she had allowed it to develop. It was entirely her own fault that she was entwined in this morass of deception upon deception. If only he had never come to Combe Abbey.

But then the memories of the previous night surged back, and her blood began to sing. How could she possibly wish that had never happened?

Peregrine left the house on Stratton Street soon after Alexandra's departure. He walked briskly to Piccadilly, where he hailed a hackney to take him to Crane Court in Fleet Street. He didn't know if he would find Nevil Maskelyne at the Royal Society, but it was likely. The discreet house where the Society had its being was a general meeting place for its members, serving almost as a gentlemen's club, where, instead of cards or dice, the pastime was scholarly discussion, frequently with vigorous arguments on minute points of research. Perry, although not a member himself, was a frequent visitor, numbering many friends among the members.

The doorman acknowledged him with a bow when he opened the door to Perry's knock. "Mr. Sullivan, sir. A pleasure to see you. We're rather light on company this morning. May I ask whom you wish to see?"

"Is Reverend Maskelyne here?"

"Aye, sir, came in not half an hour ago. He's in the library, I believe."

"My thanks." Perry took the stairs two at a time and went into the library on the first floor. It was the biggest room in the house and ran the entire width of the frontage, windows opening onto Fleet Street. Nevil Maskelyne was sitting at a table in the window surrounded by piles of leather-bound volumes of research papers.

He was so absorbed that he jumped when Peregrine appeared beside him. "Good God, Sullivan, where did you spring from?"

"I was hoping you would be here." Peregrine perched on the arm of a chair. "Can you spare me a few minutes, if 'tis not a bad time?"

"Not at all, dear fellow." But the Reverend Maskelyne didn't sound too convinced, and his eyes kept drifting back to the page of calculations he'd been working on.

"I'll be brief." Peregrine came quickly to the point.

"Among your numerous correspondents, does the name Hathaway ring a bell?"

Maskelyne frowned, then shook his head. "Can't say that it does. What's the significance?"

"Nothing much, just a personal matter." Peregrine hadn't really expected the name to resonate with his friend. He was almost positive that Alexandra had snatched the alias from the ether, but it had been worth a try. "What of Combe Abbey?" he asked. " 'Tis an estate in Dorset. Does it mean anything to you?"

The astronomer considered the question. "Douglas," he said after a moment. "Isn't that the family seat of Sir Arthur Douglas?"

"It was," Peregrine responded. "He died last year. A distant relative inherited. Sir Stephen Douglas."

Maskelyne shook his head. "No, I've never had dealings with the man. Sir Arthur wrote to me several times, though. And I met him once or twice. He had some fascinating ideas about Waring's *Meditationes Algebraicae*. As I recall, he felt Waring's algebraic notations needed improvement."

"Did Sir Arthur have any family?"

The astronomer shrugged. "I wouldn't know; we never discussed personal matters. He rarely came to town and, as far as I could gather, never for pleasure. He preferred to rusticate in Dorset."

"Of course. Well, thank you. I'll not take up any more of your time." Peregrine bowed and departed, leaving Maskelyne to his calculations.

What was he to make of all that? Peregrine reflected as he regained the street. The only facts he had were that Alexandra's father had corresponded with Maskelyne, and Maskelyne remembered corresponding with Sir Arthur Douglas. And Helene Simmons had reacted very oddly to the information that Alexandra was employed at Combe Abbey. How did those facts fit together with Alexandra's extraordinary charade at Combe Abbey?

The obvious answer was that she was related in some way to Sir Arthur. But it was absurdly far-fetched to imagine such a connection. Why was she pretending to be someone else, if that was the case?

Of course, he could ask her directly. But he was afraid that to do so would destroy the fragile trust she had in him. He had promised that he wouldn't betray her, and if she discovered that he was attempting to find the answer to her mystery on his own, she would think he had broken that promise.

He would wait, he decided. When he had the answer, then he would decide what to do with it. In the meantime, he needed to hire a horse. Or maybe borrow one. He signaled a pair of idling chairmen. "Upper Brook Street."

The chairmen deposited their passenger outside the Blackwater mansion on Upper Brook Street. Peregrine paid them and went to the door. It opened just as he raised a hand to the knocker.

"Perry, what a pleasant surprise!" The titian-haired young woman standing in the doorway smiled warmly at her brother-in-law. "Have you come to see Jasper? He's in the library, muttering over his accounts."

"I came to see if I could borrow your horse this afternoon, Clarissa. Unless, of course, you're planning on riding yourself."

"Oh, intriguing." Lady Blackwater's green eyes sparkled with curiosity. "Come in and tell me all about it." She stepped back, gesturing in invitation.

He followed her into the hall. "Are you not going out?"

"Oh, it can wait. I was only visiting my dressmaker for a fitting. She won't mind if I'm a little late." Clarissa preceded Perry across the hall and opened a pair of double doors. "Jasper, see who's come to see us with a most intriguing request."

Jasper St. John Sullivan, the fifth Earl of Blackwater, looked up from his accounts. "Perry, I thought you still in the country. When did you get back to town?"

"Yesterday. Why the glum look?" Perry regarded his elder brother with a quizzical smile.

"Damned accounts," Jasper said. "And now Aunt Augusta is demanding that the money for her daughter's debut should come from the estate revenues. 'So that she may make a good marriage in the interests of the family.'" His aquiline nose wrinkled with disgust.

"What, Cousin Sybil?" Peregrine exclaimed. "I don't mean to be unkind, but she's a positive antidote. She'd need a small fortune to find herself a husband."

"Perry, that *is* unkind," Clarissa scolded.

"Have you met Cousin Sybil?" Perry demanded.

"Well, yes, once," Clarissa admitted. "She may not be handsome, but she has a good figure."

"Skinny as a rake," her husband amended. "Anyway, I do not wish the girl ill, but neither can the estate afford to fund her debut. Augusta will have to find the sum from some other source."

"Well, I could—"

"No, you could not." Jasper interrupted his wife's hesitant beginning. "I will not permit you to use your fortune on *my family*."

"Since when, husband, did you assume the right to dictate how I choose to spend my own money?" Clarissa demanded, a martial light in the green eyes.

"Oh, Jasper . . . Jasper." Perry shook his head in reproach, his own eyes alight with amusement. "When will you ever learn?"

Jasper grinned ruefully. "Having a wife of independent means is the very devil when one is scrambling for pennies oneself."

"Jasper, you know my money is yours," Clarissa exclaimed, looking horrified. "When have I ever—"

"Never, my sweet." He rose and came around the desk, taking her face between his hands and silencing her speech with his mouth.

Peregrine discreetly averted his eyes and waited until he had their attention again. "So," he said, as if the interruption had never occurred, "I was asking Clarissa if I might borrow her riding horse for a couple of hours this afternoon."

"Well, you don't need *my* permission, Perry."

"Yes, of course you may," Clarissa said. "But why do you wish to borrow her?"

"For a lady of my acquaintance. She rides well, so you may have no fears for Griselda's mouth."

"Oh-ho?" Clarissa's eyes danced. "A lady. Who is this lady? Are we acquainted with her?"

"I doubt that very much. She is in town for a few days only and would like to ride in Richmond Park this afternoon."

Jasper's eyebrows lifted. "Does she have a name?"

"Mistress Player," Perry responded promptly.

Jasper's eyebrows lifted even higher. "Why does that sound like an alias?"

"Probably because it is." Perry shook his head. "To tell the truth, I do not know what her name is. I know the various names she uses when it suits her, but unfortunately, it does not suit her to tell me her real identity."

"Now, that *is* intriguing." Clarissa sat on the arm of a sofa, swinging her foot. "Are we talking of a lady of the night?"

"No, most definitely not."

"Are we talking of a prospective answer to Bradley's will?" Jasper inquired, his black eyes now sharp and penetrating.

Perry shook his head. "I don't know," he said honestly. "At the moment, I would say she doesn't qualify in the least. She's an intellectual, something of a scholar, and is at present employed as a librarian."

"Good God." Jasper looked astounded. "Where does she come from?"

"I wish I knew."

"Perry, you're in love with her," Clarissa said. "Don't deny it. Women can always tell these things."

"I wasn't going to deny it," Perry responded. "But what I'm to do about it, I don't know yet."

Jasper sighed. "Well, if 'tis marriage you have in mind, you had best find a way to make this lady suitable for Bradley's stipulation. You do understand that, don't you?" There was a note of steel in his voice, one that Perry had heard before whenever this vexed subject came up.

"I am aware," he said, his own voice rather cold. "If I may, Clarissa, I'll take Griselda with me now. I'll return her this evening."

Jasper said calmly, "I'll have her brought around. Help yourself to a glass of claret while you're waiting." He went to the door to find his butler.

Clarissa gave Perry a conspiratorial smile and murmured, "Don't be offended, Perry. Jasper gets irritable when he's fretting about money."

"I know." Peregrine poured himself a glass of wine. "But he ought to know I understand my obligations. I know what has to be done."

"Of course you do," Clarissa said soothingly.

"They'll bring her around in five minutes." Jasper came back into the room. "Good, you have wine." He nodded at his brother's glass and went to pour himself one. "Clarissa?"

"No, I must go. I have an appointment." Clarissa reached up and kissed her brother-in-law on the cheek. "Does the lady have a first name, at least?"

"Alexandra." He smiled. "And I do believe, for what it's worth, that that *is* her name."

"Pretty." Clarissa approved. She went to the door, saying over her shoulder, "Jasper, I will be back in about an hour. Are you going out?"

"No, I'll be here wrestling with these damn books," he responded. As the door closed on her, he turned to his brother. "Perry, forgive me for sounding harsh. 'Tis just that there are so many demands on the estate, and sometimes I despair of ever getting the family solvent again."

"I know." Peregrine put a hand on Jasper's shoulder. "I'll find a way to satisfy Bradley's conditions, I swear it. How is he, anyway? Have you visited him recently?"

"Last week. He's still as irascible and malevolent as ever, tormenting that poor fellow, Cosgrove, with his obscene meanderings down memory lane."

"So, he doesn't seem to be any closer to the grave?"

"Not as far as I can tell. He's still complaining and moaning when it suits him, but I don't think he's at death's door yet."

"Lady Blackwater's horse is here, sir." The butler spoke from the doorway. "Is Master Peregrine riding her, or should the groom lead her to Stratton Street?"

"No, I'll ride her. She's up to my weight." Perry set down his glass. "Thank you for the wine, Jasper. And if there's anything I can do to help . . ." He gestured to the account books on the desk.

"Just find yourself an unsuitable bride," Jasper said, this time without the sting in his voice.

Perry laughed. "I'll do my best." He paused as he reached the door. "Does the name Douglas mean anything to you? Sir Arthur Douglas?"

Jasper frowned, then shook his head. "No. Does he live in town?"

"He's deceased, but the family house is in Berkeley Square. 'Tis a good address. I was wondering if the family was known in Society circles."

"Not to me," his brother said.

"Ah, well, never mind." Perry raised a hand in farewell and went out to the street, where Clarissa's chestnut mare was waiting with Jasper's groom.

Jasper knew everyone, and if he had not come across the Douglas family even by name, then it stood to reason that they did not move in the first circles of London Society, through either choice or inferior social position. Maskelyne had given his impression of Sir Arthur as a reclusive scholar who rarely visited town, so it rather looked as if Perry would be wasting his time making general inquiries about the family. But he'd already come close to that conclusion, anyway. If Alexandra was prepared to show her real face in public, she must be confident that no one would know her.

So, now what?

Alexandra completed the last of her six letters and sanded the sheet before folding it and dropping hot wax to seal it. She sat back and stretched, shaking out her shoulders. The letters were all the same, a very simple statement that Sir Arthur Douglas's library was for sale and an offer to show some samples of the rare volumes. The recipients were all bibliophiles with whom her father had corresponded. She had often written the letters for him at his dictation, before everything had fallen apart with her mother's last disappearance.

She pulled the bell rope beside the mantel, and when Billings eventually creaked in, she gave him the letters. "Have these delivered this afternoon, please."

"I'll see if the lad, Archie, can do it," he mumbled.

"'Tis imperative that they go this afternoon," Alex stressed.

"Oh, aye," he said, and shuffled away, leaving Alex in some doubt about whether the commission would be executed.

Maybe she should have delivered them herself, she thought as she hurried upstairs to dress for her ride with Peregrine.

She shook out the breeches and examined the

gowns in the linen press. She had brought three with her, one dull gray, one dull brown, and one dull sludge green. She was wearing the green, but they all managed to leach any color from her complexion, and the shapeless folds concealed any feminine contours to her shape.

She couldn't bear to wear them, not here, not when she didn't have to.

For a moment, she stood deep in thought. When her mother had left for the last time, she remembered the dreadful morning when her father had instructed the servants to remove all trace of his wife from her bedchamber and boudoir. Her gowns, her shoes, her cloaks and pelisses, bonnets and shawls, all had gone up to the attics, to be locked away in iron-bound chests. Were they still there?

It was highly likely, she thought. No one would have remembered that they were up there, and when her father had died and Stephen had inherited, he and Maude had not opened the London house properly. Maude had told Alex that they were going to open it for this winter's Season, but judging by its present state of neglect, preparations were well in the future.

She made her way to the attic stairs at the back of the house and hurried up. The dust was even worse up there than in the rest of the house. The storage attic was just as she remembered it. Nothing seemed to have been disturbed. Discarded furniture lay around in a jumbled heap, chests and trunks were stacked against the sloping wall, and a faint gray light came from the small windows set into the slopes of the ceiling.

There was just enough light to see by, and Alex went to the stacked chests and trunks. She knelt down and examined them. They were not locked, there was nothing in them to steal, but which ones held her mother's clothes? She opened one at random, lifting the lid carefully. The scent of cedar filled the air, and her mother's wardrobe lay in carefully tissue-wrapped folds in front of her.

The styles would be at least five years out of date, but her mother had always dressed in the forefront of fashion, so maybe they wouldn't look dreadfully old-fashioned. She started to lift them out, one by one, laying them over an old discarded sofa. They were lovely; her mother had never spared any expense on her clothes, and her husband, to Alex's knowledge, had never complained. He hadn't really seen his wife in her full regalia, anyway, since he never accompanied her in her frequent forays to town or the Continent.

At the bottom of the trunk, she found what she was looking for. A dark green riding habit. The coat, to be worn over a cream silk waistcoat, was fitted and had a black velvet collar and cuffs. The skirt was full, with a little train, and there was even a black hat with gold edging. She could wear her own breeches beneath the skirt, and her own boots.

Alex gathered up her spoils and sped back to her bedchamber. She cast off the dull green gown and stepped into the breeches. The waistcoat fit fairly well, but her mother was rather better endowed than Alex. However, the coat would cover a multitude of sins. She buttoned the skirt to the waistcoat and shook out the folds. Then she slipped on the coat. It was not such a tight fit on her as it would have been on her mother, but it was still pleasingly shaped, she decided, examining her reflection in the spotted mirror. She twisted her hair into a knot at her nape and tried on the hat.

It was quite startling. She could almost imagine that it was her mother standing there in the mirror. It made her feel rather strange. She knew she and Sylvia both had their mother's coloring, but she hadn't given much thought to the resemblance in the last few years. She wondered what Sylvia would say if she could see her sister now as she went downstairs to await Peregrine.

He arrived punctually, as always, and Alex opened the door for him herself, before Billings could emerge from his kitchen lair.

Peregrine's eyebrows crawled into his scalp as he took in her appearance. "Where did that come from? 'Tis most fetching."

She shrugged. "I found it in the attic. I don't know who it belongs to, but since there's no one in the house but me and the caretakers, I thought it wouldn't matter if I borrowed it."

"I'm sure you're right," he said. "I, for one, most definitely approve. Are you quite ready? Shall we go?" He held the door for her, and she stepped out into the street.

"Oh, what a pretty mare," she exclaimed, hurrying down the steps to where the mare was tethered with Sam to the hitching post beside the railings. "She looks far too elegant to be a jobbing horse." She stroked the animal's silky neck.

"Oh, she's not. I borrowed her," he told her, untethering the reins. "Her name's Griselda."

"Who does she belong to?" She bent her knee so that he could toss her up into the saddle.

"My sister-in-law. Lady Blackwater."

"Didn't she mind lending her to a stranger?" Alex settled into the side saddle, leaning forward to reassure the mare with a pat on her neck.

"I assured Clarissa that I had seen you ride." He swung onto Sam.

"What else did you tell her about me?" Alex asked uneasily.

"Why, nothing at all," he responded with a fair degree of truth. "My family is notoriously uncurious, my dear girl. We don't probe into each other's business unless invited."

"How reassuring," Alex murmured, although her uneasiness persisted.

Chapter Fourteen

Lady Maude Douglas entered the librarian's corner bedchamber at Combe Abbey and closed and locked the door behind her. She had no wish to be disturbed by her husband. He was so enamored of Mistress Hathaway that he would probably have some scruples about searching her chamber in her absence. Maude had no such scruples. As far as she was concerned, the woman was a servant, and everything about her should be laid bare for her employer's scrutiny.

The chamber was neat, no stray objects lying around. Maude looked through the pile of books on the night table, but they meant nothing to her, and several of them were in Latin. She put them back and pulled aside the coverlet on the bed. People sometimes kept secrets under their pillows or the mattress, but there was nothing revealing in this bed.

She opened the armoire and riffled through the contents. Nothing she hadn't expected, just a few more of the librarian's ghastly gowns and spinster-ish shawls. The drawers of the dresser revealed only thick stockings, ugly chemises, and much-mended petticoats.

Methodically, Maude went through every drawer and explored every corner of the armoire and linen press. She didn't know what she expected to find, but she was convinced that there would be something revealing about the woman who occupied the chamber. No one could have so little personality, such a nonexistent background, as Mistress Alexandra Hathaway. She was a cipher, and Maude distrusted her with an instinctual suspicion. Quite apart from the fact that she disliked the woman intensely. Whenever she was with her, she felt as if the librarian were looking down on her in some way, felt herself to be superior. It was a feeling Lady Douglas couldn't shake, however absurd it was.

Stephen, of course, was blinded by the woman's ability to make him money. She could do no wrong as long as she continued to increase his fortune, but Maude knew when someone was taking advantage of her, or her husband. She had an infallible nose for such things, and she was convinced that Mistress Hathaway was hiding something, taking advantage of her position in some fashion, and the blanker the canvas, the more obvious it seemed to her. Stephen assured her that Mistress Hathaway had brought letters of reference, excellent testimonials from two gentlemen whose libraries she had catalogued. She was also invaluable, according to these gentlemen, when it came to acquiring rare volumes. She could be relied upon to know when a book was genuinely valuable and what price should be put upon it.

Maude had insisted upon reading these glowing references, but they were to her mind infuriatingly general. Nowhere could she discover anything about the librarian on a personal level. The woman had vaguely mentioned a village rectory in her past, an educated but impoverished clergyman for a father, but no evidence to support such a background. It was as if she had materialized from the ether. But the plain fact of the matter as far as Sir Stephen was concerned was that she was as good as, if not better than, the references had implied. As far as his wife knew, he had never followed them up.

Maude got down on her knees and peered beneath the bed. Nothing there but a chamber pot and a few dust balls. She stood up and looked around again in frustration. There must be some clue to the woman, but it was as if she inhabited the chamber without actually making an imprint upon it.

But then Maude had another thought. If there was anything suspicious to be found, surely it stood to reason that Mistress Hathaway would have removed it when she'd gone to London. Someone up to no good would not leave incriminating evidence behind. And the woman was undeniably clever. She would not make mistakes. The very fact of this chamber's sterile appearance was evidence of a kind that the woman had something to hide.

When Mistress Hathaway returned, Maude decided, she would search again. She left the chamber as she had found it, closing the door behind her.

Stephen, who was just returning from a shooting expedition, emerged from the gun room as his wife came down the stairs. He saw at once that she was in one of her moods, her mouth pursed, her eyes seeming smaller than usual. "Good morning, my dear." He tried for a cheerful greeting, hoping that it would turn aside any complaints.

"It may be so for you, Stephen," she said. "You have nothing but pleasure to occupy you. I have a host of duties and no one but incompetent servants to assist me."

"What in particular is distressing you now, Maude?" His voice was resigned.

"As I've told you repeatedly, that governess is useless. She cannot control the children. I discovered Isabel in the kitchen in a stained pinafore, eating jam straight out of the jar. A baronet's daughter behaving like a street urchin! That librarian should involve herself with the children, as I've said before. At least, she purports to have some education, unlike that useless specimen in the schoolroom."

Stephen sighed. "Mistress Hathaway is fully occupied with my affairs, Maude. I don't know how many times I must repeat that. And when she returns from London, she will continue in the library."

"When she returns from London," Maude said with a sniff. "How do you know she's conducting your business conscientiously in town? There's no one to supervise her. She could be amusing herself in any way she pleases at your expense. I would never have let her go alone."

Stephen regarded her in astonishment. "Are you really suggesting, ma'am, that Mistress Hathaway could possibly be entertaining herself in London? *Mistress Hathaway.*" He laughed. "She's such a timid mouse, I doubt she'll set foot outside the house. Think of her appearance, my dear. She's hardly dressed for town dissipation."

Maude was obliged to admit the truth of this, although she wasn't about to give her husband such a victory. "Well, I don't have time for idle conversation, Sir Stephen." She swept past him in the hall and went into her own parlor, closing the door with a bang behind her.

Stephen shook his head. He had thought their social elevation would have pleased Maude, but she seemed, if anything, even harder to satisfy. She was finding it difficult to establish herself among the Dorsetshire County families, or at least to feel that she was accepted as an equal. Her life until her husband had so unexpectedly succeeded to the baronetcy had been that of the wife of a successful Bristol trader, one of the most prominent in Bristol's lively shipping industry. She had held court as the undisputed leader of their social circle, but country and County life had very different rules and very different hierarchies. She felt looked down upon much of the time, and Stephen couldn't see how to remedy the situation if Maude herself would do nothing to ingratiate herself. She seemed to think that behaving with consequence and superiority would automatically give her both. But in this thoroughly entrenched society, she merely appeared a parvenu.

He, however, was perfectly content to be agreeable, to offer hospitality and welcome his neighbors to hunt, shoot, and fish his lands. As a result, he knew himself to be well liked. But living with Maude when she was disappointed and unhappy was a most disagreeable business.

❧

Alexandra loved Richmond Park from the first moment they rode through the gates. The shaded grassy rides through alleys of trees were almost as delightful as riding in the country. Occasionally, they would run into small parties of fellow horsemen, but for the most part, they rode in peaceful solitude, disturbing grazing deer here and there and scaring up pheasants from the undergrowth.

" 'Tis amazing to think this wilderness exists so close to London," she observed, watching a fawn with its mother disappear into the trees ahead.

" 'Tis hardly a wilderness," Perry said. "There's an entire army of gamekeepers and wardens employed to keep the wildlife plentiful for shooting and to replant the woodland when necessary. Richmond has been the playground of royalty since before the Norman conquest."

"Thank you for disillusioning me," Alex said with a mock frown. "May we gallop?"

"Certainly. 'Tis not Hyde Park, where such freedom is frowned upon."

Alex nudged the mare with her heels. "Come, then, Griselda, let us see what you can do." The horse broke into a canter and then a gallop, with Alex riding low in the saddle, leaning into the animal's neck. Peregrine watched her for a few moments, smiling at the uninhibited enjoyment radiating from the flying figures, and then gave Sam his head. The horse had been straining to follow Griselda and leaped forward, closing the distance between them.

Alexandra heard the pounding hooves behind her and whispered encouragement to Griselda, but after a few minutes, she drew back on the reins, sensing that her mare was giving as much as she had.

Peregrine drew up beside her. "Where did you learn to ride like that? The inhabitants of impoverished country vicarages don't usually have the opportunity."

Alex shook her head. "I don't know why you persist in asking these questions, Peregrine. I've said I won't lie to you, but I won't answer you, either."

"You can't blame a man for trying."

She made no response, but some of the brightness had gone out of the day, and Peregrine sensed that her lighthearted enjoyment in the ride had been spoiled.

"There's a very charming hostelry in the village of Richmond, on the river," he said cheerfully. "I thought we might take dinner there."

"And ride home in the dark afterwards? Is that wise?"

"I thought that perhaps we would not ride back afterwards," he said deliberately. "The hostelry has some very pleasant chambers overlooking the river."

"Oh, I see." Alex felt her spirits rise again. As long as she was in Berkeley Square in the morning to receive any responses to her letters, there was absolutely no reason she should return there for the night. "That sounds delightful, sir."

He smiled. "Good."

They rode for another hour, until the sun was dipping low in the sky, and then Peregrine turned his horse back to the entrance of the park. The little village of Richmond lay immediately outside the park on the banks of the River Thames. The Coach and Horses was a whitewashed, thatched-roof building with an ale garden on the riverbank. Wisteria clung to the walls, framing the mullioned windows and the front door.

They drew up outside the entrance, and the bewigged landlord emerged instantly. He bowed, his belly straining against the buttons of his brown waistcoat. He was beaming a welcome, but his eyes, like little brown buttons, were sharply assessing the quality of his potential guests. He seemed to find that quality satisfactory, as his bow deepened.

"Good evening, ma'am, sir." He rubbed his plump

hands together as they dismounted. "Welcome to my humble establishment. I'll send a groom to take the 'orses, sir." He yelled over his shoulder, and a boy appeared at a run. "Take the 'orses, rub 'em down, and give 'em a bran mash."

Peregrine nodded his approval. "Dinner and a chamber for the night, mine host. We've overstayed our time in the park, and I've no wish to ride back to town in the dark."

"Oh, right y'are, sir." It explained his customers' lack of luggage. "Yes, indeed. We've an oyster stew and roast partridges in the ordinary, but if you was wantin' a private parlor, we could do summat special fer yer dinner."

Peregrine nodded. In normal circumstances, he would not have spent good money on a private parlor, but these circumstances were not normal. "Yes, that will do fine, thank you."

"Will madam be needing a truckle bed for 'er maid?" The landlord looked around rather pointedly. In general, unattended ladies of fashion did not stop at the Coach and Horses.

"No, I won't." Alexandra spoke up with the natural haughtiness that Perry had noticed before. "My maid became unwell, and we were obliged to send her back to town early this afternoon."

"I see, ma'am." The man bowed again. There was nothing about the lady's manner to indicate that she was not the lady she appeared to be. Besides, it was all good custom, after all, whether or not she was no better than she should be. A private parlor was his business, nothing else. "If you'd follow me, sir . . . ma'am. I'll send one of the girls up with 'ot water to wait upon you, ma'am."

They followed him into the inn. Oil lamps were already lit, and there was a pleasing air of order about the establishment. They were shown first to a private parlor upstairs and then to a commodious bedchamber across the corridor, overlooking the river.

"This will do very well." Peregrine discarded his riding cloak, whip, and gloves. "I will await you in the parlor, my dear, while you refresh yourself."

Alexandra curtsied her acknowledgment with a hidden smile. Peregrine was as good a playactor as she was herself. The considerate husband was a part that seemed to suit him rather well.

Peregrine left her and went into the private parlor, where a bright fire and wax candles burned.

"And would you be wantin' to order anything special for yer dinner, sir?" inquired the landlord, who had followed him into the room.

"I don't think so. Oyster stew and roast partridge will do us very well. But you may bring a bottle of your best burgundy and a decanter of Madeira, if you please."

"Right y'are, sir. I've a good burgundy from '50. One o' the best years for burgundy, if I may say so."

"Then bring it, if you please." Perry nodded a pleasant dismissal and went to warm himself at the fire. The ease with which the gently bred Alexandra took to the life of seduction amused him as much as it intrigued him. She didn't appear to have any scruples at all. But then, why should someone who was conducting a monstrous deception every moment of her life have any scruples about any other conventional issue of morality? It seemed that what exasperated him about her on the one hand benefitted him on the other. He shook his head in rueful amusement and kicked a fallen log back into the hearth.

He turned at a light tap on the door and called, "Enter." A young serving girl bobbed a curtsy in the doorway. "Beggin' your pardon, sir, but madam says as 'ow she'll be a while, so could you delay dinner?"

"I'm sure I could, but is there a particular reason for the delay?"

"Aye, sir, madam's desirous of takin' a bath. I'm to fetch up 'ot water."

Peregrine smiled slowly. "Is she, now? Well, you may tell madam that dinner and I will await her pleasure."

"Very good, sir." The girl bobbed another curtsy and vanished.

Alexandra was full of surprises, Perry reflected, still smiling. And she appeared to be learning the art of seduction with remarkable aptitude. The landlord appeared with a crusted bottle of burgundy and a decanter of Madeira. He set them on the sideboard and drew the cork on the burgundy, sniffing it with an air of reverence. "Will you take a drop now, sir?"

"If you please, and put dinner back for half an hour. Madam is taking a bath."

"Oh, yes, sir, so Hester said. The boys are taking up jugs of 'ot water right now. I'll serve dinner in forty-five minutes, if that'll do, sir. The ladies do like to take their time over a bath." He filled a wine glass and brought it over to his guest.

"I'm sure you know best." Perry inhaled the bouquet and took a delicate sip. "You're right, landlord. 'Tis indeed a fine vintage."

The host looked pleased. "I'll send up someone to lay the table, sir."

Perry filled a second glass with Madeira and left the parlor. He lifted the latch of the bedchamber door with his little finger and elbowed it open. Steam rose from behind a screen in front of the fire, and the scent of orange flower and rosewater perfumed the warm air.

"Who's there?"

"Only me. Who were you expecting?" He stepped across to the fire screen and peered over the top, resting his arms along it, the two glasses in his hands. "What an entrancing sight."

Alexandra looked up and felt a moment's self-consciousness that vanished almost as soon as she felt it. "Is one of those for me?" She reached up a hand, and her breast lifted above the water with the movement.

A perfect breast, Peregrine thought. Rounded, creamy white, delicately blue-veined, rosy-tipped. He leaned down to give her the glass of Madeira. Her knees, drawn up in the copper hip bath, broke the surface of the water. Her hair was fastened on top of her head, revealing the slenderness of her neck and the graceful slope of her shoulders. He hadn't really absorbed her body visually the previous night, but now he allowed his gaze to drift slowly over her, guessing at the hidden pleasures beneath the water.

She took a seductive sip of the tawny wine and flicked her eyelashes at him. It was a gesture of such entrancing sensuality that it took his breath away. Where had this country virgin learned such a trick?

He set down his glass and came around the screen. "May I help, ma'am?" He hung his coat over the screen and slowly rolled up his sleeves, before kneeling on the thick sheets spread beneath the bath. He reached for the cake of soap in the dish on the floor and lathered his hands. "Lean forward."

Alex obeyed, reaching for her toes as she bent forward over her knees, exposing the creamy length of her back. Her skin was tingling in anticipation, and she could feel once more that sinking, surging sensation of desire in her belly.

Perry smoothed his soapy hands down her back, letting his fingers slide beneath the water in a more intimate exploration. Alex gave a little gasp of surprise and then moved seductively beneath the probing fingers.

He chuckled and kissed the soapy nape of her neck, his hand slipping around between her thighs, finding her center. She closed her eyes as the exquisite sensation began to build, his fingers and the wash of the water working together to fill her with a confused delight. Her back arched, and her knees lifted as the wave crested, and she gave a little cry of pleasure, folding forward again into the water.

Peregrine smiled and slowly withdrew his hand. Alex raised her head and turned to look at him. Her gray eyes were a little dazed, her cheeks delicately flushed, but she managed to say with a fair assumption of normality, "Is that the way you usually wash a person's back?"

He laughed and kissed the corner of her mouth, before pushing himself back onto his heels and standing up. "I can't say washing a lady's back in the bath is a habit of mine. But I find it a most pleasing activity." He took a towel from the screen and shook it out. "Will you step out, ma'am?"

Alexandra rose in a shower of drops and stepped over the edge of the tub, turning into the towel as he held it out. He wrapped it around her, saying, "I suspect I'm quite competent at drying."

"I think I should do this myself," she said firmly. "But thank you for the offer, sir." She wrapped herself tightly and bent to pick up her glass, which she had set beside the bath. That delicious little interlude had scrambled her senses, she discovered, making her movements unusually clumsy. She took a steadying sip of Madeira.

Peregrine moved the screen aside and picked up his own glass. He regarded her towel-swathed figure with a raised eyebrow. "Have you given thought to what you might wear to dine in?"

She grimaced. "Actually, I hadn't considered the question, but I don't want to put sweaty riding clothes on top of my nice clean skin." She glanced around the chamber for inspiration. "Oh, I know. I'll fashion something out of the bedsheet." She pulled back the coverlet and extracted the top sheet. "This will do very well."

Peregrine watched with some astonishment as she wrapped, folded, tied, and tucked until she was clad in something resembling a Roman toga. "Ingenious," he commented.

"Oh, Sylvia and I as children often fashioned costumes from—" She stopped abruptly. That line of conversation could become dangerous.

"From?" he prompted.

She shook her head and went to the washstand. "It was nothing." She brushed damp tendrils of chestnut hair from her forehead and then abruptly unpinned the knot and let the whole cascade to her shoulders, muttering, "I wish I had a brush," as she ran her fingers through it, pulling out the tangles.

Perry didn't pursue the topic, fascinating though he found it. "Shall we go in search of dinner?"

"Oh, yes, I'm famished." Alex gathered up the folds of her toga and hurried to the door. "Can you bring the glasses? I daren't let go of the sheet in case it comes loose."

"Which would be no disaster," he murmured, picking up their glasses and following her into the corridor.

"It would in the middle of a public passage," she retorted, casting him a grin over her shoulder as she went into the private parlor, where the table in the window was set for two.

Perry merely smiled. So, she and Sylvia had dressed up as children, wherever it was that they had grown up. Maybe that explained the ease with which Alexandra assumed her various parts. Could they possibly have come from a family of traveling players?

It would explain so much, but not the education and her passion for intellectual interests. Traveling players, much like Romanys, never spent long enough in one place to acquire a decent education. He refilled his glass. "One might almost think you grew up on the stage, the ease with which you play so many parts."

Alexandra laughed, thinking of her father's horror. But then she thought of her mother. Luisa had much of the actor about her. She could play many parts, the apparently dutiful wife, the doting mother, the Society grande dame, the dilettante courtesan. Could her daughters have inherited that facility?

"Why do you look puzzled?" Perry inquired, watching her expression. "Or surprised, is it?"

She shrugged. "Neither. I just had a strange notion. But 'twas not important."

"Oh, I doubt that," he murmured. "I doubt very much, my dear girl, that you have strange and unimportant notions."

She flushed, but reprieve came in the form of the landlord directing servants with laden trays, and in the bustle of setting dinner upon the table, she was able to recover her composure.

⟋⟍

Alex drifted up from a deep sleep much later that night. The curtains were still drawn around the bed, but the soft glow of candlelight illuminated the enclosed space. She blinked, confused. The candle was lit on the bedside table, and Peregrine was lying beside her, leaning on one elbow, watching her with an intensity that almost frightened her.

"Is something wrong?" she whispered.

He shook his head. "No, I was just looking at you and thinking."

"Thinking what?" She pushed herself up against the pillows. "'Tis still the middle of the night."

"'Tis near dawn," he responded. "And I was thinking that I don't know who you are, or what you are, but I do know that I love you." He moved a hand up to brush wisps of hair from her cheek. "I said once before that I would not ask for a response, but now I find I must. I love you, Alexandra."

She looked at him, her eyes misting as she shook her head with inarticulate distress.

"Does that mean you cannot love me in return or you cannot *say* that you do?" His voice was very even, very quiet.

There were some truths that could not be denied, she thought. The absolute crystalline truths that existed in their own solid bedrock of certainty. And she knew that she was facing one now.

"I cannot, *may* not say it," she murmured.

He nodded and leaned sideways to blow out the candle. "I will be satisfied with that for the present." He slid down in the bed and drew her into the circle of his arm. "Let us sleep awhile longer."

Chapter Fifteen

On the doorstep of the house on Berkeley Square, Peregrine helped Alexandra dismount. He held her hand for a moment before saying, "Would you like to go to the theatre this evening? I can borrow a box at the Drury Lane Theatre. I assume you could find a suitable gown from the treasure in the attic?" He raised an interrogative eyebrow.

Alexandra's eyes glowed. "Oh, I should like it of all things." Then a shadow crossed her face. "But there will be friends of yours there."

"Maybe," he agreed easily. "And if so, I shall introduce you as Mistress Player, as we agreed."

"But will they not ask questions?"

"Maybe," he repeated. "But they will not ask them of me or of you. My friends are in general too well bred to show an impertinent curiosity."

Alex hesitated. It was very tempting. And once again, she told herself that no one would know her. She didn't know anyone in London who would recognize her. "Then I should love to go. What play is it?"

"I believe 'tis to be Garrick playing Hamlet."

Her delighted expression filled him with warm pleasure. She clapped her hands with all the excited eagerness of a young girl, and he had a glimpse of the lighthearted child she had once been. "I will come for you at eight. And after the play, we shall have a light supper."

"I can hardly wait." She blew him a kiss and ran lightly up to the front door, raising the knocker.

He watched her inside and then mounted Sam and rode to Blackwater House to return Griselda to her rightful owner and beg the loan of the theatre box from Jasper.

Alexandra hurried into the house as soon as Billings opened the door for her. "Any post for me, Billings?"

"Aye, ma'am. A few letters come for you."

"I'll read them in the breakfast parlor. Please ask Mistress Dougherty if she could bring me some coffee." She was hastening up the stairs as she spoke and remembered belatedly that she had not yet had a discussion about supplies with the housekeeper, so presumably, coffee was not going to be on offer yet. In her own chamber, she changed into a more workaday gown, deciding to dispense with the makeup until she knew she would have visitors.

She found the housekeeper in the breakfast parlor setting a pot and a cup on a table. "You'll not be wantin' breakfast, then, ma'am?" Mistress Dougherty asked pointedly. "Seein' as 'ow you've not slept in your bed these last two nights."

"I have relatives in town. I've been staying with them," Alex stated with a haughtiness intended to thwart any further comments. Mistress Alexandra Douglas was unaccustomed to having her movements questioned by housekeepers.

"Well, there's no coffee in the pantry, but I've brought some 'ot chocolate. That do ye?"

"Admirably, thank you. I'll pour it myself." She nodded dismissal and picked up the small pile of letters on the table. She riffled through them. There was one from Sylvia in the middle of the batch. Her heart leaped with pleasure at the thought of reading it, but she set it aside for later and sat down at the table, absently pouring herself a cup of chocolate as she slit the wafer on the first one.

Dear madam,

Lord Dewforth was most intrigued to hear that Sir Arthur Douglas's magnificent collection is to go on the block. He was not well acquainted with that gentleman, but he feels it would be a great sadness for him to see such a carefully built and maintained library dispersed amongst different collections. I have the honor of acting on behalf of Lord Dewforth, who, as I'm sure you're aware, is a biblio-

phile of distinction. I would be most grateful if I could view the sample volumes you mentioned in your letter, at your earliest convenience, in the hopes of coming to some arrangement.

Yours truly,

Andrew Langham.

Alex nodded to herself and sipped her chocolate. Lord Dewforth would be a worthy recipient of her father's treasure. She slit the wafer of the second letter and ran an eye over it, then put it aside. The writer was interested in only certain volumes. He would pay well for them, but Sir Arthur's daughter did not intend the collection to be sold piecemeal. She continued her reading. Of the six responses, two were promising, two only interested in single volumes, and two, she suspected, were merely curious. She looked longingly at Sylvia's unopened letter but resolutely set it aside and gathered paper and ink, sharpened her quill, and sat down to answer the inquiries.

She offered to meet Lord Dewforth's emissary at three o'clock the following afternoon in Berkeley Square and then offered an appointment at four o'clock to the learned Mr. Murdock, whose wealth was on a par with his insatiable appetite for rare books. If the visits overlapped, as she intended they should, it would be an incentive to the two prospective buyers to bring out their best bids.

She penned politely vague responses to the other

four, sanded her labors, folded and sealed them, and went in search of Billings. Instead, she found the lad pushing a mop over the parquet floor in the hall with remarkable lack of enthusiasm. "Ah, Archie, isn't it? Could you take these letters for me, please? I'd like them delivered immediately, and wait for an answer in each case."

Archie looked pleased at the change of employment. "Right away, ma'am." He dumped his mop unceremoniously into the bucket, wiped his hands on the back of his breeches, and held one out for the letters. He squinted at the writing on the top one. "This where I took 'em yesterday?"

"Yes. One is to go to number twenty Albermarle Street, this one here." She indicated the address on one of them, guessing that the boy was unlettered. "You see the number there."

"Oh, aye." He tucked it into his waistcoat and peered at the next one.

"This is to go to number six Park Street." She pointed out the number to him. He nodded, and Alex was confident enough that they would end up in the right place. But she decided to keep back the four less important ones. She didn't want to confuse Archie too much. He could deliver them later that afternoon.

She went back to the parlor, eager now for Sylvia's letter. She had hoped that Sylvia would write to her here but hadn't counted on it. Her visit to town was to be so short, and she had seen her sister so recently, but

she knew she would have been disappointed if Sylvia
had not written as usual.

She settled by the no-longer-smoking fire and slit
the wafer.

Dearest,

*I hope things are going as planned in town.
Everything has settled into the old routine here
after the excitement of your visit, and I must
confess, I find it sadly dull and can't wait for an
accounting of your activities and London's glorious
dissipations to liven our country existence. But I did
have an unexpected visitor yesterday. Helene paid
a call, something she very rarely does these days,
although she is always sending little messages and
gifts of fruit from the orchard or preserves and jams
from St. Catherine's kitchens. But her call was a
little disturbing. I hope 'tis nothing to alarm you,
but I thought you should know without delay.
Helene said she received a visitor a few days ago.
A gentleman by the name of Sullivan. He made
inquiries about a Mistress Alexandra Hathaway;
apparently, he wished to know if she was qualified
to undertake a librarian's work. Helene told me
she assumed he was referring to you and that for
your own reasons, you were using a different name.
She simply answered that she would recommend
you without hesitation. But she then said she was
a little disturbed by the fact that this Mr. Sullivan*

had come across you in Combe, in Dorset. She asked if you were working at Combe Abbey for our cousin, under an assumed name. I told her the story we had concocted, that you had seen Sir Stephen's advertisement for a librarian, and since you knew the library as well as anyone alive, we had thought it the perfect employment for you. Since you must, after all, have employment. But, for obvious reasons, you could not present yourself as yourself. I said something about your not wanting to appear the poor relation asking for charity, which I thought Helene might sympathize with. She didn't say very much, just nodded when I'd finished, and said she must be on her way. All she said as she was leaving was that we should both know that if we are in need, she will do what she can to help, and there is always employment for you at St. Catherine's. I don't really know what to make of this, except that Peregrine has a close interest in you and, I would like to believe, for the best of motives. I don't believe he is making inquiries to do you harm, but you will, I trust, by now be in a better position to judge. Write to me soon, dearest, and reassure me that all is well.

My love as always,
S.

Alex sat with the letter in her lap for a long while. *How dare he?* After everything she had said, after beg-

ging him to accept her as she was, he was still probing, asking questions, trying to catch her out. He was
making her position untenable without beginning to
understand the stakes involved. Had he no sense of the
danger she stood in if she were found out? And now
he was no longer confining his questions to her. He
was spying on her behind her back, putting *her* friends
into impossible positions if they were to protect her.
Forcing Helene to lie to protect her. Oh, it was unforgivable.

She wrestled with the urge to search him out immediately, track him down wherever he was, and confront
him with such a dastardly cowardly betrayal. She was
half out of her chair but then sat back again. Acting on
impulse, particularly when her temper was roused, had
always been a mistake. And maybe there was some excuse for his actions. Maybe loving someone who would
give him nothing of herself could explain a need to discover what he could for himself. He was not a passive
man, not someone who would run from a challenge.
Could she blame him?

He did truly love her. She knew that in every fiber
of her being, just as she knew now how much she
loved the Honorable Peregrine Sullivan. It was a love
tinged with sadness, because it would come to nothing. And that was why she could not speak the words
he wanted to hear. He could sense her love, intuit it,
experience it, but she could never speak it.

The sons of earls did not marry the bastard daughters of insignificant baronets, let alone those daughters who were also master embezzlers.

But maybe there was an answer, one that Peregrine had already suggested.

Alex let her head fall back against the cushions of the chair and closed her eyes, indulging herself for a moment in a dream that she could almost imagine a reality. A *mistress* of independent means.

❧

"Any news of Seb and Serena?" Jasper asked his brother as they sat before the library fire in Upper Brook Street. "D'you expect them back soon?"

"I know no more than you, Jasper." Peregrine sipped his sherry. "Sebastian's been an unreliable correspondent on this voyage. I feel quite bereft of news."

"They had three years of wreckage to repair," Jasper said, indolently resting his boot on the andiron. "We mustn't begrudge them a few months to themselves."

"Certainly, I don't," Perry responded. "But I own I do miss them both. Seb, of course, but Serena grew on me, once I got to know her."

"We both had our prejudices," his brother agreed. His eyes, which had been half closed, snapped open abruptly, and their sharp black gaze fixed on Perry. "So, tell me about your mysterious theatre companion."

"I can't," Perry said simply. "I don't know anything myself. Oh, I know she's clever, I can't defeat her at chess, she can talk astronomy with Maskelyne, and she rides like a gentlewoman, but I also know she's practicing some monumental fraud on the world for purposes that I strongly suspect are probably criminal, and I love her. Hopelessly, helplessly." He shrugged and drained his glass. "Does that answer your question, Jasper?"

"Merely raises a whole host of others," the earl replied. "Does she return your regard?"

"I believe so. But for yet more reasons of her own, she cannot say so." Perry uncurled himself from the chair and stood up, stretching. "I never expected to find myself in this pickle, Jasper. 'Tis the very devil."

"What are you doing about it?"

"Persistence, just persistence." Peregrine went to the door. "I must go. I'm engaged to join a discussion on a new translation of Homer's *Odyssey*. It promises to be lively."

"I'm certain it does," Jasper murmured. "Enjoy Garrick tonight. I gather he's magnificent. Clarissa saw him the other night while I was engaged in a debate in the Lords."

"I have every expectation of doing so." Perry raised a hand in farewell and left his brother to his brief repose.

He spent a pleasant afternoon in White's Coffee House with a group of like-minded Homer scholars and returned to Stratton Street to dress, dine alone, and then collect Alexandra for the theatre.

◈

Alexandra, having achieved a degree of reconciliation with herself, went up to the attic for further exploration among her mother's long-discarded wardrobe. She found a pink silk robe à la française embroidered in an enchanting sprig pattern in palest apple green. Darker green velvet banded the sleeves at the elbow, and a cascade of lace fell to her wrists. The décolletage was deeper than she had ever worn before, and this gown had no fichu. But then, she was no longer a virginal debutante, Alex thought with a wicked chuckle. She could bare her breasts with the best of them. She found a delicate mother-of-pearl fan and pink kid slippers with a small heel. There was no jewelry in the attic chests, but then, she hadn't expected there to be. If her mother had left any, her father would have kept it. But Alex didn't think her mother had left anything of value. As flighty as Luisa could appear when it suited her, she had a shrewd head.

Something else that she had inherited from her mother, Alex thought as she examined herself in the glass. The resemblance to Luisa was as striking tonight as it had been before. Her décolletage was not as stunning as Alex remembered her mother's to be, but side by side, everyone would know them for mother and daughter.

She went down to the breakfast parlor with no great hopes for dinner. She had given Mistress Dougherty some money and asked her to prepare a simple meal, so she was pleasantly surprised at the dish of sautéed calves' livers with creamed leeks, removed with a fine piece of Stilton cheese and an apple pie. It was certainly simple but well cooked. When she had finished, she went into the kitchen to compliment the cook.

The caretakers and Archie were eating their own dinner when Alex entered the kitchen. She raised a hand as they pushed to their feet. "No, please, don't disturb yourselves. I came only to thank you for an excellent dinner, Mistress Dougherty."

"Well, I'm glad it pleased you, ma'am." The housekeeper sat back at the table. "We're 'avin' a bite o' beef 'earts, but I thought as 'ow ye'd prefer summat a bit more refined like."

Alexandra smiled her agreement. "Well, thank you again, and enjoy your dinner. I shall be going out later."

"An' will ye be comin' back t'night, ma'am?" Billings asked through a mouthful of fried onions.

"You may leave the key above the ledge at the side door, as usual," she said, resorting to the haughty tone of the mistress once again.

"Oh, aye. As you say, ma'am." Billings reached for his ale pot and buried his nose in it. Mistress Dougherty merely nodded, and Alex took her departure.

It was close to eight, and she reread Sylvia's letter, trying to decide whether, now that she had cooled off, to challenge Peregrine with the contents or leave it be. Was anything to be gained by challenging him with it? By opening the discussion herself, she would be giving him the opportunity for more questions, and she was beginning to feel increasingly vulnerable under his probing. She tried to keep up her guard, but it was so hard to do now. How could she keep her innermost self from him when she opened her body to him with such wholehearted delight? In those glorious sensual tangles on the bed, when her skin melded with his, when she could feel his heart beat as if it were her own, she wanted nothing more than to share every thought, every hope, every inch of herself with him.

No, Alex decided. For the moment, she would let this particular sleeping dog lie. She folded Sylvia's letter and took it up to her chamber. She tucked it into a concealed pocket in her portmanteau and took up her cloak and gloves, then ran downstairs just as the knocker sounded. She reached the door before Billings emerged from the kitchen and opened it herself.

Peregrine stood smiling on the doorstep, dressed in rich black velvet with creamy Mechlin lace frothing at his throat and wrists. His fair hair shone guinea gold against the deep black, and his blue eyes took on an almost purple hue. He absorbed Alex's appearance with a wordless nod of appreciation as he bowed and offered his arm.

"What a magnificent conveyance," Alex said, seeing the large coach in the street behind him, its panels emblazoned with the Blackwater arms. "The earl's?"

"Yes, I borrowed it to go with the theatre box," Perry said, escorting Alex to the carriage. "We might as well start the evening appropriately."

The coachman had let down the footstep and bowed. "Good evening, madam."

"Good evening." She returned the greeting with a

smile and stepped up into the coach. The interior was well-worn but still comfortably luxurious despite its rather old-fashioned appearance. Perry stepped in beside her and draped a fur robe across her lap.

"What luxury." She settled back as the coach moved forward. "I feel as if I'm living under false pretenses."

"As indeed you are," Perry said. "You should be used to it by now."

"I suppose you're entitled to that," Alexandra responded, stung.

"Oh, I didn't mean it unkindly," he protested, taking her hand. "I was just stating a truth."

"I'd like to enjoy this evening without being reminded at every turn."

"I don't think I do that, do I?" he asked seriously.

"I don't think you can help it." She took her hand back and plaited her fingers restlessly. She had to accept that she was living a lie, but there was no reason she should feel happy about it.

Peregrine was silent for a moment, then he said, "I pledge to do everything in my power for the rest of this evening not to give that impression." He reached out and turned her face towards him in the darkened carriage. "Will that do?"

She smiled with a hint of sadness. "Thank you." He might promise such a thing, but *she* wouldn't be able to forget.

But once they reached the theatre, Alex discovered that in the magic of the glittering crowd, the brilliantly lit theatre, the velvet and brocade box, the noisy, chattering throngs in the pit, she forgot everything except the moment. She gazed transfixed with fascination around the boxes, with their lavishly dressed occupants, the ladies with high powdered coiffures, peering through opera glasses at the inhabitants of the neighboring boxes, fanning themselves under the heat of the chandeliers and the humid press of highly perfumed bodies. She was quickly aware that many of those opera glasses were trained upon the Blackwater box, and she could almost hear the buzz of gossip as people whispered and pointed.

"We seem to be as much of an attraction as the stage," she murmured to Peregrine behind her fan.

"We'll have visitors in the interval, I daresay," he returned. "But they'll know nothing, and they'll discover nothing. People just love intrigue, particularly when it smacks of an illicit *affaire*."

"Which is, after all, for once entirely the truth," Alex said with a mischievous chuckle that gladdened her companion's heart. The part of the Honorable Peregrine's unknown mistress was one she could enjoy playing without an ounce of guilt. She leaned forward, resting her arms along the padded edge of the box, looking down into the pit.

One or two of the young bucks were ogling the occupants of the boxes through quizzing glasses, and Alex returned their stares with unabashed curiosity until Perry said urgently, "Sit back, Alexandra. That's the worst kind of attention you can attract. 'Tis one thing to be the discreet object of interest among the fashionable set, quite another to be an object to be ogled by the bucks in the pit as if you were no better than a denizen of a nunnery."

"Oh, I beg your pardon." Alex sat back instantly. "I'm not accustomed to drawing any kind of attention, so I'm not adept at telling which kind is good and which is not."

"Mistress Hathaway, of course, makes it her mission in life to fade into the background," Peregrine said. Then he sighed. "Forgive me, I was forgetting my pledge."

Alex made no response. She was too fascinated by the scene around her to be bothered by such reminders this evening. The initial appearance of the actors stepping onto the stage did little to quiet the buzz of the audience throughout the first scene. People were still entering the theatre, taking their seats in the boxes, waving and calling greetings to acquaintances across the theatre.

Alexandra was outraged as the actors struggled to make themselves heard throughout the first scene, but it all changed in the second scene, when David Garrick as Hamlet strode onto the stage. He was a man in his mid-forties, but his lithe figure, his utter assurance in the part, the wealth of power and emotion that invested his performance made it irrelevant that he was playing the part of a man less than half his age. The theatre fell completely silent the moment he began to speak, and Alex leaned forward again, her gaze riveted to the stage, and she barely moved a muscle until the interval.

Only when the last actor had left the stage did she sit back and draw a deep breath. She gazed at Perry. "I have never been so transported."

"No," he said with a smile. "I could see that you were. Garrick is magnificent." He turned as the door to the box opened behind him. "Ah, gentlemen, good evening." He greeted the trio who crowded into the box.

Alexandra responded to introductions with what she hoped was a mysterious smile. One set of visitors was replaced by a second and a third, and throughout she kept her seat and spoke only as much as courtesy demanded. Peregrine was giving nothing away, either, engaging only in the most innocuous small talk. Their visitors were all gentlemen, the ladies remaining in their seats to receive their own visitors. When movements on the stage indicated that the play was starting again, the gentlemen returned in leisurely fashion to their own seats, and the chatter died down again.

Once again, Alex was transported until Garrick made his final bow to tumultuous applause, shouts, and cheers. Only then did she take her eyes from the stage to glance around the theatre again. And her breath seemed to stop in her chest. In the box directly across from her sat a lady in a gown of crimson damask, a diamond pendant nestled in her deep décolletage. Her dark chestnut hair was unpowdered but dressed over pads in a high coiffure studded with diamond pins. Her gray eyes were unusually large and bright, and they were fixed in bemused question upon Alexandra.

Luisa. What in the devil's name was her mother doing in the Drury Lane Theatre? Alexandra dragged her gaze away, just as Luisa turned to her companion. Alexandra scrambled to her feet, and Perry seized her arm. "What is it? You're white as a sheet. You look as if you've seen a ghost."

"I have," she mumbled. "I must go, *now.*" Blindly, she tried to push past him to the door, but he blocked her path.

"Yes, we will go," he said in a calm, low tone. "But not in such disorder. Everyone will stare at you, and I know you don't want that. Now, take a breath."

"I have to get out of here before she finds me."

"You're making no sense. But we are going now. Just take my arm, and walk steadily. We won't stop, and if anyone speaks to us, leave it to me."

The cool steadiness of his tone calmed her, and she swallowed the rising panic. Her mouth was unpleasantly dry, and she seemed to find it difficult to draw a deep enough breath, but she took Perry's arm and let him lead her out into the thronged foyer. The doors stood open to the freedom of the Piazza just a few feet away, and she found it easier to look down at the floor and let Perry guide her, moving through the crowd with a touch on an arm here, a shoulder there, stopping for no one.

They were almost at the doors when she heard what she had been dreading. "Alexandra? Alexandra, is that really you? Wait a moment."

Alex put her head down and pushed through the throng, heedless of Peregrine's attempt to restrain her with a hand on her arm.

Peregrine let her go and turned to look behind him. A chestnut-haired woman with striking gray eyes stood a few paces away, staring after Alexandra's retreating figure as it disappeared through the doors to the street beyond.

Peregrine turned and hurried out of the theatre into the Piazza, where a light drizzle had started. He glimpsed Alexandra almost running along the colonnade. The Blackwater coach was waiting in the line of private carriages, and he jumped in, instructing the coachman, "Go slowly towards King Street. We will pick up Mistress Hathaway there." He pulled the door closed but leaned out through the open window as the coachman set the horses to a slow walk, following Alexandra.

As she turned onto King Street, Peregrine opened the door, blocking her path. "Get in, Alexandra." She stared at him, her eyes wide with fear. "Come," he insisted, reaching down a hand to her. "You'll catch your death. It's raining." He spoke quietly, calmly, hoping his voice would reassure her. The fear in her eyes astounded him even as it horrified him.

Slowly, she took his hand and climbed into the carriage. He pulled the door closed as she sat in the corner, abruptly closing her eyes. Peregrine sat opposite and said nothing as the carriage moved through the crowds.

Not a word was spoken throughout a journey that to Alexandra seemed interminable. She was afraid every time the vehicle was brought to a near stop by a surge of pedestrians or a stray dog or an oncoming vehicle that she would see her mother peering through the window at her. She knew it was an irrational fear, but she couldn't seem to shake free of it.

At last, the carriage drew to a stop in the quiet of Stratton Street. Peregrine jumped out and lifted Alexandra down to the street. "Thank you. I won't need you again tonight," he informed the coachman.

"Right y'are, Master Peregrine. Good night, madam."

She managed to acknowledge the courtesy with a vague gesture. Peregrine ushered her to the door, opened it with his key, and almost thrust her inside.

"There, you're safe now," he said with a touch of grimness. "You can stop looking like a petrified cat and start breathing normally." He opened the door to the sitting room and urged her inside. "Let me pour you a cognac. 'Tis very good for shock, I'm told." He poured a generous measure into a goblet.

Alexandra was standing by the fire, her hands shaking as she took the glass from him. She was still as pale as a ghost, and her eyes as she looked at him were desperate. She cradled the glass, inhaled its powerful fumes, and took a tentative sip. It warmed her and did seem to steady her.

Peregrine poured his own goblet and drank it slowly, watching her all the time. "Finish it," he instructed when she was about to set it aside. "And when you've done so, we shall have the first truly honest discussion of our association."

There was a harshness to his voice now that paradoxically restored her composure more quickly than gentle compassion and understanding might have done. She drained her glass and stood turning it between her hands, staring down into the fire.

"That lady was your mother," he stated after a moment. There was no question in his mind. The resemblance had been startling. "Who is she?"

Alexandra shrugged slightly. "Who knows?"

"That's no answer, and you know it," he snapped.

She looked up at him. "Well, it is and it isn't." She saw his expression darken and real anger flash in his eyes. She explained with another tiny shrug, "No one ever knows what part my mother is playing."

"I see," he said drily. "Like mother, like daughter."

"You may think that's fair, but it is not."

Peregrine took a deep breath and said with more moderation, "Come, take off your cloak and sit down. I'll pour you another cognac while we thrash this out."

He unclasped her cloak and took it from her, laying it over a chair back, then refilled her glass. "Sit down."

"No, I would prefer to stand." She took the glass, however. "The last I knew, my mother had eloped with the Conte della Minardi. But as that was about six years ago, who knows who she has moved on to now. My mother devours men like a black widow devours its mates." She sipped the cognac, feeling her body loosen, the rigidity dissipating.

"An Italian . . . did she go to live in Italy?"

"Apparently. She was not very good at keeping her family apprised of her movements." Alexandra gave a tight smile, setting her glass aside on the chimney piece.

"And now she's back in London." Peregrine nodded. "So, I need the truth now, Alexandra. Who was your father . . . or is he still living?"

She shook her head. "No."

"You do know how easy it will be for me to discover everything about your mother, and thus everything that you are hiding," he said quietly. "But if you force me to do that, and I will, make no mistake, then there can be nothing more between us. If you will not trust me sufficiently to tell me yourself, then . . ." He shook his head, and a bitterness entered his voice. "Then I cannot trust you, and without trust, there can be no love. Either you tell me everything now, or I take you back to Berkeley Square and we will never see or speak to each other again."

The ultimatum shocked her even as she understood that she should have expected it. It was all over now, anyway. Once Peregrine knew the whole story, the outcome would be the same as if she had left him to discover the truth for himself. Not even love could withstand this truth.

"There is no need for ultimatums, Peregrine. I am well aware that you have no scruples when it comes to asking questions about me." It came out as an accusation, and she made no attempt to soften it.

"What does that mean?" he asked quietly.

"I know you went looking for information from Helene Simmons. What possible right did you think you had to do that?" It felt good suddenly to be the accuser, but the moment didn't last.

"Yes, I did," he said. "And I make no apologies for it. You were . . . *are* . . . in trouble, Alexandra, and I love you. It is not in my nature to stand aside when those I love could use my help."

"You cannot help me, Peregrine. Only I can help myself, and you are just making it more difficult for me." She stood staring into the fire, her fingers pressed to her lips.

"You can stop me asking questions if you tell me the truth yourself, Alexandra." His voice was quiet but utterly determined. "Trust me."

She had reached the Rubicon, it seemed. Her voice was dull with resignation. "You leave me no choice. But you should understand that what I have to tell you will give you such a disgust of me that you will never wish to lay eyes upon me again."

"Why don't you let me be the judge of that?" A sudden smile lightened his expression and warmed his eyes. "Believe me, Alexandra, I have imagined you to be engaged in every criminal activity short of murder, and I haven't shrunk from you yet. So, try me."

"'Tis hard to know where to begin . . ." She started hesitantly but gradually gained confidence as she saw that his gaze never wavered, his expression never changed, even as she described her scheme to defraud her cousin out of the twenty thousand pounds she considered hers and her sister's just inheritance.

"So, there it is," she finished at last. "I promise I have told you everything to the last detail."

He rose to throw another log on the fire and then stood with his back to the warmth, sipping his cognac and regarding her thoughtfully. "How much have you managed to squirrel away thus far?"

It was asked in a matter-of-fact tone that was as surprising as the question itself. "About five thousand."

"Not bad for only three months. How long do you think it will be before you can cease this felonious activity?"

Alexandra stared at him. Was it possible that he wasn't going to try to stop her? She said hesitantly, "Well, I intend to make a certain amount on the sale of the library, and if my own investments prosper—" She stopped as he held up an arresting hand.

"No, don't tell me any more," Peregrine stated. "The less I know about the details, the better."

"You did ask."

"Yes, and 'twas a grave error. I have the salient facts,

that's all I need to know." He shook his head. "Well, all this unusual truth telling has made me hungry. Mistress Croft will have left a light supper in the kitchen for us. I'll fetch it."

Alexandra wasn't sure how to interpret his reception of the story. Why didn't he show the revulsion she had expected? The revulsion any man of honor would show? She followed him into the kitchen, feeling a little like a lost sheep. "Are you going to say nothing?"

He was examining the covered dishes on the kitchen table. "What is there to say? I asked for the truth, and you gave it to me. Shall we eat this in here? The range is still hot, and 'tis quite comfortable."

"Yes, if you wish." She lifted the covers off the remaining dishes while Peregrine took a candle and went down to the cellar for a bottle of wine.

"It looks a very fine veal and ham pie," she commented when he reappeared. She felt as if she were acting yet another part, that of a perfectly normal woman in a perfectly ordinary situation. But if Peregrine could behave as if nothing momentous had occurred, then so could she.

"One of Mistress Croft's specialties." He uncorked a dusty bottle and set it on the table. "There should be some glasses in the dresser."

Alex found them, and Peregrine filled them, before sitting on the bench on one side of the table. Alex took the opposite one and cut into the pie, placing a slice on his plate, while he carved wafer-thin slices from a glistening ham.

They ate in silence for a while, until Alex could bear it no longer. She said abruptly, "You must have something to say, Peregrine. I've just told you I'm a bastard, an embezzler, a thief, in essence. How could you say nothing? Aren't you shocked? Outraged? Disgusted?"

"No," he said cheerfully. "None of those things. As it happens, I'd imagined much worse."

She began to feel as if the world had spun off its axis. "What could be worse?"

He shrugged. "Murder, certainly. A different kind of stealing, perhaps." He smiled. "Be that as it may, I appear not to be as shocked as I'm sure I probably should be." He forked a mouthful of pie. "Eat your supper."

Alexandra relaxed. And slowly, a little bud of happiness opened within her. She had told the worst, and the worst had not happened. An immense lightness seemed to flood her, as if somehow all the miseries and anxieties, the dread and the tension, the terror of discovery, became as nothing, as if she had never experienced them. And she thought how delighted Sylvia would be—Sylvia, who had seen this possibility almost from the first. Of course, it was not over yet; she still had to complete her self-appointed task, but at least she was no longer deceiving Peregrine.

She ate veal and ham pie, a thick slice of ham, rice pudding, and spiced pears and drank her share of the wine. Peregrine ate well, too, but he watched her covertly with a secret smile. Alexandra was still presenting him with a few hurdles, but once they were jumped, he would be on the home stretch, and his own happiness would complete his familial obligations.

At last, Alexandra set down her spoon. "I have never eaten so much at one time," she declared in wonder. She yawned. "But I am most unaccountably sleepy."

"Hardly unaccountably." Laughing, Peregrine stood up. "Come, let me get you to bed. You have much to sleep off and, I think, to sleep on."

"So astute, as always," she murmured dopily, letting her head fall on his shoulder. "My legs don't seem as strong as usual."

He supported her up to his chamber, unlaced her gown, divested her of petticoats and chemise, untied her garters, and slipped her stockings down the smooth length of her legs and over her narrow feet. He dropped one of his nightshirts over her head and bundled her under the covers. "I must go down and snuff the candles, but I'll be up in a moment."

"Mmm," Alex murmured from the depths of the coverlet.

Peregrine smiled and left her. He extinguished the candles downstairs, all but his carrying candle, and returned upstairs. As he'd expected, Alexandra was deeply asleep. He undressed and slipped in beside her, sliding an arm beneath her to roll her into his embrace. She murmured but didn't awaken, merely curled against him.

He lay holding her, watching the firelight flicker on

the ceiling, thinking how best to extricate her from a situation in which he knew she would fight tooth and nail to remain. He knew his Alexandra by now. She would not give up until she had completed what she had set out to do. But there was no need for her to do that now. So, how to convince her?

Chapter Sixteen

Alexandra awoke from a sleep as deep and relaxing as any she could remember. She rolled onto her side and looked at the sleeping Peregrine. He lay on his back, his arms flung above his head, his breathing deep and regular. He seemed as untroubled as she felt herself to be that morning. She touched his mouth with her fingertip, and his eyelids fluttered. She leaned over and brushed his lips with her own, a light butterfly kiss, and with the growl of a bear awakened from hibernation, he seized her and rolled her beneath him. He leaned over her, his eyes wide awake and filled with laughter.

"Beware the sleeping beast," he said, nuzzling her neck, his hand sliding down her body to part her thighs.

She laughed and opened her body for him, curling her legs over his hips as he entered her, pressing her heels into his buttocks with the rhythm of his thrusts. It seemed so deliciously familiar now, this lovemaking, familiar and yet always different. She found that she approached her peak from many different angles, and the intensity was as varied. Sometimes she felt as if she were torn apart, her body disintegrating into a diffused scatter of little pieces, and other times it was as if she was sliding gently into a warm whirlpool of delicate sensation that left her soft and formless. But this morning, it was a long and wonderful climb as the ultimate promise built within her, ever tightening, growing ever closer. She heard herself beg her lover not to stop, not to slow his movements, to keep the tightness building within her. The glorious explosion hung just on the periphery, and when she reached the edge, she heard her own cry, mingling with Peregrine's as he fell heavily atop her, gathering her up tightly against him as their bodies throbbed and pulsed in unison.

At long last, Perry rolled sideways, lying on his back, his breathing still fast, his skin damp with sweat. He turned his head to smile at Alex, who lay prone in a similarly exhausted condition, her own skin glowing, her eyes dreamy with fulfillment. He moved a hand to rest indolently on her belly.

"I think I died a little," Alex murmured when she could catch her breath again.

"*Le petit mort,*" he said. "It happens sometimes when one is incredibly lucky."

"Did it happen to you?" She put her own hand over his as it rested on her stomach, twining her fingers with his.

"I do believe it did," he murmured with a soft chuckle. The little clock on the dresser chimed. "Eight o'clock. I think 'tis time to put on the day."

Alexandra groaned in faint protest as he swung himself out of bed. "I don't have anything to do until this afternoon, when I have to meet someone at Berkeley Square. He wishes to look at the volumes then, and after him, there is one other gentleman at four o'clock. I am hoping they will bump into each other, just to stimulate a healthy rivalry. It should drive up the price."

"Well, I have a few things to do this morning." Perry thrust his arms into a dressing gown. "You may stay abed for as long as you wish." He bent down and kissed the corner of her mouth. "I'm going to ring for hot water, so stay where you are behind the curtains while Bart is in here."

Alex lay back against pillows in the seclusion of the bed curtains, her tranquility disturbed as the image of her mother drifted into her mind. Just what was Luisa doing in London? Was she still married to the Count? Did she know how her daughters' legal status had changed when her husband divorced her? It was not a fact that would have interested her particularly, and it was equally possible that she didn't know that Sir Arthur had died without making provision for them. Quite simply, it wouldn't have occurred to her to ask about them. And she wouldn't be interested now, even if her curiosity had been momentarily piqued by seeing her daughter at the theatre. She would soon forget or assume she'd been mistaken. But the thought that she might accidentally bump into her mother again in town was an alarming one.

She couldn't risk it, so her outings with Peregrine would have to be curtailed.

But in a few days, she'd have to return to Combe Abbey, anyway, and this delightful idyll would be over. But maybe only temporarily over, she thought with a little frisson of excitement. Why shouldn't she be the Honorable Peregrine's mistress? When she'd first had the thought, it had seemed both exciting but impossible; now, however, she could see nothing impossible about it. She would be her own mistress financially, no burden on Perry's already overburdened finances. There was no reason at all why she shouldn't lead her life exactly as she pleased. That had been the aim of this charade from the very beginning, although then she had thought only of a quiet, comfortable, independent life with Sylvia and Matty.

Now she remembered how Sylvia had expressed reservations at that vision, at least as far as Alex was concerned. And Sylvia was, as usual, probably right. Alex needed more in her life than rustic tranquility. She was still a very young woman with her life ahead of her, once the reins of that life were firmly in her own hands.

So, when would be the right moment to present my vision to Peregrine?

She heard the door open and Peregrine's voice talking to the lad, Bart. The sounds of movement in the room were followed by the door closing again, and the bed curtains were opened once more. Peregrine was fully dressed. "I'm just going out. But there's hot chocolate, and the fire's ablaze." He tossed a brocade dressing gown onto the bed beside her. "That should keep you warm when you're ready to leave the bed."

"How long will you be?" *Would this morning be the right time?*

He considered. "It depends . . . but an hour, maybe a little more."

She nodded. "Hurry back. I shall miss you."

He laughed and kissed her lightly. "The sooner I go, the sooner I'll be back."

The door closed behind him, and Alexandra pushed aside the coverlet. She reached for the gown, thrusting her arms into the sleeves. When she stood up, the garment enveloped her and puddled around her feet, tripping her as she walked to the fire. The rich material was imbued with Peregrine's special scent, and she buried her nose in the crook of her elbow, inhaling deeply, smiling a reminiscent smile. She poured herself a cup of hot chocolate from the jug on a tray by the fire and sat down on an ottoman.

She was still sitting there, contemplating the glories of her grand plan, when Peregrine returned within the hour. "Good Lord, are you still abed, lazybones?" he greeted her as he came in, bringing the coldness of the fresh air with him, his blue eyes sparkling, diamond bright.

"Not exactly," she defended herself. "I am up, in a manner of speaking." She lifted her face for his kiss, running a caressing finger along his cold cheek.

"In a manner of speaking," he agreed. "Have you broken your fast?"

She shook her head. "The hot chocolate is sufficient. Where have you been? Or may I not know?"

"Oh, 'tis no secret," he responded easily, shrugging out of his riding cloak. "I went in search of your mother."

Her face paled, and the dream exploded. "You're doing it again . . . prying and spying. *Why?* I told you everything you wanted to know."

He sighed. "I was not spying, Alexandra. There was nothing underhand about it. I thought you would probably wish to know where your mother was living, how long she was staying in town, and maybe even what her circumstances are. On the principle of better the devil you know." He quirked an eyebrow. "Was I right?"

"Well, yes, but—"

"No buts," he declared. "You may cease your castigation forthwith, unless you don't wish to know what I have discovered." The smile in his eyes belied the mock sternness of his tone. He pulled the bell rope by the fireplace.

"You didn't let her know it *was* me last night?" She couldn't hide her anxiety.

He shook his head in reproof. "Don't be silly, I didn't speak to her myself, just asked a few questions of those who might know. The Contessa della Minardi is putting up at Grillons, a suitably fashionable spot and a most expensive one, I should add. Oh, Bart." He turned to the door as the lad came in. "We'll take breakfast in the parlor in half an hour. And bring me a tankard of ale up here as soon as possible, if you please." The door closed behind the boy, and Peregrine resumed his account. "I gather she has been staying there without her husband for a week, and when the Count arrives, they are intending to travel to Paris."

"Oh." Alexandra stretched her toes to the fire, wriggling them in the warmth. "How did you find out?"

"I have an Aunt Anne who is a notorious gossip. She knows everything about anyone who is anyone . . . or who thinks they are," he added with a sardonic smile. "And if there's ever a breath of scandal attached, Anne's interest is even more likely to be piqued. I reasoned that an Italian countess of dubious reputation would probably attract some attention in town, particularly as she goes out in public. And I was right. Anne knew everything there was to know about the Contessa. Of course, she wouldn't acknowledge the lady in public; that would not do for a Blackwater at all." The sardonic smile deepened.

Alexandra couldn't help flushing. "She's unlikely to acknowledge me, then."

Perry regarded her for a moment with his head to one side. "Well, that remains to be seen, my dear. I am sure you bear little or no resemblance to your mother except physically. You are, if you don't mind my pointing out, her living image."

Alexandra looked down at her fingers curled in her lap. She had to acknowledge that, just as she had to acknowledge that she had found the realization pleasing the other day. There was nothing to be ashamed of in resembling an undeniable beauty, and her mother was ever that. "Well, for as long as she's in town, I cannot go out," she stated, moving the subject down a different path. "I must complete my business here as soon as possible and go back to Combe Abbey."

Peregrine hesitated, wondering if this was the right moment, but maybe there was never a right moment. "You no longer need to continue with this criminal and dangerous charade, Alexandra. Take what you have, use it to ensure Sylvia's well-being, and call it a day."

She shook her head. "I can't do that. I must finish what I began. How else am I to live?"

He scratched his ear, looking for the right words. "You will live with me. We will be married as soon as I can procure a license, and you will resume your real identity. No one will associate the downtrodden Mistress Hathaway with the wife of the Honorable Peregrine Sullivan. You'll be free and clear."

"For God's sake, Peregrine!" she exclaimed, jumping up from the ottoman. "Didn't you hear anything I said last night? You cannot marry a bastard, quite apart from my criminal activities in the last months."

"I can marry whom I choose, ma'am," he returned smartly. "As can you." He looked at her in silence for a moment, watching her expression. It was difficult to read. Was there hope there? Or simply incredulity? He took a step towards her, his hands outstretched. "Love conquers all, they say, Alexandra. If you'll let it." He took her hands. They were cold, but her fingers twitched against his.

"Come, what do you say?" he pressed.

After a moment, she said so softly he could barely hear her, "I say 'tis a pipe dream."

"Then indulge it." He tipped her chin, looking deep into her eyes. "I promise it is no pipe dream. I wish to marry you more than anything I have ever wished for, Alexandra."

"It will ruin you," she stated flatly.

He shook his head, and now a flicker of laughter appeared in his eyes. "Not so, my dear. Oddly enough, it will do the opposite."

"How?" She looked at him with an arrested expression.

He chuckled richly. "It is the most perfect concatenation of circumstance. Do you remember my mentioning my perverse Uncle Bradley and the devious conditions he has written into his will?"

Alex looked bewildered. She remembered something he had said about an uncle but hadn't really taken it in. It hadn't seemed particularly relevant. What could some Blackwater uncle have to do with herself and Peregrine?

"My uncle, Viscount Bradley, is a man of immense wealth. He was a nabob in India and the Far East and amassed a huge fortune. He is also debauched, even to the point of depravity, and he has taken it into his head to be avenged upon our somewhat straitlaced family for their ostracism by offering to leave his fortune to Blackwater, Sebastian, and myself in equal parts, on one condition."

Alexandra gazed, fascinated, into the deep blue eyes fixed upon her countenance. "What condition?"

"That we each wed a fallen woman, for want of a better description." This time, his laugh was short and humorless. "The idea, as I understand it, is that Bradley will force the family to accept a woman of neither status nor reputation into its holier-than-thou bosom. So far, Jasper and Sebastian have managed to find ways to satisfy that condition, but if I do not do so before our uncle's death, then none of us will inherit. The devil of it is that Blackwater needs the money to tow the family out of the River Tick. Our father's gambling debts and general profligacy have brought the estates to the verge of ruin. Bradley is prepared to settle all the mortgages on the estates, in addition to leaving the remainder of his fortune to the three of us."

"I don't see what this has to do with me." Alexandra sounded as confused as she felt.

"My dear girl, it has everything to do with you. You are illegitimate, and by your own description, you are an embezzler and a thief. How more unsuitable could you be as a Blackwater bride? Something, I may remind you, that you have pointed out to me in no uncertain terms. And to put the icing on the cake, I love you. There will never be anyone else I could ever wish to marry."

She gazed at him, stunned, as she absorbed his words. "Oh, Perry, 'tis absurd."

"The entire situation is absurd," he declared roundly. "But the old man holds all the cards. So, Mistress Douglas, marry me and save the Blackwaters."

"I had thought to be just your mistress," she said, considering. If she could contemplate one, why not the other? Both would give her a loving life with Peregrine. "Once I'd completed my work at Combe Abbey, I had thought we could set up house, and I wouldn't object if you chose to marry someone—"

"*Enough!*" he bellowed, giving her shoulders an inadvertent shake. "How insulting can you be? I do not want a mistress, *any* mistress. I want and *need* a wife. And I want *you*. Now, your answer, if you please."

Why not? She felt a little jolt of excitement. Maybe everything could work out in the end, once this tangle was unraveled. "You are very persuasive, sir." She dropped him a mock curtsy. "How could I refuse such a tempting and elegantly phrased offer?"

"Hornet," he said appreciatively.

"But I must finish my work at Combe Abbey first," she said, and all warmth and appreciation fled from his countenance. "I have to ensure my own independence and Sylvia's."

"That is not necessary," he stated, tight-lipped.

"Yes, it is," she responded simply. "I will not let injustice stand. Stephen owes us our portions, and he will pay them. He just won't know that he's done so."

Abruptly he swung away from her and stalked to the window, standing with his back to her until he had himself under control. "And if I will not permit you to do this?"

"You will not have that right," she said simply. "I will marry you after I've completed my work."

Peregrine wrestled with himself for long minutes while she stood where he had left her, unmoving, quiet, her hands clasped against his robe, waiting. Finally, he turned back to the room and said curtly, "We'll leave it there for the moment. Get dressed and come down for breakfast. I am sharp set." He left the chamber, the door clicking shut behind him. It wasn't a slam, but it was definitely expressive of irritation.

Alexandra took a deep breath that was more like a shuddering sigh. She should be feeling so happy; indeed, a moment ago, she had been. It was an extraordinary solution, one she wanted more than anything in the world, but she could not bring herself to abandon something over which she had sweated so much blood, so many tears, so many terrifying moments. Even if she could give up her own portion, she could not leave Sylvia destitute. Even if Perry swore to support her sister, she knew that Sylvia's pride would resist such an offer as strongly as her own. Maybe she could compromise. Tell Peregrine that she would continue her charade only until she had enough for her sister and Matty to live in comfort for as long as needed.

She washed and dressed in the pink silk gown, thinking of how to convince him.

Breakfast was laid out in the parlor, but she saw no one as she made her way downstairs. The fire burned brightly in the parlor, and enticing aromas arose from the covered dishes. Peregrine was lifting the lids of the dishes and glanced over his shoulder as she came in. "What may I serve you, ma'am? Eggs, bacon, mushrooms, kidneys . . . ?"

"Just an egg, please." She poured coffee and sat down at the table. "Thank you." She offered a tentative smile as he placed a plate in front of her.

He nodded briefly before heaping a plate with mushrooms, kidneys, and bacon for himself. He reached for the ale jug and poured himself a tankard, buttered a hunk of wheaten bread, and began to eat.

"I own I'm surprised that my mother is still married to the Count," Alex observed, trying to lighten the mood.

"She is still using his name and title, so one must assume that she is."

Alex's laugh was cynical. "It probably means that she has not yet found a good enough substitute."

"You really do loathe her, don't you?" Peregrine regarded her across the table with a slight frown, wondering if this extreme depth of feeling was what lay beneath her powerful need for justice.

"She is responsible for ensuring that her daughters are destitute," she said fiercely, her gray eyes burning now with the years of accumulated anger and bitterness. "And she didn't give a damn. What am I supposed to like about that?"

"Nothing, of course," he said, his voice mild. "My own mother was a recluse and had nothing to do with us as children, so I understand how you feel, to a certain extent."

"Oh?" She sat forward in her chair. "Tell me about it."

Perry shrugged. "Our father died when Jasper was about eleven, so he became the fifth Earl while he was still at school. Seb and I were six or thereabouts. Our mother became an invalid; she shut herself up in a wing of the house and never saw us. I don't think she even asked after us. We were cared for by a succession of nursery maids, our affairs controlled by trustees. We were sent away to school a year later, where, thank God, we had Jasper to look after us."

He smiled, remembering. "Jasper stood up for us, protected us from the worst of the bullying, fought our battles while teaching us to fight them ourselves. Eventually, of course, we were able to stand on our own feet. But in essence, we were orphans throughout our childhood."

"But you had your elder brother," she said softly.

"Yes. And you only had yourself, and your sister

was your responsibility. I understand that, Alexandra."

"She still is." She looked at him with a plea in her gray eyes. "I must complete that responsibility, Peregrine. Please understand that. I promise I will no longer fight for justice for myself, but I must ensure that Sylvia is taken care of whatever might happen to me."

Peregrine sighed. "And you won't allow me to assume responsibility for you both?"

"No." It was a flat negative, and he understood that he had reached point non plus.

"Well, for the moment, we'll leave it there," he temporized. He had no intention of accepting her condition, but nothing would be gained by butting heads with her now. He sipped his ale, then said, "Since you have, in principle, anyway, agreed to marry me, would you be willing to do me a favor this morning?"

"Of course," she said swiftly. "Whatever you would like." She could deny him nothing when he was willing to accept her own need.

He smiled, crumbling a piece of bread between his fingers. "I would like you to accompany me on a visit to my Uncle Bradley."

"Your uncle?" Alexandra looked horrified, remembering what he'd said about the man. "*Why?*"

"Well, I have to present him with my entirely unsuitable choice for a bride. And the sooner 'tis done, the better for everyone."

"But we will not marry yet," she pointed out.

"I would like to establish the fact and your credentials with my uncle," he said patiently. "It will be a weight off everyone's mind. But if the idea alarms you—"

"No," she interrupted. "I mean, it's a little scary after what you've told me about him, but since 'tis part of the plan, then, of course, I will do whatever you wish."

He nodded, and there was a gleam in his eye. "In fact, you might find the idea rather appealing, since it involves another part for you to play. And you are a consummate actress, my sweet."

Alex looked for a sting in the words but felt none. He seemed to be genuinely amused by his idea. "Go on," she prompted.

"For the visit to my uncle, I would have you don those breeches you wore in Lymington—a guise, my dear, that is most enticing. We shall see how it plays with the old man."

Alexandra pondered this for a moment and then nodded with a little chuckle. She would find it much easier to deal with the fearsome uncle if she was acting. It was just another part, tailored to suit a particular situation. And she was adept at such playacting. "You'll have to direct me how to play it."

Peregrine smiled. "I will do that on the way. But first, you must fetch your costume. I'll send Bart to summon a hackney. Tell him to wait at Berkeley Square for you, and he can bring you back here to change."

❦

Billings greeted her return to the house with a characteristic sniff. "Letters come for you." He gestured to the hall table, where two sealed letters lay on a tarnished silver salver.

"Thank you." She snatched them up and hurried up to her bedchamber, reading the letters as she went. Andrew Langham, on behalf of Lord Dewforth, would do himself the honor of visiting her at three of the clock that afternoon. And Mr. Murdock would do himself the same honor, one hour later. She would have to come straight back here after the visit to Lord Bradley.

She bundled up her male costume, thrust it into a small cloak bag, and hurried back to the waiting hackney.

Chapter Seventeen

Back in Stratton Street, Alexandra dressed in the breeches and jacket. She twisted her hair into a knot on top of her head and crammed the cap over it, pulling the brim low.

"How do I look?"

"Delicious," Peregrine said. He'd been watching the transformation with a lascivious gleam in his eye. "Let's go before I yield to temptation and ravish you on the spot."

She laughed delightedly, loving the lustful light in her eyes. It made her feel both desirable and powerful, two sensations that hitherto were unfamiliar to Mistress Alexandra Hathaway. She followed him downstairs and out to the waiting hackney. The jarvey's eyebrows disappeared into his scalp when he saw his two passengers emerging from the house. The well-dressed young lady he'd taken to Berkeley Square appeared to have undergone some considerable transformation. He shrugged. It was none of his business, and the pair was providing him with a lucrative morning's work.

Peregrine gave him the address and jumped into the carriage behind Alexandra. "The secret to handling Viscount Bradley is to show no sign of discomposure," he began as soon as the vehicle began to move. "He will do everything he can to discompose you, and if he senses the tiniest crack in your armor, he'll pry it loose until 'tis a gaping hole."

"An unpleasant image," Alex murmured with a shiver of distaste.

"He's a thoroughly unpleasant person. He'll probably have in attendance a truly pathetic victim of his malice, Father Cosgrove. He's my uncle's personal priest and father confessor." Perry gave a short, sardonic laugh. "Bradley is forcing the poor man to act as his amanuensis as he writes his memoirs. Disgusting, lascivious, and perverted they are, too. He may oblige you to read some portion. If he does, you should do so without objection, but whatever you do, do not show him that they affect you in any way at all. Treat them as the disgusting fantasies of a perverted mind, beneath contempt."

"And this man holds you and your brothers in the hollow of his hand?" she asked in wonder.

Peregrine's mouth thinned, and his eyes took on a glacial cast. "Thanks to our father's profligacy, he does. Blackwater won't see the estates destroyed and the family honor with them. Bradley holds the winning card, so we must play to it." He regarded her through slightly narrowed eyes. "Does that make any sense to you?"

"You could say 'tis similar to what I am doing myself," she returned. "Stephen holds the winning card, and I am playing to it to win freedom and justice for my sister and myself."

He hadn't considered Alexandra's situation in that light before. "With one difference," he pointed out drily. "My brothers and I are not engaged in any criminal activity."

Alex flushed angrily. "That is not just. I am merely claiming what's mine and my sister's. Some quirk of the law took it away from us, and I am getting it back."

"And by doing so, you are breaking that very law," he said, wishing he had not started on this track again but unable to stop once he'd started. "It may be an unjust law, but it *is* the law of the land. Attempting to break it makes you a criminal, Alexandra. And I ask you again, give it up now, before anything bad happens. You need never return to Combe Abbey. Leave the books in Berkeley Square, take up your real identity, and show yourself to the world as my wife. I swear to you on my family's honor, Sylvia will be provided for until her dying day."

Her mouth was set in the stubborn line he recognized and dreaded. "Until your uncle dies, and until you can be sure that his will is a true one, you cannot make such a promise. Oh, I might be willing to cast my own fortunes in with yours but not my sister's. I will see her independently established, and there's no point at all in your continuing to flog a very dead horse."

Perry sighed and closed his eyes in frustration. He knew he should have kept his thoughts to himself, at least until they had no other distractions. He had no intention of giving up, but now was not the moment for forceful persuasion. "Very well. The horse is dead." He leaned to look out through the window aperture and said in a very different tone, "We are nearly there. How do you feel?"

"Curious, actually." Alex accepted the change of tone and subject with some relief. "But I do have it right, I am not really pretending to be a boy, am I?"

"No. Just follow my lead. And if he wants me to leave you alone with him, just trust your instincts. I begin to think they are probably infallible when it comes to acting a part." The carriage came to a stop as he spoke.

Alex stepped out onto the wide thoroughfare of the Strand. They were in front of a large double-fronted mansion, its windows for the most part shuttered. "It looks uninhabited."

"It is, almost. My uncle, his valet Louis, Father Cosgrove, and a handful of servants are the only occupants. Bradley does not entertain; indeed, he keeps to his own chamber almost exclusively." He raised the brass knocker and let it crash back against the brass plate with a resounding clang.

The door was opened eventually by a liveried gentleman in a powdered wig. He bowed. "Good afternoon, Master Peregrine, sir." His gaze flicked over Perry's companion but did not linger and showed no surprise.

"Is my uncle receiving, Louis?"

"He is alone at present. I will ascertain, sir. If you and the . . . um . . . young gentleman would care to step up to the antechamber . . ."

"Thank you." Peregrine stepped into the hall, Alexandra on his heels.

It was a huge, gloomy, pillared expanse of marble and gilt, and Alex looked around with unabashed curiosity. She followed the servant's measured progress up a wide, curving staircase to a square landing. Louis opened a set of double doors and progressed across another gloomy expanse, crowded with furniture and objets d'art, to open another set of doors at the far side. He stepped beyond them and turned to close them gently behind him.

"What an extraordinary place." Alexandra looked around the chamber. Every surface was covered in objects, strange foreign pieces for the most part. She began to examine them more closely and then looked in astonishment at Peregrine, who was watching her with a mischievous grin.

"Amazing, aren't they?"

"'Tis hard to believe this is even possible." She bent for a closer examination of a copper urn. The pedestal was carved with an intricate series of perfectly rendered figures all engaged in some form of sexual congress. "How could they contort their bodies like that?"

"According to the viscount, the Indians and the

Japanese are renowned for their imagination when it comes to varying the customary positions," he informed her with an assumption of gravity. He went over to a glass-enclosed bookcase and turned the tiny gold key in the lock. "Come and see this. My uncle is convinced that there isn't another copy in the known world."

Alexandra came over to look as he reverently removed a folio of pages bound in calf's skin. He laid it on the table and opened it up. "What language is it in?" She peered at it.

"Sanskrit, according to my uncle. He maintains 'tis a manual on the art of sexual activity. I gather he stole it from some temple. I don't understand the language, but some of the illustrations speak for themselves."

Alexandra gazed in awed fascination, turning the pages delicately. "'Tis beautiful but a little shocking."

"Not really, compared with the obscenities on offer in the kiosks in the Piazza," Perry replied. "They have no redeeming features at all. This is, as you say, utterly exquisite."

"Does it have a name?"

He frowned, trying to remember. "Something like the *Kama* . . . *Kama Sutra,* that's it. But 'tis one of a kind, if my uncle is to be believed." He turned as the doors opened and Louis slipped soundlessly into the antechamber. "Will my uncle receive us, Louis?"

"For a few minutes, sir. He wished to know the name of your companion."

"Mistress Player."

Louis bowed and went back into the room. A minute later, he came out and held open the doors. "His lordship will receive you now, Master Peregrine."

Peregrine went a little ahead of Alexandra, wanting to shield her from the initial blast of his uncle's attention. Viscount Bradley sat beside a blazing fire, wrapped in fur rugs despite the stuffiness of the overheated chamber. The velvet curtains were drawn tight at the windows, blocking any possibility of a draft, and the room was lit by numerous candles, whose wavering flames sent strange shapes across the paneled walls.

Alexandra's first thought was that she had walked into some elaborate stage set prepared for a sacrilegious ritual of some kind. The images in the antechamber were probably responsible for the fancy, she thought as she gazed around with unabashed curiosity. Only as she looked more closely did she see the black-robed figure hunched over a writing table in the far corner of the room, as far from the fire as it was possible to get.

"So, come to see how the dying's going, have you, boy?" the old man rasped from the depths of his rugs. His hands, long and surprisingly elegant, rested on the fur across his knees. A massive ruby carbuncle shot bloodred light from the fire's fierce blaze.

"Merely a courtesy call, sir," Perry said easily. "May I introduce my companion, Mistress Player?" He turned and gestured towards Alexandra, who instantly focused her attention on the old man and stepped up beside Peregrine.

She bowed with admirable aplomb. "Your lordship, thank you for receiving me."

His eyes were sharp, belying the general appearance of extreme old age, and their gaze grew even brighter as he took in her appearance. "Well, well, well. You Black-waters never cease to amaze me. You have a fancy for laddish play, then, nephew?" He gave a crack of laughter and was instantly convulsed with a fit of coughing. Peregrine moved to his side at the same moment the black-robed priest appeared with a goblet of brandy.

"Give it here." The old man seized the goblet from the priest and drank it down. The coughing subsided, and he leaned his head against the brocaded back of his deep chair and took a labored and stertorous breath. After a moment, Peregrine left his side and came back to Alexandra.

"So, is it true, boy? Ye've a fancy for arse play?" the old man asked with a lascivious chuckle. "Come here, girl, let me look at you."

Alexandra came forward and stood in front of his chair, unmoving, meeting the challenge in the sharp eyes. "Turn around, let's see what you've got." He made an imperative twirling movement with his finger, and she turned slowly, her eyes meeting Peregrine's. He nodded imperceptibly and winked.

"Well, nice enough, I suppose. A bit skinny, though," was the viscount's eventual judgment. "What nunnery are you from, girl? The only one I remember who specialized in such arts was old Abbess Liza on Suffolk Street."

"No nunnery, my lord," she responded with perfect composure. "I am my own mistress."

"Are you, now?" He swung his lorgnette on its velvet ribbon, regarding her with renewed interest. "Free enterprise, eh?"

"If you would call it so, my lord."

"And where do you conduct your operations? Not, I'll hazard, from behind a pillar in the colonnade." He raised his lorgnette to examine her more closely.

"Indeed not, sir. I choose my clientele with some care. I have rather high standards." She heard Peregrine beside her draw a swift breath and controlled an inconvenient bubble of laughter. For some reason, she was enjoying herself.

The viscount chuckled, a deep, volcanic rumble from within the swathing rugs. "Of what family are you, girl? You're too well spoken to be ill-bred."

"I have no family, my lord. I fend for myself."

"Nonsense. Everyone has a family. Who was your father?"

Alex smiled. "I have none, my lord. I have no family name. I am a bastard."

"Mmm . . . is that so?" He clicked his fingers over his shoulder. "More brandy, you black crow."

The priest came forward with the decanter and silently filled the viscount's goblet, before retreating to his corner. Bradley took a deep draught and leaned back, regarding his nephew's companion with a skeptical frown. "So, Mistress Player is a bastard who plies an independent trade. How have you kept yourself free of the abbesses' clutches? Those ladies do not tolerate independent trade on their doorsteps."

"My trade does not interfere with theirs, my lord. I make certain of it."

Peregrine decided that it was time to step in. "I think that is sufficient catechism, Uncle Bradley, do you not?"

"Well, that rather depends on Mistress Player," the viscount said. "That is the name you have chosen, girl, or one that was given to you?"

"'Tis my stage name, my lord," Alex responded with a cool smile. "Since I have no right to a family name, I choose my own according to the circumstances in which I find myself."

She was surpassing herself, Peregrine thought. He hadn't expected ever to be surprised by Alexandra again, but he had been wrong.

Bradley gave a sharp crack of amusement. "Tell me about these other circumstances."

Alexandra shrugged. "Why, my lord, in order to maintain my independence, I find myself in many situations where I must assume a part. I have many to choose from, and I choose whichever is most appropriate to the circumstances at hand."

"A mountebank, no less," he stated with satisfaction.

"A roving player, a counterfeit." He chuckled richly. "And light-fingered to boot, I'll lay odds." He took another swallow of brandy. "Best watch your purse, nephew, when you've enjoyed yourself."

"'Tis possible, my lord, that you mistake me," Alexandra said with a small bow. "But then again, 'tis possible that you are perfectly correct in your assumption."

His eyes were suddenly hooded. He looked at Peregrine and then back to Alexandra. "Go away," he said peevishly, waving a hand at them. "I'm tired of this banter. Take your whore, boy, and leave me."

Peregrine bowed. "As you wish, sir. Forgive the intrusion, but I wished to present my affianced bride for your approval."

"Did you, now?" the old man muttered. "Did you, indeed?"

Peregrine gestured to Alexandra. She bowed to the viscount. "Thank you for receiving me, my lord."

"Don't thank me," he rasped. "Just take that pretty little arse out of here. 'Tis a temptation in which I can no longer indulge, and I don't care to be reminded of it."

Alex heard herself say, "Should you ever change your mind, my lord, I'd be very happy to oblige you."

In the next breath, Peregrine had whisked her from the chamber. "What the devil, Alexandra?" He passed a distracted hand over his brow. "That was a step too far."

"I don't see why," she protested. "I was playing a

part, and it seemed the right line." The door from the landing opened as Peregrine was still deciding whether to laugh or not.

"Perry, have you been paying a visit to the Gorgon's den?" Jasper came into the antechamber. He was in riding dress and tossed his high-crowned beaver hat onto a side table together with his whip. He took in Alexandra's presence with a raised eyebrow and a smile, before he bowed.

"Your most obedient, ma'am."

Despite the different coloring, Alex knew instantly that she was in the presence of Peregrine's oldest brother. She bowed. "Your powers of observation are acute, my lord. I would curtsy, but in my present guise . . ." She passed an expressive hand down her body.

"Quite so," Jasper agreed. "An introduction, Peregrine?"

"I beg your pardon." Perry took Alexandra's hand. "Mistress Alexandra Douglas . . . the Earl of Blackwater."

It was a curious shock to be introduced once again by her real name, particularly dressed as she was. Alexandra proffered a faint smile. Another bow seemed superfluous.

"So, how was the old man?" Jasper indicated the doors to the viscount's chamber with a jerk of his head.

"Not much different," Peregrine said. "But Alexandra met him thrust for thrust."

"I congratulate you, ma'am." Jasper smiled at Alexandra. "Meeting Viscount Bradley is not for the faint-hearted."

"I suspect, my lord, that you and your brothers can only succeed in your enterprise with women who show no frailty in your uncle's company," she said.

"You are correct, Mistress Douglas. And Perry is indeed fortunate to have found his own Boadicea," Jasper said. "You must meet my wife. Clarissa will be delighted if you would come to dinner this evening. Can that be done?" He addressed the question to Alexandra rather than Peregrine, a fact she noted with a degree of pleasure.

"I have some business to transact this afternoon, my lord, but if Peregrine is free this evening, then I would be honored to accept your invitation."

"I am free," Perry said with a dry smile. "I am entirely at your disposal, Alexandra, once you have completed your business."

"Good. Then we shall see you in Upper Brook Street. Clarissa will be delighted. She detests Gluck . . ." He turned as the valet emerged from the bedchamber. "Is my uncle ready to receive me, Louis?"

"Yes, my lord."

Jasper bowed again to Alexandra, patted his brother's shoulder, and went into the bedchamber.

"What has Gluck got to do with it?" Alexandra asked. The last few minutes had vanished in a whirlwind, and she was still trying to grasp the details.

"Not sure," Perry said. "I gather the opera house is

putting on a performance of his *Don Juan*. Maybe Clarissa was expected to attend."

Alexandra decided that was answer enough. She looked anxiously at the tall clock as they went out onto the square landing. It was already past one-thirty. "I must get back to Berkeley Square, Perry. It takes at least half an hour to put on my other disguise."

She didn't miss the flash of distaste that crossed his face as he hardened his eyes.

"I'm sorry," she said softly, putting a hand on his arm. "But I must do this. I am playing your game; allow me to play my own, too."

For a moment, Peregrine stood at the head of the stairs, his nostrils flaring, his eyes closing with his frustration. Why couldn't she see that her own charade was now unnecessary? And yet he had to admit that it was Alexandra's skill at performing that was going to ensure the successful completion of his own obligation to his brothers.

"We'll be in Stratton Street in a quarter of an hour," he said. "You can change out of those breeches and be in Berkeley Square by two-thirty."

"Thank you," she responded. What else was there to say?

❧

In the quiet of her bedchamber in Berkeley Square, Alexandra assembled her disguise. She fastened the pad between her shoulder blades and was surprised to find how quickly her body resumed its hunch. After so many months of wearing the pad, it seemed that her body adapted instantly. She donned the dull gray gown and sat at the wavery mirror to paint her face. She decided against graying her hair. The lace cap would cover the rich chestnut, and there was no Peregrine to snatch it from her head.

The memory brought a tiny smile of reminiscence. At least, he wouldn't see her like this again. When she returned to Combe Abbey, he would not be there. She would complete her task, concentrating only on Sylvia's portion, and within a few months, she would be free and able to assume her own identity as the wife of the Honorable Peregrine Sullivan.

It was a prospect she hugged tightly to her as she made her way down to the breakfast parlor, trying to ignore the fact that her entire being now quailed at the prospect of returning to that existence. So much so that she was beginning to doubt her ability to assume that identity with the same utter conviction as before. And that struck terror into her heart.

She laid out the precious volumes on the table in the breakfast parlor, and the feel of the books, the simple business of ordering them, restored her to Mistress Hathaway's self. When the door knocker sounded precisely at three o'clock, she was ready to receive her first potential buyer.

Andrew Langham was a young man of serious mien. He was dressed in somber hues and wore his mouse-brown hair in a severe queue pinned at the nape of his neck. He bowed to the librarian, who rose to greet him when Billings showed him somewhat unceremoniously into the breakfast parlor.

"Mistress Hathaway. This is a pleasure."

"I trust you will find it so, Master Langham." She gave him her hand as she dropped a responding curtsy. "Let me show you what I have." She indicated the volumes laid out upon the table and took her place alongside them.

Master Langham took a magnifying glass from the inside pocket of his jacket and with a murmured "May I?" bent to examine the first book.

His air of reverence reassured Alexandra, who came closer. "You see the binding on this volume?" She ran a finger down the gilded spine. "I understand the engraving originated in a monastery in Perugia in the fourteenth century."

Master Langham lifted the book and held it to the light, examining the spine through his glass. "'Tis exquisite," he murmured. "I have never seen its like, ma'am."

"'Tis one of a kind, sir. Which I believe is true of every volume in the collection. Lord Dewforth will be purchasing a priceless library."

"But I daresay, ma'am, you have a price in mind," he observed drily, raising his head to look at her.

"That, sir, is a matter for the market," she responded

with a cool smile. "There are other interested buyers. I would be doing a disservice to my employer by taking a first offer."

"Mmm. Indeed," he muttered, returning to his examination of the remainder of the volumes.

When the door knocker sounded at four o'clock, she said, "Forgive me, Master Langham, but I have another interested purchaser." Smiling, she moved to the door to the library. "Perhaps you would let me know your decision at your earliest convenience."

He moved with her to the door. "May I ask who my rival might be?"

"I believe Mr. Murdock is interested, sir."

He grimaced a little but then said, "I suppose that was only to be expected. I will consult with Lord Dewforth immediately."

"I will wait to hear from you most eagerly, sir." She bobbed a curtsy in response to his bow and hid a smile of satisfaction. She was doing Stephen a great service, but at the same time, she was going to ensure that her father's precious library went to a worthy owner. She was going to keep just one volume for herself: the Chaucer, which her father had long ago promised to her. Yet another promise that he had forgotten to keep. She had it at the bottom of her portmanteau in her chamber abovestairs and had already decided to leave it with Peregrine for safekeeping when she returned to Combe Abbey. Stephen would never notice its absence, if indeed he had ever remarked its presence. She had no intention of selling it, but simply to possess it filled her with a sublime pleasure.

"A Mr. Murdock, ma'am," Billings intoned from the doorway.

Alexandra turned with a smile and an extended hand. "Welcome, sir."

Silence reigned in the library while the prospective purchaser examined the books. Finally, he straightened, letting his quizzing glass fall to his chest. "Your employer is Sir Stephen Douglas, is that so?"

"It is."

"Why the devil's he want to sell the library? Any man would be honored to own it. Sir Arthur would be spinning in his grave."

Alexandra concealed her expression by turning away for a moment. When she spoke, she said softly, "That's as may be, sir. But 'tis not relevant to the sale of his library. Sir Stephen has instructed me to sell it, and I am obeying instruction."

"Hmm." He stroked his chin, regarding her with a frown. "There was a Chaucer in the library, as I recall. Beautiful piece. 'Tis still there, I trust."

"No, sir. Sir Arthur left the Chaucer to his daughter on his death. But 'tis the only volume missing."

"Pity," he muttered. "It was the gem of the collection."

"There are many gems, sir."

He said nothing, continuing to stroke his chin,

frowning at the volumes on the table. "Well, ma'am, I will think about a bid, and I will let you know."

"Thank you, Mr. Murdock." She curtsied and moved to show him to the door. He left without a backwards glance, and Alex stood for a moment in the hall, wondering if she'd overplayed her hand. But then she shook her head, dispelling the notion. The library was her hand, and it was impossible to overplay it with hungry bibliophiles such as Lord Dewforth and Adam Murdock.

Chapter Eighteen

Peregrine was sitting beside the fire, staring morosely into the flames, a glass of claret in his hand. He couldn't imagine what Alexandra was doing at the moment. He knew her when she was playing the diffident Mistress Hathaway with her employers, and he knew her when she was flamboyantly displaying her talents as Mistress Player. He knew her as a passionate lover, eager to learn, and he knew her as a learned scholar, demon chess player, and outrageous manipulator.

Which of these roles was she playing that afternoon as she played one prospective buyer off against another? A mélange of several roles, he decided. But she would be in control. Of that he was confident. He was about to abandon his fireside and go in search of some outside stimulation when he heard a carriage draw up outside the house. Curious, he went to the window.

The carriage was a hired post chaise, and the postilion was letting down the footstep. Peregrine knew who its passengers were the instant before his twin stepped down to the street. Sebastian stood for a moment, straightening his coat, looking up at the house, before he turned and lifted a young woman with hair the color of jet down to the street beside him.

Peregrine felt a surge of delight. He and Sebastian had spent so little time apart over their lives that the last months of separation had been a sore trial. He hurried from the parlor and wrenched open the front door. "Seb, I'd almost despaired of hearing from you." He flung his arms around his twin, who hugged him in a close, wordless embrace. Only then did they break apart as Perry turned to greet his twin's companion, who was standing placidly to one side, watching the brothers' reunion with an understanding smile.

"Serena . . ." He bowed over her hand and then laughed and kissed her warmly. "Why didn't you warn me? We have nothing prepared."

"And we need nothing prepared, Perry," Serena reassured him. "As long as there's still a bedchamber and Bart to bring up hot water—"

"And as long as there's claret in the decanter, m'boy," Sebastian declared. He turned to direct the postilion and the coachman to untie their luggage from the chaise. "So, Perry, what have you been up to?"

"Oh, rather a lot," his twin said with a chuckle. "Come in out of the cold." He ushered his sister-in-law into the house with an arm around her shoulders. "I'm sure Mistress Croft could rustle up something."

"I only need to get out of my travel dirt," Serena said. "We've come from Dover this morning, and the crossing from Calais was brutal. I feel as if I have salt encrusted on my eyelids."

The housekeeper appeared in the hall as they came in from the street. "Why, Lord love us. Master Sebastian and Lady Serena. I wish you'd given a bit of warning, sir."

"We need very little, Mistress Croft," Serena said swiftly, shaking the housekeeper's hand. "'Tis so good to see you again. May I ask for some hot water and maybe a cup of your spiced wine? I've been dreaming of it since we left Calais." Her warm smile brought a beam to the housekeeper's countenance.

"Aye, that you can, my lady. I'll have it up to you in a trice. You go on into the parlor, Master Sebastian. I daresay Master Peregrine will take care of you."

"Ah, me, relegated to the tender mercies of my brother," Sebastian said with a mock sigh. "While my darling bride has the undivided attention of the admirable Mistress Croft." He blew Serena a kiss as she hurried up the narrow staircase, laughing over her shoulder at him.

The brothers went into the parlor. Peregrine filled a wine glass for his twin. "All is very well, I gather."

"Couldn't be better," Sebastian said, standing with his back to the fire. "And with you, Perry?" His gaze was sharp and knowing as it rested on his brother's countenance. "Something is afoot, I'll lay odds. I know that look in your eye, brother." He raised his glass in a toast.

"I can't deny it," Perry said placidly, raising his own glass in response. "But tell me, are you home for good now?"

"Yes, I think we've satisfied our wanderlust. Serena wishes to rent a house in town—"

"Whatever for?" his twin interrupted. "There's room to spare in this house, and why waste money when 'tis in such short supply?"

Sebastian shrugged. "If it were up to me, we would certainly make this our home, but Serena has some notion of being mistress of her own household. And besides, we don't wish to cramp your style."

Perry shook his head in swift demurral. "You won't be doing that." But even as he denied it, he wondered how Alexandra would feel after their marriage about sharing a house with her in-laws.

"Ah-ha," Sebastian said with a triumphant chuckle. "You've just thought better of that, haven't you?"

His twin grinned ruefully. "I have missed you, Seb."

"And I you," Sebastian said warmly. "But come, tell all."

"In a nutshell, I have found my unsuitable bride."

"Congratulations." Sebastian's smile was a little twisted. "I hate to say it, but 'tis a considerable relief, Perry."

"Oh, I know it," Peregrine said without rancor. "But it took me rather longer than you and Jasper to reach an epiphany."

"So, who is she? Or, rather, *what* is she?"

"A bastard, an embezzler, a fraud, an actor of some considerable skill, and an out-and-out bluestocking. To put it simply, Alexandra has a brilliant mind and happens to be a gross manipulator."

Sebastian whistled. "Well, that is a catalogue, indeed. She certainly sounds as if she fits Bradley's stipulation. What does Jasper say?"

"He's only met her briefly. We are bidden for dinner tonight. You and Serena will come, too, of course."

"Oh, wouldn't miss it for the world. And Serena will be happy to see Clarissa again. I was going to call at Blackwater House later this afternoon, but I'll send Bart with a note inviting us for dinner." He took another sip of wine, regarding his brother thoughtfully. "So, where is this paragon of unsuitability at the moment?"

"She's selling a library of rare books, intent on driving a hard bargain by setting two of the richest bibliophiles in the country at each other's throats."

"Intriguing. And where exactly is she doing this?"

"In Berkeley Square, her family's town house, to be precise."

Sebastian sat down, stretching his booted feet to the andirons. "All right, Perry. Let's hear the rest of it. You can't keep feeding me morsels; I feel like Tantalus."

"Hear the rest of what? Morsels of what?" Serena came into the room, speaking through a mouthful of hairpins, twisting the thick mass of black hair into a knot at her nape. "Or am I intruding?" She stuck the pins into the knot in a somewhat haphazard fashion.

"Not in the least," Perry said. "It will be easier to tell you both at once; then I won't have to repeat myself."

Serena took a seat with an air of expectation. "Could I have a glass of wine while I'm listening, please?"

Peregrine poured her a glass and brought it over for her. "If you're sitting comfortably, I will begin."

His audience listened to his tale, their faces registering amusement, astonishment, and finally a fair degree of awe. "She sounds like a remarkable woman," Serena said when he fell silent.

"Oh, she is," Perry agreed. "But she is also utterly exasperating and as stubborn as can be."

"That seems an inevitable quality, if you can call it such, with unsuitable brides." Sebastian chuckled, looking at his wife. "They get themselves into absurd situations and then refuse to be rescued. The knight in shining armor doesn't appear to figure in their romantic fantasies."

"If, indeed, we have such fantasies," Serena retorted. "I think we're all too pragmatic for such flights of fancy. We have too much to do to make the world work for us."

"Has she seen the viscount yet?" Seb asked.

"This morning. She dressed in breeches."

Sebastian gave a shout of laughter. "That was a happy thought. Right up the old man's alley. Did he salivate?"

"Oh, he licked his lips once or twice, but Alexandra gave him his own back. It was a pleasure to watch."

Sebastian nodded. "I can imagine. And when's the happy day?"

Perry sighed. "I have it in mind to go to Doctors' Commons in the morning and procure a marriage license. We could be married around the corner in the church on Bolton Street as soon as we wish, as I've lived in the parish for well over the necessary fifteen days. But I haven't as yet presented the case for a speedy wedding to Alexandra."

"Will she object?" Serena asked.

"Probably," Peregrine said honestly. "But I intend to override those objections."

"As we're all meeting her tonight for the first time, maybe Serena and Clarissa could work a little womanly magic," Sebastian suggested, glancing interrogatively at his wife.

"We'll see," Serena said firmly. "I know 'tis vital that the marriage take place quickly, but I'm not dragooning anyone into anything."

"The old man could slip his mortal coil at any moment," Sebastian pointed out.

"I understand that. But if Perry can't persuade her, then I doubt two complete strangers can do so." Serena set her lips in a way that Sebastian recognized. He shrugged and gave his twin a rueful shake of his head.

"No, Serena's quite right," Peregrine said. "I'll talk with Alexandra tonight." He glanced at the clock. "'Tis almost five-thirty. You should send your note to Clarissa, Seb. I told Alexandra I would fetch her at six o'clock, so I'll walk around to Berkeley Square now and bring her back here. We can all share a hackney to Upper Brook Street."

"In that case, I must dress for dinner." Serena followed Perry from the parlor. "Are you coming up, Seb? You're looking sadly travel-worn."

"On your heels. One must look one's best on such an occasion." Sebastian uncurled himself languidly from his chair and went upstairs on the heels of his wife. In their own bedchamber, across the hall from his twin's, he looked around, smiling at its familiarity. He and Perry had shared the house on Stratton Street for more than six years, since they had first dipped their toes into London's social scene, but it was time now to set up his own household, particularly in the light of Perry's news. The house was too small for two married couples, particularly when the wives in question were as strong-willed and independent as he guessed Alexandra was and knew Serena to be.

co∞o

Peregrine strolled to Berkeley Square and banged the tarnished knocker on the Douglas house. The door was eventually opened a few inches by the ancient retainer, who peered at the visitor through the crack.

"Is Mistress Hathaway at home?" Perry tried to keep the impatience from his voice.

"Reckon so. She's 'ad visitors all afternoon, bangin' at the door, givin' a man no peace." Billings remained holding the door half closed, still peering around it.

"Well, you may admit me," Peregrine said firmly, pushing the door wider and stepping swiftly past the old man into the dingy hall. "Inform Mistress Hathaway that I am waiting to escort her to dinner."

Billings sniffed and shuffled off into the back regions. A moment later, a young lad scampered across the hall and up the stairs. He came down within moments and scampered back towards the kitchen without so much as a glance at the visitor.

Perry tapped his cane against his boot. He had to assume that the boy had taken the message to Alexandra. He paced the hall, examining the various pictures on the wall. A few gloomy landscapes and several portraits of severe gentlemen, all of whom were members of the Douglas family. He stopped in front of one and looked closely. It was of Sir Arthur Douglas. He had the air of an unhappy man, preoccupied and disappointed. His curled white wig sat above a very broad forehead. His nose was Alexandra's, shapely and aquiline; his mouth was thinner, though, and his eyes were green instead of gray. But then Alexandra had her mother's eyes, as Peregrine had already noticed.

"My father," Alexandra's voice said softly from the stairs.

Peregrine turned from the portrait. "Yes, so I see. You have his nose." He smiled, as always delightfully surprised at the pleasure he found on seeing her after even a short absence. She was wrapped in a hooded cloak, and he couldn't see if she'd found yet more discarded treasures in the attic, but that was a pleasure to be anticipated.

"But little else," she responded, jumping off the last step. "Oh, except for his love of books."

"Was he also a superb chess player?"

"I learned at the knee of a master," she conceded, coming over to him. "Are we to go immediately to your brother's house?"

"Not immediately. We'll walk back to Stratton Street; 'tis but a step or two, and the evening is not overly chill. There are some people I would like you to meet."

"Oh?" Her eyes sparked with curiosity. "Who?"

"My twin brother and his wife. They arrived back from the Continent this afternoon."

"And you have told them about me." It was statement, not question. She had long since sensed the bond between Perry and his twin and knew he would not have kept his own circumstances a secret.

"Yes. I hope you don't mind." He opened the front door.

"No. How should I? In the circumstances, they have a right to know that when and if we wed, I will satisfy your uncle's stipulations." She moved past him into the street.

"What do you mean, *if*?" he demanded, closing the door behind him with a bang. "We are agreed, are we not?"

She paused, turning to look at him. "As long as you accept that I have to complete what I started."

"God help me," he said roughly, taking her arm. He began to walk swiftly in the direction of Stratton Street.

Alexandra found that she almost had to trot to keep up with his long stride and swift pace. "Oh, please, don't let's quarrel, Perry, *please* slow down."

He moderated his pace somewhat. "So you expect me to stand aside and watch while my wife continues her criminal career?"

"No, you'll be watching me as your betrothed," Alexandra pointed out. "We will still be connected, partnered, if you will."

"Sometimes I would like to shake you until your teeth rattle," he stated. "But let us not start this evening on a bad footing." He stopped on the corner of Berkeley Street and Stratton Street and turned her to face him. "In the morning, I intend to go to Doctors' Commons and procure a marriage license. We can be married in the church on Bolton Street. My brothers will stand as witnesses. Do you agree?"

"When the time comes," she said. "I understand the need for speed, and I will make all haste to complete provision for Sylvia's future, and then we may be married."

"There's no point having this discussion in the middle of the street," he stated.

Alexandra sighed and tried once more. "Don't you understand, Perry? I must do this alone, because otherwise, as my husband, you would be implicated."

"Do you think I don't know that?" he demanded harshly. "Once we are married, I am legally completely responsible for you, your debts, and all your actions."

"Exactly," she said with a calm that infuriated him.

"God help me," he muttered again as they turned onto Stratton Street. At the house, he unlocked the door and ushered her in.

He opened the door to the parlor. It was deserted, but the fire had been made up and the decanters on the sideboard replenished. "Let me take your cloak."

Alexandra tossed back the hood of her cloak. Her chestnut hair was braided in a double plait at her nape, confined with a tawny gold velvet ribbon. Peregrine reached around and unclasped the cloak at her throat, drawing it away from her. He couldn't help a smile of appreciation. "Who did these clothes belong to?"

She looked at him. "Can't you guess?"

He frowned for a moment, then gave a shout of laughter. "They were your mother's, weren't they?"

Alex nodded, laughing, relieved that the earlier tension had passed.

"A lady of considerable taste," he observed.

"Oh, she's certainly that," Alex conceded. "They don't even seem to be that outdated, do they?"

"Barely at all."

"Well, she was always in the forefront of fashion." She traced the neckline of the gown. "Of course, she's rather better endowed than I am, so the gowns are a little loose. But I don't think 'tis too noticeable."

"I hadn't noticed at all," he lied gallantly.

"Liar."

He laughed. "No, 'tis true. The whole impression is what counts; a minor imperfection here and there is not worth mentioning."

"Oh, so, 'tis an imperfection." Her eyes danced.

He threw up his hands in disclaimer. "Never say so. It is a most beautiful gown, and you are perfection, my dear."

She gave a complacent smile. "I thought that since we were dining with Lord and Lady Blackwater, I should be a little more formal than usual." She shook out the tawny velvet folds of the overgown that opened over an underskirt of bronze damask, spread over wide panniers. The décolletage was particularly low, her breasts rising in a creamy swell almost to the nipples, and the width of the skirts accentuated the smallness of her waist.

Before Perry could respond adequately, the door opened, and Sebastian came in. "Ah, Mistress Douglas. An honor." He swept her a formal bow, his eyes dancing, and she responded with an equally deep, perfectly judged curtsy.

"Mr. Sullivan."

"Oh, Sebastian, please," he said, dropping the formality instantly. "Or Seb. My friends call me the latter." He regarded her with an appreciative smile. "I must say 'tis hard to picture you in the guise of the dowdy spinster lady Mistress Hathaway."

"That is my most fervent hope, sir," she responded with a mischievous smile that instantly endeared her to Sebastian. She looked between the brothers. "If you were not standing side by side, I confess I would be hard pressed to tell you apart."

"Most people have that problem," Perry said, turning to the decanters on the sideboard. "Sherry, or claret, Alexandra?"

"Sherry, if you please."

"Seb?"

"Claret, thank you. Serena will be down in a moment."

On cue, Serena came into the parlor. "Forgive me for keeping you waiting." She advanced with a warm smile and an outstretched hand to Alexandra. "Mistress Douglas . . . or may I call you Alexandra?"

"I do hope you will . . . or just Alex, if you prefer." Alex clasped Serena's hand. "I am delighted to make your acquaintance, ma'am."

"Serena," Serena corrected. "I will have sherry, Perry, if I may, and Alex and I are going to get better acquainted on the sofa." She moved to a sofa on the far side of the parlor and sat down, arranging her lavender silk skirts around her so that she left sufficient room for Alexandra.

"I won't ask for all of your secrets immediately; you'll only have to repeat them for Clarissa later," Serena said comfortably. "But I am most intrigued about selling a library. Perry was telling us that was what you were doing this afternoon?"

"Yes, I was. Pitting two rivals against each other is surprisingly amusing," Alex said. "I left them to fight it out between them. Each is as acquisitive as the other, so I'm hoping I'll get a better than satisfactory price for what is, after all, a priceless collection." Her smile was a little wan suddenly. "'Tis hard to see it sold out of the family."

"I'm sure it must be," Serena said with swift sympathy.

"Tell us of your travels," Peregrine invited, deftly removing the attention from Alexandra. "Did you go to Paris?"

"Yes, and mightily tedious it was, too," Sebastian said. "No one is in Paris—"

"There are a few Parisians, Seb," Serena corrected with a sly smile.

"Don't be obtuse," her husband retorted. "What I meant was that the entire court is ensconced at Versailles. 'Tis like its own little country, tucked behind its borders."

"And so rigidly ruled, you wouldn't believe," Serena said. "There are times for eating, hunting, sitting, attending church, listening to music . . . and woe betide you if you do something out of turn."

"It sounds miserable," Alexandra said. "How long were you there?"

"Oh, Serena couldn't stand more than two days. We went on to Rome as soon as we decently could take our congé of the Vicomte de Lasalles."

"He was one of our father's relatives, wasn't he?" Peregrine asked. "I seem to remember Jasper mentioning him."

"Some cousin by marriage," his twin agreed. "Jasper said it would cause grave offense if we didn't make ourselves known to him while we were in Paris. Of course, we didn't realize that that meant imprisonment in Versailles."

The long case clock in the hall chimed seven. "Speaking of Jasper, we should be on our way." Peregrine picked up Alexandra's cloak. He draped it around her shoulders and went to the door, calling for Bart. When the lad appeared, he sent him off to fetch a hackney.

Half an hour later, they descended to the street outside Blackwater House on Upper Brook Street. Alexandra was conscious of a flutter of nervousness as they went past the butler into the house. She was now well and truly in the midst of Perry's family. Could she fit in, become a part of this clearly close-knit group? And she found that she yearned to belong somewhere, *to* someone. Apart from Sylvia, she had never felt she had any real emotional connections with anyone. Even her father had been only a distant mentor rather than a close and loving part of her life.

"Serena . . . Seb . . . how wonderful that you're back." A titian-haired woman flew into the hall in a whirl of emerald skirts just as the butler closed the front door. "You look wonderful. Did you have a splendid time?" And then, without waiting for an answer, she spun towards Alexandra, her hand outstretched in welcome. "Mistress Douglas, I bid you welcome."

"Lady Blackwater." Alexandra curtsied as Clarissa took her hand in both of her own, her clasp warm and reassuring.

"Oh, we don't stand on ceremony in the family, Alexandra. You must call me Clarissa."

Alexandra smiled her acknowledgment of the invitation and turned to make her curtsy to the earl, who had followed his wife into the hall. "My lord."

"I don't stand on ceremony, either, Alexandra," Jasper said. "Welcome. Now, come to the fire, all of you. 'Tis drafty standing around here, and in honor of the occasion, we are broaching a couple of our few remaining bottles of pink champagne."

He ushered them all into the library, and Alexandra without volition walked instantly to the shelves, her knowing eye sweeping along the titles. "Do you see any treasures?" Perry inquired with a chuckle in his voice.

She flushed and spun back to the room. "Oh, I do beg your pardon. 'Tis a habit so ingrained I don't realize I'm doing it."

"Well, you must tell me if there's anything in there that's saleable," Jasper said cheerfully. "The family coffers are in sore need of an injection, and I doubt that any of us will miss a volume or two." He eased the cork out of a bottle of champagne. It emerged with a discreet, carefully controlled pop.

"I would be more than happy to look for you," Alexandra said. "If you would really like me to."

Jasper handed her a glass of the pale, faintly pink-tinged bubbles. "If you wouldn't think me a hopeless Philistine, Alexandra, I should be most grateful."

She smiled at him over her glass. "As Perry will tell you, sir, I am quite knowledgeable, and I'm sure I could direct you to a suitable buyer. I'm sure there must be some treasures on these shelves."

"Well, I, for one, would prefer it if you did not work this evening," Peregrine declared. "You may return in the morning and comb through the shelves then."

"An unforgivable host, forgive me, Alexandra." Jasper bowed with a penitent smile. "But do return when you can spare the time."

"I am at your disposal, sir." Alex began to feel comfortable. And the feeling only progressed as the evening went on. Perry's brothers and their wives were so easy together, such pleasant companions, amusing but also serious when the subject warranted it, that she began insensibly to slide into their shared familiarity.

"So, when is the wedding to take place?" Jasper asked as they rose from the dining table and returned to the library.

There was a short, awkward silence, then Perry said, "We are still discussing the date. But it will be in the church on Bolton Street. You'll be there, of course?"

"Of course," his elder brother responded. "It will be, as always, a family affair." He raised his port glass in a toast to Alexandra. "We will all be there to welcome Alexandra into our ramshackle family."

"I hope she knows what she's getting into," Sebastian said with a laugh. "But no doubt, Clarissa and Serena will give you all the gory details."

Alexandra felt as if she was being swept along on a tide of inevitability. She said hastily, "We shall be wed as soon as I return from Dorset. I expect to hear from the potential buyers by tomorrow evening, and once I have settled the purchase, I will complete my business at the Abbey and return as quickly as possible."

Peregrine's expression darkened, and he drummed his fingers on the arm of his chair. Jasper broke the awkward silence. "Well, that's between you and Perry, of course. But nothing need prevent us from preparing for a wedding and a wedding breakfast. Clarissa and I will host the celebration." He shot an interrogative glance at his wife, who nodded.

Alex said little for the remainder of the evening, and the party broke up soon after. As Perry was handing her into the hackney, she said sotto voce, "I will return to Berkeley Square tonight. I would give your brother and Serena some privacy. And tomorrow I must complete the business of selling the library. The negotiations will take all day, I imagine."

Peregrine's mouth tightened, and then he said, "As you wish." He called up to the jarvey. "Berkeley Square first."

Outside the house, he stepped down, waiting for Alexandra to make her farewells to Sebastian and Serena. Then he held up his hand to assist her to the street. He held her hand tightly. "I will respect your wishes. And I will leave you alone tomorrow to complete your business here. We will talk about this further the day after tomorrow. I will come after breakfast, and we will go riding to Richmond, where we may talk undisturbed."

"I will look for you then," she said in a low voice.

He raised her hand to his lips and then, without further word or salutation, climbed back into the hackney.

For the first time since she'd arrived in Berkeley Square, Alexandra made her way around the house to the side door. She reached up to the lintel, and her fingers located the key. It fit a little stiffly, but the door eventually swung open, and she stepped into the dark passage. Her reflection that the caretakers might have left a sconced candle burning to light her way was quickly amended. After all, she hadn't needed one before. Why should they assume that she would return to her own bed tonight?

She groped her way down the corridor and into the hall. It was almost as dark as the narrow passage, but she managed to feel her way to the stairs and thus to her chamber. The fire was a mere ashy glow, but there was enough heat to light a taper and from that a candle. She riddled the ashes and threw on some more wood, then unlaced her gown, ridding herself of the stiff petticoats and panniers.

She climbed into bed at last, lying against the pillows, watching the firelight on the ceiling, and wishing that she hadn't parted company with Perry in such an unfriendly fashion. She could imagine how frustrating it was for him, but if she was to be in any way true to herself, she had to complete what she'd started. And that meant she had to leave him before he found a way to prevent her.

Chapter Nineteen

Alexandra awoke the following morning with a feeling that something was not right. It didn't take her many minutes to realize what it was. She was lying alone in a strange bed, or at least it felt strange after the last few nights when she had awoken curled against Peregrine in the deep feather-bedded warmth of Stratton Street. She got out of bed, shivering. The fire was almost out, and a brisk wind was rattling the badly fitting windowpane.

She threw more kindling onto the embers in the grate and crouched in front of it until the first flames flickered into life, then she wrapped herself in a dressing robe, pushed her feet into a pair of slippers, and left her bedchamber. It was reasonable to assume that the caretakers didn't know she had slept in her own bed, and they were not sufficiently attentive to come and check. She made her way down the backstairs into the kitchen, where the lit range provided welcome warmth.

Mistress Dougherty was frying eggs and looked

startled as the door opened. "Eh, Mistress Hathaway. Didn't know you was 'ere."

"I came in last night." Alexandra sniffed hungrily as she warmed her hands at the range. "I would like some breakfast."

The housekeeper looked a little doubtful. "I'll see what's in the pantry."

"No, I'll look," Alex said hastily. "Don't stop what you're doing." She went to the pantry and rummaged among the mostly bare shelves. She found two eggs in a bowl at the back of a shelf, half a loaf of bread, and a crock of butter and brought them out to the kitchen table. "I'll fry these myself. Don't let me disturb you, Mistress Dougherty."

The housekeeper was sliding her own eggs onto two plates at the table and merely nodded, seating herself as Billings came in from the backyard privy, adjusting his belt. He glanced at Alexandra with surprise. "Didn't expect to see you this mornin'."

"Then I expect it's a pleasant surprise," she returned. "Would you please light a fire in the breakfast parlor for later?" She added butter to the skillet and turned her attention to the range. She set a pan of milk on the heat to warm for her chocolate, fried her eggs quickly, buttered a thick slice of bread, and took her breakfast away with her up to her chamber, where at least the fire would be blazing by now.

There was nothing she could do until she heard from the prospective buyers, which left her with the whole day to herself. And whose fault was that? she asked herself ruefully. She had told Peregrine that she wished to be alone, and he was abiding by her wishes. Ordinarily, the prospect of an entire day to herself would have pleased her, but now it seemed a rather bleak prospect, as much as anything because she knew he was angry with what he saw as her intransigence. To make the prospect even bleaker, rain was now beating against her bedchamber window, and she imagined how it would be in Stratton Street for Perry and his brother and Serena. They would probably be breakfasting together and making plans for the day. While she spent the time in lonely discomfort in this cold and unwelcoming house, with only memories for company.

And then she remembered Jasper's invitation, almost a request, that she examine the contents of the library on Upper Brook Street. Was there any reason she shouldn't do that today? With a renewed surge of energy, Alex wrote a note to Clarissa asking if it would be convenient for her to look at the library that morning. The invitation had come from Jasper, but etiquette demanded that she communicate with his wife. She went in search of Archie, sending him off to Upper Brook Street with instructions to await an answer, then returned to her bedchamber to dress before going down to the breakfast parlor.

Archie came back half an hour later with a note. "Butler give me this, ma'am. Said it was from 'er ladyship."

"Thank you." Clarissa took the note and slit the wafer. Clarissa had written briefly but warmly.

My dear Alex,

Come, by all means. Jasper is engaged with a riding party this morning, so the library will be entirely at your disposal. You would be doing us a big favor if you can find anything of value. I will be waiting for you.

C.

Alexandra threw her cloak around her shoulders and went out into what was now a persistent drizzle in search of a chair. She alighted at Upper Brook Street, and as soon as the butler admitted her, Clarissa came running down the stairs.

"Oh, there you are. How nice. I was anticipating a very dull morning," she said, kissing Alexandra on the cheek. "'Tis such a miserable day, and you're all wet. Come into the library. Could you dry Mistress Douglas's cloak and bring coffee?" she asked the butler with a smile.

"At once, my lady." The butler bowed before disappearing in stately fashion into the back regions with the visitor's dripping cloak. Clarissa ushered Alexandra into the library.

"There," she said with an arm flung wide towards the shelves. "See what you can unearth, my dear. I doubt some of them on the top shelves have been dusted in a decade."

Alexandra laughed. "I'm accustomed to a little dust, and sometimes 'tis best if they're valuable that they not be disturbed by rough hands."

Clarissa smiled and sat down by the fire, taking up her sewing. "I shall sit and sew while you explore, and we can chat if you feel like it."

"What are you sewing?" Alexandra moved a set of library steps up to the first bookcase.

Clarissa flushed a little and held up the tiny garment she was embroidering.

"Oh, a baby!" Alexandra cried. "You are with child, Clarissa?"

The other woman nodded. "But 'tis still a secret. I am fairly certain, but I wish to wait a little longer before I tell Jasper."

"Oh, I can keep a secret," Alexandra declared. "None better, believe me."

"Oh, I do," Clarissa assured her with another smile. "But I'm guessing you will be glad when there is no longer a need for those secrets?"

"With all my heart." Alexandra stepped onto the ladder and reached up to the top shelf of books.

"If 'tis any comfort, my dear, both Serena and I had our secrets that we had to keep for others' sakes," Clarissa said, keeping her eyes on her sewing. "We both know how hard it is."

"I am comforted," Alex said sincerely. "And I thank you, Clarissa. The baby is wonderful news for you. I'm sure Lord Blackwater will be beside himself with joy."

"To be honest, I suspect he will become a mother hen and drive me to distraction," Clarissa said with a rueful chuckle. "He'll be asking me how I am, watching what I eat, constantly telling me to rest. I just know it."

"He doesn't strike me as the fussy kind . . . ah, what have we here?" Alex slid a slender volume off the shelf, opening it delicately with the tip of a finger.

Clarissa watched her, making no response to Alex's comment. Alex was suddenly gone from the room in all but her physical form as she stood on the ladder, lips pursed, gently turning the fragile pages, and Clarissa waited patiently for her to return in full to her surroundings.

The butler came in with a tray of coffee and little cakes, setting it down on a side table. "Will that be all, my lady?" He glanced curiously at the lady on the ladder as he spoke.

"Yes, thank you." Clarissa poured coffee into two shallow cups. She helped herself to one of the little cakes and sat back in her chair, nibbling it, watching Alexandra. After a moment, she ventured to say, "Have you found something of interest?"

Alex seemed to have to shake herself to awareness. She looked up, blinking as if startled to discover that she was not alone. "Yes . . . yes, I believe so. If this is what I believe it to be, then 'tis certainly a treasure. I would be loath to part with it if I were Lord Blackwater." She stepped off the ladder, carrying the book.

"What is it?" Clarissa was intrigued. It was impossible not to be touched by Alexandra's awe.

Alex sat down on the sofa beside her and laid the book carefully on her lap. "I think it may be Francesco Petrarch's *Canzoniere,* first published in Venice in the fourteenth century. There are very few copies left." She turned the fine vellum with a fingertip. "I should really be wearing gloves."

Clarissa looked at the vellum page lying open on Alexandra's lap. "I wish I read Italian."

"I would need to consult another bibliophile to be certain," Alex said.

"Whom would you ask?"

The two women jumped, turning as one to the door, where Lord Blackwater stood in riding breeches and damp boots. "It seems you have found something of value, Alexandra?" He came into the library, closing the door behind him.

"I think so," she said. "But I will consult with either Lord Dewforth or Mr. Murdock, depending on which of them wins the battle for my father's library." Her mouth took a wry twist. "I daresay, if I am correct and they corroborate my opinion, then you would have your buyer on the spot."

Jasper nodded and went to the decanters on the sideboard. Clarissa hastily put her sewing away, exchanging a conspiratorial smile with Alex. "You're back early from your riding, Jasper."

"Carlton's horse threw a shoe, and with this rain, we

called it a day before noon." He poured a glass of claret and came back to the fire, standing in front of it, warming his backside. "Should I be encouraged by this find that there will be others, Alexandra, enough to return this family to full solvency?"

She shook her head. "It would be extraordinary to find more than one such treasure, sir. As far as I can see, there is nothing like this on the lower shelves, but I will look at the other top shelves. 'Tis always possible. Was one of your ancestors a bibliophile, do you know?"

Jasper gave a short laugh. "No, reprobates, the lot of 'em, as far as I know. Of course, they were all prudish and prim as nuns on the surface, married stiff-necked women who spent more time on their knees in church than they did in their husbands' beds, and turned a blind eye to whatever their lords and masters were up to outside the family. But woe betide anyone who broke the rules publicly and threatened to bring the family name into disrepute."

Alexandra would have laughed, except that she realized his lordship was in deadly earnest, his voice full of angry disgust. "That's why your uncle wishes you to make these unusual marriages?"

"In a nutshell. His own early love was forbidden him, and unlike his brothers, ever afterwards he made no attempt to pretend that he was anything but a rakehell and a debaucher, as they all were underneath. 'Tis my opinion that this ridiculous will is designed to avenge himself. That and his filthy memoir," Jasper added with a grimace.

Alex nodded. "Perry said something of the kind but not quite so succinctly. I think I understand it better now."

" 'Tis good that you do," Jasper stated. "This is not a family to enter into with your eyes half shut."

"Jasper, there's no need to sound so bitter," Clarissa protested gently. "We and your brothers are our own family. Oh, 'tis necessary to pay court to the aunts and uncles on occasion, but 'tis not a very great trial, Alex. You mustn't be put off by Jasper's jaundiced view."

"No, indeed, you must not," Jasper agreed, shrugging off his momentary bitterness. "Clarissa is quite right. My brothers and I are creating our own branch of the family, with our own values." An almost gleeful smile lightened his expression. "In fact, much as I hate to admit it, we have much more kinship with Uncle Bradley than we do with any of the rest of 'em."

❧

It was early afternoon when Alex left Upper Brook Street with Jasper in his curricle. She carried with her the *Canzoniere* carefully wrapped in silk. It was the only treasure she had found on her search through the shelves, but its worth should fill a considerable hole in the Blackwater coffers. Jasper drew rein outside the house in Berkeley Square and turned to his passenger. "So, if we do not see you before, Alexandra, we will see you on your wedding morning. We look forward to it most eagerly."

Once again, she felt caught up in this tide of inevitability. They were all so anxious for her to play her part, so ready and willing to accept her into their close-knit circle, but *she* wasn't ready yet.

"As do I, my lord," she said, stepping down to the street. He handed his tiger the reins and jumped down beside her.

"I'm certain you understand the importance of this, my dear," he said as he banged the knocker. "There is a degree of urgency."

"I understand that, my lord." She curtsied briefly as Billings opened the door, and she stepped quickly into the hall, only breathing a sigh of relief when she heard it close behind her. "Any letters for me, Billings?" She drew off her gloves, aware that her hands were quivering a little.

"Aye, there's two of 'em." He gestured to the dingy salver on the table, where two wafer-sealed letters lay. "Thank you." She scooped up the letters. "I trust the fire's well lit in the parlor?"

"I'll send Archie in with a fresh scuttle of coals." He shuffled off to his own lair, and Alexandra went into the parlor.

The fire was low, but it wouldn't take long to bring it back to life. She kept her cloak on, however, as she examined her correspondence. Lord Dewforth's seal adorned one, Mr. Murdock's the other. She slit the wafer of the first. It was short and to the point and gave the price his lordship was prepared to pay for Sir Arthur Douglas's library.

Alex whistled soundlessly. It was even better than she had hoped. She slit the wafer of the second, and her eyes widened. Mr. Murdock's offer pipped Lord Dewforth's at the post. She sat down to write a letter of acceptance to Mr. Murdock and a polite rejection to his lordship, which she softened with the offer of the *Canzoniere*.

She sent the letters off with Archie and returned to the library, fighting back unexpected tears. The reality was now inescapable. The library had been a joyful part of her life ever since she could remember, and in the last months at Combe Abbey, she had realized what it must have meant to her father as she examined every detail of the collection. But it was over now.

In less than an hour, she received answers to both of her letters. Lord Dewforth's was curt but accepting that he had been outbid. However, he expressed a desire to see the *Canzoniere* if it could be delivered to his house. Mr. Murdock's was brisk and to the point. He would himself collect the library from Combe Abbey, but he required that Mistress Hathaway assure him that she would see to the crating personally. If, in addition, she had any knowledge of the missing Chaucer, he would be delighted to offer a separate price for it.

Alexandra wrote her replies. Halfway through her

letter to Murdock, she paused, holding her dripping quill over the inkwell. What should she say about the Chaucer? Could she just ignore his comment? But why not tell the truth? She resumed her letter, saying that as far as she was aware, Sir Arthur Douglas had left the Chaucer to his daughter. She knew nothing more. She told Lord Dewforth to send his secretary to collect the *Canzoniere* from Berkeley Square at his leisure and sent the always willing Archie off with the letters.

Only then did she sit back, close her eyes, and let the sense of accomplishment warm her. The collection would be in the hands of one who treasured it, valued it for what it was, not just its monetary worth. The volumes would no longer lie neglected and unvalued on the shelves in Stephen's library. All she had to do was return to Combe Abbey, see the collection crated and on its way, and then devote all of her time to making money. As much as she safely could in the shortest time available.

With a sudden burst of determination, she got up and went in search of Billings. She found him dozing in front of the kitchen range. He jerked awake when she laid a hand on his shoulder. "Eh . . . eh, wass' this, then?"

"I'm sorry to disturb you, Billings, but I need you to arrange a post chaise for me for dawn tomorrow. I am returning to Combe Abbey." It was better this way, she told herself, even though the voice of conscience told her that she was being cowardly. She owed Peregrine an explanation, and the thought of leaving him without a proper farewell tore at her, but she couldn't be certain that she would hold to her determination if he really put his mind to stopping her. And with the support of his brothers . . . no, she knew she could not prevail against the Blackwater brothers in force. A letter would have to do, however cowardly.

Billings muttered something under his breath, but he dragged himself out of the chair. "The Bell at Cheapside will 'ave one. Dawn tomorrow, you say?"

She nodded, and he stomped out of the back door into the drizzly late afternoon.

They'd be glad to see the back of her, Alex reflected, going up to her chamber to put together her meager possessions. She returned her mother's wardrobe to the trunks in the attic, smoothing each one into neat folds with a reminiscent smile. They had brought her so much pleasure. Then she went to her own chamber to pack up her own belongings. She couldn't bring herself to leave behind her own dress, the one Sylvia had packed for her. She would conceal it with her boy's disguise in the bottom of the portmanteau. As soon as she finally left Combe Abbey, her task completed, she would resume her own identity, in her own gown.

In Stratton Street that afternoon, Peregrine could settle to nothing. Every ounce of his being yearned to go to Alexandra; it was almost like being pulled apart in a tug of war. And he didn't know why he was depriving himself of the pleasure of her company. It was cutting off his nose to spite his face, he thought irritably as he got up from his chair for the second time in five minutes. Why couldn't he simply resign himself to the inevitable, let her get on with her mission, and look forward to starting their life together when she had satisfied herself that she had taken care of Sylvia's future? It wasn't as if he were in a position himself right now to guarantee that future. But he knew that he couldn't do that. Every moment she spent in Combe Abbey endangered her, and she didn't seem to understand the reality of that danger. Fraud was a capital offense; stealing as much as a penny loaf was a capital offense. He couldn't possibly stand aside while the woman he loved stubbornly persisted in putting herself in such an impossibly dangerous position.

"Why so glum, Perry?" Sebastian came into the sitting room, rain dripping from his hat. "'Tis foul out there. You're much better off in here by the fire."

"It doesn't feel like it," his twin said, flinging himself back into his chair. "I am so angry with her, Seb, and yet I can't bear to be away from her."

"There's no point in being angry, believe me." Sebastian stood in front of the fire, drying his damp boots. "For some reason, we Blackwaters are drawn to exasperatingly independent, stubborn women who won't see reason, let alone do as they're told." He shrugged with a light laugh. "Accept it, Perry. 'Tis our fate."

"I don't believe in fate," Peregrine muttered, but already his mood was lightening. "Oh, to hell with it, Seb. You're right. I love her. Sometimes it feels as if there was never a moment when I haven't loved her . . . even in that ghastly gown, with the humpback and the birthmark and the gray hair. How could that be?" He shook his head in amazement.

"No idea, since I've only ever seen her looking utterly delectable," Sebastian responded cheerfully. "Put it down to fate, if I were you. So, did you get the license?"

"Yes, I have it." He patted the inside pocket of his waistcoat. "I just have to get through the rest of today without rushing around to Berkeley Square. I just hope she's as miserable as I am," he added, and then joined his twin in laughter at the absurdity of such a declaration.

"Where's Serena?" Peregrine asked suddenly, once his amusement had died down.

"Oh, she's visiting an old friend, Mistress Margaret Standish, I believe she said. She lives on St. James's Place." Sebastian had visited the house once, when he and Serena had met again after three years of estrangement. He remembered the occasion all too well. It was at that meeting that he had realized that however angry and hurt he had been with Serena since her betrayal, he had never stopped loving her. And he had the first inkling then that it had been the same for her.

"I'm going to change into dry clothes," he added, going to the door. "Then I suggest you and I go to White's for a mutton chop and a bumper of porter." With a grin over his shoulder, he went out.

Chapter Twenty

The next morning, before sunrise, Mistress Alexandra Hathaway entered a post chaise outside the house in Berkeley Square and began the long journey back to Combe Abbey. The dreadful sense of being completely alone flooded her once more. It seemed like an eternity since she had felt like this, before Peregrine had come into her life—had taken over her life, it seemed sometimes. And the feeling was worse than ever now that she knew what it was like not to be alone. If only they could have parted company properly, with words and kisses and the promise of renewal.

She told herself that it was better this way; indeed, it was the only possible way for this to happen. She had to tear off the bandage in one sweep, otherwise everything would become muddled and tangled again. She would need the whole journey alone to assume once more the internal character of Mistress Hathaway. The physical characteristics were one thing, but once more, she had to subsume her self into the character of the self-effacing, timid little mouse of a librarian. Already, she was beginning to feel as if the manifest glories of the last few days had been no more than a chimera.

⁂

Peregrine ran lightly up the steps to the house on Berkeley Square, a smile of anticipation on his lips. He could feel the crisp presence of the marriage license in the inside pocket of his coat. The leaves in the square garden were turning, their rich autumn red, yellow, and copper aglow in the sunlight. The previous day's rain seemed to have washed away the summer's accumulation of dust and grime, and the city air smelled fresh for once.

He banged on the door with a vigor to match his mood and waited impatiently, tapping the railings with his silver-knobbed swordstick. The door opened, and Billings surveyed him with a jaundiced air.

"Yes?"

"Good morning," Peregrine said cheerfully, stepping adroitly past the retainer. "Will you tell Mistress Hathaway that I am come to call?"

The old man blinked at him. "She's not 'ere."

"Oh?" Perry looked surprised. It was still quite early in the morning. "I'll wait, then. Did she say when she would be back?"

Billings shook his head. "No, left in a chaise afore dawn this morning." He turned and shuffled to a dusty table in the corner of the hall. "Said I was to give you this."

Peregrine stared at him, feeling a cold certainty

lodge in his belly. *She has gone . . . left me.* Wordlessly, he held out his hand for the package the old man proffered. For a moment, he stood, holding it, looking around him. He could feel Alexandra's absence in the chill, neglected air of the house. He turned, still silent, and left the house, walking quickly back to Stratton Street.

Sebastian called out to him from the parlor as Perry entered the house. "You're out early, Perry. Have you breakfasted?"

Peregrine ignored his brother and ran upstairs to his own chamber. He closed the door and stood leaning his back against it as he slit the wafer on the package. There was a book and a letter. He turned the book over in his hands. It was the Chaucer, the one volume that Alexandra said meant more to her than any of the others in her father's library. Slowly, he opened the folded letter.

My dearest Perry,

Forgive me. I have to complete my mission before we can be together. I cannot risk any harm coming to you through my actions. I must do what has to be done, and when it is over, we can come together without hindrance. But I will understand if my actions now kill whatever love you have for me. I know it's cowardly to run away, but I don't trust myself when I am with you. You can be so very persuasive, my love. Please keep the Chaucer for me in the certainty that I will come back as soon as my work is done. If you will still have me.

    A.

He read the missive twice, noticing the smudges on some of the letters. He wondered distantly if they were tears, and he hoped they were. He hoped she was in pain, suffering from her own selfish stupidity. A red burst of rage banished the cold shock of his initial realization that she had left him, and he crumpled the letter, hurling it into the fire.

"Perry?" At his brother's voice from the corridor, he moved away from the door as Sebastian lifted the latch. He turned as his twin pushed open the door.

Sebastian took in Peregrine's ashen countenance, the hollowness of his eyes, the air of one stunned by some disaster. He came quickly towards him. "Oh, God, Perry, what has happened? Has there been an accident? What is it?"

"She's left me," Perry said. "Alexandra . . . she's gone back to Combe Abbey to put her head in a noose for this foolish compulsion of hers, and she didn't even have the courage or the basic courtesy to face me with it. Does she think everything that has happened between us can be dismissed like that? What of *love*, Seb? We spoke of love, declared love. And she can throw it away on a whim and without a word of warning." He turned from his brother with a gesture of disgust.

Sebastian said nothing for a moment. He knew how

his brother was feeling; he had gone through that agony himself a long time ago, when Serena had betrayed him in much the same way. And his brothers had been there with words of comfort when he needed them and silent supportive sympathy when that was what he needed. Now he wondered what to offer Perry.

"Did she leave a letter?" he asked.

"Yes . . . she left a damned letter with the caretaker in Berkeley Square."

"Did she say anything about coming back?"

Peregrine shook his head in the same disgust. "Once she's finished her work, she'll come back if I'll have her. I'm supposed to accept that, sit here twiddling my thumbs, out of my mind with worry that she'll be exposed . . . every minute she's down there, she's risking her neck."

"She's managed to avoid exposure so far," Sebastian pointed out.

"By some kind of miracle," his twin snapped. "I found her out quickly enough. Why won't someone else?"

"What are you going to do?"

"Nothing," Perry said harshly. "She's made her bed; she must lie in it."

Sebastian hesitated. He had never heard Perry use such a tone, but he could feel his twin's hurt, the rage it fueled, and he understood it. "The journey will take her several days," he observed, thinking that would give Perry time to think clearly again.

"At least," Peregrine agreed shortly. *Will she make a detour to Barton again?*

To hell with it. She can do whatever she wants. She made it clear that she wants nothing from me, and I am happy to oblige.

Throughout the tedious journey, as the wearisome miles rolled under the iron wheels of the chaise, Alex wrestled with her unhappiness and a growing sense of uncertainty. *Have I done the right thing? How did Peregrine respond to my letter?* It would have angered him, she knew, but maybe he also understood. She had tried so hard and so many times to explain the need, the compulsion she had to complete this mission. Apart from her burning need for justice, Sylvia's future had to be secured. *But what if he doesn't understand?* That fear seemed to exaggerate the widening distance between herself and Peregrine as they crossed the county line into Dorsetshire.

She arrived at Combe Abbey in the late afternoon of the third day. There had been no time to write to Stephen telling him of the success of her mission and when he should expect her return, so she was not expecting a welcome when she stepped stiffly from the post chaise and stood on the gravel sweep looking up at her childhood home.

No one came to the door, and the coachman unloaded her portmanteau and the tea chest of books directly onto the gravel and drove off, leaving her standing at the front door, her hand raised to the knocker.

Her knock was eventually answered by the butler, who greeted her with an unsmiling bow. "We weren't expecting you, Mistress Hathaway."

She ducked her head in a self-deprecating gesture. "So sorry to have disturbed you . . . such a nuisance in the afternoon, of course. I'll just go straight to my chamber to take off my cloak and hat. If it wouldn't be too much trouble to ask one of the footmen to bring in my portmanteau . . ." She gave him a shy, slightly scared smile as she indicated her bag sitting in lonely state on the driveway.

Her request was met with another frosty bow, which she took to mean assent, and she scurried up to her bedchamber. Its Spartan quiet was a relief, and she went to the window to look out at the familiar, well-loved view that always calmed and reassured her. A tap at the door announced a boy with her portmanteau, which he set down just inside, vanishing before she could even thank him.

Alex took off her cloak and hat and hefted the portmanteau onto the bed to unpack it. Concealed in the bottom with her silk gown and her boy's costume was a velvet pouch that contained her father's heavy gold signet ring and his diamond fob. She hadn't wanted to leave them behind at Combe Abbey and had had a passing thought that maybe she would try to sell them in London. But somehow, when it came to it, she couldn't bear the idea of parting with them. They were all she had left of her father. But with all of the momentous and glorious things that had happened in London, she had never given them a second thought, and they had traveled undisturbed to and from.

She left the pouch where it was at the bottom of the portmanteau, together with the garments that might well come useful for her midnight flight from Combe Abbey. Her hand stilled for a moment as she contemplated that prospect. When she finally left here, she would be free . . . and Sylvia would be free. And Peregrine would be waiting for her. He *had* to be waiting for her.

She unpacked the remainder of her clothes and shoved the portmanteau under the bed and was just straightening up when a maidservant tapped and came into the chamber. "Sir Stephen would like to see you in the library, ma'am, as soon as you're able."

"I will go to him at once, Mabel." Alex checked her reflection to make sure that everything was exactly as it should be. The birthmark was in the right place, the crow's-feet and little lines around her mouth were in place, her hair was newly streaked with gray, and the pad was set firmly between her shoulders. Then, with a resolute tilt of her head, Alexandra went downstairs to see her employer.

She found both Maude and Stephen in the library as she entered after a discreet tap at the door. "Ah, Mistress Hathaway, welcome back," Stephen greeted her with a gust of bonhomie. "Your errand was successful, I trust."

"Yes, indeed, Sir Stephen . . . Lady Douglas." She curtsied to her employers. "Mr. Murdock has offered a very good price for the library." She told him the sum, lowering her head to hide her disdain at the predatory greed sparking instantly in his eyes.

"Excellent . . . most excellent." Stephen rubbed his hands together. "Very good, indeed." He nodded vigorously before appealing to his wife, "Mistress Hathaway has done very well, has she not, m'dear?"

Maude regarded Alexandra with a slightly wrinkled nose, as if something offended her. "I'd like to know why it took so many days to complete your task, Mistress Hathaway."

"Oh, let's not quibble about such matters," Stephen put in hastily. "Mistress Hathaway knows her own business, and now it is completed, and that's all that matters."

Alexandra bobbed a diffident curtsy. "I do apologize, ma'am. These things do take a while to set in motion. There were several interested parties who took time to consider their offers."

Maude sniffed but made no further comment, taking up her tambour frame once more. Stephen coughed in a moment of awkward silence before saying, "So, how do we proceed now with the sale, Mistress Hathaway?"

"Mr. Murdock will arrange transport for the library, sir, but he has requested that I take personal charge of crating the books. It is a matter of considerable delicacy, as I'm sure you understand. Some of the volumes are almost priceless, and 'tis understandable that their purchaser wishes to be certain that they arrive in mint condition."

"You're to be spending your time packing boxes, then?" Maude looked up from her embroidery. "Such employment is hardly worth the sum my husband is paying you."

"I think you will find, ma'am, that it requires both skill and an intimate knowledge of the books to accomplish the transfer successfully." Alex offered her diffident smile, but she could hear the involuntary note of steel in her own voice, and the alarming thought occurred that maybe because the end of this ordeal was in sight, she was allowing her guard to slip a little. It wouldn't do. Not so close to fruition. "Mr. Murdock *was* most insistent, ma'am, that I take charge of the crating myself, but if Sir Stephen objects, then of course . . ." She looked inquiringly at her employer, careful to keep her tone soft and conciliatory.

"Not a bit of it," he declared. "Nothing must go wrong at this stage. Indeed, Lady Douglas, I do think 'tis best you leave me to conduct my own affairs as I see fit."

Maude flushed with annoyance at being taken to task in front of the despised librarian. She declared with a dismissive gesture, "Well, on your own head be it, sir. If you wish to be taken advantage of, then that is, of course, your prerogative." With that, she gathered up her sewing and swept from the room, the door closing with a decisive bang behind her.

Stephen sighed. "How long do you anticipate this crating to take, Mistress Hathaway? Her ladyship is right to say that it will take you away from your proper employment. I desire you to find time to attend to my financial affairs even while you are occupying yourself with the library."

"I shall, of course, do as you wish, sir." Alex curtsied again. "But I was employed first and foremost to take care of the library, and this will be the final stage in that employment. I do not myself consider it to be outside the remit of my employment here." She saw the flash of surprise cross Stephen's eyes and cursed herself anew. He was not used to hearing her stand up for herself. She was going to have to be doubly careful in the next few days.

"Well, that's as may be," he said stiffly. "Nevertheless, it will please me if you spend some time each day on my financial affairs."

"Of course, sir." Alex lowered her eyes demurely. "If you wish it, I will take a look at the books now. I can begin with the crating first thing in the morning."

He looked somewhat mollified. "Yes, well, why don't you do that? 'Tis more than a week since you last looked them over, and there may be some adjustments we should consider."

"Indeed, Sir Stephen." She moved to the desk, setting her plain glass pince-nez on the end of her nose. "I will start right away."

"Good . . . good." He hesitated for a second before heading for the door. "I'll leave you to it, then. You will join us for dinner, as usual."

"It will be an honor, as always, sir."

The door closed behind him, and Alex sat down behind the desk and rested her forehead in her palms. She could feel the house closing around her minute by minute, trapping her once more in this ghastly charade. For some reason, the knowledge that she could bring it to an end at any moment by simply walking away seemed to make it even harder to endure.

❧

Sebastian entered the parlor in Stratton Street. "D'you care to accompany me to White's, Perry? Serena's out house hunting, and I could sorely use some entertainment. What d'you say?"

Peregrine looked up from his book, closing it over a finger to keep his place. "I don't think so, Seb, if you don't mind. I'm in an ill mood for company."

His twin still looked as if he'd been hit by a runaway coach, Sebastian thought. But he wouldn't talk about Alexandra, merely sat with his books by the fire, rarely leaving the house. "I'm happy to bear you company if you'd rather stay in," he offered.

Perry shook his head with an attempt at a smile. "I'm poor company, Seb."

Sebastian took a breath and said, "I know you don't wish to talk of it, Perry, but what are you going to do about Alexandra? You love her, my dear boy. You can't just lose that in the blink of an eye . . . I know that from my own experience."

Perry leaned his head against the chair back, closing his eyes briefly. "I know that, Seb. But I don't know what to do . . . I don't know what I *want* to do. At the moment, I'm so angry I almost think she deserves whatever might happen to her. Even if it means a trial at the assizes."

"No, you don't," his twin said flatly.

"No," Perry agreed with a heavy sigh. "I don't suppose I do. But Alexandra's made it very clear that she wants nothing from me, so nothing is what she will get. I don't know how I'll feel when it's all over, one way or another." He shrugged. "Go and enjoy yourself with some congenial company, brother. I'm not fit company for man or beast."

Sebastian hesitated for a moment. "Have you talked to Jasper?"

Perry grimaced. "He called yesterday afternoon, when you and Serena were out. He didn't say much. But he didn't really need to. You know how he is when one of us is in trouble."

Sebastian nodded. "Like a rock." He turned back to the door. "I'll leave you, then, if you're sure you won't come out."

"Positive. Have a good evening." Peregrine returned to his book as the door closed behind his brother.

Chapter Twenty-one

Alexandra got up from her knees in front of a packing crate and wearily arched her back, pressing her hands into her spine. It was back-breaking labor, moving between shelves and crates with piles of books, carefully wrapping each one individually before laying it in the crate. And with each book she stowed away, she felt a little piece of herself going with it. There were so many memories attached to almost every volume, memories of a first reading, of a discussion with her father, of long afternoons of solitude curled up on the sofa, the very same sofa that still stood alongside the fireplace.

She was about to resume her labors when the library door opened and Sir Stephen entered, a letter in his hand. He looked somewhat puzzled. "Mistress Hathaway, I have had a communication from Mr. Murdock about the library."

"Indeed, sir?" She looked at him inquiringly. "Does he have some special instructions about the transport?"

"No." Stephen shook his head. "But he has an inquiry about a particular volume . . . Chaucer, he says here." He regarded her with a frown. "He writes that the gem of Sir Arthur's collection was a volume of the *Canterbury Tales,* whatever they may be, but when he asked you about it, you informed him that Sir Arthur had left that volume to his daughter."

Alexandra felt the pit opening beneath her. She sought for a response and managed to say, "I had not found the volume, sir, so I just assumed that Sir Arthur had given it away. His daughter seemed a logical choice."

"And how did you know he had a daughter? Were you acquainted with Sir Arthur Douglas?" he asked, still looking more bemused than suspicious.

"I had heard some talk in the village," she improvised rapidly. "Some mention of two daughters, I believe. In the absence of the Chaucer, I made an assumption."

"Did you, indeed?" The new voice was Maude's; she had been standing in the shadows behind her husband, unnoticed by either Alexandra or Stephen. "And why would you make such an assumption, Mistress Hathaway? I feel sure, Sir Stephen, that if your predecessor had given away such a valuable piece of his estate, it would have shown up in his will. That lawyer said nothing about any extra bequests made to his bastard daughters."

For a moment, rage swamped Alexandra's terror as she saw everything falling apart around her. How *dare* this usurper at Combe Abbey refer to herself and Sylvia with such contempt? And yet prudence prevailed, and she lowered her eyes. "I would not know about that, sir. There is no volume of the *Canterbury Tales* in the library, and I merely took a stab at an explanation. I was unaware that Mr. Murdock wished to pursue the matter."

"I told you, Sir Stephen, the woman's up to no good," Maude announced with that odious air of triumph. "I'll wager anything that she has stolen the volume, and who knows what others, while she's been busying herself all alone in here."

"Not so, ma'am!" Alex exclaimed, even as a little voice said that her removal of the Chaucer could indeed be considered theft, even though it was rightfully hers.

"We must search her room, go through her possessions," Maude stated. "We'll see what else the woman's stolen away. You would never know what priceless volumes are missing from the library. She could have half a dozen books hidden in her room."

Stephen looked at Alexandra, and she saw the growing suspicion in his eyes. "I agree, my dear. You will come with us, Mistress Hathaway, while we search your chamber."

They would find nothing, she thought. If she continued to deny all knowledge of the Chaucer, she should brush through this somehow. "As you wish, sir," she murmured. "I have nothing to hide."

A touch of uncertainty crossed his eyes, but Maude said, "Come, there's no time to lose." She swept from the room, and Stephen followed on her heels. Alex came behind them, filled with dread despite her knowledge that there was nothing incriminating among her possessions.

In her bedchamber, she stood immobile by the door while Maude began to go through her clothes in the armoire and the drawers in the chest, tossing her shabby, pathetic garments aside as she searched in every corner of every drawer, even shaking out her shoes to make sure there was nothing concealed in the toes. Stephen simply stood by, watching his wife with a somewhat awkward air. But he said and did nothing to stop her, not even when she pulled back the bedclothes and felt beneath the pillows. "Sir Stephen, help me turn the mattress," she demanded.

"Is that really necessary, my dear?"

She quelled his faint protest with a glare, and he helped her lift the mattress from the bed, holding it while she swept her hand along the rope springs beneath from one end to the other. "Ah, what's that?" she said, suddenly bending down. She hauled the portmanteau out from under the bed.

Alexandra turned to stone, remembering for the first time what was concealed beneath the false bottom of the bag.

Maude opened the bag and tipped it upside down. She shook it, and there was a distinct chink. She ran her hand over the bottom and found, as was inevitable, the little tab that lifted the false bottom. She looked up at her husband and then at Alexandra, then raised the piece of stiffened leather, revealing the small compartment beneath. In a silence that was now thick and heavy with dreadful anticipation, she took out the little pouch.

Maude pulled apart the drawstring and upended the contents onto her palm. Sir Arthur's diamond fob and signet ring, both engraved with the Douglas arms. "So!" she declared, extending her hand, palm up, towards Alexandra. "*So,* where did you get these, madam?" Without waiting for an answer, she extended her hand to her husband. "Look. I warned you about her, husband, but you wouldn't listen." Her eyes glittered with an almost manic satisfaction as she thrust her opened palm under his nose with a dramatic gesture that made him take an involuntary step back.

He stared down at the contents of her palm. "What are these?"

"*These,* sir, belonged to Sir Arthur Douglas. See the engraving." She gazed up at him with that glitter still in her eyes. "Hidden in this thieving, deceitful mountebank's baggage." She turned back to Alexandra. "These belong to the Douglas family. Where did you steal them from?"

Alexandra felt faint, as if the world were fading around her. Maude didn't wait for an answer. "I knew there was something wrong with her, something not right with her namby-pamby, oh-so-shy, oh-so-demure, butter-wouldn't-melt manners. She's no middle-aged spinster, husband, she's a thief, with some connection to Sir Arthur. She must have stolen the ring and the fob from somewhere, and I don't know what else she's stolen from us, but by God, we shall find out."

"No . . . no, you are mistaken, ma'am." Alex found her voice at last. "I have stolen nothing."

Maude gave a short derisive crack of laughter and turned back to the portmanteau, pulling out first the silk gown and then the breeches and jerkin of Alex's male costume. "Look at these." She held up the garments, waving them in front of her husband. "Look at this gown . . . and breeches, Sir Stephen, breeches and a jerkin. Why would the shameless hussy have such garments in her bag unless it was for some piece of trickery?"

"Just a minute . . . just a minute." Stephen held up his hands for quiet. "I can't make head or tail of this rigmarole. What is all this about, Mistress Hathaway?"

"'Tis obvious," Maude said. "Look at her." She pointed a finger. "Guilty as sin. Fetch the beadle, Sir Stephen. I demand you fetch a beadle. You're Justice of the Peace, 'tis for you to have her arrested."

Stephen looked across at the ashen Alexandra. "Can you explain any of this, Mistress Hathaway?"

Alexandra could see no way out. To protect Sylvia, she must continue to conceal her real identity. She had no choice but to maintain a steadfast silence, and with that knowledge came an almost fatalistic acceptance of whatever path fate had now laid out for her. "I have nothing to say."

"Condemned by her own mouth," Maude announced triumphantly. "The deceitful, thieving baggage."

Stephen waved her down impatiently, addressing Alexandra once more. "Come, woman, you must have an explanation."

"No," she answered simply. "None that I am willing to divulge."

"And what about this mysterious volume?" Maude demanded. "This Chaucer that's so valuable and is no longer part of the library. You told this Mr. Murdock that Sir Arthur had left it to his daughter, but such a bequest was nowhere in his will. You have stolen it."

Alexandra felt the guilty flush flood her cheeks even as she shook her head vigorously. "Not so, ma'am. I have stolen nothing."

"Then where is the missing volume?" Stephen demanded. "If you cannot tell me, then I have no choice but to assume you have stolen a priceless piece of the estate, and as the Justice of the Peace, I will have you arrested for theft. You will be committed to the cells at Shire Hall to await the quarterly assizes, which are set for one week hence. We will let a judge decide what should be done with you."

He gestured to his wife. "Come, Lady Douglas." He swept the lady in front of him out of the chamber, and Alex heard the key turn in the lock, imprisoning her.

Her mind was racing. She knew full well that once she was locked up in the prison cells beneath Shire

Hall, she would to all intents and purposes have disappeared off the face of the earth. She would be just another piece of human flotsam who had somehow fallen afoul of someone in power. No one would know where to look for her.

If she could get a message to Perry . . . but would he come? After she had left him without a word, would he care enough to come?

But even if she could reach him and he came, the case against her was impossible to disprove. They had Mr. Murdock's letter. She had certainly offered a seemingly false explanation for the volume's absence from the collection, and the law would look no further. There was no legal document to say that Sir Arthur had left her the Chaucer. It was all the evidence a court would need to hang her. A cold shiver went through her. Would they hang her?

The awful reality was undeniable. Hanging *was* the usual sentence for thievery. Perry had pointed that out to her often enough. Even stealing a penny loaf could put your head in the noose. If she couldn't prove that the volume belonged to her all along, then she was guilty of stealing it. And not even the Honorable Peregrine Sullivan could protect her.

Alexandra fought the waves of despair as she sat alone in her chamber waiting for the beadle. Could she write to Sylvia before he got here? But she dismissed the idea even as it came to her. Sylvia must not be implicated in any way.

What would they allow her to take with her into prison? Money. She had some; it might smooth her path a little and would certainly help her buy food. She didn't think prisoners were fed in jail. She thrust her coin purse into the bottom of her pocket. For an instant, the forethought made her feel marginally more in control, until reality swamped her yet again and she sank down on the bed.

Oh, God, this was such a nightmare. How could she find herself flung from the peak of happiness to the depths of this hellish pit in a matter of days?

The key turned in the lock, and the door opened. The beadle stood there with Sir Stephen. "Come along, then, mistress." The law officer flourished his staff of office. "You goin' to come quietly?"

"Yes, of course," Alexandra said with a quiet dignity that she did not feel. She wrapped herself tightly in her cloak. "What may I take with me?"

"Ye'll not be needin' much," the man said. "There's little enough in the ways of the gentry where you're goin', mistress." He gestured that she should precede him through the door. "The cart's waitin' below."

Stephen said nothing to her, merely stepping aside as Alexandra moved through the door. The beadle stated, "You'll be makin' formal charge down at Shire Hall, sir?"

"Aye," Stephen said shortly. "In the morning." He didn't move as .the beadle hustled Alexandra down the stairs and across the hall, where she was conscious of greedily curious eyes on her from the shadows.

Outside, a rough farmer's cart stood with an old nag between the shafts. The beadle jerked his head upwards. "Climb in, then, mistress. 'Less you'd rather walk."

Alex didn't deign to reply. She climbed into the cart, stepping fastidiously over the rotting straw covering the floor, and sat down on the single wooden bench with her back to the driver. Her jailer climbed onto the box and took up the reins, and the horse started wearily down the driveway.

It was a rough journey in the ramshackle cart to Dorchester, the County town, where the assizes were held. The narrow streets were crowded with farmers, horse traders, yeomen and their wives, country folk who had come to the thriving market from miles around, to sell or buy. They looked with naked curiosity at the well-known cart, driven by the unmistakable figure of the beadle, and the cloak-wrapped figure on the bench behind. Alex shrank into her cloak, pulling the hood low over her head. She didn't think anyone would recognize her, but word would get about soon enough. The servants from Combe Abbey would be the first to spread the tale of the thieving librarian.

Shire Hall was a stone building where all County business was transacted. The beadle drove the cart around to a narrow, fetid courtyard at the rear and drew rein. He clambered down and tethered the horse to a hitching post before beckoning to his passenger.

Alexandra climbed down without demurral, although her heart was thudding painfully. She could see the dark flight of steps at the rear of the building that led down to a barred door at the bottom, and a hard nut of nausea settled in her throat. For a moment, she contemplated making a run for it into the busy street behind, but she knew she would never outrun the ensuing hue and cry, not with such a crowd about, and it would only worsen her position. She might even find herself held in irons. Instead, she followed her escort's wordless instruction to go down the steps. He came close behind her, hemming her in, dogging her every step. At the base, he fitted an enormous brass key into the lock, lifted the heavy bar, and pushed the door open onto a pitch-black space, reeking of bodies and ordure, of damp and tallow.

Alex swallowed the nausea, trying not to breathe as her jailer slammed the door behind him. He felt in the dark to strike flint on tinder and lit a tallow candle on a rickety table by the door. It illuminated a narrow corridor lined with wooden doors, the top halves of which were barred gratings. She looked around, shivering now in the dank, mildew-smelling cold. She saw fingers curled around the bars of the gratings, eyes peering at her, and heard a low murmur that sounded to her terrified ears utterly menacing. As if they were caged animals welcoming new prey. It was nonsense, of course. The inhabitants of these cells were as unfortunate as she was herself. But the sound still terrified her.

The beadle moved in front of her, fitting a key into

one of the wooden doors, pulling it open. "Y'are a lucky one, you are. Sir Stephen says y'are to be kept alone, not in the common cells. In with ye, then." He gestured to the dark interior of the cell.

Alexandra sent a swift prayer of thanks for her cousin's merciful impulse. Maude wouldn't approve of her husband's charitable instruction, she thought grimly as she stepped into the small, fetid space. Before the man could slam the door on her, she said swiftly, "I have a little coin. I would like you to furnish me with a candle, some wine, and some bread and cheese. Oh . . . and a blanket," she added, finally taking in the contents of her new home. A stone bench, a pail, a rickety three-legged stool, and some foul straw for floor covering.

The beadle looked at her through narrowed eyes. "Show me yer coin?"

Alexandra felt for her pouch in her pocket. She had no intention of showing her jailer how much she had and opened the purse without taking it out, feeling for a half sovereign. She drew out the coin and held it up and away from him, so it glinted in the light of his candle. If Stephen had thought to have her housed away from the rest, she reckoned the jailer would not dare to assault her. At least, not until she had been tried, convicted, and sentenced. She pushed the gloomy thought away from her. She had sufficient troubles for the moment.

The man's eyes sharpened at the glint of gold. "Mebbe I can do summat for ye."

"A candle, wine, cheese, bread, and a blanket," she

repeated steadily. "You shall have the coin when you have brought me those. I daresay Sir Stephen will wish to be sure that I am well treated until the assizes."

He looked uncertain, and then, with a muttered "Hoity-toity," he banged out of the cell, leaving her in darkness. And now the sounds of the jail seemed magnified, separating into whispers, coughs, rustles of small animals, and then an unearthly scream that brought the hairs on the back of her neck to life. She felt her way to the stone bench. It was cold and damp to the touch. A day in here, and she'd have an ague, Alex reflected wretchedly, huddling even deeper into her cloak, closing her eyes against the darkness.

She didn't know how long it was before the dim glow of the tallow candle appeared in the grating of the door, but the key turned, and the beadle came in. He set down his candle, a leather flagon, and a napkin-wrapped bundle on the stool and threw a horsehair blanket onto the bench beside Alexandra. He took out the stub of another candle from his pocket and lit it from the other one.

"Leave me the longer one," Alexandra instructed. "That stub won't last the night."

"Twopence more," he demanded.

She debated for only a moment. She knew that a night in the pitch darkness inhabited by those ghastly sounds would drive her out of her mind. She felt for two pennies in her purse and silently held them out to him along with the half sovereign. He replaced the candle stub with his own and left her. She heard the key turn in the lock and his steps receding down the corridor. She heard the bang of the door to the outdoors slam, heard the heavy bar drop into place outside, and fought the growing sense of desperation.

Was she truly helpless?

Here, alone in the dim flicker of the tallow candle, she knew she was. Until the judge arrived to conduct the assizes, when they would bring her out of the dark prison and into the courtroom above, she was invisible.

The night passed somehow. In the windowless cell, she couldn't distinguish between day and night, and with no timepiece, Alexandra had no way of telling the time. She tried to sleep and then gave up all attempts and sat up, shivering despite the blanket and her thick cloak, on the cold stone bench in her cell. The beadle did not appear again, but at some point—morning, she assumed—his place was taken by an elderly, toothless man in ragged breeches and jerkin, armed with a heavy wooden club. Half a sovereign bought her a fresh candle, a flagon of wine, and a tepid bowl of indefinable soup. A hunk of stale bread and a cup of water had also been provided—prison rations, she gathered. Around her, the noises continued, and occasionally she caught snatches of conversation, but for the most part, she seemed to be existing in a dim circle of light surrounded by the whispering darkness.

She grew grimier and hungrier as the hours passed, and her sense of helplessness at times threatened to overwhelm her. What was going on beyond the walls of her prison? People were leading their ordinary lives, performing their accustomed tasks. Combe Abbey would be running along its accustomed course. Did anyone wonder about the disgraced librarian? Or had she come and gone as such an insubstantial presence that once out of sight, she was out of mind altogether?

She had no idea what time it was when the door to her cell opened and the beadle appeared. For one glorious moment, she thought that perhaps he had come to say that Sir Stephen had withdrawn the charges and she was free, but one look at his expression banished such a forlorn hope.

"Just takin' a look at ye. Justice likes a report on the prisoners every day or so."

"Would you tell Sir Stephen I'd like to talk to him?" It was another forlorn hope, she was certain, but nothing ventured . . .

The beadle shook his head. "Bless you, woman, he don't come down 'ere. Too afraid of catchin' summat, if ye asks me. Doubt he'll be back in town until the assizes. Ye'd best save your talk till then, when y'are brought up afore the judge."

Alexandra sighed, swallowing her disappointment, blinking back a surge of tears. She realized she had still been nurturing the tiniest hope that her cousin would reconsider. And now there was nothing left. She would rot in this filthy hole until the assizes. And if no one knew she was there, there would be no one to speak up for her to the judge, and once she was sentenced and condemned, there would be nothing anyone could do to help her. She turned her face to the wall, and after a moment, the beadle went out. The key grated in the lock, and the heavy bar came down with a crash.

Chapter Twenty-two

Peregrine awoke one morning after another tormented night and realized that it had been over a week since Alexandra had left. Just what was she doing at this moment? Sitting at breakfast with the poisonous Maude or already at work in the library, creatively moving sums of money from one account to another?

He found to his surprise that the thought brought familiar exasperation but not the cold, despairing anger of the last days. Perhaps it just wasn't possible to maintain such fury for any length of time; it was far too debilitating. He went to the window and looked out upon a bright, crisp day. And the blood once more stirred in his veins. He'd done enough sitting around and moping for a lifetime. He'd deal with Alexandra when the time came.

He went down to the breakfast parlor, telling Bart in the hall to go to the mews and bring Sam around. The horse had been eating his head off for more than a week and would be chafing at the bit. Serena and Sebastian were already at breakfast when he went in. They both looked at him with shrewdly assessing glances that he now realized had been their habitual expressions for the last week.

"Good morning," he greeted them. "A fine one, it looks."

"You noticed?" Sebastian said with a quirked eyebrow.

"Yes, finally," his twin agreed, examining the offerings on the sideboard. "I have it in mind to ride in Windsor Park this morning, get rid of the fidgets. D'you care to join me?"

"I wish," Sebastian said with a mock groan and a grimace at his wife. "But Serena insists I must look at two houses with her, as she can't make up her mind between them. My wife is being unusually indecisive."

"Well, you do have to live there, too," Serena pointed out. "You're looking more yourself, Perry?"

"I am a little less enraged," he conceded. "I still don't know what to do for the best, but there's nothing I can do about the wretched woman at present, so I'll take my life back for now."

"Good." Sebastian's smile was relieved.

Perry gave him a rueful smile of his own. "I'm sure I've been very difficult to live with."

"No, just not really here," his twin said, burying his nose in his tankard.

Peregrine left soon after, riding Sam through the still quiet streets of fashionable London and out into the countryside towards Windsor Castle and its parkland.

He was glad his brother had declined his invitation; it was good to be alone in the fresh air, feeling Sam's easy stride beneath him, feeling the dusty, tangled web of his thoughts clearing. He still couldn't forgive her for leaving him without a word, and yet finally, he could feel some compassion. She had been abandoned, betrayed by a father she had trusted; maybe it was to be expected that she would need time to trust another man again.

He still intended to make his point more than forcefully when . . . *if* . . . she returned to him. Melancholy loomed again, and he urged Sam into a gallop along a broad ride along the river, letting the horse have his head until the animal slowed of his own accord, and his own melancholy was expunged under the sheer exhilaration of the exercise.

It was mid-afternoon when he was once more in the city, Sam picking his way wearily over the cobbled streets, Perry's own body aching pleasurably. He left the horse in the mews and walked around to Stratton Street. Just as he reached his door, it opened, and Marcus Crofton stepped out into the street.

"Oh, Perry, I've been looking all over for you. No one's seen you in days, and your brother and his wife are not at home."

"Good to see you, Marcus. Now you've found me, will you come in, take a glass of wine?"

"Gladly. I've some news that might interest you."

Marcus turned back to the house, his host moving ahead of him into the hall.

An icy shaft of apprehension ran down Perry's spine. He tossed his hat and whip onto the bench by the door and shrugged out of his riding cloak as he opened the door to the parlor, ushering his guest into the warmth.

"Sherry or claret, Marcus?"

"Claret, thank you." Marcus sat down, crossing one elegantly booted foot over the other. He took the glass with a nod and sipped appreciatively.

"So? News?" Perry prompted when he had sat down with his own glass.

"Oh, yes . . . I had a letter from my mother this morning. 'Tis the damnedest thing . . . Mistress Hathaway, your pet librarian, if you remember?"

"I remember," Perry said, his gaze fixed steadily on his guest, his expression like stone.

"Well, it seems she's been thieving bits and pieces of the library all the while," Marcus said. "Some precious volume . . . Chaucer, I think they said . . . and no one knows what else has gone, because only she knew what was there in the first place."

Peregrine had been living with this possibility for so long that he felt no shock, not even surprise, just an icy clarity. He needed help at this point, and he couldn't wait for Sebastian to return. Besides, Marcus was connected to the whole mess, albeit without his knowledge. "Let me tell you a few things in the strictest confidence,

Marcus." Quickly, he told Marcus everything about his friend's stepsisters and their circumstances.

Marcus blinked, shook his head as if to clear his mind, drained his glass, and said, "Good God in heaven . . . that's appalling. How could such a miscarriage of justice go unnoticed?"

"Because there was no one who cared to notice it," Perry pointed out. "Alexandra decided to reset the scales of justice. And this is where it's led her."

"To Dorchester jail and the assizes," Marcus stated, setting aside his glass. "If we take my curricle, change horses every couple of hours through the night, we can be in Dorchester by tomorrow afternoon."

"I was hoping you'd say that," Perry said, setting aside his own glass.

"Well, of course I would," Marcus declared forcefully. "These are my stepsisters, and I feel a responsibility to right what wrongs have been done them by the fact of my mother's marriage." He was on his feet. "I'll fetch you here in half an hour."

Peregrine knew he could not get to Dorchester on horseback in that time. He stood up. "I'll be ready." He went into the hall to let out his guest. "Do you know when the Dorchester assizes are to be held, Marcus?"

"The first Monday of the month . . . the day after tomorrow," Marcus said as he stepped out into the street. "Half an hour, Perry."

Once Alexandra was in the dock, all hope would be lost. They had to get there by tomorrow. Peregrine took the stairs two at a time. They would change horses and share the driving. Barring highway accidents, they could do it . . . just.

The next morning, just after dawn, they were on the coastal road into Dorset as a pale sun broke through the clouds, warming the air a little but not enough to combat the sharp sea breeze. It was a relief to turn inland, away from the gray green sea with its white-capped waves surging onto the pebble beaches below the cliff. They were both tired. They had kept up such a pace that it had been difficult to catch a few minutes' sleep when the other was driving. They had changed horses, courtesy of Marcus's purse, every couple of hours, so the animals were still fresh.

They drove into the town of Dorchester soon after noon. As they passed the stone building of Shire Hall, Perry averted his gaze. He didn't want to be distracted now by worry for Alexandra, by wondering what was happening to her in the dungeons below. Marcus was driving as they turned into the yard of the Red Lion.

Perry jumped down from the curricle. "I'll go in and order some food, Marcus. We're famished." Every moment's delay hurt, but he knew he could be no good to Alexandra if he was fainting from fatigue and hunger.

The landlord greeted him jovially. "Aye, I can give you a good pot of rabbit stew, sir. Good job you'll not be wantin' a chamber, mind. The assizes start tomorrow, and there's not a chamber free in town. Such a to-do as 'tis, wi' all the folks 'ereabouts come to watch the felons sentenced. There'll be a public 'anging a few days after. O' course," he confided as he ushered Perry into the taproom, "depends on the judge. We likes the 'angin' judges around 'ere. Some of 'em prefer sendin' criminals to the hulks or to that there 'Merica place. What's the fun in that, I ask you?"

"None, I daresay, for anyone," Perry observed drily.

A few hundred yards away, Alexandra nibbled a hard crust of bread and watched her candle flicker and die. The jailer had not appeared since that morning, and she had no way of replenishing her light. Once the flame guttered, she would be in that peopled darkness, with nothing to distract her from the sounds. But somehow, she had achieved a strange kind of resignation. She no longer felt hope or purpose, and without those, there was really nothing to fear. She was lost, the world was lost to her, and she slipped into a void, a dark place empty of all emotion, aware only of physical sensations, of the cold and the damp, hunger and thirst. Her only thoughts now were how to alleviate those discomforts. They seemed the only things of any importance now.

Marcus mopped his bowl with a thick slice of wheaten bread and heaved a sigh of satisfaction. "So, are we going to bribe the jailers to let her go? I doubt they'll be averse to a healthy sum."

"No." Peregrine drained his ale tankard, setting it down on the deal table with a thump as he pushed back his stool. "'Tis too risky, Marcus. Sir Stephen's her accuser, and he's the Justice of the Peace. It won't be worth their while to take a bribe and face his wrath. They'll lose their livelihoods. It won't do."

"No, I see your point. So?"

A grim smile hovered around Peregrine's mouth. It was time to play the game his way now. Alexandra had insisted on playing it her way, and it had landed her in a prison cell. It was past time he asserted himself. "She'll be out of there within the hour, if I have to kill someone first."

"But we'll do our best to avoid that, I trust," Marcus murmured wryly as he followed Peregrine back outside.

Peregrine's fatigue had vanished. He was infused with purpose now, his plan forming and reforming in his mind. First a visit to the prison to see how many jailers they would have to contend with, and then they had to gain access to the prisoner. Money would do that much, he was certain. He refused to allow his imagination to wander, to start thinking about how she was, what conditions she was living under. He must concentrate only on getting her out of there.

But what if she is in the common cell, among the rogues and ruffians of the highways and byways? Not even Alex, fighter though she was, would be able to hold her own among a mob of rough, thieving women. For an instant, the ghastly thought intruded, and it took all of his willpower to dismiss it. He could do nothing to alter the past but everything to change the present. He would adapt his plan to whatever conditions he found her in.

"Do you have a pistol with you?" he asked Marcus as they went into the stable yard.

"Yes, and my sword." Marcus touched the hilt of the sword at his hip. "So, we *are* going to be fighting our way out of there?"

"Not if I can help it," Perry said. "But sometimes a show of force is necessary. I have a pair of pistols and my sword."

"We'll play it by ear," his friend stated. "Dorchester is a sleepy market town. I doubt that the jail will be bristling with armed guards."

"Let us hope not." Suddenly, Perry veered off towards the stable block. Marcus waited, and his friend eventually appeared with a rope halter that he pushed into the deep pocket of his coat. "Let's go, then." Perry set off at a brisk walk in the direction of Shire Hall, Marcus falling in beside him. "Here's what I need you to do."

Chapter Twenty-three

Alexandra paced the small cell back and forth, forcing her cold, cramped limbs to move, swinging her arms as vigorously as she could. She had the stub of another candle, begrudgingly provided by the old jailer when he'd brought her bread and water a few hours earlier. As always, she wished she had some sense of the passing of time. The old man had also produced a bowl of watery porridge on production of a silver shilling, but the price for these creature comforts, if they could be called such, increased day by day, and Alex was beginning to worry now that her supply of coin might not last until she was brought before the judge. As time inched by, she became increasingly impatient for the moment that hitherto she had been dreading. Anything was better than these interminable dark hours of inaction, not knowing what the future might hold for her.

She had begun to exercise her body as much as she could and had started cataloguing the library in her head, going through the shelves one by one, methodically seeing herself pack and crate each individual book.

When she missed one, she made herself go back to the beginning. It kept her mind off the sounds, which were as unbearable as ever, and gave her at least the illusion of a purpose.

⟨≈⟩

Above Alexandra, in the afternoon sunlight filtering through dusty windowpanes, Marcus Crofton idly twirled a gold sovereign on the table so that it caught the pale sun, winking seductively at the old man who hadn't taken his eyes off it. He didn't know his visitor, but everything about the young man bespoke authority.

"As I said, I am Sir Stephen's agent," the visitor repeated when it seemed the man was so mesmerized by the dance of the coin that he wasn't listening to him. "Sir Stephen wishes me to see your prisoner at once." He caught up the coin and folded it into his palm, fixing the old man with a cold stare. "I would like you to take me to her now, if you please." He tossed the coin into the air and caught it again.

"Aye, sir. But I ought to ask the beadle, sir. Master Gilby's mighty fussy about 'is prisoners, sir. He don't like folks goin' down to visit less'n he's 'ere 'imself. I don't 'ave no orders, sir.'

Marcus smiled and flicked the coin with his thumb so that it fell onto the table beneath the jailer's watchful eyes. "You do now. And I should remind you that Sir Stephen Douglas does not take kindly to having his orders countermanded."

The man's hand in fingerless mittens shot out and scooped up the coin. "If 'tis Sir Stephen's orders, then I s'pose it'll be all right, sir." He shuffled to a hook on the wall, where hung a ring of keys. "If'n ye'll follow me, sir. Mind yer step, 'tis dark an' a bit damp like." He took up a horn lantern and held it aloft as he opened a narrow door in the far wall of the chamber.

Marcus grimaced and followed close. A flight of stone steps led down into darkness. The lantern offered a swaying path of light, revealing a long corridor lined with wooden doors, all with gratings at the top. Whispers filled the air and grew louder as the lantern's light swayed from side to side, offering momentary illumination in the barred windows of the cell doors. Marcus felt the hairs on the back of his neck lift. The jailer stopped at a door in the middle of the corridor and hung his lantern on a hook above the door before inserting a key.

"'Ere's a visitor fer ye." He pushed the door open a crack. "I'll 'ave to lock it after ye, sir. 'Tis the beadle's orders, sir."

Marcus gave a quick thought for Perry, who should by now be in the chamber above, waiting for the old man. If their luck held, Perry would only have to immobilize the one jailer. He nodded his agreement and stepped swiftly into the dimly lit cell, grimacing at the reek of damp straw and ordure. The woman standing in the middle of the cell was immobile, staring at him, blinking as if she had never seen his like before.

"Mistress Hathaway?" He had never called her anything else, and since, as far as he could see in the dim light, she still looked like the middle-aged spinster librarian he knew, he couldn't think how else to address her. He looked more closely and saw that her appearance was, in fact, altered. Normally trim and neat to a fault, she was disheveled, her hair hanging lank and bedraggled to her shoulders. Her eyes were deeply shadowed, her skin waxen in the dim light of the tallow candle. Her gown was the same shabby one he remembered, but the humpback was gone, and the material hung in loose, limp folds around a body that seemed thin and frail.

"Dear God, what have they done to you?" he heard himself exclaim as the jailer closed the door and the key turned in the lock.

For a moment, Alexandra didn't recognize her visitor. She hadn't known her stepbrother well, indeed had only seen him as an occasional visitor at the dinner table at Combe Abbey. Now she shook her head as if dismissing confusion. "Master Crofton . . . I . . . what are you doing here?"

"Never mind that. Can you walk?"

"Yes . . . yes, of course." She could feel the blood beginning to flow again. Somehow, someone, someone with no reason to hurt her, knew she was there. He could get a message to Perry. "It's only been a few days, I think, but in truth, 'tis hard to tell day from night down here."

"I don't wonder," he said with a shudder. "Peregrine will be dealing with the old man. As soon as he gets down here, we have to walk out. We have to walk out as if we have simply been about our legitimate business in the council chambers above." He cocked his head, listening for a sound from above, but the walls and ceiling were so thick that no sound penetrated the dungeons from the upstairs chambers.

Alex wrestled with her confusion. How did Peregrine get there? How was her stepbrother involved? But the question lost all significance as she registered what he had said. "Just tell me what to do," she said simply.

Peregrine had insisted on immobilizing the jailer himself. If the man was hurt, he didn't want Marcus involved. So far, as far as they could tell, there was only the one jailer on duty, and if the gods smiled, their luck would hold. He could certainly handle one old man single-handed. It was also immensely reassuring to know that there was no reason for the elderly jailer, or indeed the beadle, to recognize either of them. He himself was completely unknown in Dorchester, and Marcus would have had no previous dealings with men such as the jailer and the beadle. If they could make their escape cleanly, without pursuit, they could be free and clear before anyone knew what had happened. The prisoner would have vanished off the face of the earth, the librarian a mere memory. And no one would look for the timid, mousy spinster in the radiant and assured wife of the Honorable Peregrine Sullivan.

At least, that was what he was counting upon. As he sauntered carelessly into the council chamber a few minutes after Marcus had entered, he remembered wryly the old aphorism: if you touch pitch, expect to be tarred in your turn. Marry a criminal, and find yourself on the wrong side of the law. He, Peregrine Sullivan, a thoroughly upright member of Society, with a strict code of honor, whose primary goal in life was to uphold the honor of the ancient Blackwater name, was about to commit a crime, quite possibly violent, that could bring him to the gallows.

The council chamber was empty at first when he entered. A door in the far wall stood ajar onto a dark space, and he walked over to it. The smell of damp and rotting straw rose up in noxious waves from the darkness at the base of the flight of steps. He cursed Stephen Douglas with silent vehemence that was nonetheless powerful for being unspoken and stepped back quickly at the sound of shuffling steps below.

He moved into the middle of the chamber, waiting with the appearance of nonchalance. The owner of the shuffling steps emerged from the gloom of the stairwell. He held a brass key ring and a horn lantern, which he hung on a hook beside the door. Suddenly aware that he was not alone, he turned back to the chamber, leaving the door ajar behind him.

He coughed and shuffled to the table. "Didn't realize anyone was 'ere, sir. Master Gilby ain't 'ere at present. I'm expectin' 'im soon. If'n ye'd care to wait."

"No, I don't think I would," Peregrine said. He had his pistol in his hand, tucked behind his back. He raised it with a smile he hoped was reassuring as he stepped up to the old man. "I don't intend to hurt you. But I'd like you to face the wall for a moment."

The jailer blinked at him in bemusement, his eyes darting to the pistol and back to Peregrine's smiling countenance. "Do what, sir?"

"Face the wall," Peregrine said quietly, laying a hand on the man's shoulder, turning him around. He took the rope halter from his pocket and swiftly bound the jailer's wrists. "Forgive me. This will only be for a few moments."

A sudden noise behind him brought him whirling around. The beadle stood in the doorway to the street, his expression momentarily confused. It was the moment that gave Perry his opening. He had secured the old man and now, swiftly, hand outstretched in greeting, stepped towards the beadle.

"Master Gilby, I believe. I'm delighted to make your acquaintance."

The beadle shook his head as if to dispel confusion. Everything looked as usual. But his eyes fell on the open door to the cells. His startled gaze moved from his smiling visitor, still extending his hand in greeting, to the old man, who was slowly turning back to the room, his hands securely fastened at his back. But the visitor was a man of Quality, his coat and breeches of the best superfine, the tailoring exquisite. And he was smiling, that hand outstretched in familiar greeting.

Master Gilby hesitated a moment too long. Peregrine's outstretched hand became a fist, which connected with a satisfying thud against the beadle's chin. The man toppled sideways, reaching for the table to steady himself. The table slid away from him under Peregrine's swift kick, and then Peregrine slammed the street door, which the beadle, in his surprise, had left open. The grating of the key as he turned it in the lock seemed as loud as a thunderclap in the strange, uncomprehending silence of a room that ordinarily saw only orderly business.

Peregrine slipped the door key into his pocket and regarded the results of his few moments of action. They were all safely locked in; no one could disturb them from the street. Neither of his victims appeared badly hurt, but Master Gilby, now sitting on the floor, was rubbing his jaw with an aggrieved air that boded ill. The old man, with his hands still bound at his back, looked from one to the other, his head swaying from side to side as he tried to make sense of this extraordinary upset in the normal, peaceful sequence of his daily life.

Perry decided that Master Gilby was probably going to be a nuisance, so he used his fist for another neat touch to the beadle's chin, which rendered him satisfactorily immobile. Hoping that it would be long enough,

Perry took the key ring off the wall, together with the horn lantern, and descended into the darkness.

"Marcus?"

"Here. Where you see the light," came the answer, and the yellow flicker of a candle showed in the grating above one of the doors halfway along the passage. Perry heard the sounds, the whispers, the rising voices, as the inhabitants of those dark spaces began to realize that something different was happening in their prison.

He ignored them, concentrating on the glimmer of light. He reached it, his fingers fumbling with the key ring. "God damn it, I don't know which one is the right one. Marcus? Is Alexandra all right?"

"I'm all right, Peregrine."

Her voice, strong, infused with her own clear intonations, filled with her own self, was the sweetest thing he had ever heard. And paradoxically, it brought a surge of anger. He loved her, but he wasn't sure he had forgiven her yet.

He found the key, and the door creaked open onto the fetid space. Alex stood wrapped in a cloak in the middle of the cell, offering him a tentative smile as she pushed a lank strand of hair from her forehead.

"I don't know what I look like," Alexandra murmured, suddenly absurdly conscious of how dirty she was, how greasy her hair must be. She wondered if she smelled bad and reflected that she must reek after so much time in this damp filth.

"Like the very devil," Perry said drily. "Pull your

hood low, and when we get upstairs, you need to shuffle out of the building like some old woman supplicant to the council chamber. You've sufficient experience at charades to pull that off without any trouble."

Alexandra bowed her head in acceptance. She couldn't blame him for his harshness. She had forced him to accept a situation that he had detested from the first moment. But tears pricked behind her eyes nevertheless. She wanted him to enfold her, to hold her, to tell her he loved her and that the nightmare was all over. But perhaps she had forfeited that comfort. Perhaps he was there only because of the past, those few glorious days they had shared.

She drew the hood over her head. She had long since discarded the pad between her shoulders. It was unnecessary in this prison cell, where no one saw her, and desperately uncomfortable, but now she hunched her shoulders in the remembered way and gave him a clear-eyed look. "I can do whatever is necessary, Peregrine."

He nodded curtly and gestured to the cell door. "Hurry, then. Walk between us."

"What about upstairs?" Marcus gestured upwards with a jerk of his head. "Anyone likely to cause trouble?"

"I hope not. The beadle still should be in the land of dreams," Perry responded shortly. "I'll go ahead; you bring up the rear." He stepped out into the corridor, and a crescendo of voices and shouts arose from the cells around them. A tin pot clanged against the barred grating of a door at the far end, and he grimaced. *"Hurry."* He grabbed Alexandra's hand. "Get up the stairs before the racket brings the whole town down upon us."

She stumbled slightly in her haste as she half ran behind him to the stairs leading up to the council chamber. She could hear Marcus behind her as the noise from the cells grew ever louder. Perry was pulling her behind him up the stairs, and she nearly fell into the chamber, blinded by the bright light of day. "I can't see," she gasped.

Perry ignored the comment, but his hand tightened around hers. "Your hood," he instructed. "Shield your face." His eyes darted to the old man, who stood with his back to the wall, hands still bound, gazing in mingled fear and curiosity at the intruders.

Peregrine raised his pistol in a threatening gesture, hissing, "Make a sound, and you'll join your friend on the floor." He sensed that the jailer, emboldened by the noise from the cells below, was preparing to add his own voice to the hubbub. The beadle, still curled on the floor, stirred and groaned, and the old man shrank back against the wall.

Alexandra was astounded at this new side to Peregrine. She could never have imagined him threatening anyone, let alone a helpless old man. But then, she could never have imagined present circumstances, she reflected, pulling her hood low over her forehead, hunching her shoulders even tighter. Behind her, she heard Marcus slamming the door to the cells, and the tumult below grew fainter.

The beadle struggled to his knees. Perry bent over him. "My apologies," he murmured, and applied his fist once more. Master Gilby toppled sideways with a soft exhalation.

"Serves him right," Alexandra murmured with ill-concealed satisfaction, remembering the greedy paw that had swallowed her money in exchange for the pathetic candle stubs and watery soup that had kept her just this side of utter desperation since he'd turned the key on her.

Perry shot her a quick glance and thought that she looked better already. Her spirits were certainly improving, judging by her present expression. "Hurry," he instructed. "Keep your head down." He unlocked the street door and strolled out into the cold afternoon air, glancing casually around. The street was quiet, with a Sunday hush to it. Alexandra's hunched figure shuffled out behind him, and Marcus, with the same insouciant air as Peregrine, stepped out, closing the door firmly behind him.

Perry turned casually back to the door and surreptitiously relocked it. "That should hold them for a while." He dropped the key into a cracked and empty flowerpot at one side of the door.

"I'll fetch the horse," Marcus murmured, and strode off down the street to the Red Lion.

Peregrine turned aside into the alley running beside

the Shire Hall, and Alexandra followed him, keeping to the shadows. "What's happening?" she whispered.

"Just stay where you are," he instructed. "We're waiting for Marcus." He stood just inside the entrance to the alley, watching the street. No one seemed aware of anything strange happening around the Shire Hall. There were few people on the street, but as the church bells began to ring for the mid-afternoon service, doors opened, and more folk appeared. A few urchins darted among them, earning random backhanded clouts when they got in the way.

Alexandra stayed in the shadows, still closely wrapped in her cloak. Her eyes were accustomed to the brightness now, and her lungs seemed to expand as the fresh air filled them after the noxious dampness of the last days. "How long was I there?" she asked abruptly.

The question startled Peregrine. And then he realized what it meant, and the thought of her enduring endless hours in that fetid darkness, not knowing even the time of day, filled him with a savage rage against the men who had put her there.

"About a week," he said. "But it's over now."

"Unless they catch us." An involuntary shudder lifted the fine hairs on her nape, and she was very cold.

"That's not going to happen." His voice was calm, reassuring, confident. "Here's Marcus now." He stepped back into the alley as Marcus, riding a horse from the inn's livery stable with a portmanteau tied to the saddle, turned into the entrance. He dismounted swiftly.

"Quickly." Peregrine gestured imperatively to Alexandra. "You'll have to ride pillion. I'll go up first, and you come up behind me." He mounted. "Put your foot on my boot." He held his hand down to her.

Alexandra took it and felt his fingers tighten around her wrist. She put a foot on his boot, and he yanked her upwards as she jumped, then settled into the saddle behind him.

"Hold me tight, and keep your face averted," he instructed. "Just until we get out of town."

"We can avoid town by taking the back way through the privies," she said. "If I remember aright, this alley will lead to the fields behind town."

Of course, this was Alexandra's home country, Perry remembered. She had grown up there, after all. "We'll pick up the coast road from there," he said, holding out his hand to Marcus. "My thanks, my friend."

Marcus took the hand in a warm grasp. "My thanks for the adventure. I look forward to calling upon my stepsister in town." His smile was mischievous. "I need to hear the rest of your story. Indeed, I believe I am owed it. But for now, I shall put fresh horses to the curricle and head for a quiet afternoon at my fireside in the Dower House. Where it shall be said I have been all day nursing a cold. The horse is not a patch on Sam, I'm afraid, Perry, but he was the best I could get. He should carry you to a decent town, where you can hire a chaise. You can sell him there, and we'll settle up over a good dinner in town." With that, he raised a jaunty hand in farewell and headed out of the alley into the main street.

"Let's find a way out of this maze." Perry set the horse towards the rear of the alley. "We have about half an hour to get well clear, before the town falls about our ears."

Alexandra said nothing, her arms tight around his waist, her head resting against his back. She would not allow herself to believe that she was safe until there was no possibility of pursuit.

The horse picked his way over the slimy paving stones at the rear of the buildings where the outhouses were situated at the bottom of kitchen gardens. The gardens in their turn opened onto the fields. Peregrine dismounted to open a gate beside a stile that gave onto a narrow path leading around a stubble field. He kept the horse close to the hedgerow, but they saw no one and after a while reached another stile that led onto a lane.

"God knows where we are," Perry murmured, dismounting to open the gate once again.

"Go right on the lane." Alex spoke for the first time in an eternity, it seemed to her. "Can't you smell the sea?"

He paused, taking a deep breath. He could, indeed, smell it, the faint salt tang to the air. "The coast road will take us into Hampshire."

"Yes," she agreed. "But I don't wish to involve Sylvia."

"If you think your sister is going to permit you to call the tune any longer, Alexandra, you are much mistaken," Peregrine said firmly. "Any more than I am. And when we're all living in London under the same roof, you will find yourself outnumbered, my dear. For now, we are going to stop at the nearest hostelry, where I shall have a few things to say to you, after which I intend to get some sleep. You, not to put too fine a point on it, need a bath before anything else. You have a prison reek about you."

"That's hardly surprising," she retorted, astonished at how quickly she was returning to her self.

Peregrine didn't dignify the retort with a response, and they rode in silence for the next half hour before a small, whitewashed hostelry bearing the sign of the Hare and Hounds appeared on the outskirts of a little village. Peregrine drew rein outside and dismounted, offering a hand to Alexandra to dismount. "Stay here," he instructed, "and keep your face hidden."

The door to the inn opened directly onto the tap-room. He called out, and a woman appeared at the counter, pink-cheeked from the kitchen range, wiping her hands on her flour-dusted apron. "Good evenin', sir." She looked a question.

"Do you have a room for the night, for my wife and me?" he asked pleasantly. "Our carriage broke an axle a few miles down the road. Our coachman is seeing to the repair, but it will not be ready before morning."

"Oh, aye, sir. I've one nice chamber at the back," she

said. "If you'd follow me." She led the way up a narrow staircase to a small landing with only one door. Behind the door, Perry found a small dormer room, clean and simple. "I'll 'ave a fire goin' in no time, sir. Would you be wantin' supper?"

"Yes, indeed," he said. "And my wife would like a bath. Is it possible you could provide sufficient water?"

"Enough for a hip bath, sir, if that'll do."

"Amply. And could you bring the ingredients for a punch bowl when you light the fire, please?"

"Aye, sir." She hurried away, calling, "Josh . . . Minnie . . . we've customers."

Peregrine went back outside to where Alexandra still waited by the horse, her hood drawn up around her head as instructed. "Come inside." He gestured that she should precede him up the stairs. "Sit on the window seat, say nothing, keep your face hidden, and leave the talking to me."

It was oddly comforting to obey these simple instructions, Alexandra found. She knew that Perry was still angry, but she knew, too, that he would forgive her now. He would have his say, but he *would* forgive her.

She sat mute and still while the bustle in the chamber continued around her. The fire blazed, a hip bath was brought and filled from steaming jugs, and a punch bowl and all that went with it was set upon the hearth.

"Will that be all for now, sir?" The landlady looked around the chamber, her gaze lingering for a curious moment on the figure on the window seat.

"For the moment, thank you." Peregrine smiled his thanks. "Could you serve supper in here in an hour?"

"Aye, sir. Will a mess of fresh-caught river fish do for you and the lady? Tossed in brown butter with a few onions an' some wild garlic?"

"Admirably." He nodded dismissal, and she curtsied and left the chamber. "Now, get out of those filthy clothes, Alexandra, and get into the bath."

"As you command, sir," she murmured, sliding off the window seat. "The only problem I see is what I should put on afterwards."

"I have what you need." He was peeling oranges for the punch, his back to her as he knelt before the fire.

It was a relief not to have his eyes on her as she stripped away the prison foulness, kicking the pile of filthy garments into a corner, before lowering herself into the copper bath. After a moment, she said, "Perry, would you pour water over my hair so I may wash it?"

He dropped the orange peel into the mixture of rum and brandy and stood up, turning to the bath. Resolutely, he refused to consider the temptation of her nakedness as he matter-of-factly poured a jug of water over her bent head. He waited while she soaped her hair vigorously and then rinsed it with another jug of water, before returning to his punch.

She was still some way from forgiveness, Alex reflected ruefully. She stood up in a shower of drops and wrapped herself in the towel hanging over the fire screen. "Did you say you had something for me to wear, Perry?"

He pushed back on his heels and stood up again. "Yes." He went to his portmanteau on the chest at the foot of the bed. "It was intended as a wedding present, but you had other plans." He took out an exquisite garment of white lawn edged with the finest alençon point lace and tossed it lightly onto the bed.

Alexandra picked it up and held it against the candlelight. The lawn was so fine it was almost transparent, and the lace was almost too delicate to imagine that it could have been spun by human hands. "Oh, Perry, 'tis exquisite." She held it against her cheek, relishing its delicacy. Her eyes filled with tears. "Will you ever forgive me?"

"Oh, yes," he said, and now a tiny smile appeared at the corner of his mouth. "I appear to have done so already. But listen to me, and listen well, madam. We will be married as soon as we get back to London. You will become my wife, Mistress Sullivan, and Alexandra Hathaway will no longer exist. And . . ." He came over to her, taking her damp, bare shoulders in a firm clasp. "Understand this. If you ever fail to trust me again, I will lock you in an attic and feed you bread and water until your dying day. Is that understood?" He gave her a little shake.

"Oh, yes," Alexandra said. "Quite understood, but unnecessary, my love. I will never make that mistake again."

He looked into her eyes and then said softly, "See that you don't."

He kissed her, a hard, affirming kiss. She leaned into him, losing herself for the moment in the familiar reassurance of his body, in the ineffable joy of his love. And much later, when supper was done and the fire banked for the night, she reached for him, pressing her body, clad in the thin nightgown, against his.

She ran a hand over his back, caressing the muscular, taut backside through his tight-fitting knee breeches. "I love the feel of you," she murmured, sliding her hand around to the bulge of his penis, which stirred into life at the merest brush of her fingers.

With a swift movement, Peregrine lifted her bodily from the floor and took the two steps necessary to the bed, where he dropped her onto the coverlet. His eyes glowed with the pure light of lust, and something else, she thought . . . triumph. The triumph of a warrior, a victor of the field. And Alexandra found that she gloried in it. He bent over her, pushing the delicate nightgown up to her waist. He straightened and looked down at the long pale length of her bared legs, the dark curly nest at the apex of her thighs, the smooth white belly framed in the white lawn.

Alexandra felt her nakedness as an exquisite vulnerability, even though a mere movement of her hand would cover her, shield her from the burning intensity of his hungry gaze. The essential core of her body was revealed for him, delineated in a way more pointed than complete nakedness. Her skin grew hot; her blood seemed to be racing through her veins. She wanted to cover herself, and yet she didn't. She simply lay there, feeling absurdly like a virgin laid bare upon a sacrificial altar.

Slowly, Peregrine unlaced his breeches, and his engorged penis sprang free. His eyes met hers as he swung himself over her, straddling her, the tip of his penis brushing her belly. "I want you now." His voice sounded strange, almost harsh, pulsing with desire. He lifted her legs onto his shoulders, opening her wider for the first thrust of penetration. She heard herself give a little cry that could have been of surprise, and again she had the sensation of time running ahead of her while she desperately tried to catch up. But he was growing within her, filling her with his presence, possessing her with each hard thrust, his eyes never leaving hers as he asserted some primal need for ownership. She was his, she belonged to him, only to him, and he played on her body until she could no longer deny it herself. She was his, and with a cry of surrender, she let him take her with him in a free fall down below the dark waters of a need as ancient as man himself.

He sprawled on the bed beside her, his breathing fast and uneven. He moved a hand to cup the damp mound of her sex, his fingers moving through the tight black curls. His free arm was flung above his head, and they lay with tangled limbs, unspeaking for a long while. Finally, Alexandra said, "What was that?"

He turned his head to look at her, his hand still clasping her center. "I have no idea, sweetheart. But it was wonderful. I didn't hurt you?"

She shook her head with a weak laugh. "No, quite the opposite. But you did take me by surprise."

"And long may I continue to do so," he responded, finally moving sufficiently to hitch himself onto one elbow to look at her. "You do look adorably wanton like that."

"I feel wanton . . . like a lady of the night behind one of the pillars in the Piazza," she said.

"What do you know of such things?" Perry demanded, only half in jest.

She wriggled beneath the bedcovers, drawing the sheet up to her chin. "I read, my love. And I have always read anything that catches my attention. I know a lot more than you might imagine about the seamier sides of life. There are many ancient texts discoursing on the lives of courtesans, even common whores. Not much of a life they had, either," she added with a grimace.

"No, I don't suppose they did," he agreed drily, standing up and throwing off his clothes. "But you, my sweet, are intended for the utterly conventional life of Mistress Alexandra Sullivan. And you had best accept it with all good grace." He climbed back into bed and rolled her into his embrace. "It is clear, is it not?"

"Crystal," she said, nestling into his shoulder. "I love you, Peregrine Sullivan."

"And I love you, Mistress Douglas."

Epilogue

❧

The door closed behind Viscount Bradley's visitors, and he rested his head against the cushioned back of his deep armchair, adjusting the rug over his knees. Visitors tired him, and six at once was really overdoing it. A spurt of flame flared in the grate as a log crumbled beneath the fierce heat. He reached sideways to the small table beside his chair and took up his brandy goblet, inhaling the powerful aroma before drinking.

So, they had done it. All three of his nephews had finagled their way into satisfying his condition for their inheritance. A thin smile played over his lips as he reflected on his just-departed visitors, his three nephews and their wives. Blackwater had found his wife, Clarissa, in Mother Griffith's nunnery in Covent Garden. An unimpeachable address for a high-class whore. But whatever she'd been doing under that roof, the viscount was convinced that she had not been peddling her flesh. But he couldn't prove it, and she had certainly entered Jasper's protection straight from the nunnery, Nan Griffiths had sworn it. So, whatever his suspicions, Bradley had, in honor, no choice but to accept the situation as it was presented to him.

The smile flickered again. *In honor,* indeed. Honor was not a quality he possessed in a great measure, but he was a gambler, and if he was outbid, then so be it. And when it came to being outbid . . . Sebastian's bridal choice, the lovely Lady Serena, had definitely played on the outer fringes of respectable society. A gambler, one of faro's daughters, the stepdaughter of an out-and-out rogue, who had not thought twice about selling her to the highest bidder. Sebastian had happened to have the correct coin.

And then there was Peregrine. He had married a sharp-tongued actor with a predilection for deception. There was no knowing who this Alexandra truly was, but Bradley recognized a player when he met one, and the lady was most definitely a player of considerable talents.

So, he supposed, he had achieved his wish. Three completely unrespectable, unsuitable brides foisted upon the hypocritical, prudish Blackwater clan. Oddly, the vengeance was not nearly as sweet as he had expected it to be. His nephews were all uxorious to the point of nausea, and their wives clearly adored them in turn. Clarissa was radiantly blooming with child, and Bradley rather thought the other two would not be long following suit. Not that he'd actually wished his nephews ill; if truth be told, they were the only human beings he could tolerate, but he had rather hoped to see his wretched family squirm. They had thrown into the street the woman he still loved even after all the years that had passed since the destruction of his youthful passion, and he had nursed his bitterness and the prospect of the perfect revenge as if it were his lifeblood.

But now he didn't seem to care one way or the other what they thought. His nephews certainly didn't appear to give a damn about how their relatives viewed their marriages. The whole idea of his vengeance now seemed insipid, a waste of his time and energy.

He heard a faint rustle behind him, and his eyes sharpened despite his bone-deep fatigue. There was one recipient of his malice whom he could still prick a little. "Cosgrove, you black crow. Where are you going? Come over here."

The black-robed priest had been trying to slide from the room while his employer seemed to be sleeping. Now he swallowed a sigh of dismay. The old man loved to torment him, dictating his filthy memoir one vile detail after the other, and the priest's only recourse was to appear unaffected as he wrote to dictation. He came forward to the fire. "Yes, my lord?"

Bradley looked up at him, the tall, curved black figure, and suddenly everything seemed pointless, a complete and utter waste of his time. There was no satisfaction in tormenting this man of God with the detailed confession of his sins, both real and imagined. He didn't repent of them, and he certainly didn't expect divine forgiveness for an ill-spent life. He'd enjoyed most of it hugely.

"Bring me the manuscript," he rasped.

Father Cosgrove glided silently to the table in the window where he had spent so many wretched hours listening to the dripping poison from the old man's diseased mind. He picked up the sheaf of papers covered in his own neat script and brought it to the viscount.

"Burn it," Bradley instructed curtly. "All of it."

Father Cosgrove looked at him in amazement. "Burn it, my lord?" So many hours of labor over the last two years.

"Yes, every page. Get on with it. I want to see it done."

Slowly, the priest fed the pages one by one into the brightly burning fire. Flames flared as the paper caught, curled, and crumbled to gray ash against the logs. The viscount watched, his eyes on every page, and when it was done, he leaned back in his chair and closed his eyes with a little sigh. "Get out now."

Father Cosgrove slipped from the chamber. If his work as amanuensis was over, then maybe so, too, was his servitude in the house of the devil. Maybe he could return to the quiet of the Benedictine monastery and resume his life of prayer and meditation.

Louis, the viscount's valet and general factotum, appeared on the landing outside the antechamber to the viscount's bedchamber as the priest emerged. "Is his lordship resting?"

"I believe so," the priest said. "He sent me away."

Louis nodded and entered the antechamber. He

opened the door to the bedchamber and stepped soundlessly into the room. The viscount was immobile in his chair, eyes closed, his head resting against the cushioned back. Louis went to the bed to turn down the coverlet, prop up the pillows, preparatory to helping his lordship to bed. He set a candle on the bedside table and stepped over to the viscount's chair.

"My lord, will you go to bed now?" His voice was soft, and he laid a hand on Bradley's shoulder. Instantly, he knew that his lordship was no longer in the room. The paper-thin, blue-veined eyelids did not flutter. The mouth was slightly open, and when Louis put his hand against it, there was no breath.

Louis stood for a moment looking down at the dead man. Not many would mourn the old man's passing, but Louis had been with him for close on forty years, and the two had shared a bond of a kind. Louis would miss him.

He stepped quietly from the chamber, closing the door behind him. A message must be sent to Lord Blackwater on Upper Brook Street.

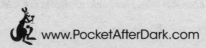